ENDSVILLE

OUTLAW ARCANA BOOK 1

BY CLAY SANGER

The shifter looked up, and its empty eye sockets lit with pale, hungry white light—a cold, merciless radiance like stars in a black sky.

It worked its mouth, slurping blood. *"Maglo et tun'y-eth,"* it gurgled.

Then it charged, lurching forward.

Gabriel back-pedaled and lined up two shots: *Boom-Boom*. The muzzle strobed like a camera flash in the dark alley; the reports flat and hard. The first round hit the thing in the forehead, the second in the cheek, but it didn't even break stride.

Now it really had Gabriel's attention. Fading back towards the Couatl's compound, he retreated, skipping fast, to put space between him and the lumbering creature. His pistol went back in the holster, but his knife came out, and his trot turned into a run as the creature with the glowing white eyes picked up the pace and gained on him.

Gabriel managed to keep the thing at a distance while he prepared his workings. His mind was moving fast, and his body tried to keep up. The creature was closing in, picking up speed.

Knife in hand, Gabriel pulled the flask from his breast pocket and poured honey-thick oil over the blade. He screwed the cap back on the flask, dropped it back in his pocket, switched his knife into his other hand, and drew his cigarette lighter. Then he stopped, held his ground, lit it, and whispered a pyromantic charm as the flames licked the dripping oil.

The oil caught, lighting the blade with a brilliant golden radiance, swelling and redoubling until it blazed in Gabriel's hand like a torch.

The creature paused, cocked its head to the side. A disturbingly curious expression for a mangled corpse with burning white eyes.

"Yeah," Gabriel grunted, bringing the blazing knife to bear, lips peeling back from his teeth in a Viking snarl. "Come on, motherfucker."

DEDICATION

For my wife Kerri, who always hangs in there and patiently waits for me to catch up. I love you. So big.

PART ONE

We Are Bad People

No one loves a crow. Scavengers. Thieves. Liars. Harbingers of death. Loyal to and beholden to no one but their own kind. Drawn to the chaos and carnage so they can pick gold from the bones. Good, bad, indifferent. A crow does what a crow does. Nothing commands a crow. Not men. Not kings. Not gods.
The House of the Crow lives up to its namesake.

Appended by Elijah Berdeaux, Master Knight of the Watch
to *A Modern Study of the Great Houses*
by Bahadir Fadel Satik, Lord Commander of the Watch

1

Dollars, deeds, or blood. The Crows of Los Angeles didn't carry balances. All debts came due.

Gabriel St. John took a ride with a dead man out to Pomona to settle the books. Frankie Pallone played the part of the dead man. Gabriel played the part of the Reaper. The sand running through the hourglass took care of the rest.

Gabriel rode in the backseat with his pistol on his knee and Frankie did the driving. The old goombah kept flicking nervous glances in the rear-view mirror, his eyes wide and bright with fear. Like he expected that forty-five might suddenly speak up and have an opinion of its own. Gabriel wished he'd quit doing that.

"I knew when I saw you show up with them gloves on that I was in deep shit," Frankie said, trailing off into a nervous snort.

"Shut up and drive, Frankie," Gabriel replied. Every time Frankie had something to say—every time he poked at Gabriel with those terrified eyes—it twisted a knife in his belly. They went back a long way, him and Frankie Pallone. Everything about this was a bad day.

For his part, Frankie shut up and drove. The old man knew how this game was played.

They turned onto Val Vista Street, into the dark heart of suburbia under bluebird skies. Palm trees, tall cedars, low ranch-style houses with little brown yards. Frankie had a fucking magnolia tree in his front yard.

"Is Angelina home?" Gabriel asked. Angelina was Frankie's wife.

Frankie's eyes flicked back to the rearview mirror. This time, there was a little fire with the fear. "You asked me that already."

"I'm asking you again. Is Angelina home?"

"In Chicago all week. With her sister."

"What about Gillian?" He'd already asked him that, too.

Frankie shifted uncomfortably at the mention of his daughter. "At her Mom's until Tuesday."

"You need to be sure, Frankie," Gabriel said.

"I'm sure, okay?"

Gabriel nodded. "Pull in the garage."

Frankie rolled up the short driveway, hit the garage door opener and drove inside. He pulled in next to his wife's little Lexus and parked.

Gabriel ground his teeth. "You sure she's not here?"

"I dropped her off at the airport last night. Good enough for ya?"

"Good enough," Gabriel agreed. "Close the door."

Frankie did so, and the garage door rumbled down behind them, sealing out the harsh white afternoon glare—foot by foot—like a closing tomb. The daylight disappeared in a final flare at the bottom edge. Only the dull yellow glow of the overhead fixture remained.

Gabriel reached forward. "Keys."

Frankie handed them over.

"Let's go," Gabriel said, popping open his door and swinging out of the backseat. Frankie followed suit.

The two men were a stark contrast. Gabriel was thirty-two, long, tall, and handsome, with coal black hair and arctic blue ice-chip eyes. He was tattooed and grim, hard and lean, like iron pipes dressed in a Johnny Cash funeral suit. He looked like a boxer, a mercenary, or a mafia enforcer—the sort of guy who fought for a living.

Frankie Pallone, on the other hand, was short, and twenty years soft around the middle. No amount of Brylcreem and comb-overs could hide his receding hairline. He looked like a retired porn star in his tracksuit and gold chains.

Frankie led the way into the modest ranch house, and Gabriel followed behind like a shadow, his Sig .45 couched alongside his leg. In his experience, you didn't have to keep a pistol trained on somebody to keep them on their best behavior. That was a matter of will. A matter of intent. A guy who clearly didn't mean to use it wasn't all that intimidating, even if he had his piece stuck in your face. A guy who *did* have the stones to use it didn't even need to have it in his hand to make his point. They both knew Gabriel was the latter.

Frankie stopped in the kitchen and turned around. Slowly. He shrugged—a gesture of frustrated surrender. "Now what, kid?"

"Go get it," Gabriel replied. Blunt. To the point.

Frankie found the balls to meet Gabriel's glacial stare. "We already been through this. I told you. I ain't got it. You wanna know what went wrong, you're gonna have to get on a plane, go to Tokyo, and talk it over with Takagi."

Gabriel let the bald-faced lie hang in the air for a few beats, long enough that Frankie's resolve wavered just a hair. "It's in the safe in your den."

The proclamation landed like a judge passing down a death sentence. Gabriel watched the numbness and fear crawl its way up into Frankie's face in place of where the color used to be. *Yeah, that's right. You* know *I* know.

Frankie stood there, frozen, while what little bluff and indignation he'd mustered up bled away like the air leaking out of a balloon.

Gabriel raised the pistol, fat suppressor can screwed onto the muzzle, and leveled it at Frankie's face. "Go get it."

The old man flinched away from Gabriel's forty-five caliber Cyclops stare and without further protest, turned and headed for the den, walking like there was lead in his shoes, while Gabriel followed.

Frankie's den looked out on the backyard and patio. Gabriel pulled the chain and closed the blinds, bathing the room in blue shadow. For a moment, Frankie didn't do anything at all. He just stood there in the middle of the room, presumably watching his life flash before his eyes.

"You're making this real hard, Frankie," Gabriel said, lowering the pistol. "Let's get this over with."

Frankie gave a half-hearted nod, licked his dry lips, and went to the wall. He took a framed family portrait off the hook and set it aside, revealing a sizeable safe concealed behind it. The strongbox itself was surrounded by a constellation of faint black runes, barely visible in the blue afternoon shadows. A similar array of mystic symbols was inscribed on the safe door. Wards to hide its contents from prying eyes. To hide its entire existence from all means of divination other than an old-fashioned physical investigation.

But, Gabriel knew what was in Frankie's safe as sure as he knew what color socks he'd put on that morning.

"Did your mom or sister find it?" Frankie asked.

Gabriel declined to answer. "Open it up."

Frankie didn't argue. He opened the safe.

The bread box sized safe swung open on its oiled hinge without so much as a squeak. The interior was adorned with ward runes just like the exterior and the surrounding wall. Inside, Gabriel could see a few stacks of cash, some paperwork, a clear tube of gold coins, and a manila envelope standing on edge.

Gabriel could just see the grip of a pistol peeking out from under the manila envelope. He knew Frankie saw it, too. The old bastard paused and just sort of stared at it for a full ten seconds without so much as twitching. But Gabriel wasn't worried. It had been a long damn time since Frankie had pulled the trigger on anybody. He didn't figure he was apt to start back up now. "Probably a bad idea, Frankie. That'll make this go real hard."

The old man got the hint. He pulled the manila envelope from the safe and left the hardware be. With an expression that was equal parts guilt, regret, and fear, he passed the package to Gabriel.

Gabriel nodded to Frankie's comfy chair. "Have a seat."

Frankie sat and put his hands on his knees. Gabriel took a seat across from him, the room's narrow coffee table between them. He laid his pistol down on the table with a soft *thunk* and fixed Frankie with a meaningful glare. *Stay put, old man,* that glare said. Then he inspected the envelope. Its contents bulged with rectangular mass. Twisting the brass enclosure pins open, Gabriel slid the item from inside.

It was a small, artfully bound leather tome, dyed a brilliant green.

The rich emerald cover and binding were hand-gilded, engraved with strange and wondrous symbols. Holding it as if it were fragile, he turned it over and inspected the back cover. There was a slight semi-circular discoloration in the lower right-hand corner near the binding. That little imperfection meant something to him.

He opened the book and checked through a number of pages, turning them with the care of a museum curator, inspecting the hand-illuminated illustrations. Where there was text, it was presented in a precise and regal hand. Alien symbols and formulas covered the pages. This tome had been hand-written, not printed.

After several minutes of inspection, Gabriel turned to a particular page with purpose. He ran his fingertip over a smaller image hidden within a larger illustration. That of a tiny frog with a crown of six stars encircling its head. It was concealed within the larger spectacle of an orgy scene. The image of the crowned frog was all but lost in the cascading hair of a buxom female participant as she bent over a tree stump. The disturbing image of a blindfolded man with three large penises servicing three women at once dominated the illustration. From between his jagged teeth protruded a lolling forked tongue. In his left hand, he held a bloody rabbit by the scruff of the neck.

After a breath of contemplation, Gabriel closed the book and slid it back inside the envelope. "Who was your buyer?" he asked. Then he corrected himself. "I mean, your *other* buyer."

Frankie chewed that around for a bit before answering. "Jessica Kard, up in San Fran. But she canceled on me out of the blue. Not long before you showed up. Guessing she got the impression the book already *had* a buyer. Somebody she didn't want to tangle with. Got cold feet. Which means you're probably asking me questions you already know the answer to."

Gabriel shrugged, and as hard as he tried, he couldn't keep himself from looking wounded. "Why'd you do this, Frankie? Angelina takes good care of you. You got rental houses. That good old-fashioned retired shit. Far as I can tell, you're doing okay. You got a kid."

Frankie sniffed and looked away but said nothing.

"That's it?" Gabriel asked.

It was Frankie's turn to shrug. "It don't matter now anyway. We all got our issues, kid."

We all got our issues. Shit, wasn't that true?

Frankie Pallone. Frankie Vegas. Uncle fucking Frankie. The guy who had showed up with a PlayStation for Gabriel's twelfth birthday party. Who'd slipped him a pint of gin and a dog-eared issue of *Hustler* for his fifteenth. Told him with a wink to stash both of them somewhere his Lady Mother wouldn't find.

"Goddammit, Frankie," Gabriel said with a shake of his head.

"Yeah. Goddammit," the old man agreed. "So. Now what?"

"You know how this ends."

"It doesn't have to. I can just *go away*. Better than gone. Like I never existed at all," Frankie said. Tears welled up in his eyes. "All you gotta do is give me five minutes. Less than that. Give me one minute. Shit, less. Just … let me walk out the door."

"You know I can't do that," Gabriel replied.

"That's your old man's rules, not yours," Frankie said and scrubbed a tear from his cheek as it fell free. "C'mon. Please. You *can*."

"But you know I won't."

Frankie didn't offer a reply to that. Probably because he knew it was true. "We go way back, you Crows and me."

"You ain't a Crow, Frankie," Gabriel replied.

"Next closest thing."

"There ain't no 'next closest thing,'" Gabriel said. And that line of bargaining died.

Frankie shook his head as if trying to will the Reaper away. "There's gotta be something we can do here. There's fifty large in the safe. More. Take whatever you want. Something that—"

"You stole from us," Gabriel said. "You stole from my

Crows. You don't cut us out of the middle, Frankie. That's not how this works. Ever."

"We can work it out. We can..."

"It's already worked out." Gabriel tapped the book with the tip of his finger. The grim *rat-a-tat-tat* of a drummer at a firing squad. Then he stood up and raised the pistol.

"Jesus," Frankie hissed, eyes flying wide with panic, turning his face away as far as his neck would crane. His whole body started trembling, and the old man pissed himself. "Oh, Jesus. Oh, Christ. Don't do this. *Please*."

That hung Gabriel up.

They *all* did this. Tough guys. Nobodies. Whenever it came time to meet the Reaper, they all bargained. They all begged. One way or another. Some quiet. Some loud. But all of them did it. Tried to make one last deal. Tried to throw the dice one more time. All of them.

Gabriel forced the breath he was holding out and then another one back in.

Maybe Frankie sensed a chance to survive in Gabriel's hesitation. He rolled his dice. "Don't make my girls come home and find me like this. Please." He stared bug-eyed at the wall, gripping the arms of the chair until his knuckles were white.

That hit Gabriel hard. Poked at him in places he didn't like to talk about.

"C'mon." Frankie's voice was soft. Tears spilled down his cheeks. "Please."

"Okay," Gabriel replied.

Frankie's body uncoiled a notch in hopeful relief. "Okay?"

"Yeah. Okay," Gabriel said.

The old man sagged in the chair letting out a long quivering breath. His head slumped forward, a relieved sigh draining the tension from his body. He closed his watery eyes and crossed himself with a trembling hand. "Thanks, kid."

Then Gabriel pulled the trigger and put one in his head.

Frankie jerked with the shot, and Gabriel put two more into his sternum to seal the deal. The shots from the suppressed forty-five sounded like a hammer striking a two-by-four. Nothing the neighbor's gardener would write home about.

Frankie Pallone, Frankie Vegas, Uncle fucking Frankie deflated by degrees and sank into his chair. An empty sack of meat. Better than gone. Those had been his words. Better than gone.

Gabriel tucked the book up under his arm, and thirty seconds later, he was better than gone himself.

2

Three hours later, Gabriel was sitting up on Mulholland Drive, watching the sun go down, trying to get right. He had a smoke or two and kept to himself. No one bothered him as he watched the sky over Los Angeles turn pink then red, then violet. The city below came alive in an ocean of light. Eventually, his phone rang.

Gabriel answered. "Yeah?"

"How'd it go?" the voice on the other end asked. Victor. Gabriel's Lord Father.

"We're good with the package," he replied.

There was a long pause. "And the rest?"

Gabriel gave his father the only answer he could muster. "Handled."

And that was that.

Gabriel settled up with his Lord Father and Victor headed to Burbank to deliver the merchandise. Gabriel didn't. He was in no mood for it.

Instead, he went to a hotel and made a couple of phone calls to occupy his time. Her name was Celeste. Or so it said on her business card. She was *that* kind of call girl, the kind with beautiful business cards who you sent a limo to pick up.

The sex was a vicious thing, anger and hurt erupting in the act. She gave back as good as she got. It was helpful. Therapeutic. The company of a stranger was better.

Gabriel sat naked on the edge of the bed, smoking a cigarette, staring out the hotel window across the Los Angeles skyline. The suite was non-smoking. He had a whopper of a penalty fee to look forward to when he settled the bill. That didn't much concern him. He wanted a cigarette.

His reflection in the dark window stared back at him, a ghostly apparition. Gabriel looked right through it.

Celeste traced her fingers along the great black and crimson tattoo that filled his back to spread dark wings across his shoulders. The Crow. *His* Crow. Like his father, he'd earned it—the hard way.

First had been the Perched Crow, wings folded, the mark of the House Militia. A servant. A task gopher trusted to clean up messes, expected to provide support, and brought to fight if the bodies were needed.

Then the Perched Crow spread a new pair of wings and flew. The Four-Winged Crow of the Soldier. The family muscle. You weren't a Soldier of the Crow until you'd demonstrated your willingness to turn problems into wreckage. After that, there was no turning back.

A crimson laurel had been tattooed behind it when he'd first shed blood for his House. A Ruby Cross was added beneath the beak when he'd suffered his first wound. Gabriel sported five Ruby Crosses.

When he became a Knight, the elite of his father's house, a spear was added, clutched in the talons of the Four-Winged Crow. And when Gabriel became a Captain, a swallow-tailed banner was inked entwined around the shaft of his Knight's Spear.

Blood. Violence. Ruthlessness. Family and above all—loyalty.

That was the Crow. The Crow came first, and the Crow came last.

There were more. Full sleeves, shoulder to wrist, creeping down over the backs of his hands. Ink like a rock star. A crucifix over his heart. A rune-filled triangle and a leering death's head opposite it on his chest. Some were artwork. Some were arcane.

But none mattered like the Crow.

"What does this mean?" Celeste asked, gently outlining the wings of the Crow with her acrylic nail, a little chip of glistening mulberry, like frozen blood. She wrapped her other slender arm around his shoulders, cuddling up close to his back.

Celeste smelled like cinnamon and sex. Gabriel liked that. "What?"

"I see a lot of ink. Never any quite like this. If you can tell me, what does it mean?"

Gabriel contemplated that question. He contemplated it for a good long while. "It means we're bad people," he said with a ghost of a smile. "We lie. We cheat. We steal. We kill. So long as we take out the trash and keep the peace with the other liars, cheaters, thieves, and killers, nobody really cares."

"Didn't mean to pry," Celeste said gently.

"You're not," Gabriel replied. And he figured she knew that.

"So how do you feel about that?"

He considered it. "How do you feel about being a whore?"

If Celeste took any offense, she didn't show it. "I am what I am. I *know* what I am. I know *who* I am and what I'm good at. And I make a living doing it that most people couldn't even dream of. So, what do I have to be ashamed of?"

Gabriel nodded. "Yeah. Kind of like that, I guess."

Celeste kissed him on the back of the neck. "I thought so."

Gabriel figured she did.

Her fingers skimmed over his skin, following the lines in the ink. Following the shapes of the scars. She didn't ask about the story behind those. She didn't have to. "Do you want me to stay?"

"No," Gabriel replied. That was all the heart-to-heart satin pillow therapy he had in him for one night. Snap of the fingers. That quick. That much. No more. "But, uh, leave the card?"

Celeste kissed his cheek. "Of course."

Then she left Gabriel alone to slay his own demons.

He had lots of them.

3

Victor St. John made it to his appointment in Burbank in the small hours.

The Lord Crow was a sinister echo of his son, plus twenty-five years or so. Tall and lean, descended from New York Black Irish. Blue-collar Vinegar Hill Brooklyn to be precise. Salt and pepper mane. Granite face creased with frown lines and crow's feet. Eyes like old iron twinkling beneath a brooding brow in a perpetual mixture of scowl and bemusement. As if perhaps Victor knew the punchline to a joke that no one else got, and just maybe, he was willing to shoot you over it. Old jailhouse ink crawled up out of the collar of his expensive shirt. Wherever he walked, he walked like he owned the place.

The buyer was one Dante Washington, Mr. Dante Washington to everyone but his own mother. His business was venture capital and real estate. His *other* business was complicated. Heroin, coke, guns, and money laundering. Puppetmaster and godfather to half a dozen Los Angeles gangs that paid him tribute like a patriarch.

In his teens, he'd been a thug, but always too intelligent to be petty. By twenty he was an up-and-coming prince of L.A.'s mean streets. By thirty he'd served a nickel as a guest of the state of California and learned how to avoid ever repeating that mistake. By forty, Dante Washington was a king.

Over the course of his illustrious career, he'd made some strange enemies. Necessity dictated that he make equally strange allies. Those most trusted he kept close. Like his dearest Miss Althea Gentles. Others he did business with at a distance. Such as the Crow. Mr. Dante Washington was a believer in a world of the willfully ignorant. That gave him an advantage.

Dante Washington ruled an empire, an empire maintained and protected by weapons and the skilled hands to wield them. Not every weapon came out of a gun crate, no more than every enemy came out of the 'hood. Part of Mr. Washington's success was understanding that and a willingness to accept that which others thought comical or impossible—all ingredients in his kingpin's recipe.

As a successful businessman, Mr. Washington had a supply for his every need and demand. His coke came through diverse channels in Mexico. His heroin was an East Coast import, a redundant supply chain years in the making. His guns he got from the Russians, or in the event of a supply snafu, a backup series of pipelines from his friends in Mexico.

When he needed *other* weapons, he reached out to his *other* dealer.

The Crow.

Victor St. John met after-hours with Mr. Dante Washington and Miss Althea Gentles at Mr. Washington's Burbank office. Nothing was mentioned about the speed bump in the book's delivery, nor the nature of the delay, and nothing needed to be.

Mr. Washington waited patiently while Miss Althea inspected the tome in meticulous detail, much the same way Gabriel had sitting in Frankie Pallone's den earlier that day.

"The Vert Grimoire of Jean-Francois Mercier," the priestess said reverently as she scrutinized the tome. "Are there any other copies?"

Victor smiled. It was a sly question. "If there were, then it wouldn't be genuine, would it?" A grimoire was more than just words on paper. It was more than just a mystical textbook. Magic begets magic. Even into the writings of such craft, craft was expended. Handing it to a scribe for duplication or running it through a printing press produced a *book*. A real grimoire was not a *book*. It was a culmination of arcane acts designed to instruct and reproduce arcane acts. To copy it would be to consume it. Sometimes such things were done, compiling lesser works into greater works or transferring the work into a new copy as the preservation of the original failed. Results varied.

Not all grimoires were created equal. The Vert Grimoire of Jean-Francois Mercier was a masterpiece.

"Clever man," Miss Althea said with a nod. At length, the mysterious priestess gave a faint smile of approval. "The Goddess will be pleased."

Victor inclined his head in a respectful nod. "And what goddess are we pleasing today?"

"Mr. St. John," Miss Althea said gently, passing the tome to her boss, "As the Goddess keeps my heart, I keep her secrets."

"Fair enough," Victor conceded. He looked to Mr. Washington. "The price is satisfactory?"

"It is," Mr. Washington replied.

The Lord Crow shook hands with Mr. Washington and sealed the deal.

"There's another matter I'd like to discuss with you," Mr. Washington said.

Victor was all about doing business. He got comfortable in his chair and held up his pack of smokes. "Do you mind?"

With a chuckle, Mr. Washington passed Victor an ashtray.

They got down to it.

4

Fiona St. John was the earliest riser in her home. Her husband Victor often kept late hours working. Her mornings were entrenched in routine, quiet time that she enjoyed while the rest of the house was still sleeping.

She turned on a single kitchen lamp and no more, preferring the cool gray shadows of the house in the early morning. Fiona woke with tea, sometimes coffee. There was no newspaper or television in her morning routine. Only the peace and quiet of her bathrobe, a cup of tea, and the morning breeze on the patio of their hillside Malibu home. Sometimes, two cats, Axel and Calypso, would join her as it pleased them if it pleased them.

The family estate stood off Latigo Canyon Road, wrapped around four very private acres of a westward-facing slope. The western patio afforded a magnificent view of the Pacific Ocean and the homes below; the bulk of the estate, its water garden, guest house, and outbuildings, was nestled deeper back in the shadow of the canyon.

Fiona reveled in the cool blue dawn, looking west down the shadow-draped hills as lines of white waves marched toward the shore far below.

The wind kissed her cheeks and stirred her snow-white hair. No color from a bleach bottle. Her family line came by it naturally. Pale and statuesque, Fiona was a beautiful creature. Her fifty years were gaining on her oh so very slowly. Also common to her family line. With each year, it was slower by degrees.

Finely drawn vine work of pale green tattoos encircled her arms from shoulder blade to fingertips, faint, meticulous, and delicate. When she crossed her legs, the hem of her bathrobe pulled back just enough to reveal a far more heavy-handed tattoo climbing up her thigh to disappear beneath the silk. Deep black and rich crimson. The tail of the Crow that perched on her right hip and thigh.

Its wings arched forward encircling her waist—front and back—while its up-turned beak climbed the curve of her ribs beside her breast. She adjusted the hem of her robe, and the sliver of black tail feathers disappeared.

An hour and a half of peace and cool morning breeze. It was a fine start to the day.

She could hear from the kitchen inside that Victor was up and shortly thereafter, he joined her on the patio with a cup of coffee in his hands, still dressed in a white wife-beater tank top and gray pajama pants.

Elaborate ink covered most of Victor St. John's scarred and muscled hide. Wrapping around the left side of his chest and back, like a cloak hung from his shoulder, was his great Crow, mostly obscured by the shirt. But his shoulder, adorned with the Crow's bowed head, was clearly visible. A crown anointed in three stars hovered above it. Victor St. John was a Lord of the Crow and thus had the right to wear the Crowned Crow with pride. Victor was one of three lord Crows, and the only one to be found on this side of the Atlantic.

"You didn't sleep much," Fiona said. Her voice was rich with her native Ireland.

"Late night. Early morning. Lots of irons in the fire."

"Something to be worried about?"

Victor shook his head, sipped his coffee. "Just business. I'll know more tonight. Fill you in over breakfast?"

Fiona nodded.

Some Crows kept their spouses or significant others out of the family business. In the dark. Ears full of lies. That's how things had been with Victor's first wife, Isabel, Gabriel's birth mother. Perhaps a contributing factor to her very bad end. Not so with Victor and Fiona. They were, quite literally, partners in crime.

"I left word for Gabriel to come by this morning. Fill him in too."

"And where's he at? He didn't go up to Burbank with you?"
Victor shook his head. "Eh. Probably drowning his sorrows."
Fiona considered that. "Rough day at the office?"
Victor shrugged. "Yeah. I suppose so. You need a warm up?"
"I don't, I'm fine," Fiona said, setting her cup aside.
Victor bent down and kissed her on top of the head. "Okay. I'm gonna get a shower then. I feel like old luggage."
She touched his cheek and tipped her head up to kiss his chin. Victor went back inside.
Alone, in the quiet, the Lady Crow enjoyed her morning.

5

Gabriel came by the house as ordered around nine o'clock, still wearing yesterday's suit and smelling like he had drowned himself in perfumed rental ass. Nobody was inclined to question where Gabriel spent his nights. Everybody had their vices, and Gabriel's family knew his well enough.

Nobody said a word about Frankie Pallone. Not a single, solitary word. Like it never happened. And it was apt to stay that way. After a cup of coffee and some familial pleasantries, Victor, Fiona, and Gabriel sat in the plush den and discussed matters at hand. Victor and Gabriel took a seat across the coffee table from each other and Fiona wandered to the windows to watch the distant waves roll and churn.

"So," Victor said, pinching a thumbnail down the crease in his slacks, "The esteemed Mr. Washington had some secondary affairs he wanted to discuss with me when I delivered his merchandise yesterday."

"Such as?" Gabriel lit up a smoke and sank back into the cushions of his parent's comfy sofa.

"He believes it's time for us to upgrade our relationship. Wants us to take a look into a little problem he has that goes bump in the night."

"Did he give you any intel on his, uh, *problem?*"

"Track with me," Victor said as he leaned forward. School was in session. The Lord Crow spoke, and Gabriel paid attention. "Now, we all know Dante Washington and crew moves a lot of serious weight. Coke, meth, H, the works." Victor gave a knowing smirk. "That's nothing compared to the weight he moves in cash."

The international drug trade was still the most lucrative criminal enterprise in California. Trafficking in drugs, and all the sins that went with it, was how the money was made. And it was the money that made the world go 'round. But you couldn't spend *dirty* money, not in the quantities the rich and powerful did. To make money clean, you had to *launder* it.

That was where California rose to special distinction.

California was the world's seventh largest economy, rife with opportunities to launder money by the tens of billions of dollars a year. Then California afforded myriad ways to smuggle those clean dollars right back out again, very often through the same channels the illicit trade was smuggled in on to begin with. That way, Columbian drug lords could buy horse ranches, and Mexican cartels could fund private armies and pay the mountains of bribes they needed to grease the gears.

California was one of the greatest dirty money laundromats on earth. The business of turning dirty money into clean money was booming. And Dante Washington was a serious player.

"So, roll the dial back to two weeks ago," Victor said. "Mr. Washington wakes up one morning and finds that a laundering depot under his control has been knocked over."

"So how bad did he get hit?" Gabriel asked.

Victor cleared his throat. "Thirty-four million dollars. Cash."

The young captain tried not to choke on his coffee. "Shit," Gabriel wheezed, setting his cup aside and leaning forward. "Whose money was it?"

"Mr. Dante Washington's very own."

"Wow," Gabriel said. That meant one of Southern California's money laundering barons just got stepped on for thirty-four million of his own scratch. That was the kind of money that could put a guy out of business. Thirty-four million dollars earned the hard way. By supplying distribution weight to neighborhood dealers, slinging one eight ball on one street corner at a time. That thirty-four million dollars represented a metric shit-ton of work and risk. Depoted so it could be turned into off-shore investments, private loans to clean fronts, housing developments, strip malls. Anything but piles of small, grubby bills laying around in shrink-wrapped bundles in a basement somewhere in the hood.

If word of him getting ripped off hit the streets, every client he did business with would begin thinking about moving their money somewhere else, somewhere they deemed more secure. Mr. Washington would have to regain their confidence.

It would have to be handled. The money found and the security breach closed. Washington would need to be in a position to claim victory before anybody who mattered learned that something had gone wrong. And somebody was going to have to take the fall for it.

That left Gabriel with one question. "Okay. So where do we figure in?"

Victor retrieved a bound file folder from the end table to his left and slid it across the coffee table to his son. While Gabriel perused the file, Fiona stood by the wall of windows watching the distant surf move restlessly along the coast. Outside it was a picturesque postcard Friday. A good day for skipping work and heading down to the beach instead. Alas, for the Crows, work had a way of intruding.

Gabriel opened the file and found a stack of color eight-by-ten photos inside. They were date and time stamped and looked like they were printed from security footage.

"Where are these from?" he asked, flipping through the pics.

"Security cameras from Mr. Washington's office up in Burbank."

Five familiar faces stared back at him from the pages. They were all young for the most part, as eclectic and oddly matched as a five-token-band sitcom cast.

There was Edwin, a blond-headed white suburban action figure straight out of a West Hills stereotype. His parents had been expecting him to be a doctor or lawyer or maybe an accountant. But he was more into bartending and beach bumming.

Alex, a tall, lanky black kid from Reseda. Everybody always wanted to know if he played ball or *where* he played ball. Alex didn't play basketball though. He played the cello, played it at serious scholarship levels for a middle-class kid from the Valley. At least until his life had taken a turn in a different direction.

There was Naomi. She was an adorable little freckled-nose redhead who had banked on making the Chatsworth porn-queen-dream come true. That had been her plan rather than college. A general dislike for taking it in the ass, court-ordered rehab, and shooting her stepfather had knocked a promising porn career off track though. She had beaten the rap on shooting stepdad, mostly because he *had* just pounded her mother into a coma before coming after her with a kitchen knife. Mom never woke up, and stepdad was DOA at county. Naomi never quite got back in front of the camera. She had heavy baggage.

Next was Felipe, a stylish young Puerto Rican cat with a decent family pedigree of competent practitioners. Felipe was estranged from all of them though, hence, his affiliation with this crew rather than the family clan. Felipe had talent, and he wasn't afraid to use it. He was never the kind to roll hard though. He tended to stay on the whiter side of gray when it came to practicing the Art.

Then there was a pretty young Mexican girl. She was all class and attitude, and she wasn't the sort of lady you pissed off unless you were ready to take the pain.

Her name was Mahri. She was the *real* talent in the group.

Gabriel paused, frowned at the photo. A lump pushed up in his throat, and he swallowed it down. Mahri Ramirez. They had history—lots of history.

She and Gabriel used to be an item back in the days before she was old enough to know better and he was still too young to care. She'd taught him to talk dirty in Spanish. It was a marketable skill in Southern California. Mahri was good news if you were a friend; bad news if you were an enemy. She was a spooky girl. Her mentor, Dr. Angus McCoy, kept her on the level—most of the time.

These people only had one real thing in common. They all ran with the Circle Odd. A coven of petty practitioners based in University Park. A few philosophical differences aside, the Circle Odd was a friend of the Crow. In particular, friends of Gabriel and his sister Delilah.

The Odd had a couple of rockstar types—Mahri and Felipe and the coven's founder, Dr. Angus McCoy. For the most part, it was a low-key, low-impact sort of outfit. They didn't run hard and fast like the Crow. They turned a little easy trade and stayed out of the real knuckle-busters. Back in the day, Dr. McCoy used to get it on, but The Odd was more schoolyard than street these days. Nobody equated them with hardcore anymore.

"What the hell were they doing sniffing around Washington's turf?" Gabriel asked, perplexed.

"Mahri," Victor replied. "I guess her and, uh, Ol' Doc McCoy had a little difference of opinion about what direction the coven was moving. She wanted to up their game. Heard Washington was shopping, so she went selling."

"Selling what?"

"The usual for the Odd. Something of his went missing. They were helping him find it."

"Washington hired them to find his missing cash?" Gabriel asked.

Victor nodded. "And to figure out how it went missing."

"How'd that work out?"

"Not so good," Victor replied. "Mahri and the kids apparently got close enough to get their asses handed to them then they shit the bed and ran; scattered like quail and left Washington holding the bag and the blowback."

Gabriel thought of the t-shirt's he'd seen that said *I'm A Bomb Technician*. Practitioners were sort of like bomb techs. *I'm an occult expert. If you see me running, try to keep up.* "Bet he's real happy about that."

Victor shrugged. "He's on the fence. Mostly interested in getting the right somebody on the job."

Gabriel mulled that over. If Washington had hired Mahri and her crew to track down his missing cash, it meant whoever hit him—and how they did the job—was something he couldn't sort out the old-fashioned way. That indicated a real hardcore player. It wasn't very likely that a player of that caliber would be willing to give up his ill-gotten gains without a fight. And there was no telling just how much fight they might have had in them. Dicey prospect, getting in the middle of that mess.

"Okay, so whoever ripped off Washington, how'd they do the job?" Gabriel asked.

"Strong. Right in through the front door."

Gabriel cocked a dubious eyebrow. "Somebody just walked in, knocked over a heavily guarded gangland depository, and walked out?"

"Not exactly," Victor replied. "Apparently the guards got a bad case of homicidal madness and turned on each other. Tore each other to pieces, and nobody even hit the panic button. Once the screaming stopped, somebody walked in, stepped over the bodies, and helped themselves to the cash. Then they split."

"That's unusual," Gabriel said.

"So, you can understand Mr. Washington's interest in our services."

Yes. Yes, he could. Something that went bump in the night, indeed.

"Any survivors?" Gabriel asked.

Victor shook his head. "Don't know. Washington had a crew of nine on the site at the time. He came up with five dead and four MIA."

Gabriel sighed. Missing men smelled like an inside job. Inside jobs had a way of getting messy because they called into question who you could trust. "Does Washington think his, uh, missing men are sitting on a beach somewhere earning a percentage?"

"Not ruling the possibility out, but he doesn't have any intel that says so. Washington thinks someone or something is coming after him. Retaliation, maybe, for whatever landmine the Odd stepped on. Somebody trying to convince him that chasing his lost money ain't worth it. He ain't sleeping real good when the sun goes down."

"So, Washington's got some talent on staff, right? His resident priestess? What does she think this is?"

"To be honest, if she knew, they wouldn't be hiring us."

"She bullshit or the real deal?" Gabriel asked.

"As far as I can tell, she's the real deal. This just blindsided them and they need a boost."

Gabriel pondered the last order they had filled for Washington. The Vert Grimoire of Jean-Francois Mercier. It was a master-work of the Merovingian Discipline, focused on protection from spiritual attack and binding hostile practitioners and entities. They had requested it on the quick, fronted the cash like they meant it, and the Crow had the connections to make it happen in record time. It added up.

"What do we know about her? The priestess." They had all seen it before and more than once. Some outsider hires on their very own spiritual consultant, mystic, occult advisor, whatever, and they turned out being the problem.

"We're still putting her puzzle together, you get me?"

Gabriel did. He'd keep his eyes and ears open, and one of them on Mr. Washington's trusted priestess at all times. He asked the million-dollar question. "So, Washington would like us to ...?"

"Find his money. Find out who took it, how they did it, and how to prevent it from happening again."

"And when we find them?" Gabriel asked.

Victor shrugged. "That's going to depend on what we find and when we find it."

Gabriel nodded. "What about the Odd? Mahri, the Doc, and the other kids?"

"I don't know yet," Victor said. "They blew a bomb up in Washington's face and then cut and ran. He's not gonna be real quick to forget that."

Gabriel felt a little unsteady about that prospect, and his expression shouted it loud.

"I get you," Victor said, holding up a conciliatory hand. "First things first, we clean up the mess. That's what we're getting paid to do. How we handle The Odd is our business. Me and Doc McCoy go way back. And I know, you and Delilah both got ties. They're friends. We don't shit on our friends."

Not unless they shit on us first, Gabriel thought, the image of punching a forty-five-caliber hole in Uncle Frankie's skull still fresh in his mind. He stowed that thought. Fast.

Silence hung in the room, the expectant hush of the other shoe waiting to drop.

Gabriel looked back and forth between Victor and Fiona. "What?"

Victor nodded toward the photos in Gabriel's hand. "Flip to the back of the stack."

Gabriel did. He saw the photo of a man, plain and dull, some middle-aged white guy dressed in a gray suit that reminded Gabriel of a Texas rancher on a Sunday afternoon. He wore a thin goatee and a long brown ponytail. Dude had glasses that belonged on a cartoon character. He looked like he sold lawn equipment at Home Depot and collected butterflies on the weekend. Maybe he had lived with his mother until she died, after which he had inherited the house and all her *Precious Moments* figurines. Gabriel didn't know him from Adam.

He looked up from the stack of photos. "Who's Mr. Magoo?"

Victor looked to Fiona to explain.

"His name is Hector," she said.

"And we know him?"

"I do. He's a hunter. A Knight Commander of the Helitori."

Gabriel gave that a second to sink in, to stretch to size, and went back to studying the mousey, bespectacled stranger in the photo.

The Helitori had been giving militant witch hunters a bad name since the Crusades. They operated very discreetly, even by the standards of the sort of people that populated the Crow's world. You didn't just ring them up for a sit-down and a pint. You had to know somebody who knew somebody to even make contact with them. They were ghosts, independent, diffuse, a hydra that never seemed to run out of heads. What the Helitori may have lacked in strength of numbers, they made up for in dogmatic devotion and the sheer independence of their many secret cells. They didn't have many allies. They had fewer friends. What they did have, was a *mission*.

The Helitori hunted demons, abominations, and abusers of black magic with fanatical zeal. Getting on the self-righteous shit list of the Helitori was a declaration of war for an organization like the Crow, and a death sentence for easier prey.

It was never good news when the Helitori came to town.

"So, what do they want with Mr. Washington?" Gabriel asked.

"Nothing yet," Victor replied. "They're looking for Mahri. They're after the Odd and whoever hit Washington."

Gabriel sniffed. "Shit."

"Yeah. Shit."

That was bad news, and Gabriel was slow to swallow it. "Does that mean the Helitori thinks the Odd was an accomplice to the Washington heist?"

"We don't know what it means yet," Victor admitted, "but yeah, it does kinda cast a suspicious light on Mahri and her crew, don't it?"

"What does Washington think about that?"

"I convinced him to reserve judgment for now," Victor said, "but make no mistake about it. If he gets the idea that Mahri fucked him, well, you know how that ends."

Yeah. He did. "How did the Helitori even catch wind of this?"

"It's what they do, son," Fiona replied. "Don't underestimate them."

It made for a complicated mess. Throwing the Helitori into the mix only served to make matters murkier. Whoever got between the Helitori and their prey would be at war by association. If that blowback landed on Mr. Washington's operation, it would be the Crow's fault, and their list of enemies would skyrocket.

Gabriel thought of his father's working-mantra-number-one. *If it was easy, anybody could do it.* And of course, its companion mantra. *If you're good at something, never do it cheap.*

"So how do we want to handle this?" Gabriel asked.

"I don't think I'm quite ready to rule on that yet. We'll have Church tonight and get everybody to weigh in. Eight o'clock. I'll get the word out."

Gabriel nodded. That was good. This Washington gig wasn't shaping up to be just another day at the office. Best to let the Crows be heard before laying down the law.

Mulling it over, he arranged a couple of the pictures on the coffee table and snapped a few shots of them with his phone.

Victor was curious. "What are you thinking?"

"Well, I'm thinking we've got all day until Church tonight, and there's no time like the present." He flipped to a picture of Mahri and her wayward Oddies. "If Mahri's got her tit in a ringer, there's a short list of places she'd go asking for help. The Odd was pretty quiet before she started shaking things up. If she and the Doc weren't seeing eye-to-eye, maybe the best thing we could do is get his side of the story first. Tracking down Mahri and the Doc is as good a place to start as any."

Victor nodded his consent. "Put your sister on dealing with the Doc. If he has something worth knowing she'd be the one he'd talk to."

"Will do," Gabriel said. He might need to roll her out from whatever rock she was under, but he'd get Delilah on task. "So, how's the payday look?"

"Mr. Washington fronted a hundred last night against five percent of whatever we help him recover. Since we're sweeping up after somebody else's mistake, we keep the front money if the job's a bust. We shake hands and walk away, do business another day."

Gabriel cocked an eyebrow. A hundred grand front and five percent of the recovery made this a million-dollar job. Depending on who they brought in for this gig, it would cut eight to ten ways or so, plus paying out workday gravy to Crows who weren't senior enough for a full share. That was definitely worth getting out of bed in the morning. The promise of cash did indeed inspire a certain unique kind of enthusiasm.

"Where to first?" Victor asked.

"Scene of the crime," Gabriel said with a smirk. "I want to see where the bad man touched them, maybe pick up a trail. We got a number for Washington's crew?"

Victor provided a name and number. Jonathan Markus. He ran security for Mr. Washington's outfit. "Warehouse is in Burbank."

Gabriel nodded, tucking the notes in his pocket. "Got it."

As he rose to leave, his mother called out to him. "Son?"

"Yeah?"

"Be careful out there."

That hint of worry. That little ghost of doubt Fiona St. John rarely, if ever, showed. It was a stark reminder for Gabriel that the stakes were high. The pieces on the board were just starting to move, and they were bigger and meaner than usual. Miscalculations were ill-advised. He turned back and kissed her on the cheek. "Thanks for the coffee."

Then he set out to track down his sister.

6

Delilah St. John's week was on a significantly different trajectory before her brother Gabriel came calling. On the day he was settling up with Uncle Frankie, she'd made a trip out to Palm Springs chasing a payday and drove her '66 Toronado as far as the directions she'd been given would take her.

She didn't usually make house calls. If people wanted her services, she normally insisted they come to her, not the other way around. But for five thousand bucks, she was willing to make an exception. She had it on good authority that the Godfather was good for it.

The Godfather—that's what they called the dude who ran this outfit—like in the movies. He'd already sent one of his cronies to bring her a down payment of a grand as a show of good faith. Money talked, and that was enough to get her out here from L.A. anyway.

The route came to an end in the lonely desert east of Palm Springs at a dirt driveway blocked by a chained gate. She pulled off the highway and up to the barred drive, taking one more look over the map, her notes, and her phone. The sun-weathered sign above the drive read *Bodecker Automotive* in faded green letters. She sighed. This was the place. Halfway between the ass-crack of nowhere and the land that time forgot.

Beyond the gate and the sagging chain link fence that surrounded the lot, buildings rose up out of the scrub like sandblasted ghosts. Dull metal boxes, skin burnished to the color of the desert by decades of neglect, sun, and dust. Business must have been positively booming at *Bodecker Auto*.

Martian landscape stretched in every direction broken by a

single ribbon of sun-bleached highway. Brown, empty desert dotted with crisp olive-green scrub. Jagged black mountains dimmed in blue haze. To the west, the tallest peaks were dusted with snow; to her south, the shadowy peaks faded into the distance like islands floating in a whitewashed sky.

The wind was a living thing in this country, always groping with insistent fingers, pulling hair and tugging shirt tails.

She pulled her jacket tight around her skinny frame and stepped out of the car for a smoke. The wind protested but eventually yielded enough flame to allow her to get her cigarette lit. Delilah and fire were old friends. It wasn't cold, but it wasn't really hot either. Which meant it was spring. Or winter. They were interchangeable in this country. She squinted into the setting sun and took a drag off her smoke.

Delilah was a little thing, five foot six and rail skinny, with a shoulder-length bob of snow-white hair that the wind pulled at like a merciless, shitty little brother. She wore a battered old motorcycle jacket, some ratty canvas high tops, and jeans that had seen better days. She was punky on accident—not really on purpose—it just sort of worked out that way.

An old Caddy appeared out of the cluster of buildings from the east and rattled its way down the chalky dirt drive on the far side of the gate. A minute later it arrived and parked opposite Delilah's Toronado, its tires crunching to a stop in the grit.

The passenger door opened and a scroungy meth-head popped out. "Miss Delilah?" he asked, and she nodded in response.

He was young, twenty-something—not any older than her—all knobby knees and elbows, with stems for arms and legs, and lank, dirty-blond hair.

There was a blurry tattoo of a swastika on the back of his right hand, yet he appeared meek as a mouse. He smiled a lot, and did so as he introduced himself, "Hey, I'm Connor."

She cast another glance at the sinking sun. "Hey, Connor, clock's ticking." The window to get it right and get it sharp was closing fast. That, and she wasn't much on small talk. "I'll follow you."

"Right," Connor replied with a nod and gestured to the driver. "Uh, this is Levon."

"Ayyyy, girl," Levon said, calling out from the driver's window with a lecherous yellow smile.

"Uh-uh," Delilah said with a shake of her head. "Just drive, Levon. I'm here for business." She crushed her smoke out under the toe of her shoe and dropped into the driver's seat of her car.

Connor snorted and chuckled. "Swing and miss, dude."

Levon rolled his eyes. "Fuck off. Get the gate, fool."

"Right," Connor said as he unlocked the chain and dragged open the gate. With a nod he stuck the padlock in his jacket pocket and hooked a thumb over his shoulder, smiling that dopey puppy dog grin at her. "I'll leave it unlocked for you."

"Brilliant," she said with a smile, then made a good show of looking irritable and impatient while Connor mounted back up with Levon. The cruddy old Caddy whipped around and headed back down the dirt drive.

Delilah pulled the .38 Bodyguard from the black leather satchel on the seat beside her and checked once more to make sure it was loaded and within easy reach should she need it. After a deep breath and a check of her nerves, she pulled out and fell in behind Levon and Connor.

Victor, her Lord Father, didn't condone his people doing work on the side without his say-so but, what he didn't know wouldn't hurt him, and better yet, she wouldn't have to split with him. Delilah had taken a bath on the Super Bowl and needed to scrounge up some cash fast. No big deal, really. Nothing worth pissing the Lord Crow off. He got a little testy when his people—especially his own kids—did stupid things like lose their hat and ass on a huge Super Bowl bet they'd booked while they were high as a kite. It wasn't really about the money—it was about reputation. Victor St. John didn't like to look bad, even by proxy.

So, there was Delilah. Daddy didn't need to know, and frankly, neither did these folks. She hadn't exactly thrown the family name and her resume on the table when she heard the Godfather was hunting for some pay-as-you-go-talent. And she didn't plan to.

Delilah had a moment of doubt, that nagging realization that this would be a great place for a couple of tweakers to get out of hand and try to leave her dead in a ditch. That little flutter of anxiety continued to crawl around in her belly until she saw there were several other vehicles here waiting for them.

A jacked-up pickup with knobby tires and lights on its roll bar, with some men and women reclining in the truck bed in lawn chairs, sipping beer.

There was an old Dodge Charger, a big blower on the hood, primer gray, still a work in progress, and several motorcycles— big old gnarly choppers, with ape-hanger handlebars and saddle bags.

Across the lot, she saw a pair of big, mismatched SUVs with fifteen, twenty people milling about. Tattooed thugs, bikers, speed-freaks and their special lady friends mostly. They had a couple of fires burning in rusted out barrels, and as the sun sank into the horizon, they clustered around the burn barrels in the gathering gloom.

The ratty Caddy parked on the edge of the crowd and Delilah pulled in beside, following suit.

"Here we go, Miss Delilah," Connor said as he stood up out of the passenger side of the Caddy. He even came her way and opened the door for her like a parking attendant at a high-rent hotel. Levon dismounted the Caddy but paid her little mind. He cupped a hand over his mouth and lit up a joint instead, wandering off into the deepening gloom to join the party.

With the sun sinking and the wind rising, it was getting cold fast.

"After you, miss," Connor insisted.

Delilah took up her black leather satchel and hooked it over her shoulder as she climbed out of the car. Then walking with Connor, she moved in toward the crowd.

The wind howled, creaking through the cracks and empty windows like cold air through the pipes of an old organ. Music, radiating from the muscle car, nearly drowned it out. A harmonica squealed as Led Zeppelin's *When The Levee Breaks* echoed over the derelict lot.

Connor trotted over to the gaggle and approached a man

who was reclining on his bike like a king surveying his domain from his lofty throne.

That would be the Godfather.

The guy was tall, hard-looking as cut granite, lean and mean, decked out in biker leathers, with short-cropped gray hair and a stubbly beard. He wore a large silver ring on each finger of his right hand and a gold wedding ring on his left. The man leaned down and Connor spoke to him in confidence. With a nod, he patted the young man on the shoulder and stood. He raised a hand in Delilah's direction and beckoned her to come over.

The Godfather strode forward to meet her, extending his ring-laden right hand to her in greeting.

"Miss Delilah," he said with a crooked smile, his voice a gravelly baritone. "You come highly recommended. I take it finding the place wasn't too much trouble?"

Delilah took in the scene. Some of the revelers paid her no mind, others eyeballed her with interest. The nagging awareness of how alone she was out here bruised her usual bravado. She nodded.

"Good," he said, glancing to the west. The sky was the color of blood and the sun was gone. "It's my understanding that this sort of thing is a matter of particular timing. Correct?"

Again, Delilah nodded. "There is the matter of the balance owed."

The Godfather reached into his leather jacket and produced an envelope stuffed with bills. With a friendly smile, he passed the cash to Delilah.

She thumbed through the bills, giving a quick count and then stuffed the envelope into her satchel.

"Should we get started then?" the Godfather asked.

Delilah was a little taken aback. "Right here? In front of everybody?"

"Of course," the Godfather replied.

"It's just that usually most folks want to do this kind of thing in private," she said.

He grinned. "My money, my show, right?" His cronies were getting quiet, zeroing in, taking notice. "It *is* my show, right?"

He was all smiles, his voice even, but there was a dangerous insistence to it that Delilah dared not ignore.

She cleared her throat and summoned up her courage. *Never let them see you sweat.* "Of course," she said with a bat of her eyes. "What's a girl gotta do to get a drink around here?" She managed a crooked smirk of her own.

There was something almost paternally approving about the Godfather's smile. He waved over at the muscle car with a flick of his fingers. "Cut it," he ordered, and a few seconds later the music died, leaving only the moan of the wind, the crackle of the fire barrels, and the soft murmur of the crowd. "What are you drinking, little lady?"

"Tequila," she replied, and the Godfather nodded to one of his people to fix her up. He led her like his personal guest to a tailgate of a pickup truck scattered with an array of beverages, and in a moment or two, one of his girls produced a shot of tequila. Delilah nodded her thanks and downed it. She set the empty shot glass down and said, "One more time." A black-haired girl with a gargoyle tattooed on her left forearm and a ruby stud in her bottom lip poured her another.

"What do they call you?" Delilah asked.

The girl gave a wicked smile. "Ruby."

Delilah nodded. "That figures." Ruby had a shine about her that Delilah could sense. A minor hedge witch maybe. A featherweight, but a practitioner nonetheless.

Delilah looked at the second shot while the first one crawled down her throat into her belly, drowning the fluttering wings of nervous butterflies. She looked up at the Godfather and nodded. "I need blood."

His brow twitched in amusement. A dead hush fell over his gathered troops. "How much?" he asked.

"Just a drop or two," she said.

He obliged at once. A little pocket knife flicked open with a mechanical *snick,* and he pricked the tip of his finger. A bead of blood welled from the small wound and wound down his finger in a crimson ribbon. "Where at?"

Delilah picked up the shot glass and approached the Godfather, holding it up to catch a couple drops of blood as they fell from his finger. The little crimsons beads swirled in the golden tequila.

Delilah's eyes met the Godfather's, and she managed a final confident smirk. "Bottoms up," she said and downed the shot.

The reaction in the crowd was mixed. Some didn't bat an eye. Others chuckled at the display as if watching a sideshow act. Still more watched in rapt attention. Ruby stared narrow-eyed in simmering anticipation.

Delilah felt the tequila burn its way down her throat. She kept her eyes locked with the Godfather's the entire time. One heartbeat ... Two heartbeats ... Three. The booze bloomed warm in her stomach ... Four heartbeats ... Five.

The whole world seemed to pause. To take a deep breath before the plunge.

Then it all rushed away in a red haze.

The sensation of falling, of sudden vertigo, always made her gasp. Her head lolled back. Her eyes rolled up, and the lids closed dreamily. She was lost, lost in a strange Red Dream.

She saw the Godfather. Muffler roaring, motorcycle tearing down the desert highway in the crimson gloom. She saw him with a handful of a lady friend's raven black hair getting his dick sucked. He wasn't cheating, just getting his nut. The wife that belonged to the golden ring on his left hand was long dead. Noise, mundane events, mundane memories. She rode them down deeper into the Red Dream.

She saw a killing, one long past. The Godfather's first. A beating, vicious blows from a pipe bashing some poor bastard's head in until brains flew.

The Red Dream twisted and shifted, a painful change in direction, a dizzying turn through the bottomless crimson fog. Running ... fast ... she was running, the cold, crisp crimson night racing by as she loped through the scrub. A man screamed, making her heart race. The stink of his fear filled the air, and she was on him, the Godfather was on him ... teeth slashing, hounds howling ... blood bubbling through the hooks of her teeth.

Until again ... the Red Dream twisted and violently changed course.

She saw the Godfather... and she saw the man behind him raise a gun to his head. She both saw the shot and *felt* the pain explode through the back of her skull.

Then nothing.

She gasped.

She opened her eyes.

The world was purple twilight, not crimson fog.

The only sound was the crackle of the burn barrels and the howl of the wind. Otherwise, you could hear a pin drop. Nobody in the Godfather's posse even breathed.

Delilah steadied herself, took a few deep breaths through her nose, and with a shaking hand, set the shot glass down on the tailgate. "Another," she said with a grunt. "Please."

Delilah had worked a lot of Red Dreams in her life. She'd seen a lot of fucked up things, peeking up the metaphysical skirts and into the cosmic souls of other people.

She'd never seen *anything* quite like that. She'd never ridden a Red Dream all the way to the moment of somebody's death before. It was an ill-advised thing to do. The living mind had a hard time coping with the experience of dying. It shook her up.

Ruby poured her another shot of tequila, studying her with pregnant expectation. Delilah took the shot gratefully and downed it. This one knotted up her stomach on the way down, and she had to suppress the urge to gag. She wiped her mouth with the back of her hand and took a slow, steadying breath.

She could feel the Godfather's eyes on her, like lanterns in the twilight gloom. "Well?" he asked softly. "What'd you see?"

Fear crawled into Delilah's belly like a scavenging crab. What could she say? What did she dare say? "I don't ..." she muttered impotently, shaking her head, eyes wandering around the crowd closing in around her, all staring at her expectantly.

That's when she saw him. The man from her Red Dream. The one who bushwhacked the Godfather and blew out the back of his head. Her hands threatened to tremble, to betray her. "Maybe we should talk privately," she said, looking up at the Godfather with knowing, serious eyes.

He shook his head, his expression resolute. "No. Right here, right now. You tell me what you saw."

Lie, she thought desperately. *Make something up. Say something, say anything, just don't say* that. *Buy some time. This isn't what you signed on for.* But it was virtually impossible for her to lie right now—not to him.

The blood magic of the Red Dream was a double-edged sword. She'd tasted the Godfather's blood, and while that opened a window on his soul and his fate, it gave him a little leverage over her in return. At least until the sun rose and the Red Dream broke for good.

"Tell me," he insisted, and she couldn't deny the compulsion that pulled right through her gut.

Clenching her jaw, but unable to stop it, the truth leaked out through her teeth. "That man is going to kill you," she said, jabbing a finger at the crony she'd seen in her vision. The one who'd blasted the Godfather in the back of the head.

There were cries of outrage, of alarm.

"Fuck you, bitch!" the would-be assassin snarled.

"Thank you," the Godfather said. There was some pushing, some shoving, and some threatening words, but the Godfather paid it all no mind. "Boys. Grab Booker, please."

Four hard-hitting thugs moved into action as the Godfather stepped defensively to Delilah's side. His boys were in position before Booker ever knew what hit him.

"Let's have us a bonfire!" the Godfather roared, and his enforcers dragged Booker away to the edge of the gathering, kicking and screaming. Delilah saw a couple more of the Godfather's men stalking that way with a can of gasoline and an old tire.

Dread, bile, and tequila welling up in her throat, Delilah tried to turn away. She wanted to leave, to run. She didn't want to be here for this.

The Godfather grabbed her by the elbow and stopped her. When she tried to fight back, to pull away, he subdued her and pulled her close, grabbing her by the chin and forcing her to look.

"No, no, my dear," he chided softly in her ear. "You called it. So, you're gonna watch."

His boys beat Booker down like a dog. When all the fight

was out of him, they dragged him back to his knees and shoved that old tire down over his head and shoulders, pinning his arms to his sides. When it was firmly in place, the poor bastard started to scream, to plead.

"No! No! No!" he wailed. "Please! Please! Don't! Please!" His cries fell on deaf ears.

They doused the tire in gasoline and lit it on fire.

Orange flames and black smoke rushed up to engulf the man's body, his face, his head. Delilah had never heard a human being scream like that before. He collapsed and writhed on the ground, kicking and wailing until he'd sucked in enough fire to fry his throat and silence him. Then he trembled and thrashed without a sound. The wind turned, dragging the black stench of burning rubber and gasoline over the pack. Delilah turned her face away from the stink. Cheering the fire on, the Godfather's hounds made no effort to put Booker out of his misery. They let him burn.

The Godfather seemed pleased.

That's when it hit Delilah. "You knew," she said shakily, a tear breaking loose and trailing down her cheek, her voice a quivering whisper. "You already knew."

"Of course I knew," the Godfather replied. "What kind of chicken-shit outfit do you think I'm running here?"

Delilah had no answer. She stared at the burning wreckage of Booker in silent horror. This wasn't her *thing*. This wasn't what she *did*. She hadn't been ready for it. This wasn't what she'd come out here to do.

"See, but now I know you're the real deal," the Godfather said. "So, when I call on you again, I know I'm getting what I pay for. Right?"

That hit Delilah like a slap across the face. *Wrong!* Anger bubbled up in her then. Pure, hot, and righteous. This wasn't going to happen. She wasn't going to *let* this happen, would be *damned* if she would let this son of a bitch cow her and jerk her around on a leash. Anger erased the fear and shock, and she bristled up.

"What do you think you're doing?" she snarled, wrenching free of the Godfather's grip and pushing away. He let her go and held up a hand to his nearby men signaling for everybody to stay cool.

"No need to be hostile," the Godfather said.

Delilah's eyes narrowed dangerously. "I know what you are. And your pack of hounds and your little hedge witch don't scare me."

"The fuck's this noise about?" one of the Godfather's men asked. Delilah's revelations, what she saw, what she *knew*, raised the hackles on all their necks. But the leader of the pack waved him down with a gesture.

"Do you know what you're getting yourself into here, darlin?" the Godfather asked. Lingering behind him in his shadow was Ruby, the raven-haired girl with the gargoyle tattoo. She eyed Delilah with mounting curiosity and caution.

Delilah retreated three steps backward, coming to stand beside the nearest burn barrel while the crowd tightened and gathered in. Even on two legs, these people looked like what they were. A pack of bloodthirsty hounds, shifters, white trash dogboys and their little dabbler witch-bitch—And the pack was agitated.

"First, a murder isn't what I signed up for, and a lousy five grand doesn't even *begin* to cover it." With a hand model's grace, Delilah swept her fingers back and forth over the crackling barrel. At her caress, the flames began to swell.

Two dozen eyes reflected golden firelight back at her with inhuman intensity. Like a pack of hyenas caught in the game warden's spotlight. Dots of pearlish reflection danced in pairs in the gathering dark, all fixed on her.

Delilah had the Sight, more so than just the ability to ride the Red Dreams. She could feel the naked hostility coming her way in waves. The wish to come at her with blade and gun, fang and claw. She held her ground.

"Never without my knowledge and my permission. You want my services, you tell me what they're for." The flames swelled and crackled higher. A ribbon of fire coiled around her hand like a twining serpent.

"Last, if you *really* don't know who and what I am then your 'chicken-shit outfit' can go fuck itself and you can lose

my number forever you small-time, white-trash assholes."
Delilah pulled her hand away from the burn barrel, and
the ribbon of fire came with it, coalescing in her palm like a
boiling torchlight—then she held it out before her for all to see
before reminding them, "There's plenty of fire for everybody."

No one dared to move. No one dared to breathe.

"Now do you know who I am?" Delilah asked, a dangerous
glint in her eye, serpentine tendril of fire slithering through
her fingers.

Ruby laid a calming hand on the Godfather's arm. "I do,"
she said. "You're Delilah the Crow."

The Godfather cocked an eyebrow.

Delilah nodded.

The Godfather's demeanor changed at once.

"We don't give a shit," one of the pack hounds snarled.

"We *do* give a shit," the Godfather corrected, quieting
the pack. "Apparently we've had a misunderstanding. That's
on me." Equal parts curiosity, business-savvy, and caution
danced in his eyes. "I'd like to make that right."

Delilah had no illusions. For all her bluster and bravado,
she was miserably outnumbered, and this was no pack
of pussies. She might take a few of them with her, but the
sheer weight of numbers would crush her and then they'd be
dumping her in a shallow hole somewhere in the ass-crack of
California never to be seen again. Besides, she'd never killed
anything bigger than a mouse in her life. She was skating on
her *family's* ferocious reputation, not her own. Her face was
calm and hard. But her heart was racing, clicking in her throat
like a clock run amok.

The Godfather was savvy enough not to call her bluff,
risk the casualties, and ruin their business. So she was wise
enough to accept his olive branch. With a wave, she dismissed
the living flame from her hand.

"Consider this a down payment," she said, patting her
satchel where she'd stuffed the cash. "Ignorance and lack of
manners is expensive."

The Godfather chuckled, just a soft growling noise in the
back of his throat. But he smiled. "What's the balance?"

"I'll let you know," Delilah said. "Until then ... I don't see you, you don't see me."

The Godfather nodded. "That's fair. Have a good ride home, little sister."

Delilah didn't wait for a second invitation. She withdrew to her Toronado and tried to keep her pace casual. There were no doubt animals in that pack that wouldn't be able to help themselves if she looked like a rabbit running. And the Godfather might not be able to reel them in before the damage was done.

Keeping her foot light on the gas pedal, she found her way back down the abandoned drive, and out the route she'd come until she finally reached the blacktop. Her eyes stabbed the rear view mirror the whole way for signs of pursuit, but none came, so she grabbed the four-lane highway and was gone.

"Jesus Christ," she wheezed, blinking back tears. The sight of Booker burning and thrashing, trapped in his tire, his face twisting in the flames, screaming silent screams played on a reel in her head while the dark countryside flashed by unseen.

Her hands shook all the way back to Los Angeles.

7

Delilah's place was a little house up the hill from Dodger Stadium at the end of the Everett Park cul-de-sac. Nestled behind a screen of poorly trimmed fence brush and some withered old palms, it offered her plenty of privacy. Small apartment buildings and duplexes dominated the end of the cul-de-sac all around her, lining the street in a mix of disjointed colors and styles. For what it was worth, Everett Park, a teardrop-shaped patch of grass just big enough to take the dog out for a shit, was right out her front door. And you could see the downtown skyline from her porch. So at least there was a view.

Nobody bothered her here, tucked in behind the prickly brush and slumping palms at the top of a long flight of chipped concrete steps. That was just how she liked it.

She woke on her couch to welding arc sunlight blasting in the windows, hitting her in the face like a physical blow. The television was on, all obnoxious and brassy, shouting at her about some car dealership once in a lifetime sales event. Her head was pounding, and it tasted like a baby dragon had shit in her mouth. Desert dry, cigarette ash, weed, bile, and tequila.

She'd made it home late the night before and imbibed heavily. The lingering burn of the Red Dream held on until sunrise, and she'd had no wish to keep riding the Godfather's vision in living Technicolor.

She drank herself out of Patrón and smoked herself out of weed. It made for a more agreeable night. Somewhere near dawn, numb and dysfunctional, she dozed, tossing and turning restlessly through the remains of the crimson fog. She'd woken up in a drunken panic just before sunrise, assailed by dreamy memories. That of a massive black hound leaping at her with slavering jaws, ripping her stomach open, dragging out her entrails. After that, she'd finally slept. Well, for a few hours anyway.

Now was better. Because the remains of the Red Dream were burned away.

She was very hungover and maybe still just a wee bit drunk. She definitely didn't feel steady. When she sat up, her stomach did a somersault, and the room gave a defiant spin, sending her in a race with the devil for the bathroom. Delilah knelt and prayed, and the porcelain god accepted her offering.

Friday was off to an auspicious start. She stripped out of her smelly clothes and piled herself into a scalding hot shower. Her skin turned lobster pink, and her tattoos turned black.

None blacker than the Four-Winged Crow that stretched wings across her slender back. Her crest sported no blood laurel for kills or badges of honor for wounds suffered in the line of duty. She'd never been a knight or a captain like her brother. Delilah had other talents. In the Crow's left talon, it clutched a ring of stars. In its right talon, it clutched a banded torch with an orange and purple flame.

Delilah was a sorceress, by trade and profession. No petty dabbler. No one-trick pony. Through her mother's lineage, she came from a long and storied tradition. Most practitioners in the City of Angels spoke Delilah St. John's name in low and reverent tones.

She had other tattoos, permanent reminders of where she'd been and what she'd done. The ones that *weren't* written in ink mattered the most. Fading stretch marks swept crescent wings above her bony hips, across her midsection. A hand width below her belly button was a thin purple c-section scar.

Delilah hung her head low and let the hot water bring her back to humanity, her snowy hair hanging wet and straight down her cheeks. The clutching claws of the Red Dream were gone. Only the miserable tequila hangover remained. Of the two, the latter was the most preferable.

Scrubbed and pink as a squalling baby, Delilah stepped out of the shower a couple degrees closer to functional. She scraped the dragon shit out of her mouth with a toothbrush and slipped her steam-damp bathrobe around her shoulders, then she went looking for some Advil and a cigarette.

She rounded the corner into the kitchen and startled half out her skin at the unexpected sight of a man sitting at her breakfast table.

"Jesus Christ, Gabriel," she said with a yelp, fumbling to get her robe closed. "Don't you ever call first? Or knock?"

Gabriel shrugged. "It was open." He took two cigarettes out of his pack and lit them both. He passed one to her.

Delilah accepted the peace offering with an acidic expression. After a long soothing drag, she took a seat, hooking a stray strand of wet hair behind her ear.

"Staying busy, sis?" Gabriel asked with a smirk. He poked at a couple of burnt up roaches in the ashtray, ran his fingers over three empty wine bottles and a bottle of Patrón with about half a swallow left in it.

"Hey, we all got our thing, right? Mine's tequila. Yours is pussy. Speaking of which, back at ya. Where'd *you* sleep last night?" The corner of her mouth twitched up in a sour grin and Gabriel showed no signs of arguing. Probably because she was right. Oh, how the bobble-headed girlie-girls loved her big brother, all tall, dark, and mysterious. He was pretty fond of them too. Especially the married ones, because those were the most likely to end in a fight and he probably liked a good fight better than the girls.

His skirt-chasing was all tourniquets and scar tissue though. Her big brother was so hopelessly screwed up that finding somebody to love and cherish was probably beyond him. By her estimation, there was no beloved queen in his future.

Delilah could sympathize. Prince Charming's weren't exactly lining up at her baggage-buried door either. She had one of those once. A lifetime ago. That wasn't likely to happen twice. She didn't get misty over it. Didn't buy into the woe-is-me, self-pity, thousand-yard-stare bullshit. Most of the time anyway. Don't make any beds you didn't want to lie in. Delilah was full of tough talk. Sometimes she even believed it herself.

"You doing okay?" Gabriel asked, the barb ignored, his tone

sincere. The place was a wreck. Dirty dishes piled up in the sink. Trash needed to go out. The recliner in the living room had turned into a laundry hamper. There was a month's worth of unopened mail dumped in the box on the end table.

"Rough night," Delilah said. "You ever had one?"

Gabriel grunted. "Sometimes."

That rang a bell of recognition. "So, uh, was I right about Uncle Frankie?"

Gabriel nodded. "Settled up last night."

And that's all that was said about that. The silence that followed lingered until it got painful and stale. Delilah changed the subject. "So. What's up, doc?"

"We got Church tonight. Eight o'clock."

Delilah nodded. "Okay. Business or pleasure?"

"Business. The Helitori are in town. They're leaning on a client of ours. We might need to push back. Clean up a mess on the side."

Delilah reached out and tapped her cigarette into the overflowing ashtray. "Sounds like good ol' family fun."

"Yeah. A couple things though."

"What?"

"We got a pretty good idea who's on the Helitori's shit list."

Delilah motioned for him to continue, wondering what the hell he was tiptoeing around.

"The Circle Odd. Mahri. Felipe. Some of the others. They were working for Dante Washington, bit off more than they could chew. They fucked up, sis. Big time."

Delilah blinked, nodded, took a long slow drag off her cigarette. She had friends in the Circle Odd. The real kind. On the days when she thought giving up life as a Crow might be the thing to do, the Circle Odd was where she most often contemplated putting down roots.

She sighed, exhaling a plume of smoke. "Well. Shit." That news left her quiet for a long time. She opened her mouth to say something, realized she had nothing to say really, and closed it again.

Gabriel gave her a minute to try the bad news on for size. "You ready for the rest of the story?"

Delilah nodded. "Yeah. Hit me."

Gabriel laid it out, giving her the same briefing their Lord Father had just given him.

When he was done, Delilah's head still hurt. Maybe a little more than when he'd started. It must have showed.

"Do you, uh, want me to put on some coffee or something?" Gabriel asked at length.

"I'm out of coffee."

"Okay. You all right with this, sis?"

Delilah shrugged. "Do I have a choice?"

Her brother offered a sympathetic smile. "Not really."

"So, what's your plan now?"

"Find Mahri before somebody else does. She's the best lead we've got."

Delilah made a face. She was less convinced. "Whatever you say, chief."

Mahri had developed this bad habit over the years of getting in over her head and levering on Gabriel to come bail her out. In Mahri's defense, it usually worked. As a general rule, people who knew better got the hell out of Gabriel's way, but people that didn't woke up in the ICU or got measured for caskets.

Delilah was fond of Mahri, but more the Mahri she'd grown up with than the sketchy witch she'd become. Mahri was like that sister you had no choice but to love, even on the days you didn't like her very much. But Gabriel ... dear brother ... had a soft spot for that girl a mile wide and a decade old. And Mahri knew just how to push it until he squirmed. Not that Gabriel was ever going to admit that, mind you. Not at all. Not by a long shot.

"So, what am I doing while you're playing hide-and-seek with Mahri?" Delilah asked.

"Need you to check in on the Doc. Word is him and Mahri are butting heads about this Dante Washington thing. He might know something she's not gonna tell us."

Delilah nodded. She knew she was more likely to get the Doc's cooperation than anyone else in her family. Besides, this whole mess had her worried about the old man.

She was almost as blind to her soft spot for the Doc as her

brother was about Mahri. She'd at least admit she had one for the old Scottish hippie. There had been many a day when the only person in Delilah's orbit that didn't want something from her was Doc McCoy. That included her own father and every now then, her brother too. Not the Doc though. He just liked to talk about things he couldn't talk about with his own apprentices— that and drink. As it so happened, she was good at both.

"Don't go alone," Gabriel cautioned. "Call Dodger. Have him meet you."

Delilah didn't argue. "You gonna take your own advice there, Captain? Call in some backup?"

Gabriel mulled it over. At length, he nodded. "Yeah."

"Good," she replied.

When he was done with his smoke, Gabriel crushed it out in the overflowing ashtray and rose from the table. He bent down and kissed his baby sister on top of the head. "I'll see you at Church tonight. Don't do anything stupid, okay?"

Delilah gave a sour chuckle. "Hey, you know me. Constant as the North Star. Where are you going?"

"Washington's busted up warehouse in Burbank," Gabriel said. "And the Five's a shitbeast this morning."

Delilah nipped a short drag off her smoke. "Okay. Try to bring me back something we can work with, would you?"

Gabriel nodded then he gave her the stern big brother look. "And what are you gonna do?"

"Behave myself and have breakfast," Delilah said. "Maybe shave my head and get a swastika tattooed on my snizz." She shrugged. "I'll manage. Go. You're cramping my style."

Gabriel chuckled, and before he left, he dropped a couple of cigarettes on the table for her. "You're out of those too," he noted, pointing at the pile of crumpled up packs scattered around the table. He stepped out.

Feeling the worry pinching at her in uncomfortable, private places, Delilah got herself straightened out. She called Dodger as promised, skipped that tattoo and the head shave, and headed out to check on Doc McCoy.

PART TWO

Hard Left Turn

The Crow is the most mercenary of all the great old houses. When seeking their services, a shopper would be wise to remember that they value the terms of the deal as much as the price. If you're looking for a mercenary blind to everything but the buyer's gold, there are plenty to be had, and you should look elsewhere. The Crows have their own code, and it's not for sale.

A kingless gaggle of rogues and rebels, built on a legacy of defiance and vicious independence. To some, an alliance of outlaw princes and thuggish gangs rather than a proper house. To others, the ultimate and enviable expression of freedom. Somewhere between the revilement and the romance lies the truth. But only a Crow knows what that is.

Appended by Elijah Berdeaux, Master Knight of the Watch
to *A Modern Study of the Great Houses*
by Bahadir Fadel Satik, Lord Commander of the Watch

8

Dante Washington's busted up cash depot was a few blocks off the Five in central Burbank. It was tucked in where a narrow, sun-bleached warehouse row dead-ended at some train tracks. Across the tracks was a busy Home Depot and a block or two the opposite direction was a sketchy looking car yard behind a rusty metal fence. It looked like a chop shop, and nobody seemed much to care. In between, the world was filled with warehouses and industrial buildings. North and south, mountains rose up out of valley haze, green and brown. The day was white spring sunshine and getting warm fast.

Gabriel cruised down warehouse row in a nondescript work car—a white Nissan sedan that would have blended away into any parking lot in Southland with a registration that didn't land anywhere near him or his family. Vehicles had a bad habit of becoming rolling crime scenes when things didn't go according to plan, so it was best if the one you had to set on fire and abandon in a ditch led the authorities nowhere. As a matter of habit, Gabriel didn't touch his personal wheels when he was working. He pulled the burner Nissan into the back lot of the warehouse and parked it.

There was no one around and no sign of life—just a rust-spotted metal sign on the wall beside the loading dock that read *Foster Enterprises* and a matching, aging panel truck pulled up alongside the dock. He ran the company name through his mental Rolodex but came up dry; it meant nothing to him.

A big gray SUV rounded the block, pulled onto warehouse row, and shortly after that, into the lot behind him. Four well-dressed men dismounted. They were mature, fit, well-groomed, and athletic, and looked more like private military contractors than gangland thugs. Gabriel swung out of his vehicle in kind and they met in the middle of the parking lot.

A man stepped to the front of the pack and took the lead. He was forty-something, tall and slim, with a smoothly shaven head and meticulously trimmed goatee. He wore a tailored black suit accented with an open-collared burgundy shirt. He approached and offered his hand with a companionable smile.

"Jonathan Markus. I manage security for Mr. Washington."

Gabriel shook the man's hand and noted the heavy gold chain on his wrist. The sunlight caught it, and he noticed each thick link was engraved with Ptolemaic runework. Markus and his men were no neighborhood homeboys in business casual. They were professionals.

Professional *what* remained to be seen.

"Shall we?" Markus said, gesturing toward the warehouse.

"I assume we can speak frankly, Mr. Markus?" Gabriel asked as they made their way across the secluded back lot.

"Of course."

"Nine men babysitting this building. Five of them go out of here in plastic bags. Four of them disappear. I'd lay even odds that if you find your four MIAs, you find your money." Gabriel chuckled. "Or you at least find who you need to beat until they tell you where the money is. Yeah?"

"Maybe," Markus conceded.

"But you don't think so?"

"I do not," he replied but didn't elaborate.

"I'm assuming you guys had this place wired to the gills. Mics, cameras, the whole nine yards?" Gabriel asked.

"Of course," Markus said.

"And you got?"

"Nothing. No video. No audio. No door entry or exit times. The whole security system went haywire. Didn't even trip the outage alarm with our monitoring service."

"Really?" Gabriel asked with a cocked eyebrow.

"Yup. Didn't know anything had even gone down until shift change the next morning. By then, the scene was several hours cold."

Then someone is either good, lucky, or both, Gabriel thought. That didn't help narrow things down any. There wasn't exactly a shortage of people in Los Angeles who knew how to trick out an alarm system, even a very sophisticated one. It happened every day. "Other than the surveillance tech, did you have any other security or alarms on the place?"

Markus frowned and couched his response carefully. "I think you'd need to speak with Miss Althea about that," he said, his tone unsure.

A skeptic, Gabriel thought. *Skeptical, but not an outright disbeliever. That's good.* He wondered if Markus had seen just enough shit he couldn't explain to goad him into putting that charm bracelet on every morning, but if he still felt silly doing it.

Gabriel fished around in his jacket and came up with a smoke and a lighter. He fired it up and asked, "Have you guys already cleaned up, or is the scene still…"

Markus shook his head. "Clean as a whistle. Sorry. Couldn't be helped. Can't leave a mess like that just lying around."

They climbed the back steps toward the loading dock access door, and Gabriel began to feel the awful energy that still clung to the place. Like greasy smoke from a diesel fuel soaked funeral pyre of rotten corpses. *Not as clean as you think it is, boys,* he thought grimly. The arcane black rot still hung heavy in the air.

Markus punched a code into the panel beside the door, then produced a set of keys to unlock the mechanicals. He continued. "We had to …"

"You burned the bodies," Gabriel said, his voice low. "Good. They needed it."

An uncomfortable silence fell over Markus and his three men. "How did you know that?" he asked, pushing open the door. Inside, a dark hallway led away into the lightless beyond.

Gabriel shrugged and took a drag off his smoke. He didn't elaborate. The empty hallway loomed ahead of him, full of gruesome and unpleasant promise. He motioned inside, glancing to Markus. "May I?"

"By all means," Markus replied.

With a contemplative frown, he took a final drag off his cigarette and dropped it on the concrete stoop just outside the door. He ground it out with the toe of his shoe and stepped inside.

First things first, he inspected the wide metal jamb of the security door and its interior. It had the look of being recently re-painted, but for some reason, the paint was cracked and flaked. As if the door had been smashed by a massive impact. But there were no dents, dings, or scratches to account for the cracking paint.

Scratching his thumbnail along a flake in the paint, he was able to peel away a chip about the size of a quarter, revealing the faint traces of a blurred pale yellow rune beneath. The edges of the rune looked weathered and eroded. But they were on the inside of the door and underneath a layer of paint. The wind and rain hadn't been gnawing at them.

Running the crumbling chips of paint between his thumb and forefinger, he got it.

Someone had drawn and laid wards on this door and painted over them to conceal them. Then something else had come along and smashed them like toothpicks. He ran his fingertips over the surface of the door and along the jamb. There was a faint, disjointed, latent energy there, but whatever spells had been laid here to protect this place were spent and ruined.

There was enough pain and malice clinging to this place to taste it on the air like the stink of distant roadkill. But it wasn't enough to make use of, not directly.

Something else slithered just beneath the surface of his awareness here—something dark and foul—molten footprints left in putrid tar—but he couldn't quite see them. It warned him that something awful had been here and left its mark and the primitive instinctual parts of his mind screamed warnings that it might return. That monkey fear set the hair on the back of his neck prickling, but it wasn't useful, so Gabriel set it aside.

He sighed. The place was a dud, all sun-bleached and metaphysically threadbare, echoes of fear, and very little substance. It had been scoured clean. Even if it hadn't been, two weeks had passed. Fourteen sunrises and sunsets. Each one degrading the imprint that lingered on this place. Pulling a decent divination out of thin air here would be difficult and not likely to bear much fruit.

He regretted not bringing Delilah along. He did this kind of stuff with vocational proficiency, but she was the real expert at Reading the echoes world.

"Problem?" Markus asked.

Yeah. You guys ruined my crime scene. Figured your priestess would know better, he thought but kept it to himself. Kind of like the monkey fear, it wouldn't have been useful. "Nothing time and money can't fix," he said with a grunt.

He stood, reaching into his breast pocket and produced a three-inch-long oblong crystal tied to the end of a foot-long leather braid. Letting it dangle like a plumb bob, he incanted under his breath.

He didn't have his sister's talent and education, not by far, but Gabriel had a few tricks up his sleeve that didn't involve blades and bullets. This was one of them.

At once the rising rhythm of his minor divination spell began to thrum in time with his heartbeat. He felt light on his feet, cotton-headed. The state of his vision changed and much of the color bled out of the world. His fingertips and the tip of his nose tingled. It was a little like being high and oxygen deprived. A feathery euphoria accompanied it, fluttering around in his belly and his naughty bits, but he kept it in check.

"Don't touch anything," he advised. Then he began to move off down the hall into the dark, empty warehouse, dangling the crystal in front of him. It swung back and forth to the slow rhythm of his steps, like the pendulum of a grandfather clock.

Markus cleared his throat. "I take it you're just going to ..."

"Yes," Gabriel replied. He put Markus out of his head and kept walking, moving a bit like someone focused on passing their field sobriety test. He trailed fingertips along the wall to keep himself oriented to something real and physical.

Then the world faded away into the silken murk, echoes of the dead rose up out of the gloom, and Gabriel walked into the shadowy memories of mayhem.

9

The divination was murky, indistinct. A walk through a watercolor echo and little more. There was a sense of memory, of feeling, rather than an actual crystalline image or painful recollection of experience. The scene was stale.

The dark corridor closed down around him in soft, soundless shadow. For a time unknown, he willfully put one foot in front of the other, blind in the dark, his stomach rising balloon-like in his throat. The sense of buoyancy, of weightless steps, made it feel like his bladder was floating. It was a distraction. He wished he'd thought to step out for a piss before getting started. He chased away the butterflies of unimportant thoughts and put it out of his head. The spell wouldn't last long. It would be easy to waste it on distractions and come away empty handed. He focused.

The gloom parted, and he stepped over the shape of a body on the floor. The body was like solid smoke, the shape and form recognizable, but the details indistinct. He tried to bear down, to bring the disconnected image into focus. Around the spectral shade, the floor exploded in a wash of inky black stains. Blood, Gabriel realized. The world remained without color, but once he saw it for what it was, the blood stains filled with crimson depth.

The gloom parted further.

Footsteps tracked through the blood and moved off into the dream world of his divination. He followed them. He tried to focus his sense of hearing, not his physical ears, but his awareness of the sounds that permeated this event. There would have been screams, shouts of fear, roars of rage, and gunshots.

These men, he'd been told, had ripped each other to pieces.

The silence receded, but what filled the hollow, sonic void was a harmonic hum, a rising and falling with the rhythm of his heartbeat. Layers of noise that had not existed here in the time and place he was studying. Strange.

Heartbeat.

Not his heartbeat.

He was aware of his own heartbeat, and it was not in sync with the harmonic drone. That was someone else.

Something else, something with a beating heart had laid this metaphysical static here. A distraction. Cover. Chaff. Ahead of him, the gloom receded further, and he saw two shadowy forms beating, biting, and grappling at each other. One of them had a claw hammer in his hand, and it rose and fell. Or maybe it was a hatchet. Shadowy weapon striking shadowy face. Crimson drops flew in surreal slow motion.

He tried to dial the two combatants in, to see them more clearly, to test the effectiveness of his spell versus the noise covering the echoed memories of the event.

But he could see no more than the flowing blood. Everything else remained spectral shadow.

He pushed hard against the limits of his divination spell trying to cut through the cover with brute force. But the harder he pushed, the less control he had over the ebb and flow of the imagery. The more he turned up the pressure, the less feeling he had of time and space. The less sense events made.

His vision of events became chaotic. He couldn't differentiate between the combatants, between old echoes and newer echoes. Shades began to fragment into different versions of themselves, walking back and forth maddeningly over their own footsteps as hours' worth of impressions began to play out all at once.

It was too much, so Gabriel pulled back on the power and wrangled the divination back to straight and level like righting a lumbering jetliner rolling over out of control. He sorted through the static of broken timelines and pushed the older echoes back to where they belonged. He brought the murderous events of the night of the heist back into focus.

Gabriel turned and looked back the way he'd come,

though the sense of space was very much relative. He saw the indistinct shape of a tall silhouette, though male or female, he couldn't tell; black, white, thin, fat, old, young—none of it was discernible. The only thing clear is that they weren't part of the combat.

This was the conductor leading this symphony of fratricide and bloodshed.

Gabriel watched the mess these poor bastards had made of each other. He watched guns buck and recoil in slow motion as bullets and buckshot traced gossamer lines through the air. Sometimes shadows shattered into fragments where the spectral bullets struck, other times crimson droplets flew as they cut through manshapes.

He counted the men. Twice. Nine men tore into each other, and no one was left standing. There might have been four of them unaccounted for when Markus was counting up his dead the next morning, but none of them walked out here alive.

Their gunshots and murderous blows rose and fell as the dark figure looming in the background wove the threads of their destruction. When it was over, nine men lay in ruins on the ground, and the dark puppet master stood over them, grim and unidentifiable.

The figure moved forward, and one by one chose four of the fallen. At its touch, the dead flinched, twisted, and rose, and when the master withdrew, four of the broken dead followed with them.

The gray gloom receded, and color and light began to leech back into the world.

The harmonic whine faded away.

Gabriel's spell began to draw to a close by degrees.

He found himself standing beneath harsh fluorescent lights, blinking at the sudden brightness, somewhere deep in the bowels of the warehouse. He was looking at a row of low concrete sub-structures that looked like bomb shelters, bunkers. There were four of them, each about the size of a walk-in cooler. They were more or less concealed behind a screening sea of shelves filled with random odds and ends, rows of OEM car parts, salvage, boxes, and containers. He was standing next to a large wooden crate marked FRAGILE - AUTO GLASS.

The little bunkers were reinforced vaults, complete with thick vault doors. One of them stood open, the door was intact showing no sign that it had been drilled and tapped by a safecracker and no scars from a welder. Someone had opened this vault with one of two things: mojo or the combination. Either prospect had its own implications.

The walls were deceptively thick and plated in an armored metal liner. The cavity inside the vault itself was about the width of a wooden pallet: about seven feet high and about twelve feet deep. Overall, similar to a walk-in closet, just a little deeper and shorter.

There were fluorescent lights set into the ceiling of the vault, protected behind a screen of thick steel mesh. There were red gas cylinders at the rear of the vault, set behind a sturdy grate. The placards on them marked them as some sort of fire suppression system.

This vault stood open and empty. There were some broken metal bands, like those used to fasten cargo to pallets, discarded on the floor along with some broken splinters of bright yellow wood.

As the last remnants of his divination spell faded, a dim recollection of cubes of shrink-wrapped, banded cash stacked up on pallets came to him overlaid by a ghostly afterimage of bloody men scooping the money into contractor's trash bags. One of the apparitions had a vivid crimson flower of a fresh gunshot wound in the side of his head. Then the spell was over.

With a frown, Gabriel pocketed the crystal pendulum, which was now warm to the touch. He hoped his sister could get more use out of it then he had, but only time would tell. Then he found his way back outside.

He found Mr. Markus and his men where he'd left them, huddled along the back stoop, talking in low tones.

"Welcome back," Markus said. "Anything good?"

Gabriel pondered that, and at length, he nodded. "I need a cigarette," he grumbled. He had more questions than answers. And now, he decided, was not the time to ask them.

They stepped outside, Markus locked up the depot behind him, and Gabriel had a smoke.

"So, how does this work, exactly?" Markus asked, resetting the alarm from the panel beside the door.

"Kind of like you'd figure," Gabriel replied. "We take a look at the evidence, see where it takes us next. Kick over rocks. Follow the leads. One step at a time until we find your money and who took it."

"And you really think you can accomplish that?" Markus seemed dubious. "Like this, I mean?"

Gabriel got it. He understood Markus's skepticism. It was hard enough to take this stuff seriously to begin with. He had already seen Mahri and her crew try this on for size and fail. Things had only gotten worse. Markus had his sympathies. But Gabriel gave a crooked grin and said "'This?'"

Markus chuckled. "Yeah. This. Whatever you call it."

"Yes," Gabriel replied with confidence. "I do."

Markus seemed as satisfied as he was going to get.

"Mr. Washington's, um, spiritual advisor. Miss Althea. How long has she been around?"

Markus chuckled. "About six months. No disrespect meant, Mr. St. John, but she *does* check out. That's the part I do for a living."

Gabriel thought he sounded very sure of himself. "Where'd she come from?"

"She's an associate of Mr. Watts," Markus explained.

"And he also checks out, I assume?"

Markus gave a knowing grin. "He and Mr. Washington go back as far as 'back' goes."

"Hrm," Gabriel replied with a single nod.

"So, now we...?" Markus asked, his voice trailing off.

"Sit tight and keep your heads down," Gabriel said, juggling his keys out of his pocket. "I'll be in touch shortly. Call us if something changes." He headed back toward his car.

"Like what?"

"Like something scary," Gabriel said. Then he was gone.

10

Gabriel stopped off for a recon tour of Mahri's apartment and helped himself to a little breaking and entering, just like he planned. It was a bust, nobody home, looking like it had been tossed by angry longshoremen who like to throw things around. Whether or not they'd found what they were looking for was anybody's guess.

The kitchen trash can was dumped over and had been laying there long enough to stink and draw flies. She hadn't been home in a while. The things that were missing gave Gabriel the idea that she'd split without much intention of coming back any time soon. Her birth control pills, her valuable arcane workings; no sign of a cell phone or charger, wallet, purse, cash or toothbrush. Sure, the goons who'd tossed the joint might have made off with those things, but he didn't think so.

Lingering beneath the smell of spilled trash and Mahri's perfume and hair products, Gabriel caught whiff of a faint, unnatural odor. A touch sulfurous, a taste metallic, a tinge salty. The ozone of magical residue. Somebody had used brute force to burn through Mahri's wards.

Gabriel made his way back to the living room and pushed aside the rug in the foyer with the toe of his shoe. He found the floor beneath blackened with scorched glyphs. Burned through, indeed. The entry had been fast. Somebody with lots of arcane horsepower and little time or patience to disarm the protective spells. A metaphysical door-kicker. Gabriel filed that away and left the trashed apartment behind.

He tried to give her a call. No answer. Then he tried her other number. Still no-go. That didn't surprise him much.

After the apartment, he hit a couple of her usual haunts, but nobody had seen her in days. Since the folks he questioned knew lying to him was hazardous to their health, he mostly believed them. It didn't really matter if they were telling him the truth or not though. He was more interested in the word hitting the street that he was looking for her and being seen doing it.

He swung into a 7-Eleven on Figueroa south of USC and grabbed a bottle of water and a pack of smokes. Then he gave it a little bit to see if any chickens came home to roost. He passed the time sitting in his car, people-watching the bus stop across the street. There was a curiously light-bulb-shaped lady in leopard-print stretch pants dancing to a tune that, clearly, only *she* could hear. A tired-looking fifty-year-old grandmother tried to prevent the three small children she had in tow from playing in traffic, and there was a tall scarecrow of a kid with his nose buried in his phone who kept having violent sneezing fits.

Gabriel liked to sit and watch the local wildlife. Always had, even as a kid. All the Angelinos going their thousand different directions, bouncing off each other like debris in a cyclone. But somehow all thirteen million little pinballs always seemed to get where they were going. Except for the ones that got gutter-balled along the way, of course, in car crashes or some other unfortunate event. But statistically, those were rare. Knowing the things Gabriel knew about the world, there was some strange comfort in that. He took it where he could.

Gabriel didn't have to be patient for long. His phone rang within the hour.

Mahri Ramirez. On cue.

"Hi, *papi*," she said. She sounded equal parts tired and apologetic.

"Hey girl," Gabriel replied, lighting up a smoke with a smug grin. "You're making yourself pretty hard to find. Something up?" Of course, he already knew the answer to that.

There was a long pause. "Yeah. You could say that."

"Uh-huh. You want to fill me in?"

"I know you're looking for me." Another long pause.

"Yeah? So why you hiding from me?"

"I'm not. I ... Look, I need your help. Now." Her voice was tight with tension, dread.

Gabriel processed that in silence.

"Please?"

"Where are you?"

"Koreatown." She rattled off an address around Third and New Hampshire. Gabriel made a mental note.

"Got it. What's going on?"

"Not over the phone," Mahri insisted. "Can you get here? Please?"

The tiny spiders of suspicion crawled up Gabriel's back. He didn't like that idea. "Yeah, how about you come to me? Can you get to the Church?"

She paused, sighed. "No. Look, it's complicated, okay? I've got something up here I need your help with. Can you just come?"

Bad idea. But Gabriel bit anyway. "Give me something, Mahri. Like whether or not I'm walking into a gunfight."

"No. It's not like that. It's just ... shit. Please. I need some help. I don't have anybody else I can call."

There was that tone. That damsel-in-distress tone Mahri had such a way with. She'd been using that on him since she was sixteen-years-old and needed a ride home. Gabriel sighed. *Don't let her twist you up. This ain't then. This is now.* "Yeah, okay. I'm on the way. It's gonna take me a little while to get up there. If something's going down and you need to bounce, bounce. I'll find you."

Mahri sighed, a sound of pure relief. "I know. I think I'm good for now. I just ... Thank you, Gabriel. Thank you."

"Yeah." Then he hung up the phone and went back to watching people at the bus stop across the way.

A pot-bellied guy with a bad comb-over had joined the cast. He was huffing and puffing and juggling plastic grocery sacks containing two plastic bottles of cheap booze—quantity over quality—some cheese puffs, and a pack of single ply toilet paper. Neither his liver nor his heart seemed to approve, but who cared when you had luxuries like wiping your ass with paper so thin you could read through it in store for you?

Gabriel glanced at his own reflection in the rearview mirror, glacial blue eyes looking back at him. "Trap?" he asked, cocking an eyebrow at the man in the mirror.

It was a rhetorical question. *Be careful what you wish for.*

With a frown, Gabriel got moving.

11

Gabriel made the drive to Koreatown and dropped a couple of phone calls while he was oozing through the afternoon traffic. One was to his Lord Father, giving Victor the heads-up that the game was already afoot. Then he called in some backup.

He parked his ride at a Starbucks in the shadow of the Hollywood Freeway, perched against the rear fender, had a few smokes, and waited for his backup to arrive while an endless procession of caffeine-craving Angelinos circled the busy drive-thru.

His added muscle rolled up in a late-model Toyota Camry. The Toyota Camry. The most common passenger vehicle in the City of Los Angeles and the ultimate in low-profile urban camouflage. The man behind the wheel was Piper Keels, a Knight of the Crow and Victor's pit bull.

Two words described Piper: bad motherfucker. He had those words tattooed on his scrotum—literally. You could put Piper Keels in a three-thousand-dollar suit and not hide for a second what he really was. He looked like an ex-con, which was true, and like he hurt people for a living, which he did.

Piper Keels was a bad motherfucker.

No suit today. Just jeans, work boots, and a dark gray hoodie. His long goatee was starting to go gray, and his hairline was receding. Piper wasn't a young buck anymore, but he still smiled a lot because he loved his job.

He'd come up with Victor and Bingo back in the day when the Crows of Los Angeles were rebuilding from an East Coast has-been to a West Coast who's-who. Piper wasn't big, and he wasn't loud, but he was hard as hard got. He didn't talk about being a hard motherfucker, and he didn't brag about it, either— because he didn't have to.

Piper was also more than a little nuts. Quick to laugh, he lived life and had a good time. Piper liked his speed, his weed, his women, and his whiskey. He loved to fight, and he liked to hurt people. The man worshiped the memory of his deceased mother and sister, and God help anyone who disparaged them. They'd die screaming, probably on fire with their own genitals stuffed down their throats. It was pretty commonly accepted that Piper's mama had done some awful shit to him when he was a kid. And that was okay. She'd killed his sister before killing herself. Nobody brought that up.

He had a puckered divot of a scar in his right cheek from where he'd been shot in face twenty years earlier. There were plenty more to go with it across his leathery, scarred hide. He had the words *DEATHPROOF Blackbird* tattooed across his chest and the scars to back it up.

Piper was Victor's iron right hand. He'd open you up with a smile and take a shit in the gaping wound while telling you a knock-knock joke if that's what the job called for.

He wasn't a man with the master plan like Victor, but he was a Crow for more than twenty years, and there was a lot of sinister intelligence lurking behind that vicious smirk.

Piper rolled down the driver's side window as he pulled in beside Gabriel.

"Hey baby," he catcalled to his Captain. "How much for a half-and-half."

Gabriel chuckled and popped the trunk as he ditched his smoke. "You got radios?"

Piper nodded.

Gabriel grabbed his gear bag from the trunk. It contained his handy essentials: Body armor, assorted weapons, a first aid kit in case he or somebody else got a hole put in them, and a collection of mystical wares and trinkets that proved useful in his line of work.

He threw the bag in the back of the Camry and piled in the backseat beside it. "Let's go," he ordered, stripping out of his jacket and shirt so he could don his bulletproof vest along the way. Piper pulled out into traffic as Gabriel directed him to the south.

Gabriel briefed the Crow Knight as they drove, using Google Maps on his phone to take a bird's eye look at the address Mahri had provided, familiarizing himself with the immediate neighborhood.

It showed a long, four-story brick apartment building, dominating the block on which it stood. It was wedged in between a series of strip malls and neighborhood restaurants to the south, and a sprawling stretch of two and three-story apartment buildings to the north and west that went on for blocks into Little Bangladesh.

Gabriel eyeballed the map display while he strapped into his vest and pulled his shirt and jacket back on. At a stoplight, he passed the phone up to Piper so he could have a look at the target himself. "I'll go up alone. You hang loose outside and back me up."

"Sure that's wise?" Piper asked with a cocked eyebrow, fingertips flipping the map image around, zooming in and out.

Gabriel chuckled. "No. But I need eyes on the street. That's you."

Piper nodded. "You're the boss. Get a kabob?"

"Maybe later."

Gabriel had Piper circle the block once to give them a curbside view of the area. On the south side, a razorblade-thin alley separated Mahri's building from its multi-level strip mall neighbor. The claustrophobic gap between the buildings was wide enough for foot but not vehicle traffic, and it appeared to be gated at both ends. The west alley at the back of the building was similar, and there was no way to get an angle to see it from the street. The north alley was better. It could pass vehicle traffic, and there was no gate. It emptied right out onto New Hampshire.

On the loop back around, Piper nodded toward the curb about a block north of the apartment building where the alley opened onto the street. "Here?"

Gabriel nodded his approval. "Yeah. That's good."

Piper parked it.

Before them on the right stood the long four-story red brick apartment building where Mahri was hiding out. The position would give Piper a good view of the east side main entrance and quick access to the north alley. It was the best they could do.

Gabriel popped in his earbud and slipped his throat mic on under the collar of his shirt. They did a quick final comm check. Once the radios were talking, Gabriel set out his kit bag and drew the heavy brass zipper open.

He skinned on a pair of tan leather driving gloves. He was a firm believer in a level of caution when it came to leaving his fingerprints around. Especially when he had no idea what he was walking into. Tan, because it was less conspicuous than black. When civilians saw a guy walking around in black gloves, they had a tendency to wonder what he was up to.

Once he was gloved up, he took a rag from his kit bag and proceeded to give his carried goods a quick wipe down. He ran the cloth over his pistols and spare mags, his radio, belt knife, and cell phone. Then he did his lighter and pack of smokes. It wasn't perfect, but it was better than nothing. From that point forward, everything he touched or added to his carried gear, he wiped down.

He tucked his Sig .45 into the pancake holster at the back of his belt and pulled on a shoulder rig underneath his jacket. He threaded a short, stubby suppressor onto his little Ruger .22 semi-auto and snapped it into the shoulder rig under his armpit. The little Ruger didn't pack the punch of his Sig .45, but it was a lot easier to carry concealed with a suppressor threaded onto the muzzle. It was also a hell of a lot quieter. Humans weren't hard to break, and the little twenty-two could get the job done. He hadn't met a man yet who could walk away from a couple taps to the dome from the old deuce-deuce.

He began to pull the more exotic fare out of his kit bag. A metal liquor flask filled with a thick, viscous oil the color of honey that smelled faintly of frankincense. That went in the breast pocket of his jacket along with a three-foot-long braid of thin leather cord with a small engraved silver bead woven into it every few inches. Gabriel wound it up into a loop and slipped it inside the other side of his jacket. He pulled three carved and stained wooden sticks out of an oiled piece of doeskin. Each one was about the length and diameter of a cigar, vaguely hourglass-shaped, carved with a veritable constellation of tiny, precise runes. They were warm to the touch.

The real estate in the pockets of his street clothes was filling up fast. Burner cell, radio, a couple of spare mags for each pistol, smokes and lighter and his other assorted goodies. But that was about all the room he needed.

Gabriel never carried a billfold with an ID or credit cards on his person when he was working just in case he unexpectedly woke up in an emergency room somewhere. It would make him harder to ID. Today, his wallet went into in his kit bag along with the rest of his miscellaneous paraphernalia. As per usual, he left it there in Piper's care.

Gabriel didn't wear trinkets of protection. The defensive spells he relied on were inked into his skin. He'd already slipped his bulletproof vest on under his shirt and jacket on the ride over, so he gave himself a final once-over, took a quick rifling through his kit bag, and called it good.

Shedding his sunglasses, he pitched them in the gear bag and dismounted the little Camry.

"Keep me posted," Gabriel ordered, giving his Brother Crow a pat on the shoulder through the open driver's side window.

"Do the same," Piper replied. He tapped a finger against his radio. "Status checks. I don't hear from you, I'm gonna come looking."

Gabriel gave an affirmative nod.

Piper lit himself a smoke and settled in for a wait, his radio resting on his thigh. "So. We trusting Mahri today?" he asked, his tone flat.

"Nope," Gabriel replied. With that, he headed off down the block.

Moving causally, as if he belonged there, he crossed the street and gave the red brick apartment building on New Hampshire a once over as he strolled. He loitered for several minutes across the street on the east side of the building, taking in the sights, marking the exits in his head, watching who came and went.

There was very little foot traffic in or out of the building, but the sidewalk was busy.

Down the block, somebody was having a yard sale. All the trashy shit they didn't want any more strewn around their building's stoop for a buck or two a pop. Yard sales drew penny-pinching crowds the way shit drew flies, and there were plenty of bystanders meandering around. Neighborhood locals wandered the sun-dappled sidewalks under the shade of scraggly old trees. The block was hopping. It was bad timing. Nothing that could be done about it, though.

There was an entrance lobby on the east end of the building. Fire escapes climbed the exterior walls above it all the way to the roof. There was a windowless service door on the north side of the building, looking out onto a narrow driveway alley.

Gabriel took a peek through the narrow gate on the opposite alley and saw at least one service door on the south side of the building as well—some sort of fire code exit most likely. The gates were eight feet tall and tipped in iron spikes. A guy could shimmy over them if he had to, but it would cost him some time. Scaling a gate or a fence was a great way to get shot in the ass.

Aside from the yard sale, it looked like a pretty typical Friday afternoon—Kids were making their way home from school, traffic was trickling back and forth, folks were haggling over cardboard boxes of shit nobody really wanted anyway, and somewhere nearby, somebody had their car stereo turned up too damn loud. Nothing looked out of place, but everything *felt* out of place.

It wasn't a question of whether or not this was a bad idea. Obviously, it was. Gabriel didn't wander into disasters like a naïve greenhorn. He did this for a living. The smart move would have been to have Mahri come to him, on his terms. But that wasn't going to happen. Not today, anyway.

Some days, you had to play the hand you were dealt. If it was easy, anybody could do it.

Gabriel keyed up his radio mic. "Going up."

12

Gabriel spotted the lobby security camera through the exterior doors before he even went inside. He was an old pro at ducking cameras. A subtle dip of the head, a turn of the body, angle toward the walls, and boom. Hollywood loved to play off security camera footage as if every frame was a smoking gun. Most cops would tell you though that more often than not, the security camera footage sucked. Especially if the person on the recording made half an effort to dodge it. The lobby cam gave him no trouble.

The main lobby itself was very narrow, old walls mopped in thick almond colored paint. One wall was dominated by ranks of metal mailboxes. At the far end, an archway opened onto a long central corridor that ran the length of the ground floor and just inside that corridor, a tiled staircase wound upward.

He took the stairs up, keeping an eye peeled for more cameras and spotting none. Each floor was closed off behind a fire door. The stairwell echoed like a hollow drum. He let himself out of the stairwell onto the third floor and began searching for Apartment 316.

The place smelled like dust and cooked cabbage. The carpet was worn and threadbare. The hallways in this building were dark and narrow with doors that led out onto the fire escapes at both ends. Meager daylight filtered in through their fly-spotted windows. It wasn't a ratty apartment building, but it wasn't a particularly nice one either. It looked like the super's solution to maintenance was paint. Lots and lots of paint. Decades of it smeared thick on everything that was worth painting.

Gabriel passed an elderly Asian man in the hallway. The

old man was sleepy looking and paid him no mind. Other than that, he didn't encounter another living soul.

When he found the correct apartment, a small unit in the southeast corner, he backtracked and posted up just inside the dark stairwell, keeping an eye down the hallway on 316. Then he pulled out his burner cell and gave Mahri a call.

She answered on the second ring. "Hello?"

"It's Gabriel. I'm here. Stay on the line, step out into the hallway. Leave the door open."

"Huh?"

"Just do it, Mahri."

There was a long beat of hesitation. Then, "Yeah. Okay."

A moment later the door to 316 opened and Mahri stepped out into the hall. She looked back and forth, phone to her ear. "I'm here. Where are you?"

Gabriel didn't respond for a full fifteen seconds. He hung tight to his dark corner and watched with one eye. He waited and he listened.

Mahri's body language grew increasingly impatient. "Gabriel?"

Gabriel watched her, looking for a tell that might indicate she wasn't alone, that she was up to something. He saw none.

With a sigh, he hung up the phone and dropped it in his pocket. He leaned out from his sheltering corner and gave her a discreet wave. A look of relief swept over Mahri's pretty face. He motioned for her to come his way and she did, meeting him at the corner.

"You alone?" he asked.

"Uh, sort of," she replied with a hesitant grimace.

Gabriel cocked an eyebrow. "What does that mean?"

"It means sort of." She smiled at him, looked like she was fighting the urge to hug him. "Thanks for coming."

"Uh-huh." Gabriel drew the suppressed .22 out from under his jacket and couched it alongside his thigh.

Mahri grew noticeably nervous at the sight of the gun.

"Let's go. You first."

"Gabriel I ..."

He shook his head. "Humor me."

With a nervous sigh, she did, and they made their way back to the apartment. Once inside, Gabriel pushed the door closed behind them. He keyed up his radio. "Contact. I'm in. Standby."

"Copy that," Piper replied.

Gabriel took in the room. The place was small, sparse. He could see a little galley kitchen off to his right. There was a bathroom to his left, the door standing halfway open, and a room next to that, but the door was closed.

The rest of the small one-bedroom apartment was living room. There was a cheap, second-hand television perched atop an even cheaper second-hand entertainment center. A well-loved couch. A guacamole-green easy chair that had been born in the '70s. There was an old, well-used, wooden tray table folded out beside it, and finally, a bookcase full of paperbacks containing at least three Bibles. The place positively reeked of an elderly retiree who lived alone.

The vibe did not disappoint. Seated in the worn out easy chair was, indeed, a motionless, expressionless, little gray old man. He sat, blinked, breathed, and every now and then he licked his lips, but his eyes stared off into the empty nothing over the horizon.

"Who's that?"

Mahri shrugged. "Mail on the table says Emilio."

Gabriel was not amused. "What is this place?"

"Borrowed."

"Uh-huh. Sit down," he instructed, pointing at the couch, his eyes scanning. Mahri complied. She crossed her legs and tucked one hand under her hip. Gabriel froze and shot her the stink eye, his grip tensing on the pistol. "Keep those hands where I can see them."

"Jesus, Gabriel, I'm ..."

"This is not a debate."

Mahri moved slowly and carefully, bringing her hands into view.

"Good girl." Gabriel kept one eye on her at all times while he checked the rest of the apartment.

He poked his head into the galley kitchen, checked the pantry at the back, then checked the bathroom—all empty.

Then he gave Emilio the once over, snapping his fingers in front of the old man's face.

"He's not home right now," Mahri assured him. "Figuratively speaking."

He looked back to Mahri and nodded toward the bedroom door. "So, what's behind Door Number One?"

"That's what I called you about."

"Kinda figured." He nodded. "Open it."

She stood up, moving slowly, and did as he requested.

Gabriel took a look.

He saw a young man bound to a kitchen chair with great gobs of duct tape. The young man's forehead was marked with a spiral of Htavastian runes. Mahri's work, depriving him of energy, giving her physical power over him if he gave her any shit. A sock had been stuffed in his mouth and taped in place as well.

He looked equal parts pissed off and terrified.

"Okay," Gabriel said, a bit at a loss. "I'll bite. Who's this?"

Mahri scowled. "A Helitori witch hunter. He tried to kill me."

"Oh yeah?" He looked back to the captive Helitori hunter. To be fair, the kid didn't exactly look up to the task, and there was something so amusing about that it made the corner of Gabriel's mouth tug up into a crooked smirk. "So, how'd that work out for ya?"

The angry young hunter had no response other than to scowl and try to look tough.

Jesus, you're young, Gabriel thought as he moved in and patted the hunter down. The kid was maybe old enough to buy a beer. Maybe. He found him clean, then checked the bedroom closet and under the bed. Nobody else to be found. He turned to Mahri and frowned. *What have you done, kiddo?* "Okay, Lucy. You're gonna have some 'splaining to do."

"I know," Mahri conceded. Her eyes flicked toward her prisoner.

"Yeah, not in front of him," Gabriel allowed.

Mahri nodded.

Gabriel turned back to the prisoner and moved in behind

him. He tipped the chair back on two legs like a dolly and spun it around ninety degrees to face the bed before rocking it back down on all fours. Then he took a seat on the foot of the bed and studied the young man.

He was fit and athletic but otherwise could have been any twenty-something white Angelino. He'd have blended into any crowd in Southland. Gabriel peeled back his sleeves, checked down the front and back of his collar, saw no ink, no piercings, and no jewelry.

He mulled it over while Mahri lingered nearby, quiet and fidgety. At last, Gabriel reached out and began to peel the tape and gag from the hunter's face.

"Guy's got skills," Mahri warned, bristling. "You sure you want to do that?"

Gabriel paused, the sweaty duct tape peeled halfway off the hunter's cheek. "That right? You got skills?"

The hunter shrugged.

Gabriel reached out with his little Ruger .22 and tapped the young hunter with the tip of the suppressor right between the eyes. *Tap. Tap. Tap.* Gentle and menacing. "I. Asked. You. A. Question."

The kid's whole body stiffened when Gabriel's pistol came to rest between his eyes. At length, he nodded—tense, trembling, eyelids squinted, waiting for the hammer.

"You say anything other than answering my questions, and I will end you. You might be fast. But you're not that fast. Got it?"

The hunter nodded.

Gabriel lowered the pistol. Then he ripped the tape and gag from his mouth with a violent yank. The hunter gasped and sucked in a deep breath, licking his raw lips. "Take your time, catch your breath."

With a few deep breaths, the young hunter composed himself.

"What's your name?"

The hunter hesitated, but after a moment, he answered. "Toby."

"Hi, Toby. Do you know who I am?"

He nodded. "Gabriel St. John. Captain of the Crow."

Gabriel chuckled. "Let me guess. Somewhere in town there's a shitty motel room with a bunch of sticky notes and pictures taped to the wall, and one of them is mine?" The young hunter was slow to answer, so Gabriel prodded him along. "That was an actual question, Toby. I suggest you answer it."

"Yes."

"Where?"

"Why would I tell you that?"

"Because you don't want to die taped to a chair in some shitty apartment."

The kid licked his lips, appeared to contemplate his plight. His expression turned stoic, determined, resigned. And it wasn't for show. "Do what you gotta do."

Gabriel gritted his teeth. *Goddammit. Little fucker just checked me.* Toby was a zealot ready to die for the cause. That didn't leave a whole lot of leverage to work with. "We're getting off to a real bad start here."

The young hunter just shrugged.

Gabriel pressed the muzzle of his Ruger to Toby's right kneecap. "You don't have to die quick, kid. One piece at a time works. Everybody gets chatty when you take enough pieces off."

The young hunter stiffened but held firm. "Like I said, man. Do what you gotta do. I got nothing to tell you."

Gabriel scowled in silence, his glacial blue eyes locked on the young hunter's own frightened gaze. "Mahri. Go get me something sharp and pointy out of the kitchen."

Mahri hesitated for a beat, more in surprise than reluctance. "Seriously?"

"Yeah." *You wanna play chicken, kid? Let's play chicken.*

The young hunter swallowed the lump rising in his throat and looked away from Gabriel's icepick glare. He stared at the top of his shoes instead.

"Wow. You just fucked up," Mahri snorted at the captive hunter with a smirk. Then she headed to the kitchen. She came back with an el-cheapo, plastic-handled twelve-inch chef's knife. She passed it to Gabriel, and as he took it, he set his pistol aside on the bed.

He dangled the blade downward in his grip between two fingers like a pendulum and rested the sharp point on the young hunter's kneecap. "I don't have a lot of time. Or patience. Do you want to start over?"

The young hunter licked his lips and eyeballed the knife.

Gabriel could feel his own reservations scuttling up his back to whisper doubt in his ear. He didn't want to cut this kid up any more than the kid himself wanted to be cut up. The threat of pain was always more effective than the actual pain. Once you started hurting someone, they'd say anything to get you to stop. *Come on you little shit, flip. Don't make me do this.*

Gabriel turned the knife over and pressed the tip into the young hunter's crotch.

The kid let out a sick, frightened groan and tried to crawl back into the chair as far as his bonds would allow.

Gabriel stayed in the game, grim and resolute. "So help me, God, kid. I will split your sack." *No, you won't,* whispered the little angel of doubt nibbling at his ear. Gabriel pushed it away. If Piper were here, he'd do this without batting an eye.

But Piper's not here. That little angel of doubt was a persistent twat.

"Do it," Mahri breathed, her voice low, intense. "Fuck him up."

That gave Gabriel pause. He looked over his shoulder and saw her standing there, chewing her bottom lip, watching with feverish expectation. On the edge of her seat. *What the fuck is wrong with you?*

"Get out," Gabriel said. "Close the door behind you."

"What?" Mahri sounded shocked.

"Get. Out."

"This asshole tried to kill me, Gabriel."

"Yeah, life's a bitch. Now get out."

Mahri fumed, her eyes alight with bloodthirsty anger. That pure malice had come out of nowhere and hit her like a wrecking ball. It wasn't like her. Not at all. Gabriel wondered what it meant.

With a derisive snort and a shake of her head, she stepped

out, slamming the bedroom door shut behind her.

Gabriel turned back to the young hunter. The kid was beginning to tremble.

"I didn't try to kill her," he said. "Honest."

"Well, dude, if you're trying to get her number, lemme tell ya, she's more than you can handle." Gabriel moved the knife up and pressed the tip against the kid's belly. "If you weren't trying to kill her, what were you doing?"

"Tailing her."

"For who?"

The young hunter fell silent.

Gabriel gave the kid the stare of death and scraped the knife point up along his shirt until it came to rest against his adam's apple. "She says you're Helitori. Is she right?"

The terrified young hunter held his tongue.

Goddammit. "Kid, you better tell me *something.*"

The young hunter stood his ground.

Gabriel took a deep breath and placed the tip of the knife underneath the kid's nose, pressing it against his upper lip. "I'm gonna count to three," he warned. "Then I'm gonna cut your fucking nose off. See where that gets us." *No, you won't. He's just a kid.* "Got it?"

No response.

"One." *No, you won't.*

The young hunter's breathing sped up.

"Two." *Yes, I will.*

He swallowed, and his eyes squinted in painful anticipation. "Three ..."

"Fuck! Okay! Okay!" He cracked.

"Talk, junior. Helitori?" Gabriel twisted the point of the knife so it pricked the skin ever so slightly, the edge of the blade scraping against the kid's sensitive nostril.

"Shit. Yeah. Yeah."

"Do your bosses know you found her?"

"Yes."

"Are they on the way?"

The young hunter hesitated, but his words came bubbling out when Gabriel put a little pressure on the knife. "I was supposed to nab her in MacArthur Park. They were coming there."

"What about here?"

"I don't even know where here is, man. Okay? Please."

"You better not be fucking with me."

"I'm not. I swear. Come on, man. Please." The young hunter gulped in a shaky breath, wanted to pull away from the knife, but remained frozen and too afraid to move. "Please."

The kid was terrified. That was bad enough. But now on top of it, he was sick with guilt. He'd cracked. He'd run his mouth. Gabriel could see the reality sinking in with each ragged breath, each flinch. He looked younger and younger by the second. Tears welled up in the kid's eyes.

It shook Gabriel's nerve. *Damn it. Goddammit.*

With a shake of his head, he pulled the knife away from the young hunter's face. "We're not gonna do this."

The kid let out a long, trembling sigh of relief.

"Here's what we're gonna do," Gabriel said. He had a new plan. "I'm gonna cut you loose. And you're gonna go back to your bosses and let them know the Crow had mercy on you today. We don't want any beef with the Helitori."

The young hunter nodded. Sweat rolled down his temples. The overload of adrenaline made his whole body shiver.

"You tell them the Odd and Dante Washington is Crow business. And they need to pack up their shit and get out of Dodge. I look over my shoulder one more time and see one of you assholes there, it ain't gonna end like this." Gabriel made sure the kid met his gaze. "Got it?"

He nodded.

"If I ever see you again, I'm gonna bust you up. Clear?"

Again, a nervous nod.

"Sit tight. This is almost over." With that, Gabriel got up, policed up the knife and his pistol, and went into the living room. He pitched the unused kitchen knife onto the dinged up old coffee table and leaned against the arm of the sofa, buttoning the Ruger back into his shoulder rig.

Mahri paced back and forth a few feet away like an angry animal.

"What the hell is wrong with you?" he asked.

Mahri's eyes flashed with indignation. "Really? That motherfucker tried to kill me. Let's start there."

"And?"

"Seriously? Naomi's been missing for days. Our best guess is the Helitori already got her, and I can't find Alex, Edwin, or Felipe either—you do the math."

"But you don't *know*. Right?"

Mahri looked dumbfounded. "What? Are we trying to convince a jury here?"

Gabriel shook his head. "It's not like that."

"Then tell me—what it *is* like."

Gabriel felt a bubble of anger rise up out of his belly. "All it takes is one fuck up, and we've got a war with the Helitori. One oops, and this shit is on. Then it's not just you and the Odd in the crosshairs. It's all of us."

Mahri contemplated that. "Okay. So, what do we do?"

"He goes home. You come with me."

Mahri shook her head, rolled her eyes. "So that's it, then? You're just going to let this guy walk?"

"Yeah. I am."

Mahri threw up her hands in exasperation. "You do that, and that little motherfucker will shoot you in the back tomorrow. They're animals. You ought to blast that fool, and you know it."

Gabriel's temper flared. His tone turned sharp, agitated. "Who do you think you're talking to?"

She flinched, pressed her lips tight, held her tongue.

"I'm not your goddamn firing squad, Mahri. Got it? Now, do you want a pound of flesh that bad, or do you want to play this smart? Your choice."

She fumed but was silent.

"Yeah. That's what I thought." Gabriel shook his head, sighed, struck up a fresh cigarette. "If you want that kid dumped, do it yourself."

It wasn't an offer or a suggestion. Just a smart ass, aggravated comment.

Then Mahri dashed left, snatched up the knife from the

coffee table, and bolted for the bedroom.

"Shit!" Gabriel snorted and took off after her.

It was five steps to the bedroom door, and she was two steps ahead of him.

The young hunter's eyes flew wide as Mahri barreled down on him, snarling.

"Mahri!" Gabriel shouted, grabbing a handful of the back of her shirt. He pulled.

But not before she put six inches of that knife into the side of the kid's neck. She twisted and ripped as Gabriel pulled her away and the knife tore free of the gruesome wound. She tried to slash the young hunter again, but Gabriel hauled her out of the room thrashing.

"God damn it!" he snapped, wrestling Mahri away from the kid. He stripped the bloody knife from her grasp and shoved her into the living room where she piled up on the floor, cussing and snarling in Spanish.

He spun back to the captive hunter.

Blood, bright red and hot was pumping from the purple gash in the side of his neck in spurts. His eyes bulged in horror. The kid's whole body was quivering. He gasped, choked, and tried to scream but the sound only whistled through the hole torn in his neck.

"Help..." the kid grunted in a thin, wet voice. "*Help.*"

"That's what you get!" Mahri snarled at him as he sat there trembling, gagging, and gushing blood. She'd hit all the good stuff.

For ten seconds, Gabriel just stood there in shock.

"Help," the kid wheezed.

There wasn't a damn thing Gabriel could do for him, and he had presence of mind enough to not spring to his aid and get doused in incriminating blood.

The kid's lights went out fast. His wheezing and thrashing tapered off as blood pumped down his body and onto the floor. His eyes went in and out of focus and his head sagged.

A couple shallow breaths, then he stopped breathing at all. The kid's bladder released and he leaked a puddle of yellow piss around his bloody shoes.

"That's right!" Mahri barked from her sprawl on the floor. "Fuck you!"

Gabriel was too stunned to speak. He marveled at how he'd managed to let this get so dicked up so fast. He trusted Mahri; he knew her; they had history. She was ...

Mahri giggled. She *giggled*.

That snapped Gabriel out of his fugue. "You called me all the way up here just to stick a knife in this kid? You could have done that yourself!"

"He had it coming," Mahri snorted.

Don't we all, Gabriel thought numbly. Gabriel looked toward the old man, the pawn Mahri had charmed for the use of his apartment. Nothing about his condition had changed. He kept right on staring off into nothing, but every now and then, he blinked. Gabriel's heart sank even further.

"Is this guy a witness?" he asked, pointing at the enspelled old man.

"He won't remember shit," Mahri replied.

"You sure about that?"

Mahri rolled her eyes.

"Are you sure?" Gabriel barked, his voice rising. *Fuck you if I have to get rid of this old man as a witness. Just, fuck you.*

"Yeah. I'm sure." Scowling, she got back to her feet. "Jesus, what's your problem?"

All Gabriel could do was blink and stare. *Who are you?*

His ear bud buzzed. Piper called in. *"Heads up, boss. We got company. A whole shit-pile of it."*

Gabriel grunted and damn near laughed. That added up because when it rained, it poured.

13

Gabriel looked around the apartment, mind machine cycling up to full speed. No time to dwell on the awful shit that had just happened. The apartment had a window that faced east onto New Hampshire. Gabriel angled a look outside to see what he could see.

"What do you got, Piper?"

"A van just pulled up in the parking lot across the street and there are six dudes heading your way. Don't exactly look like they live here."

"You gotta be fucking kidding me," Gabriel said with a groan.

He keyed up his radio. "Copy that. I see 'em. Standby."

He glowered at Mahri. "You expecting company?"

"Huh?"

"Who knows you're here?"

"Nobody."

"Nobody? What about him?"

He hooked a thumb toward the deflated corpse of the dead hunter in the next room.

"No. He started tailing me over by MacArthur Park. I nailed his ass in a bathroom. I didn't have this place yet."

"Get your shit," Gabriel ordered, jabbing a finger at Mahri. Then he gave the apartment a quick once over himself, a final check to make sure he left nothing behind. As he did his quick survey, he spied a collection of miscellaneous pocket items on the corner of the ratty old entertainment center. It included a decent pocket knife and Glock pistol.

"That his shit?" Mahri nodded.

Gabriel went to inspect the dead hunter's belongings. His eyes seized on the cell phone.

"Jesus, Mahri. You didn't ditch his cell?"

Mahri opened her mouth, paused, then closed it in silence and shook her head.

"Are you *trying* to get us killed?"

"I didn't think about it!"

Son of a bitch. "Come on. Let's go."

"Okay, gimme a second."

"You got half a second. Hurry." Gabriel went to the front door and took a quick look out into the hallway—nobody home.

Mahri breezed around with a quickness and scooped up her backpack. It looked like she had been ready to bounce before the proverbial shit hit the fan, which was good.

Piper buzzed in his ear. *"All six of them just came in through the east doors."*

"Copy that," Gabriel replied. "Come on," he grunted and gave Mahri a nudge toward the hall.

In the hallway, he flipped a mental coin. He had six men coming in from the east doors and two stairwells to choose from, one on the east end of the building and one on the west. They were coming in from the east, so he turned the opposite way. It was a dice roll at best.

Gabriel continued toward the west stairs, Mahri in tow. He yanked the door open and came face-to-face with a resident—a thousand-year-old woman with a wispy head of curly white hair. She paused and looked him and Mahri up and down. "Excuse us," Gabriel said, and he and Mahri moved past her and onto the stairs.

They started down, Gabriel pausing at the turn above each landing to check the way ahead.

As they were approaching the second floor, footsteps began to echo up the stairwell from below. Gabriel skidded to a stop, grabbing Mahri by the wrist and pulling her to a halt behind him.

"Shit. Go back," he whispered, giving Mahri a nudge in the upstairs direction. As they rounded the stairs to the third floor, he heard voices on the landing below them. It sounded like a man, muttering into a radio, then the scratchy echo of a reply, saying something about the third floor.

It seemed like the team of hunters had split up into pairs, probably at least one coming up each set of stairs—and they had the third floor on their minds. Hearing that, Gabriel passed the third floor and kept trucking upward.

"Where are we going?" Mahri asked in an urgent whisper.

"Fourth floor. Best chance that they pass us by and we can slip past them. If they tracked his cell, they may or may not know what floor he's on. They'll be searching the building."

"There are fire escapes. Or the roof?"

Gabriel shook his head. "There's probably a camera on the door to the roof. And even if there isn't, I don't want to wind up getting trapped up there with nowhere to go." He shrugged as they stopped at the fourth-floor fire door. "Let's call the roof Plan B. Fire escape is a maybe though."

He cracked the fire door open and peeked into the fourth-floor hallway. All was quiet. He pushed open the door, let Mahri go through first and followed her into the hallway, easing the fire door closed behind them.

They ducked around the corner and hugged the wall, pausing for a brief moment while Gabriel weighed their options.

The exterior fire escape just screamed *hey world look at me!* If they had spotters out, they'd be busted. But both interior stairwells were likely to end up with them running head-long into a pair of Helitori hunters—assuming they were Helitori, that was, and not some entirely new brand of assholes. Gabriel sighed. He had enough assholes to juggle.

"So, where are we going?" Mahri asked.

Gabriel peeked around the corner and looked the fourth-floor central corridor up and down. "Heh. Probably to jail." He looked to Mahri. "Okay, kiddo. Fire escape it is. Go."

They dashed into the fourth-floor main corridor and headed toward the west end fire escape. Thankfully the door to the fire escape didn't appear to have an alarm. More attention was the last thing they needed. They pushed through and out onto the red metal landing.

Gabriel took a quick survey of the back lot and found it

empty, narrow and shaded; damn near butted up against the neighboring building to the west. A long-forgotten dumpster sat on the fractured old asphalt down there, heaped in trash that was never going to get collected. The opposing buildings were tall enough, and the west alley narrow enough, that the ground rarely ever saw the light of day. Nobody was in sight. That would do.

Leading the way Gabriel began to descend the western fire escape, pulling Mahri along behind. The metal fire escape clanged like the percussion section of a drunken marching band as they made their way down the steep switchbacks of stairs.

They moved from the fourth floor to the third floor, made the hasty turn around the metal catwalk, ducked under the stairs, and began down toward the second floor.

Halfway there, the door to the second-floor fire escape burst open and a hunter lurched onto the catwalk below.

So much for the question of whether or not they had a spotter out there somewhere with eyes on the west side of the building. They were made.

Gabriel didn't hesitate. He grabbed the inside rail to his right and swung down over the side of the stairs like a kid on the monkey bars. As he swung down, he reared back both feet and delivered a double-booted kangaroo stomp toward the surprised hunter.

The man had a split second to cover up, and he did, taking the brunt of the booting on his shoulder. But Gabriel's strength and momentum was still enough. With a surprised cry, the hunter cartwheeled over the rail and dropped fifteen feet to the cracked pavement below. He landed on his side with a hard bounce, crawled a few stunned, breathless feet, and then collapsed.

Gabriel dropped to the second-floor catwalk and got a look through the fire escape door into the second-floor main corridor. A second hunter was charging his way at a sprint; some big corn-fed white dude with a sandy buzz cut. "Go!" he shouted to Mahri, pointing toward the ladder that would take her the rest of the way down to the back lot.

Then he bolted inside to face the oncoming hunter.

He was Gabriel's height but packing a heavier build. Unlike the hunter Gabriel had just booted over the railing, or the poor dead kid upstairs, this no-neck son of a bitch looked like he whipped ass for a living.

They slowed and eyeballed each other.

Gabriel didn't want to go for his gun because once the shooting started, it would be mayhem, cops, and corpses and bad would only get worse.

For his part, the big hunter didn't seem too interested in going for his noisy troublemaker either.

The big bastard feinted left, charged, and he was a lot faster than he looked. He had the size and speed of an NFL linebacker, and he put it to good use. He came in swinging and Gabriel was on the defensive, covering up, fading back.

He tried to shuck and jive, to squirt past his opponent, but the dude wasn't having any of that. Gabriel ducked and dodged, and the big bastard slammed him against the wall, leaving him breathless and grinding his teeth.

A big meaty fist slipped past his guard and caught him behind the ear, loosening his knees by a degree. The hunter tried to hook a long, muscled arm around Gabriel's neck but lost his grip and his nerve when Gabriel rammed a fist into his nuts and an elbow into the side of his throat. The big man staggered backward, and Gabriel spun around, bouncing him off the opposite wall with a mulish front kick to the gut.

Gabriel went on the offensive hard and the big man covered up against the short barrage of fists. *Whop, whop, whop* up high, and *boom*—Gabriel planted a kick in the big man's right kneecap.

The hunter yelped and his leg wobbled. His guard slipping for half a second, and Gabriel landed two solid overhand rights into the side of his head.

In desperation, the hunter lurched forward and tried to wrap Gabriel up around the hips for a takedown. Gabriel was able to twist and shoot out of the grapple, and the big man missed his lunge, staggering across the narrow hallway into the opposite wall with a thud. That exposed his back to Gabriel for a split second.

The big hunter lurched upright, spinning with a growl just

in time to catch a thunderous kick to the side of the head from Gabriel's right foot.

All the bones melted out of the big hunter's body, and he keeled over into a broken pile on the hallway floor. Gabriel followed the momentum of the kick down and gave the big bastard half a dozen good hammer fist parting shots to make sure he stayed down.

Gabriel left the big man in the hallway bloodied, unconscious, and limp as a boned fish, and bolted for the fire escape door. The fight had been noisy but hadn't lasted more than fifteen or twenty seconds. He was back on the fire escape before the first curious resident had even poked their head into the hallway.

Gabriel's eyes swept the back lot and down between his feet beneath the fire escape catwalk. Mahri was huddled close to the building looking up at him with big, bright eyes. Ten feet to her left, the hunter Gabriel had booted over the railing was still piled up on the ground, down and out.

Gabriel swung onto the ladder, riding it down with a rattling clang. He was off the ladder and moving before it even hit bottom.

"Go!" he shouted at Mahri pushing her toward the north alley.

Then he keyed up his radio. "Piper. North alley. Pick us up."

"Copy," Piper drawled over the radio.

Together, Gabriel and Mahri took off down the narrow back lot, sprinting north toward the alley and their escape.

Ahead of them, a third hunter rounded the corner, cutting them off, plowing headlong into them at a dead run.

Gabriel had a split second to react, and he used it to shove Mahri out of the way. It cost him half a step and half a second, and the newcomer barreled in without hesitation.

As Gabriel pushed Mahri clear, the other man slammed into him like a freight train.

The third hunter was a boxy white guy in a casual gray suit. He was a head shorter than Gabriel, but he was stout, and he knew how to throw a tackle. With a winded grunt, he and Gabriel went down in a tangle, slamming into the broken pavement with a hard bounce.

Gabriel twisted and rolled, managing to buck the hunter off rather than allow him to mount up and start pummeling.

Both men scrambled to their feet with athletic grace. There was no fear in the hunter's eyes; no hesitation. This dude was a fighter through and through, and he was in it to win it.

His hand snapped to the tail of his jacket and came back brandishing a big fuck-you-knife. It was no ordinary blade. It was a vintage Roman pugio: ancient, pitted, and made for killing. As the hunter's knuckles tightened on the dagger's hilt, a wave of lightless energy, like a heat-shimmer on a desert highway, blossomed along the length of the blade.

Then he came on in a rush, teeth bared, jaw set, dagger leading the way, shimmering through the air with each violent thrust and feint. Each swipe of the blade gave off an angry harmonic hum.

The man was fast, and that blade moved like an extension of his hand, his attacks strong and sure.

Gabriel backpedaled on the defensive, no time to break and go for his gun, no time to get out of the way. Three steps and the wall of the building met his back. The hunter grabbed the shoulder of his jacket. If a guy could put a hand on you, he could put a knife in you.

And they both knew it.

The dagger came in, and Gabriel was able to twist enough to keep it out of his chest, but not avoid getting cut. The shimmering blade bit through Gabriel's jacket, shirt, and bulletproof vest like paper. A hot gash opened up low along his ribs, and blood welled from the wound, slick and hot under the torn Kevlar.

The hunter turned the blade and pulled it back again, renewing his attack, intent on pumping the knife like a piston until he hit enough meat to put Gabriel down. But Gabriel locked hands on the man's wrist and trapped the dagger when he came back in. Turning, pushing off from the wall, he used his superior size and strength, heaving his attacker around in a violent circle.

Bones snapped in the hunter's wrist; he howled, his elbow buckled and bent. Snarling and grappling, the two men locked both their hands on the dagger, fighting for control.

Gabriel twisted, bringing the knife point up and around. He drove a knee in behind it and the shimmering dagger buried to the hilt through the hunter's sternum, cracking against his spine on the far side.

The man let out a winded gasp in Gabriel's face. His eyes bulged. Gabriel rammed into the knife again, ripping it deeper through muscle and bone, cutting ribs, splitting meat. A gush of hot blood poured down over his hands, and with a shoulder, he shoved the mortally wounded hunter away.

The hunter staggered, clutching the ruins of his chest, hands disjointed, uncoordinated with shock. He fetched up against the far wall and sank to the ground, choking, gasping and still fumbling at the dagger angled through his chest.

The light drained from his eyes and the tension leaked out of his body.

Gabriel stood there, three steps away, panting, soaked in blood. Most of it wasn't his. He ground his teeth together and took a deep breath. So much for that war with the Helitori he hadn't wanted to start. Too late now.

"Jesus, *papi*," Mahri breathed from somewhere to his right.

There was a howl of rage, of anguished protest from the second-floor fire escape. Gabriel snapped that direction and saw a tall, slender black man staring down at the murderous mess in the alley below, seething.

"Go," Gabriel hissed at Mahri, shoving her toward the north alley.

She flinched and fumbled but turned on her heel and took off around the corner.

Eyes blazing with fury, the hunter on the fire escape went for his gun.

Backpedaling for the corner, so did Gabriel.

Their pistols came out, and their muzzles crossed at the same instant. The narrow alley filled with the sharp bark of gunfire as they traded shots. A round hissed past Gabriel's left ear. Another pecked the wall beside him in a shower of brick shards.

Gabriel dumped shots at the man on the fire escape in forty-five caliber pairs as he withdrew. When you didn't have a wall for cover, sometimes you had to make one with lead. So Gabriel poured it on, his Sig bucking like a machine in his hands. Gunshots rang out like jackhammers on concrete.

His volume of fire was faster and more accurate than the enraged hunter. It forced the other man on the defensive, grazing the edge of his cover, exploding in plumes of red brick dust. The hunter flinched away, curled a protective arm up around his face, and dove back through the fire escape door out of sight.

Gabriel rounded his own corner and took off down the north alley, swapping his nearly spent magazine for a fresh one as he went. With blood-soaked hands, he stuffed the partially expended one in his pocket.

Mahri was sprinting off ahead of him. Piper and the little silver Camry shot past the gap at the far end of the alley. The reverse lights came on, blazing white inside the red halos of brake lights. Piper whipped the wheel and began racing backward down the alley like a stunt driver. He could drive like a champ.

"Keep going!" Gabriel instructed, then he broke off from Mahri and flipped a one-eighty, posting up behind the north alley service entrance stairs for cover. He eyeballed the now-open service door there. The hunter he'd killed in the back lot must have cut through the building and come out that way.

Gabriel reached up and swung the service door shut with a bang. His muzzle came up, and he covered their retreat as Mahri dashed toward the car.

A heartbeat later head, shoulders, and a pistol peeked around the corner into the north alley from the back lot. Gabriel drilled a pair of shots at the pursuing hunter and drove him back behind his cover.

Mahri hit the car and wrenched the back door open. "Gabriel! Come on!"

Gabriel did, angling to keep as much cover between himself and that back corner as possible, gliding backward, keeping his muzzle up.

Piper swung out of the driver's seat, pistol in hand. He posted up over the roof of the car and didn't ask any questions. As Gabriel withdrew, he laid a hail of suppressing fire down the alley, grazing the back corner of the apartment building with lead.

One of the Helitori hunters broke out, dashing across the open alley for cover on the opposite side. He crossed muzzles with the two Crows, and they exchanged a handful of shots as Gabriel kept withdrawing.

Gabriel heard a bullet hiss past his head with a loud buzz and another cratered the Camry's back glass with a sharp crystalline *pop*. The hunter disappeared behind the neighboring building to the north and Gabriel reached the car.

He threw the door open, dove inside, and before he could even give the order, Piper was back in the driver's seat. He barked the tires and had them out on the street and rolling. Out in the neighborhood, the flurry of gunfire had pedestrians lying flat on their bellies or running away as fast as their feet would carry them.

Gabriel's heart hammered like a heavy metal drummer on speed. His world was tight in adrenalized tunnel vision, his muscles were strung like piano wire, and his head was on a swivel.

"Everybody whole?" Gabriel asked, exchanging his second half-empty magazine for a full one.

"Yeah, I'm good," Piper said.

"You okay?" he asked Mahri, who was still half in the floorboard, ducked down behind the back seat.

"I think so," she replied.

Gabriel pushed himself into a sitting position, trying to get a picture of their surroundings. "Don't run the light," he said as Piper approached an intersection on Third Street.

"I got it, boss," Piper said.

"Get to the freeway and get the fuck outta here."

Gabriel put a hand on Mahri's arm. They were both trembling. Gunfights had that effect on people. "You okay? Nothing bleeding?"

She took stock of herself as much as she could manage and shook her head, "I don't know."

"Come here and let me see." During an adrenaline-fueled gun fight, people could get holes plugged in them and never even feel it. He gave her a quick once over and didn't find anything bleeding.

"That's a lot of blood, cap'n," Piper said, eyeballing Gabriel in the rearview mirror.

"Yeah. But most of it isn't mine."

Piper cocked a curious eyebrow. "Most of it?"

"Fucker stuck me," Gabriel said with a grunt. His sliced Kevlar vest was slick with blood, sliding slug-like against his skin. But other than the gash from the dagger, he didn't seem to have any holes in him that he hadn't been born with. In the haze of adrenaline, the gash in his side burned, but it didn't really hurt.

With a grimace, Gabriel peeled off his torn jacket and unbuttoned his bloody shirt. A concerned expression on her face, Mahri gave him a hand, and that fast, she was the Mahri he knew again—not the ghoul who'd been laughing at slicing some kid's throat open ten minutes earlier.

The first lances of pain started to cut through his adrenaline as Gabriel stripped out of his wrecked shirt and body armor. Mahri's hands were gentle as she helped him. Balling his shirt up into a mop, Gabriel pressed it against his wounded side as Mahri unfastened his ruined vest. He took a couple of deep breaths just to make sure everything was still functioning, then peeled back the bloodied shirt to inspect the wound.

The gash wasn't very deep, but it was nasty—angling upward across the ribs on his left side in a six-inch cut. A couple of inches to the right and the hunter's lunge would have buried the dagger in his lung instead. It was going to hurt like a son of a bitch.

Mahri helped him fish his first aid kit out of his bag, and they dressed the wound the best they could to get the bleeding under control.

"Where to?" Piper asked, piloting them up on to the freeway.

"Head to the Church. We'll figure it out from there." Gabriel sighed. He'd need to send somebody back for his own car. He sure as hell didn't have any plans on stopping by there now just to bleed all over it. One to clean up was plenty.

"Bad?" Piper asked, still eyeballing his wounded captain in the rearview mirror.

"Not too bad," Gabriel replied. "Needs to be sewn up."

Piper didn't need any further instructions. He nodded, put them on course for the Church, and called the family doctor while scanning with calm, attentive eyes, watching for signs of pursuit or cops. But neither the Helitori nor L.A.'s finest ever picked up their trail. In, out, and gone fast. By the time the noisy shooting started, the fight was over.

Time would tell how much of this would stick to them.

If some of the Helitori got picked up by the police, they might run their mouth—not likely, but it could happen.

There may be a witness who may have seen something the cops could use to make two and two add up to four; after all, they'd been seen in the apartment building, and there was security camera footage of unknown value.

Their silver Camry was going to have to do a disappearing act after taking center stage as a getaway car in front of the entire neighborhood. The bullet hole in the back glass didn't exactly speak of honest work.

Helitori assholes. None of it had to go down that way. Right, wrong, or indifferent, Gabriel blamed the Helitori for the outcome of the encounter. Make stupid choices, win stupid prizes. They didn't have to go on the offensive. The asshole with the dagger didn't have to whip it out and try to kill him. Nobody had to start shooting.

Mahri didn't *have* to kill that kid while he was taped to a chair begging for his life.

Yeah. There was that.

Gabriel put it out of his head. What was done was done, and there was nothing he could do about it now. Whatever the blowback would be, would be, and where it would land at that point was anybody's guess.

The hunter from the fire escape, that was a problem. When he saw his buddy with his chest split open in the alley, that wasn't business—it was personal—and there was going to be a reckoning, one way or another. Gabriel was still covered in the guy's blood.

He fished a cigarette out his jacket pocket and lit up. He sank back in his seat, pinched his fingertips between his eyes, and enjoyed his smoke while his ears continued to ring from the gunfire. His sore spots hurt like hell. As Murphy typically prescribed, bad had turned to worse. Because that's the kind of asshole Murphy was.

He looked at Mahri and found her staring out the window, watching the world go by as Piper piloted them along. Her expression was blank, empty, and she seemed to be a thousand miles away.

"Hey," Gabriel said, touching her arm and offering her a cigarette. "You okay?"

She nodded and replied with a hollow smile, like an empty mask. An anti-smile. All shape, no substance. No light at all. The only thing simmering in Mahri's large, dark eyes was anger. The kind you saw in a kicked dog.

She took the cigarette with a nod. "I'm good. Thanks, *papi*. I owe you."

With a flip of his Zippo, he lit her cigarette. *Yeah*, Gabriel decided, looking at her and seeing half a stranger. *Bad has definitely gone to worse.*

They rolled out for the Church.

Practicing the Art isn't safe. In fact, it's inherently perilous. Mere mortals frequently find themselves in direct opposition to that which is ancient, alien, and immortal. These things, these old spirits, these entities, these gods - they care little for the fate of mortal man. Through the Art, we are interlopers in their world, meddlers in their affairs. We tamper with the cosmic forces that define them for our own ends. Some find good humor in our trespass. Still more would rather bathe in our blood and gnaw upon our bones. It leaves us to hope that a lifetime of study ends quietly in our beds at a ripe old age, rather than in screams to the taste of our own blood. Students beware. Either is a right possible conclusion.

From the essays of
Dr. Angus McCoy, M.D., Ph.D.,
Metaphysician and Mantled Wizard of the Green Wall

14

Delilah found her way to University Park to check on Doc McCoy and made arrangements to rendezvous with Dodger as her brother had suggested. She parked her black Toronado along the tree-lined curb deep in the heart of residential suburbia and waited for her back up to arrive. She reclined in the driver's seat, listened to some tunes, smoked a few cigarettes, and ate a Snickers bar.

About twenty minutes later, she heard the throaty rumble of a Harley Davidson approaching and watched as the Dyna Glide rounded the corner, rolling in her direction. Her brother was tall, six-foot-four, and built like an oak tree. But this guy was massive with an easy four inches and forty or fifty pounds on Gabriel, and all of it muscle.

Dodger was a biracial bronze giant, a former Marine like his father, combat vet from Iraq, a Knight of the Crow. Like Delilah, he was a second generation blackbird.

He pulled up across the street and backed his bike up to the curb, peeled off his helmet, pulled his ponytail out of the collar of his leather jacket and smoothed a hand over his woolly black beard.

"What's good, little sister?" he called with a handsome grin while lighting a cigarette.

"Eh, some of this and some that," Delilah replied. She nodded towards the next block. "Did you take a look?"

Dodger nodded, exhaling a plume of white smoke. "Yup. His Beamer's in the driveway. Guess that means he's probably home."

Delilah nodded. "What do you think?"

"I don't know, this is your trouble call. Let me go do a walk-around first. I'll let you know when it's clear to come up."

Dodger dismounted and made his way down the sidewalk. The big leather-clad biker stood out like a sore thumb in picket fence-suburbia, but nobody was going to tell him that. Delilah couldn't help but smile. Dodger rounded the corner out of sight, and a few minutes later, she got his all clear text and moved on to join him.

Doc McCoy lived and worked out of a conspicuously red bay-and-gable house on Bonsallo Avenue in University Park. The home was narrow and long, its two stories as tall and pointy as a miniature gothic cathedral. It could, and probably should have been, brick red. Instead, it looked more like a fire truck, bright red, white accents, and a pine green front door. The small yard was sodded, but brown from lack of watering and the entire narrow lot was cordoned off by a low wrought iron fence. Its cracked concrete driveway filled the slender gap between the Doc's house and his neighbor's. His BMW was present and accounted for.

With nothing outwardly amiss, they let themselves in through the front gate. Along the way to the front door they passed a meticulously hand-lettered wooden yard sign affixed to an iron lamppost that read:

Dr. Angus McCoy, Ph.D., M.D.
Professional Services, Consultations, and Odd Things
By Appointment Only

They loped up the front steps, and Delilah grabbed hold of the big brass door knocker, giving it seven or eight obnoxious raps. No response. After fifteen seconds of dead air, Dodger balled up his meaty fist and gave the big green door a sledgehammer cop-knocking. Still nothing.

Delilah tried to take a peek through the front window, but the blinds were drawn tight. "Probably too early for him to be shithoused and passed out on the couch. What do you think?"

Dodger took a look up and down the street, and seeing it was all quiet on the western front, he reached out and tried the doorknob, finding it unlocked.

"Smart ass," Delilah grunted.

Dodger grinned. "I do what I can."

Delilah pushed the door open and took a peek inside. "Doc?" No one answered.

Dodger and Delilah paused at the front door, slow to enter, knowing the Doc's home and place of trade was warded, and unkind to uninvited intruders. Thankfully, Delilah was a welcome friend. She placed her palm in the center of the front door, probing with her senses until she felt the tingle of a key glyph concealed beneath the thick green paint.

She announced herself and guest in the Doc's preferred Ancient Greek. The hidden glyph warmed beneath her hand, welcoming, accepting, and recognizing her. The house would let them pass in peace.

"Don't get surly," Delilah warned, looking over her shoulder at Dodger.

"Surly? Really?"

"Loud. Threatening." She pointed at the house. "It might change its mind."

The old wizard might have been a mostly washed-up has-been these days, but he was still a force to be reckoned with. And this was his sanctuary.

Dodger gave a respectful nod. "Noted."

"Doc, you got pants on?" Delilah asked, probing deeper into the house, passing through the foyer. The lights were off, the curtains drawn, and he didn't own a television, making it dark and cave-like in the house.

She poked her head into the kitchen on the left and froze. Every cabinet had been turned out onto the floor, and every container opened and dumped along with the pantry items, pots, pans, and all the grainy shit the old hippy put in his morning smoothies.

Dodger laid a restraining hand on Delilah's arm, catching her attention. "Shhh," he whispered and motioned for her to step back behind him. As she pulled back, the big biker skinned his pistol out of his waistband holster. He press-checked it, pulling the slide back half an inch, making sure a round was chambered. He gripped the pistol in both hands and drew it up close to his chest at the ready.

Delilah's heart rate began picking up, and her adrenaline started to flow. "Do you think somebody's here?" she asked in a low whisper.

Dodger shrugged, and moved forward cautiously, with eyes scanning, head on a swivel, and ears tuned in. He took the lead and cleared their way room by room.

The Doc's place was always a little eccentric and cluttered, but now it was a wreck. Somebody had tossed the place like a tornado.

Delilah trailed Dodger at what she hoped was a safe distance. This kind of thing wasn't her cup of tea. She'd never actually been shot at or run headfirst into a pack of goons ransacking a house before. She had the skills to defend herself if it came down it, but she'd never really put them to the test. All of a sudden, this was the real deal, and her adrenaline-fueled imagination took off like a startled jackrabbit. Was it the Helitori? Had they been here? Were they still here? How many were there? Where were they? What were they looking for? She became conscious of her bare hands. No gloves. Had she touched anything? Of course she had. But what? She couldn't remember.

Her mind fumbled for an incantation, a defense, or an attack. Like a green soldier awkwardly juggling his spear and shield in the face of the oncoming horde, she thought about the pistol in her black leather satchel, both of which she'd left in the trunk of her car—because this was friendly territory and she hadn't been expecting trouble. *Stupid, stupid, stupid*, she thought, berating herself. Her nerves got raw fast.

By contrast, Dodger moved with confidence. He'd been the first man through the door more times than he could count and his actions were deliberate, paced, and seasoned. Room by room he cleared the long, narrow first floor. The only sound was that of their movement. There was no sign of anyone else home on the ground floor.

Dodger took a peek up the long, dark staircase. "You coming?" he whispered.

"Yeah," Delilah snorted, hoping her irritation masked her nervousness.

Dodger took a deep, steadying breath, and cleared the

stairwell, quick and quiet, then motioned for her to follow. Delilah caught up and froze at the top of the steps a pace behind him.

The upper floor was rank with the stink of raw meat, coppery blood, and shit. It was an awful, slaughterhouse smell. Exchanging an uncertain glance, they proceeded to sweep the three bedrooms upstairs. Both guest rooms were trashed, but clear, as was the guest bath.

They moved on toward the master suite where the raw stink of blood and feces grew stronger with every step. The door stood ajar, and the heavy curtains were open just a crack, allowing some sunlight to slant into the room, radiating out into the dim hallway. There was a bloody handprint smeared on the beige carpet, just outside the bedroom door, as if somebody had been crawling, bloody and torn, trying to escape before being yanked back inside.

Adrenaline and dread bloomed cold in Delilah's stomach and combined with the raw stench it threatened to make her gag.

Dodger looked back, held his hand out and with face grave, and eyes bright, motioned for her to wait.

Delilah stood outside the door, a swarm of conflicting emotions bouncing around in her head like ping pong balls.

Moving forward alone, Dodger began to clear the master bedroom. When he moved through the door, his shoulders hunched forward and his pistol came up.

"Hands! Lemme see those hands!" he barked in a commanding tone, startling Delilah half out of her skin.

"Now!" Dodger shouted, then he was on the move.

Delilah raced towards the door, instincts flying haywire—fear, dread, worry, disgust, anger and the unbearable unknown.

She saw Dodger grab a tall, lanky figure by the shoulder and pitch him face first onto the bedroom floor. He put his boot on the back of the intruder's neck, anchoring him to the spot.

She fetched up against the door frame and froze in her tracks. The carpet was smeared with gore. The wall and dresser to her right were splattered in blood. The bed was horror house wreckage.

Doc McCoy hung from the wall above the bed, splayed out in a Christ-like pose.

A broken shard of wood from a smashed picture frame pinned his right arm to the wall; a curving hook of glass from the shattered dresser mirror secured his left, and his belly was pierced through by a broken board like a bug on an insect collector's mat.

His face was swollen and beaten almost beyond recognition; his long gray hair and wiry goatee were mops of dripping black blood. His eyes had been torn from their sockets.

Blood.

Blood was everywhere.

The bed and wall were painted in it.

From the nipples down, the Doc's body was raw and purple. Flayed, Delilah realized with a wordless gag. His skin had been torn off in long, agonizing strips and piled on the floor and bed beneath him. Parts of his anatomy were still recognizable in the piles of withering flesh.

His belly had been opened, and his guts spilled down over his thighs and down his legs to dangle against the blood-soaked headboard.

Tunnel vision closed in and threatened to send Delilah down the hall screaming.

She looked to Dodger and saw a mirror of her own horror and revulsion.

"Oh my God," she wheezed, a trembling hand rising to her mouth.

Dodger also had no words for the grotesque tableau. Instead, he squatted over the figure he was pinning to the floor and proceeded to pat the man down. "Lace your fingers behind your head. You move or make a sound, and I'll kill you." Then he flicked a glance at Delilah. "Get outta here, Dee."

But Delilah was frozen. Rooted in place. She looked down at the figure on the floor as Dodger kicked his feet apart and continued patting him down.

The kid was young, white, mop-headed and blonde with a surfer-boy style.

Delilah flinched in shocked recognition, "Edwin?"

The young man craned his head around, cheek to the floor, trying to get a look at her. "Delilah?" It *was* him. Edwin. One of Doc McCoy's wayward apprentices of the Circle Odd. He'd fallen right into their laps.

"Shut it," Dodger ordered, cramming the muzzle of his pistol into the back of the kid's head.

Edwin closed his eyes, reigned in his fear. "I didn't do this."

"I said, shut it."

Delilah shivered. "Dodger, wait."

"Whatever this is, we can talk about it outside," Dodger insisted.

"I didn't do this," Edwin repeated, anxiety and urgency creeping into his tone.

"I don't give a fuck," Dodger grumbled.

Delilah had never seen Dodger noided out before. It gave her the chills.

Outside, a breeze stirred. It made the Doc's wooden yard sign sway and clang against the iron lamppost. *Gong. Gong. Gong-gong. Gong.*

The hackles rose up on the back of Delilah's neck when a gust of wind slammed the front of the house, rattling the windows.

The front door blew open with a resounding *bang.*

The unnatural wind forced its way through the front door, eddied and twisted down the cluttered first-floor hallway, and turned and boiled up the stairs. It raced to the master bedroom in a swirling blast and blew by Delilah, swarming around her, sucking the breath from her chest as it passed. The temperature in the room plummeted.

The Doc's mutilated corpse rattled as the gust slammed against his body and the far wall.

Everything went still.

Then the Doc's slack lower jaw snapped and popped like a jolted nutcracker. With a snort and grunt, he bit at the empty air, teeth clacking, then, slowly he turned his head and looked down at them all with those empty, torn eye sockets.

Edwin screamed.

With a snarl, the Doc began to rip himself free of the wall.

15

A multi-car pileup of emotions seized Delilah in the iron grip of indecision. For a long, brutal moment, all she did was stand and stare in grief and shock. Doc McCoy, a friend, a mentor, was dead—suddenly, horribly, and violently. He'd died screaming, defiled, tortured, and maimed. Liquid hate boiled in her heart for whoever had done this.

Ten feet away was a hungry monster, the kind that lifelong nightmares were made of.

Delilah was numb, frozen, and was forced to watch the grisly scene taking place in front of her.

Torn flesh squelched and slurped as Doc McCoy yanked against the jagged spikes pinning him to the wall. Old plaster cracked and broken wood creaked and moaned. His heels hammered and levered against the headboard, looking for purchase. The ghastly ropes of his intestines jangled between his legs with greasy slaps as he bucked. With each jerk and twist, his movements grew faster, more coordinated, a gory meat engine cycling up to full speed.

"I see you…" he hissed, his voice wet, broken and unearthly. His empty eye sockets fixed on Edwin. Snarling, he bit at the air like an angry mongrel, teeth snapping, gnashing.

The light filtering in through the windows dimmed as a shadowy sheen blossomed across the glass like ink spreading through water. Pale at first, ghostly. Bruising. Blackening. Expanding. Drop by drop, the light of the outside world was strangled away.

The Doc's left arm came free. Delilah's stunned, icy horror broke. The scene began to accelerate to tornado speed.

"Dodger!" she shouted, frantic. "Move!"

He didn't need any encouragement. Dodger hauled Edwin to his feet by the back of his jacket and heaved him toward the bedroom door. Edwin skidded sideways and fell half over himself before piling out into the hall, Dodger hot on his heels.

His left arm freed, the Doc reached across his body and wrenched the crucifixion spike from his right arm. "I see you!" the gory man-thing roared in its mutilated voice. Its head turned, neck popping, blind eyes tracking Edwin in his escape.

Delilah held her ground. Setting her feet, she planted herself in the bedroom doorway, between her friends and the fiend tearing free from the wall.

"Dee!" Dodger shouted, looking back, stopping midway down the upstairs hall. "Come on!" But she didn't budge.

Delilah St. John didn't do gunfights. That was a Knight's game; Dodger's game; her brother's game. Delilah did things that went bump in the night.

She'd faced her fair share of vengeful spirits and malicious entities. The hungry horrors that plagued those who worked in the arcane. But even in the face of malevolent specters and other practitioners hell-bent on doing harm, her experience had always been more theoretical than tangible. Metaphysical chess, rather than combat checkers. *Until today.*

The fear clawed in her belly and welled up like vomit, but she shoved it down. It wasn't likely that Dodger had anything in his arsenal that could stop this thing and Edwin just didn't have the skills, so this was on her. Delilah summoned up her courage and shot Dodger what she *hoped* was a confidence-inspiring glance over her shoulder. "Go! I got this!"

Dodger didn't argue. He shoved Edwin toward the stairs and they kept moving.

Delilah turned back to face the monster.

"I see you!" the Doc roared, his eyeless gaze still tracking Edwin through the walls.

Delilah shook her left hand, loosening the bracelet of graven charms around her wrist. She set her feet, let her muscles go slack, bled the tension out of her body. Tried to block out the fear fueled by the fading light as the hungry shadows bled across the windows and began to leak down the walls onto the floor.

The Doc roared, threatening her calm.

Delilah pulled in a deep, steadying breath, feeling the energy well in her center and the fear subsided. Time slowed. Chaos stilled.

Her breath came pouring back out in a lyrical incantation. Wind through the trees and water over stones. The rhythm of the incantation gave it form in her mind. The form in her mind shaped the energy in her center, and the energy in her center was projected by her will.

She held her ground. Unflinching, undoubting, and unwavering.

Each of those was failure, and failure was death.

It all happened in two seconds.

The creature on the wall gripped the broken plank through its abdomen with both hands. It twisted, pulled, levered its flayed feet against the headboard, and with a clattering, bloody, calamity, the Doc's mutilated corpse ripped loose from of the wall. It collapsed to the bed in a shower of broken plaster bits and a pile of shitty guts.

After a beat, the Doc sprang off the bed, lurched to his feet and charged toward Delilah. Torn fingers reached toward her like claws.

Teeth—purple gore on white—flashed as it snarled, slavering like a mutilated hellbeast. The Doc's jaws snapped, his teeth cracked, and his fingers clawed the air.

Delilah released her spell and an amoebic swath of unseen force burst before her, stretching into a shivering shield. The Doc smashed against it like a car wreck. The shield bowed and bent, Delilah gritted her teeth and leaned into it, then she threw the energy of his charge back at him. The counterforce heaved the grisly corpse back the way it had come and sent Delilah's feet skidding across the carpet. She braced the edge of her foot against the door jamb and held.

Before the staggering corpse-thing could recover, she poured more will and form into the shield of quivering invisible force. The lyrical incantation continued to fly off her lips in rapid recitation, rising, growing and changing. Delilah wrapped the

Doc in that energy, with bands, shackles, lasso and noose, then she heaved with all her metaphysical strength.

The bulging rubber band snapped back; the Doc was ripped from his feet and rocketed across the bedroom, smashing into the interior wall with the ruinous force of being fired out of a cannon. The wall caved in; studs broke, gore splattered, and untethered intestines slapped and tore. Like a wrecking ball, Delilah drove the Doc's putrid corpse halfway into the next room without using the door.

Sagging at his waist, lower half still dangling in the bedroom, he began to fight to recover. A water pipe in the master bath burst and a geyser of cold tap water stained pink with blood burst through the broken wall into the bedroom.

With a final turn and twist, Delilah changed the shape of the energy once more. Hooks and anchors. Chains in invisible gears being drawn toward the floor by unseen machinery. It locked the Doc in place like a slow-turning engine, pulling him tighter and tighter against the bottom of the ruined wall crater. Plaster continued to buckle and crack as the invisible force dragged the Doc toward the floor inch by inch. *Crack. Snap. Pop.*

"I see you!" The corpse-thing roared in rage as the plaster crumbled and the wood cracked. The Doc's bones broke, and his flesh and muscles tore.

Delilah spared a quick glance over her shoulder. Her comrades were nowhere in sight. Hopefully, that meant they were downstairs and headed for the front door.

"I see you!" the Doc howled defiantly, over and over.

Delilah then retreated herself and followed her friends, leaving the Doc to fight with the unseen shackles of her groping arcane machinery. Behind her, the grisly creature thrashed and howled in the buckling ruin of the wall.

The shadow gloom continued to spread, blackening the windows, creeping along the floor, multiplying like twisting vines. The gloomy vapor had substance, rising up clammy, and cold. It compounded rapidly as it began to spill across the upper story.

The interior of the house grew dark as night, and the temperature continued to fall.

Delilah hit the top of the steps just as Dodger reappeared at the bottom.

"No! Go Back!" he said, eyes wide, hitting Delilah with a slap of pure confusion.

A frigid black mist curled around her ankles and spilled down the staircase heavier than air. Its touch on her skin stole the warmth from her bones and siphoned the breath from her chest.

Then a translucent specter burst from the stairs beneath her feet.

Hollow, molten black eyes stared up at her, and a soundless mouth gaped in a featureless face.

The specter lunged, reaching for her with long ghostly fingers and snagging her by the wrists. Where the thing touched her, her skin burned with what felt like a swarm of wasp stings.

Her mind spun with sudden confusion and disorientation, and her ears flooded with alien whispers. Then vertigo kicked in, flipping the whole scene upside down. Before she could catch herself, the Misfortune yanked her head first down the stairs and melted away out of sight into the cascading gloom.

Delilah let out a cry as she lost her balance and the open stairwell loomed ahead of her as she teetered forward. Before her confused eyes, it spun like a drunken merry-go-round. Gravity took over, and she shot out a desperate hand managing to get just enough of the railing under her fingertips to avoid a face-first plunge down the steep steps. Instead, she twisted, her shoulder driving into the railing, her hip coming down on the stairs. She rolled over a hundred and eighty degrees, her ankle smashed into the opposite rail, her head came down, and she caught a vertical rung in the ear. Then she flipped again, smashing her knee—hard—as she turned over. At last, she got her other hand out and got enough of a grip on the passing rungs to arrest her fall.

Half a dozen hurts throbbed to life, but the adrenaline blurred the pain. She sprawled on the stairs, the frigid mist poured and eddied around her, and a drunken disorientation enveloped her. It wasn't the fall or the blow to the head. It was something else entirely.

The runes of protection tattooed along her sides in wings along her ribs grew warm and tight, constricting around her chest, pushing back against the malevolent force that was trying to lead her to her doom.

Another hollow-eyed specter crawled up out of the flowing gloom and latched its shapeless molten mouth to the side of her neck like a lover. It wrapped willowy arms around her in a frigid embrace.

Her heart palpitated, fluttering in her chest as the Misfortune stole her breath.

The runes along her sides hummed like hot light bulbs, and it was enough to buy back an ounce of her senses.

Delilah gave a defiant shout and drove the creature away with a brilliant spike of pure will and energy. With a soundless snarl, the Misfortune released its hungry grip and melted back into the flowing mist as it cascaded down the stairs.

Then Dodger was there, hauling her up to her feet.

"Easy, easy," he encouraged, putting a hand on her shoulder.

Up was down, down was up, and Delilah struggled to find the top of her topsy-turvy world. "What the hell is that?" she croaked.

"I don't know," Dodger replied, helping her lever herself into an upright position. "They're all over the house. Coming out of the goddamn walls."

"I see you!" the Doc McCoy thing roared from upstairs. The sound of his thrashing grew stronger.

Then another translucent specter rose up from the stairs behind Dodger, seized him by the back of the jacket, and pitched him over backward. His eyes rolled drunkenly in sudden disorientation. His arms flailed and found no purchase. Then he went over.

Delilah tried to grab hold of him, but as she reached out to catch his flailing hand, a spectral arm shot up through the steps and seized her by the wrist, pulling her up short. Their fingertips brushed, and Dodger fell.

He tried to tuck up, to guard his head, and two translucent shades swarmed up out of the shadows to ride him to the floor, interfering with his attempt at self-preservation, pulling his defensive arms away from his head.

He hit hard, landing at the bottom of the stairs with a breathless grunt and a resounding bounce.

"Dodger!" Delilah shrieked, tearing away from the stinging grasp of the spectral hand. She bounded down the steps, narrowly avoiding the groping reach of another ethereal attacker as it tried to snag her ankle. She cleared the steps and landed at Dodger's side, the impact of the landing stinging the soles of her feet.

He looked like a knocked-out prize fighter piled up on the rumpled mess of a paisley floor runner.

Delilah's head was on a swivel, sweeping left, right, up, down, then back. Maddening whispers assailed her from all directions. The urge to bolt left. No, right. No, run back upstairs. Or to freeze, don't move. Like the phantom whispers, these thoughts bounced around in her jangled mind like pinballs.

The spell of the Misfortunes was madness. Chaos. It levered on primal fear, the need to run, to escape. Fear of the gathering dark. Fear of being the prey. Intend to reach left and find yourself reaching right. See two steps left to go on the stairs below you when there were actually four.

Delilah pressed her eyes shut, scrubbing the tainted alien impressions from her mind as best she could, pushing them out of her body with will and energy.

Fuck you, fuck you, fuck you, she thought defiantly, a spike of anger pinning down the ratty wings of fear.

Formless specters drifted in and out at the edges of her vision. They faded away into the shadows, slipping in and out of the floors and walls as the chilling murk seeped down from above. The darkness had become profound as the ethereal mist cascaded down the walls. It was like being in the flooding bowels of a doomed ship watching the water pour in.

The hollow-eyed Misfortunes stalked, crawling up and down the halls like scuttling spiders only to sink into the hardwood floors or the plastered walls and disappear from view.

"Edwin!" she called out.

"Here!" came a terrified voice from the living room.

"Stay where you are," she ordered. There was no argument.

If Edwin was feeling *half* the burn of the Misfortune spell she was, he was also struggling to tell up from down.

She tried to rouse Dodger—smacked his face, shook him—and checked him over for injuries. The *real* fear was taking hold. The unsteadiness; the rushing loss of confidence; and the desperation of being left alone in the face of horror. The same thing the rabbit must feel when the hounds close in. Dodger groaned, but he didn't move.

She duck-walked a step away from his prone form and leaned around the base of the staircase, hazarding a look down the long central hallway. If the front door was still open, she could no longer see it in the deepening gloom. She searched the other direction and found no better. Both ends of the hall and the looming doorways of adjacent rooms disappeared into the swirling mist. Maintaining her sense of direction was nearly impossible, and she finally understood how firemen burned up in house fires within arm's reach of an exit and how people drowned in six feet of muddy water.

The banging and thrashing upstairs suddenly stopped.

Delilah felt the energy of her binding spell grow tight, like an overwound guitar string and she sucked in a sharp, startled breath—then it shattered.

The Doc McCoy creature tore free of her spell, and she took the hit from the backlash—ice picks to the ears, a belly flop from the high dive, a punch to the gut. It stole her breath and bloodied her nose. Delilah reeled and grabbed her head, gagging soundlessly on white pain. Her legs wobbled, and she collapsed to her knees.

The Doc McCoy creature snarled and snapped in triumph, a surreal many-voiced roar. "I see you!"

Seizing the opportunity, the Misfortunes swelled up into a spectral swarm and began to close in.

Delilah forced the metaphorical tweety birds from her head and ignored the jackhammer striking the brass gong in her skull. Instead, she balled up her small fist and drove it against the floor with a furious cry and a willful bark, summoning up a single word of arcane power.

There was a burst of soundless light, like the strobe of a

camera flash and the swarming Misfortunes were thrown back.

Delilah spun back to Dodger, who still appeared drunken and unsteady. She planted her palm in the middle of his chest and barked the command "Up!" A jolt of energy hit him like a live wire.

"Shit!" he shouted, snapping back to consciousness with an explosive jerk, lurching into a sitting position. His eyes were huge, his breath ragged, and his whole body was quivering.

"Go!" Delilah shouted, staggering into a standing position while she yanked on Dodger's hand, dragging him toward the room across the hall and the sound of Edwin's voice. Dodger sprang to his feet like a jack in the box. Stunned and stumbling, he staggered along beside her.

Translucent specters groped at them with wispy fingers along the way, through the walls, the floor, and down from the ceiling, but they kept stubbornly stomping one foot in front of the other. They dove through the door on the far side of the hall and collided headlong with Edwin in a tangle.

"We have to get out here!" Edwin screamed in panic. He tried to bolt past them, but Delilah grabbed his jacket and hauled him to a stop.

"Wait! Not that way!" she warned. "It's worse that way."

"There *isn't* any other way!" Edwin screeched.

Delilah and Dodger turned in frantic circles, looking for another escape route. A back door. Another hallway. Anything. They found none. Other than the faint, rapidly disappearing windows, the living room had one way in, one way out.

Delilah choked back a bark of hysterical laughter.

The Misfortunes had herded them right into a dead end, buzzing and blurring the thought from their minds as they did it. Creatures of doom, good at their game.

As if on cue, the frigid gloom began to leak through the ceiling into the Doc's cluttered living room. *Worse* was becoming a very relative term.

Back the way they'd come, the hallway and the stairs swarmed with a growing roach-like procession of spectral Misfortunes.

With a great leap, the Doc McCoy creature landed at the

bottom of the stairs in a predatory crouch. He was gory wreckage, broken and twisted by the chains of Delilah's spell. Cracked bones were peeled clean in places, his head was crushed and crooked, his jaw sagging off-kilter, but still snapping and biting.

"I see you!" it roared, fixing Edwin with its empty shredded eye sockets. Peeled and torn, crushed and misshapen, it rose and began lurching down the hallway, picking up speed with each step. The spectral Misfortunes swarmed around it like lampreys.

Where are you? Delilah lamented, thinking of the wards that protected the Doc's home. *Help. Please.*

But the house offered no protection. It should have held this attack, whatever it was, at bay. It should have kept the horrid Misfortunes out. Should have stopped whatever malevolent force animated the ruins of its creator. But it hadn't. The house and its many wards stood silent. It offered no resistance at all. Nor did it give them any aid.

Spectral Misfortunes began to claw their way down through the ceiling into the room, riding on the waterfalls of gloom.

"Oh shit!" Edwin gasped at the sight of them, back-peddling in panic toward the nearest corner.

Dodger snarled in frustration, snatched up a narrow end table in both hands, and heaved it at the dim outline of the living room's big picture window.

Two Misfortunes rose up out of the pooling mist and swatted it down, sending it crashing harmlessly to the floor.

Then four more rose up to join them.

Twice that many were wriggling their way down through the ceiling.

The creature in Doc McCoy's ruined remains filled the doorway, its empty eyes fixed on Edwin. "I see you," it hissed, its wet rasp a chorus of many voices.

The kid snapped. Shrieking in horror, he stumbled along the wall, groping and screaming until his feet twisted on an overturned lamp that dumped him into the cluttered floor.

Delilah stepped between the Doc and Edwin, and for a moment the ruined golem of twisted meat stopped. It turned those baleful empty eye sockets on her.

Delilah stood her ground, pulled the Zippo from her jacket pocket and struck the wheel. A pale flame bloomed in the lighter's chimney, and Delilah pulled the flame into her hand with a graceful glide.

"Aw shit," Dodger grunted.

"Get back," Delilah warned, the flame swelling in her palm as she raised her hand, filling the dark room with hot golden radiance. "Now." Then she began to whisper to the fire in an alien pyromantic tongue, soft, insistent, commanding, while the flame in her palm began to writhe and grow.

Dodger sprang for the far end of the room seeking cover.

The Doc McCoy thing snarled and broke into a charge with an avalanche of Misfortunes following him.

Delilah brought her hand down and let loose the fire.

Fire—the Universal Cleanser. Only those things born in flame were immune to it. Everything else burned.

The billowing burst of golden flame erupted from Delilah's outstretched hand in a sweeping lash of tendrils. They snapped in a dazzling dance of blazing ribbons—whip cracks of striking fire and blistering heat.

The onslaught drove the spectral Misfortunes away before it. The pale phantoms retreated, their silent mouths gaping, hollow eyes empty and black. The creeping mists of their disorienting spell burned away as Delilah's fire brands sliced through the murk.

Fire bathed the Doc McCoy thing in cleansing flame. It howled and shrieked then halted its charge, falling back. But Delilah whipped it again, unleashing another torrent of billowing yellow fire, twisting and turning it under her command, making it lash like a living thing as she drew it into both hands.

Whipping with her tendrils of flame, Delilah drove the creature into retreat.

Across the cluttered floor, biting at the walls and ceiling, the fire began to hook claws into things Delilah did *not* intend. Fire was fickle, hungry, and impossible to control absolutely. It began to catch elsewhere, and smoke began to rise in place of the evaporating murk.

Delilah battered the Doc and his host of hungry shades from the doorway, clearing their exit. She hammered and pounded on him until he collapsed on the floor, burning, twisting, and growling. The Doc McCoy creature retreated like a wounded crab toward the door beyond the staircase, burning and smoldering.

Shouting the lyrical peel of her pyromantic incantation, sweat streaming down her face, Delilah drove them back into the hall, up along the stairs, and further still into the unknown gloom.

"Edwin get up!" she barked, but the terrified kid didn't move.

A swarm of Misfortunes rushed at her from the left as she pushed into the hallway, but she whipped them in bursts of fire until they retreated. The phantoms repelled, and the hallway retaken, Delilah pulled her lashing flames back, clenching each fist in a blazing golden halo. The spellfire boiled and twisted up her arms but did her no harm. The air was heavy with the odor of dry heat and brimstone.

The gloom parted by a faint degree and to her far right at the end of the long hall, the silhouette of the back door could be seen. A way out.

"Dodger, go!" she shouted, pointing toward the door.

Dodger came on like a freight train. Along the way, he snatched up Edwin like a child, heaving and shoving him along as the young man shrieked in horror. They piled into the hall. Edwin fought and protested with every step. Hanging on to the kid in his horrified, spell-drunk frenzy was like trying to wrestle an angry monkey.

He broke loose from Dodger's grip, and came out swinging, kicking and punching.

Spectral hands seized the opportunity and reached through the wall, bursting out of the surface of a darkened mirror.

They grabbed Edwin by the hair and heaved him backward with sickening strength.

With a crunch, he smashed ear-first into the big mirror, and it exploded in a shower of shards. A purple gash opened along the back of Edwin's neck as daggers of broken glass rained down.

Then the blood began to flow.

Edwin staggered, clutched his wounded neck and sagged to his knees.

"No!" Delilah shrieked. A split-second distraction. The Misfortunes surged back up the hallway from the opposite direction, threatening to overrun her.

"Look out!" Dodger shouted, pointing toward the rushing swarm.

Delilah spun back to face them, fear and anger slamming together inside her like wrecking balls. She shoved both hands out before her and cut loose with a roaring vortex of fire like an angry dragon. Rugs and draperies caught at once. A dry wreath hanging on the wall below the stairs lit up like a torch. A charging Misfortune ducked under her fiery onslaught and heaved her right off her feet.

Delilah was forced to release her hold on the flames as she tumbled, extinguishing them rather than lose control completely. But the damage was already done. The house was burning now. Embers began to twist and turn on the choking air.

Two hungry Misfortunes leaked through the wall on top of Edwin. One locked its hollow mouth over his and began to steal his breath. The other sank spectral fingers into the wound on the back of his neck and pried it open until blood sprayed.

Dodger rushed in, trying to come to his aid, but other Misfortunes sprang out of the floor and the opposite wall and held him at bay, driving him away from Edwin. Dodger had nothing to combat them with.

The Misfortune who'd taken Delilah off her feet crawled up her body and latched its formless mouth between her breasts, sucking the beats from her heart. The sensation was nauseating. She felt tunnel vision close in as her heart disobeyed her brain.

Defiant to the very end, she found anger enough to fight back. Shoving with her will as much as her hands, she drove the specter off, breaking its hungry suckle. Scrambling and scampering, she found her feet again before it could overwhelm her.

She rushed toward Edwin as the Misfortunes deepened their hold on him.

The floor was slick with his blood. His face was pale and shocked. He was no longer screaming.

The wall behind Edwin exploded in a shower of plaster, broken boards, and the remains of the mirror. Delilah threw her hands up and shied away reflexively, tucking against the far wall for cover.

Twisted and shredded, burnt arms shot through the wreckage and snatched Edwin up by the back of his bloody jacket. They heaved, hammering the boy against the wall, once, twice, three times, beating him with bone breaking force until they finally managed to wrench his body into the next room through the hole in the wall.

"Oh God, no!" Delilah screamed, racing toward the broken gap, even as the lingering Misfortunes groped and pawed at her. The house shook and trembled. Hungry fire spread rapidly.

She caught only a glimpse into the next room. The floor was buckling, sinking, melting into black tar. Taking the spare bedroom down the surreal sinkhole with it. At its epicenter knelt Edwin, face frozen in bloodless terror, eyes fixed a thousand miles away on nothing.

Burned and ruined, Doc McCoy held him from behind in a bloody embrace, gnawing, chewing, ripping great hunks of meat out of his neck with each toothy bite. Scorched bony fingers pierced Edwin's chest, breaking ribs, turning them out, pulping pink lung meat, digging toward his heart.

The floor continued to bend and sink, sloughing and slipping, the furniture and decorations piling into the slurry. Obscured beneath the surface of the roiling tar, hands reached up through the molten ooze and took hold of Edwin and the Doc both, dragging them under.

They went down together in that gruesome embrace.

Just before the sinking floor and the groping hands swallowed them, Doc McCoy turned his empty eye sockets, now burnt charcoal-black by Delilah's fire, on the sorceress herself. "I see you… Delilah."

Then they were gone, and the ceiling caved in on top of them in a rush of air choked with plaster dust.

A Misfortune crawled up Delilah's side and levered against

the wall as if to drag her through the gaping hole into the impossible catastrophe of the next room.

With a tearful scream, she shrugged off the phantom and lurched stiff-legged toward the silhouette of the back door. It was open, showing the light of day beyond this shadow-bleeding, tar-boiling hellscape.

Five steps from freedom, the debt came due. All the haste, the improvisation, the raw energy. All metaphysical muscle and no finesse, no tools to lighten the load.

Her body quit, tunnel vision closed in; her knees sagged; she stumbled toward the door, and the floor tried to lurch up to slap her, but Dodger was there. He grabbed her and kept her from face planting. Sweeping her up like a rag doll, he dragged her toward the door and the outside world.

Behind them, the house shuddered. Walls cracked. Things buckled. The floor rippled. Fire spread.

The Misfortunes began to regroup and moved back in to pick up the pursuit.

Leaning on each other, limping and gimping, Delilah and Dodger burst at last through the back door and out into the light of day. Together they stumbled and took the short steps down into the backyard. They piled in a heap at the foot of the Doc's little concrete bird bath.

Behind them, the house began to burn in earnest. The Misfortunes piled into the open door, pale specters all but lost in the darkness and smoke. But they would not follow them out into the daylight.

Delilah's entire body quivered with metaphysical exhaustion. She was punch-drunk, numb. The horror dial was overloaded. Dodger was pulling on her, hauling her to her feet.

"We gotta go!" he insisted from far away in the shell-shocked fog.

Moving on autopilot, she followed Dodger out through the back gate and into the narrow alley between the two houses. From there, they limped back to where they'd parked their rides.

Dodger's tone was urgent. "We can't leave any vehicles here. Can you drive?"

She nodded.

"You sure?"

She nodded again. Mute and stunned.

Dodger piled her in her car. She sorted herself out while he got saddled up on his bike. Keys in the ignition. *Get it together. Get it together.*

Smoke was rising into the sky from Doc's house around the block. A couple of curious neighbors were wandering out on the sidewalk to have a look. Somewhere a dozen or so people were picking up their phones and dialing 9-1-1.

Get it together.

She started the car. Dodger pulled up alongside her, his bike growling and rumbling. "You good?"

Get it together. She nodded, gave a half-hearted thumbs up.

Dodger rolled out.

Doing her level best to *get it together*, Delilah dropped it in drive and followed.

Behind them, the Doc's corner of Hell burned to the ground.

16

The Church, surprisingly, was a church. Or at least, it *had* been a church.

Before it came into the possession of the Crows of Los Angeles, it had been home to a very small but very devoted neighborhood start-up congregation. The pastor had been young and enthusiastic. His meager flock was the same. Some churches had bingo night. Others had raffles and bake sales. They'd opted for a more hip vibe, like barbecues, block parties, and everybody's favorite, Nintendo Night. All good clean fun for the neighborhood. It lasted about a year until eight members of the congregation got busted for dealing crack and selling pussy. Including the pastor. The fun and games came to an end, and the Arbor Vitae Family Worship Praise Center went up for auction.

"Praise the Lord," Victor St. John had offered with a smile when he bought the place for a song. For pennies on the dollar, Victor's Crows got their very own discreet urban guild hall a few blocks from easy access to the 405 in Arbor Vitae Inglewood.

The Church had worn a lot of different hats over the years. Built in the Sixties, it was originally a community medical clinic, thrown up by somebody who was obviously getting concrete poured on the cheap. Or maybe the developer was making union buddies happy. Either way, the exterior walls were castle-thick, making the place one hell of an urban bunker. That had definitely been part of its appeal to the Crows.

It'd had a short life as a small neighborhood Christian school. Then a pretty good run as a community rec center in the Eighties. And during the Nineties, it skipped like a rock from hip little street church to a Crow Hall. It had been the urban home of Victor's Crows ever since.

The neighborhood wasn't great, but it wasn't bad either. The streets were packed tight with little bungalows, but they all had bars on their windows. There were small and medium-sized apartment buildings on every other block. Lots of trees. Mostly residential. A few shops and restaurants. Out of the way, no fuss, no muss. No touristy looky-loos. The same faces hanging around, day in and day out. No reason for anybody to be around that didn't need to be around. And that was the idea. Low profile, tucked away, and nobody hassled them. About a third of the local residents were foreign-born and about one in six didn't speak much English at all. The Crow's neck of Arbor Vitae was predominately Hispanic.

The Church even sported a partial three-story rooftop, so also like a castle, it gave a commanding view of the neighborhood at large. All the Crows put in their fair share of hours up on that roof contemplating the workings of the universe. Or drinking and smoking a little weed. Same thing sometimes.

They had a section of the place decked out like a safehouse apartment, just in case somebody needed somewhere to crash or lay low for a while. The Church had a full basement, part of which they'd walled uptight and made into an indoor gun range. Buried under all that concrete, earth, and asphalt, nobody ever complained about the noise. Hell, nobody even really noticed. It didn't really *look* much like a gun range. More like a long, weird hallway. They kept it discreet, just for those times when code inspectors happened to stop by for a visit, which was rare. Some of the Crows were convicted felons after all. It wouldn't look good for them to be hanging around an unpermitted gun range in the underbelly of Inglewood.

They had hidey holes aplenty throughout the old building and a couple of heavily warded vaults that could double as impromptu holding cells or panic rooms, just in case. Those well-prepared, masterfully warded rooms were just as good at keeping things in as they were at keeping things out.

The west wing of the Church had been converted into a combination garage, warehouse, and workshop with big roll-up bay doors. Much of the sprawling building was used as storage. This was one of Victor and Fiona's front businesses, their own personal money laundering service for the Crow. On paper, the family business was high-end antiques. Furniture, artwork, and other collectibles with four and five figure price tags. Victor didn't do showroom or gallery retail to the public, certainly not in this neighborhood and location. His crew acquired pieces for dealers and sold wholesale. Again, it kept the looky-loos at bay and was one of the ways they explained shit to the IRS.

The Crows had twenty years of history in Inglewood down on Arbor Vitae. Some of the younger Crows, like Gabriel and Delilah, they had grown up down here, running around the neighborhood with the local kids getting into trouble.

Mahri, the trouble-making queen bee from The Odd, she was an Inglewood original from Arbor Vitae. A much younger Gabriel had met a much younger Mahri hanging out at the pool hall down the block back in the day. Those were simpler times. For everyone.

17

Friday afternoon was growing stale, golden, and hazy when Gabriel and crew rolled into the Church. They'd lost an hour and change on essential detours and traffic.

The first essential detour was to dump the Camry off at one of the Crow's anonymously rented storage units. They had a dozen scattered around Southland. Weapons caches, spare equipment, burner vehicles, cash, questionable Occult paraphernalia you didn't want to leave sitting around on your coffee table as a conversation starter.

The bucket full of catastrophe that had happened at Mahri's pickup had gone down in front of a neighborhood full of witnesses, and even though it had happened in the back lot of the apartment building and an alley, there'd been a lot of running, shouting, and shooting. There were cell phone cameras everywhere these days. The silver Camry would need to stay out of sight until it could be cleaned up, the shot up back glass could be replaced, and its bogus registration could be swapped out for a new one. Maybe a paint job too. Then there was the blood, Gabriel's and the hunter he'd killed. It was smeared all over the car, and that was not something he wanted turning into a crime scene until it could be cleaned up.

They hit one of their storage boxes in South Park because it let them swap the blown burner ride for another. Gabriel rounded up his bloody clothes and torn body armor, stuffing them in a garbage bag while Piper policed up the gear and goodies.

As he was tying the sack, Gabriel noticed Mahri watching him intently. "That's as much my blood as it is his," he said. "I'd like to keep track of it."

In the darker corners of the supernatural world, letting something get its grim little claws on your blood was a recipe for disaster. Fresh blood was best. It went stale over time, eventually fading to little more than a metaphysical echo for anything but the most capable practitioner. But safe was better than sorry.

A tiny smirk tugged at the corner of Mahri's mouth. "I've probably got some of you on me too. You gonna want this also?" She tugged at the low collar of her tank top, and Gabriel found himself suddenly aware of her cleavage.

He forced a frown and didn't give her the satisfaction of letting it show. Which was mostly pointless because, clearly, she knew better. Not like they hadn't swapped plenty of fluids in the past as it was but he opted not to dignify it with an answer.

He fished a spare white undershirt out of his gear bag and slipped it on overhead, getting it spotted up almost at once with fresh blood, but it wasn't bad enough for him to care at the moment.

They locked the Camry away from prying eyes and, after throwing some plastic sheeting over the back seat of their new ride, they rolled on out in a red 2002 Chevy Tahoe. By then, Gabriel's wounds were beginning to throb merrily.

The rest of the way to the Church moods were mixed, adrenalized excitement giving way to stoic silence for Gabriel. Piper, as per usual, wasn't all that chatty anyway, but Mahri, on the other hand, seemed to slide right back into being her old self. She wanted to shoot the shit as if she hadn't just plunged a kitchen knife into a kid's neck and been caught in the middle of a gunfight between Crows and Helitori.

Gabriel didn't know what to make of that, and at least for the next thirty minutes or so, he didn't even try. By the time they rolled onto West Arbor Vitae, you'd have thought Mahri was dropping by for a social call. It could have been any other bored Friday night to her, looking to have a drink and a kill some time with old chums, maybe bullshit some shop talk.

They turned off West Arbor Vitae into the small asphalt parking lot and headed for the garage bay doors on the west side of the sprawling concrete building. Backed into a parking space beside the garage doors was a single vehicle: an old, dusty Harley Knucklehead. It was the only thing that ever parked in that spot.

Piper fished a garage door opener from his pocket, and the brown metal doors rumbled up in their tracks. They parked the red Tahoe in the shade of the Church garage and as the doors rolled down behind them, the trio dismounted.

Gabriel swung out of the Tahoe with a pained grimace.

Piper cocked an eyebrow. "You okay, brother?"

Gabriel chuckled and nodded. Sitting in the car had made him stiffen up. Getting up and stretching his tall frame to standing height was giving that fresh gash a good tug under the dressing. "I'm getting a fucking drink," he announced as they made their way inside. He headed through the garage, into the entry hall, and toward the clubhouse bar.

"You fix a girl up?" Mahri asked. Then she hooked her arm around his and leaned her head on his shoulder.

That gave him pause. It seemed like the right thing to do was to pull away and back her the hell up. But he didn't. He just kept walking, Mahri on his arm. Piper snorted, smirked, shook his head, and kept on walking. Gabriel's soft spot for Mahri wasn't exactly a secret among his brothers and sisters. Everybody knew she still came around every now and then and the two of them would knock boots for old time's sake. Today wasn't turning out to be one of those days though. Piper opened the door for the both of them, and the look Gabriel caught from the surly old Crow said he didn't like any of this.

The Crow's clubhouse bar didn't much resemble the church kitchen and community room it had been once upon a time. It was more roadhouse than righteous these days. Behind the bar stood an old, gray-bearded cowboy biker. Big and broad, he was as tough and gnarly as old driftwood, with a fading Eagle, Globe, and Anchor tattooed on his right forearm that dated back to Tet '68. That was Bingo. The old knight. Victor's first recruit when he'd washed up in Los Angeles. And like Victor, Bingo's kids wore the Crow too. Retired wasn't quite the right word for Bingo's occupation. Bingo was Bingo and holding down the Church was his domain.

They found him alone at the bar, presiding over the Holy Order of Medicinal Whiskey. His sermon was silence, his choir some Neil Young piping in over the sound system speakers behind the bar. His congregation the empty stools along the bar and the worn old couches that lined the walls. Warm brown whiskey was his holy water, some fine presidential Kush, his incense. He was making ready for Church, getting an early start, as was his custom.

Bingo sipped his cup, nipped his smoldering joint, and looked at the motley trio from under his bushy gray eyebrows. "The fuck happened to you?" he asked, eyeballing Gabriel's blood-stained undershirt. His voice was like the desert, motor oil on sun-baked gravel.

"Zigged when I shoulda zagged," Gabriel grunted, sidling up to the bar.

Bingo cocked a bushy brow and poured the captain Crow a cup at once. "How's the other guy?"

Gabriel paused, tapped a thoughtful fingertip against the glass. "Been a long day, old man."

Bingo nodded. "Ain't seen you in a while," he muttered, looking Mahri up and down.

Piper laughed. "No, you have not."

Bingo didn't get the joke, but he spotted and took note of it. He was in no hurry to ask questions. "What's the lady drinking?"

"One of the same," Mahri replied with a pretty smile, giving a nod toward Gabriel's glass.

Bingo poured. "How 'bout you, Piper?"

"Eh, I gotta take a shit," Piper replied, his tone bored, and he wandered off into the bowels of the Church.

Bingo didn't press. Now clearly wasn't the time. Instead, he passed the joint to his Captain, something to take the edge off of the pain until the whiskey caught up and something better came along. Gabriel gratefully accepted.

By the time Gabriel reached the bottom of his whiskey glass, the Crow's doc had arrived, answering Piper's call. Her name was Anna. She was Bingo's baby girl, Dodger's younger sister, and a Crow through and through.

She had a big blue crash bag under her arm, strap tight over her shoulder. She was dressed like she'd just left the gym. Bronze and tall like her brother, she was blessed with her mama's elegance, grace, and wit. What she got from her daddy was his nerve, chiseled from stone.

She frowned, eyeballing Gabriel in the mirror behind the bar. "Well, you're still upright. Is that a good sign?"

"Guess so," Gabriel muttered with a grateful smile.

"Okay. Infirmary," Anna ordered.

Gabriel didn't argue. He downed the last little swallow from his whiskey glass, gave Bingo a look, and nodded toward Mahri. "Keep her company, would ya?"

The old knight nodded catching Gabriel's drift.

After that, the captain Crow followed Anna back to the infirmary.

Anna was an ER trauma doc. Victor St. John had seen to it that there was a tuition fund set up to send Anna through med school when Bingo's baby girl had shown interest in the profession. Nothing like having a loyal-from-birth doctor in the family. Time and time again, it had proven a powerfully worthwhile investment. Outside the Crow, she sold her services as a shot doc to a number of clients who didn't have the luxury of running to an ER if they wound up with a bullet in them. Over the years, Anna had made some connections with L.A.'s underground rings of off-the-books trauma specialists. Doctors, as well as mystics and metaphysical healers.

If Anna couldn't put you back together, she knew who could and how to find them. Better yet, they'd make themselves available if she called. Either that or you died. If Anna or one of her associates couldn't fix you, then you had two choices. Go throw yourself on the mercy of legit trauma center and hope for the best, then enjoy your jail time. Or get measured for your casket.

Competent and intelligent in the extreme, unshakably frosty—that was Anna. She'd done her time in L.A. County Hospital's infamous C-Booth, and now, post-residency, she was looking at staying right where she was.

"You could go anywhere in the country, baby," Bingo had

said to her once. Not imploring her to leave. Just letting her know he'd support her decision if she did.

In the end, Anna had only kissed her daddy's scruffy cheek. "My family's here, pop." And that was that. Anna was like her mother. A Crow to the end.

She took Gabriel in the back and patched him up. "Well, most of it isn't all that deep," Anna murmured, inspecting the gash across the left side of Gabriel's chest. She noted the fresh strawberry on his chin, the black-and-blue racing stripes coming up along his ribs on the right side. She worked her fingers along his banged-up ribs, and he grunted. "Sore?"

"Peachy."

"Hurt to breathe?"

"Nah."

"How'd this happen?"

"I almost got my ass kicked. Twice. Take your pick."

They shared a smile, and Anna gave a snort. She tended the cut, poked some needles into it for a local, cleaned it up, and stapled it shut. She reinforced the wound with some tape and then dressed it back up tight. "You're fine. Your warranty was already voided anyway. I'm gonna give you some horse pills for infection. Take them. And stop getting hit for a day or two."

"No promises," Gabriel replied.

While Anna finished up, Gabriel sat up on the table and straightened himself out, feet dangling over the side. He lit a cigarette, and the family doc cocked an eyebrow. Then she took it from him, had a drag, and passed it back. Like two kids smoking in the locker room. It made him smile. Gabriel clenched his fist, flexed his arm, and turned gingerly at the waist, feeling the nice fresh dressing on his ribs holding firm. "Thanks."

"Busy night ahead?" Anna asked, digging around in her big blue crash bag.

"Yeah, I'm sure."

She pitched him a small brown pill bottle. "Just a little something to take the edge off. Because if that doesn't hurt enough now, well ... this is you we're talking about. Something will before too long."

"Your confidence is overwhelming." Gabriel pocketed the bottle. "I'll be a good boy."

"Yeah, yeah." Anna wasn't so convinced. "And for the love of God, don't smoke in my infirmary."

Gabriel gathered up his stuff to leave while Anna went back to cleaning up, but the contemplative expression on her face stopped him. "What?"

She shrugged, her expression somewhere between amused and concerned. "You okay?"

Gabriel wasn't sure how to take that. "Yeah. You?"

After a thoughtful pause, Anna nodded. "You're still all bloody."

Gabriel looked down at his hands, the thought of it having escaped him. She was right. There were crusty brown stains in the creases of his knuckles, between his fingers, caked in around his nails, smeared up his forearms.

Anna set out a pile of white towels, ripe with the scent of heavy bleach. She nodded toward the sink basin. "I'm done here. Why don't you clean up. Get straightened out, you know? Stick them in the burn bag when you get done. I'll take care of it."

Gabriel considered that, nodded in appreciation. "Yeah."

"I'll give you a little bit," Anna said. She laid a kind hand on his shoulder and then left him alone in the infirmary.

Gabriel took the towels, set the water running into the big stainless steel basin, and began to wash up. From time to time, he looked up at himself in the mirror. He had a faint smear of brown blood down the side of his face, and he *looked* a lot more strung out than he *felt*. At least, he didn't think he felt as strung out as he looked. It had been a bloody couple of days. Definitely not business as usual. The guy staring back at him looked tired.

"Fuck it," he grunted. Then he hung his head under the tall goose-neck faucet and let the cool water wash away some of the day's bullshit.

Get straightened out, he thought. *Good advice.*

He did his best to take it to heart.

Once he was cleaned up, he pulled his shirt back on and headed back to the clubhouse.

He arrived to find Bingo and Dodger conspiring at the bar. Mahri was nowhere in sight. Dodger had recently arrived, looking whipped, exhausted. He was holding a plastic baggie full of ice against the base of his skull. The big man looked spooked. Gabriel wasn't used to seeing Dodger spooked. The room stank like a house fire. Charred wood, singed upholstery, burned plastic.

Bingo looked up from his son, his gaze landing on Gabriel. The old knight's face was lined with worry. He nodded toward the ladies room.

Delilah appeared in the doorway, pale, shaken, looking like what the cat dragged in. Mahri wasn't far behind her, watching Delilah as if she expected her to fold up like a punch-drunk boxer at any moment. Delilah's face was flushed, she was holding a damp towel in her hand, wiping it across he mouth as if she'd just gotten done puking.

"Hey," she said with a humorless smirk, her voice small.

"Hey," Gabriel replied, dread settling into the pit of his stomach.

Then Delilah's knees gave way and she went down in a heap.

PART THREE

Off Plan

I am often asked, particularly by those newest in service to the Watch, why we do not do more to intervene in the bloodshed and other immorality that is often exchanged between the Great Houses. There are plots and killings. Retributions and crimes. Loathsome powers are touched and brought into this world where they do not belong.

They question, "Why do we not stop these things?"

And I ask them, "Where should we begin?"

We are not the policemen of the world. We are humble gardeners, pruning only the rotten apples and the blighted blossoms while leaving the orchard to grow as nature would will it. The garden is full of rot in need of pruning. And haunted by many hungry beasts who would otherwise devour it. The Watch does not lack for work.

Anything more would find the whole thorny garden turned against us in common cause.

From the Personal Journals of
Bahadir Fadel Satik, Lord Commander of the Watch

18

Michael LeMay watched his five-year-old son Samuel wear out the twisty slide at Soule Park. Samuel was the best thing in his world. When all else failed, that was what it all came down to. His little snowy-haired boy ran a lap around the slide roaring like a dinosaur.

"I am the greatest!" Samuel growled in his dinosaur voice, and his father was inclined to agree.

In the nearby parking lot, back-dropped by a sun-dappled orange grove across the street, car doors opened and closed. Michael glanced that way and saw the three men he'd come here to meet exiting their vehicle. He went back to watching his son play, as the evening sun slanted through the trees, cool and golden.

The approaching trio made an odd crew for a local park on the outskirts of Ojai, California.

The first was Enzio, a tall Italian with a big chip on his shoulder. By Michael's estimation, he was a dildo with ears. Enzio was a scarecrow-slender white man decked out in a very fine gray suit. His hair was on its way to graying to the same color, and there was a little more of it that shade since Michael had seen him last.

Beside Enzio walked Bahadir Fadel Satik. Lord Commander of the Watch. Better known simply as the Turk. He was a small, tidy man, balding and gray with a meticulously trimmed goatee. His skin was rich and bronze, face forever weathered by the sun and sea. He had pale jade eyes wreathed in deep crow's feet and a brow creased with frown lines. He wore a brown cardigan sweater and a starched white shirt. He could have been anyone's grandfather.

Running point for the pack was Dutch, the man who taught Michael everything he knows about things that go bump in the night. Dutch was a sharply dressed middle-aged black man. His hairline was starting to retreat by degrees, and there was a touch of gray in his goatee, but beyond that, he might as well have been sculpted from marble. He had the effortless, smooth glide of a jazz man skating on oiled glass. Being in the same zip code with him made Michael feel like a bearded, flannel-wearing, white-bread redneck, which to be fair, he was.

If the Turk was dropping Dutch on him, he was pulling out the big guns.

Enzio and the Turk lingered at a respectful distance while Dutch continued on to make first contact.

"He's getting big, Michael," Dutch said, watching Samuel take a roaring ride down the slide. He offered Michael his hand in greeting.

Michael shook it. "Pull up a seat."

Dutch copped a squat on the bench beside his old pupil.

Michael sighed. "You know I don't want to be having this conversation, right? Technically, I'm still on leave." He nodded toward his son. "We had plans for the next thirty days or so."

Dutch nodded. "I know that."

"You know I'm only doing it for you."

"Know that too."

Michael sat with his old friend, and for a long while they were quiet. Birds chirped in the trees. A tyrannosaurus rex in the guise of a five-year-old boy bellowed and howled in the distance. Somewhere halfway down the slide, it transformed into a starfighter pilot, complete with blaster sounds.

Michael broke the silence. "So. What are we doing here?"

"The Helitori posted a formal declaration."

"And we care?"

Dutch nodded. "They're gonna take out the Circle Odd. In your backyard."

Michael processed that. "What for?"

"Officially? They claim treating with the powers of the Outer Darkness."

"And I claim I got a foot-long dick. Proof?"

Dutch grunted. "Yeah. That's the sketchy part."

Michael snorted and shook his head. "Usually is."

Dutch took a deep breath and gave a nod toward Samuel. "When's the last time you spoke to his mother?"

Michael considered it, shook his head. "I don't know. A while."

"A week? A month? A year?"

"Been a couple of months."

"Do you know where she is?"

Michael chuckled. "Why? What'd she do now?"

Dutch was slow to answer. The silence was uncomfortable. "Dutch?"

"We're looking into the Helitori's claim about the Circle Odd. Points back to Dante Washington."

"Heroin, coke, guns, and real estate? That Dante Washington?"

"Uh-huh. The Crow. Word is they're getting pretty cozy with Mr. Washington's operation these last few months. Turning some trade. Making friends."

Michael shrugged. "They're mercs, Dutch. That's what they do. Why do we care? Let the cops deal with it if there's some kind of street crime to handle." Michael affected his best downtrodden Southern dialect. *"We ain't da po-leese."*

Dutch chuckled. "Don't I know it. But it might be more complicated than that."

"How so?"

"The Helitori's declaration. Named the Circle Odd. Named Dante Washington and his enterprise. Tainted by association. Unclean. In collusion with rogue practitioners of the Dark Arts."

Michael closed his eyes. "Jesus fucking Christ." Then he watched his little snowy-haired boy chase his shadow and make several awkward leaping spins accompanied by lightsaber sound effects. The Force was clearly used at one point.

"So I don't have to tell you what happens when the Helitori starts bumping up against Dante Washington."

Michael's face was grim. "They start bumping up against the Crow."

"Which means, your vacation is over."

Reluctantly, Michael nodded.

"Figured with the history you and Delilah St. John have. Well. I didn't want you to hear it on the street first."

"I wasn't even listening," Michael admitted. "My son and I were ... Yeah—Were."

"Somebody's gonna throw the first punch. If they haven't already. When that happens, the Helitori will not stop. Every member of the Circle Odd. Everybody associated with Dante Washington's enterprise. Every Crow. They *all* become targets."

Michael wasn't sure how to take that. His world was probably a better place without Delilah St. John in it. Samuel's world was definitely a better place without her in it. From Michael's perspective. But not from Samuel's.

Their little snowy-haired boy worshiped his largely-absent mommy.

In the end, Michael and Delilah had a lot of baggage. There was a lot of hurt and a lot of distrust between them. Just as many scars as there were hugs and kisses. But there would always be a part of Michael, somewhere well out of the light of day, that loved his son's mother. He didn't want to see any harm come to her. Or her family.

"Well. Goddammit," Michael grunted.

Samuel made a valiant effort to climb the slide backward, but instead slipped and got pitched unceremoniously onto the playground turf like laundry down a chute. He bounced up like he was made of flubber.

"I'm okay," the little boy shouted and went right back to firing his imaginary blaster rifle.

Michael took a deep breath and let it out slowly. "You better go say hi to him, Uncle Dutch."

Dutch patted Michael on the shoulder and put his shades back on. He stood and offered a nod in the direction of the Turk and his grumpy Italian guard dog. They began to approach. Then he put on his happiest Uncle Dutch face and went to say hello to little mop-headed Samuel. There was roaring and pew-pew and squealing in abundance. From both of them.

"How have you been, Michael?" the Turk asked, offering him a friendly handshake. The Turk was a very soft-spoken man. It was a product of his authority. He had no need to talk large.

Michael accepted the handshake and nodded. "Hanging in there. And how about you, sir?"

"I have few complaints," the Turk replied with a smile. Then he got down to it. "This business. It is very unfortunate."

"That's one way to put it."

The Turk nodded toward Samuel. "Does she see him very often?"

"No."

"Her doing or yours?"

"Little bit of both."

"I'm sorry to interrupt your family time, Michael. But ... duty."

Michael nodded. He knew all about the shit sandwich of duty. He had a set of jump wings tattooed over his heart and G.I. Bill money he'd never made any use of. Before the Watch, he'd been a soldier, an Afghanistan vet. He was well versed in the way duty could rip the rug right out from under your feet.

The Turk withdrew a silver-plated cigarette case from his sweater pocket and removed a hand-rolled cigarette. He packed it lightly against the cover of the case and lifted it to the corner of his mouth. Enzio offered him a light as he slipped the case back into his pocket.

He took a few thoughtful puffs before he continued.

"You have a very special relationship with the Crow. It could prove most useful."

Michael sketched a sideward glance the Lord Commander's way. "Don't do this to me, Satik." For his son's sake, for his own sake, he had no interest in getting mixed up in the middle of Crow business.

The Turk pressed his case. "By blood, you are family. Closer to Victor and Fiona's Crows than any of us. You are the father of their grandson. Their daughter was your—"

"I know who Delilah was and is," Michael interrupted as politely as he could muster.

The Turk sighed. "She is not her father or her mother, Michael."

"No, she is not," Michael agreed, tone tight with irony.

The Turk took a different approach. "All I'm suggesting is that you reach out. See where all the cards land, because you are the best suited for the task. And we'll leave it at that."

"Meaning?"

"This is not an order. I understand your boundaries are for the sake of your son." The Turk placed a hand over his own heart. "A voluntary favor to an old friend and brother in arms. Nothing more. There is much at work here we do not know. And there may be great advantages to leaning close to the Crow. It is not as if we have the same luxury with the Helitori. They will slap away any olive branch we offer them, now that they are on the hunt."

Michael sighed. His head sagged. He nodded. "This is going to get bloody, Satik."

"Perhaps we can mitigate that. An ounce of prevention is worth a pound of cure. Yes?"

"Assuming we aren't already too late. Feels like we're too late."

The Turk conceded the point silently. "We can make arrangements for Samuel if you—"

"I'll take care of my son."

"Very well. I can consider you returned to duty then?"

Michael nodded.

"Good. If we have anything new to report, I'll see to it that you hear about it directly. We would appreciate the same in return."

"Sure."

"Where do you intend to begin?"

Michael shrugged. He only had one real option. "Horse's mouth. You want to hug the Crow? Guess I'll go hug the Crow."

"Thank you," the Turk said, his tone sincere. "Your boy is growing up very beautiful, Michael. Peace be upon both of you."

With that, the Turk and Enzio retired to the car.

"That was the plan," Michael muttered when they were well out of earshot.

When Michael looked back toward the playground, he saw his little snowy-haired boy charging his direction at full sprint while Dutch made long-legged strides to keep up.

"Daddy!" Samuel cried, waving something triumphantly overhead. "Lookit! Uncle Dutch made me a bird! It's got lasers!"

Samuel was waving a little origami crane back and forth like a tiny lunatic. The lasers were entirely imaginary. Everything had lasers this week. Even the dinos.

Michael laughed. "Oh yeah? Let me see."

"You okay?" Dutch asked when he caught up to the father and son duo.

"Yeah," Michael replied. "Good enough."

"I'm sorry about this."

Michael shrugged. "Me too. But, he's not wrong."

Dutch nodded. "No, he is not."

"Doesn't make it any better though."

"No. It does not."

Michael glanced back toward the parking lot. "Your ride's trying to get away."

Dutch chuckled. "They won't leave without me. They have no idea where they are." He reached down and patted Samuel on the head and Michael on the shoulder. "Whatever this is, you call me first. You can bow to the Lord Commander as time allows. Understand?"

"Yessir."

"And if you need something, you just say it. I'll drop a mountain on this, so help me God."

Michael nodded. That meant a lot coming from him. "I'm sure it'll just be a couple days, Dutch. Pin the tail on a couple of donkeys. Then I'm back to Mr. Mom and mac'n'cheese. The Turk can work out the diplomatic mission."

"Mac'n'cheese?" Samuel echoed hopefully.

"I need some bodies for surveillance. Whatever you can send me."

"All right," Dutch said. "Next?"

"I need a face-to-face with a Helitori shot-caller. I need it like a week ago."

"No promises, but I'll see what I can arrange. Anything else?"

Michael paused, weighed it all against his gut. "Eh, I'll keep you posted."

"You got it. Watch your back."

"Yeah. Thanks, Dutch." They shook hands.

Dutch turned to Samuel. "You stay cool, little man."

"Yup!" Samuel replied, his tone happy, distracted. He was playing with his little paper crane.

"I'll be in touch," the Master Knight said, and then he walked up the hill to rejoin his traveling companions.

"You want to go get some pancakes?" Michael asked his son when they were alone.

"*And* mac'n'cheese?"

"Yeah. Why not."

"Cool," Samuel said. Then he took off at a run, flying his origami laser crane at warp speed across the park while his daddy followed.

19

Delilah was dreaming. Dream was a generous word for the experience. It was somewhere closer to a nightmare, or maybe a bad acid trip.

It was the night her son Samuel had been born. She'd been alone because she and Samuel's father, Michael, could never seem to keep the peace for any longer than it took to fuck. She knew that was more her fault than his, but she would never admit it—least of all to him.

Michael … she hated him almost as much as she loved him.

Blood. There was blood everywhere. One minute she'd been getting out of the shower. The next she'd been lying on the bathroom floor. Cold. Wet. Her thighs and the floor underneath her slick with blood. There was no single experience likely to induce more instant, animal terror in a young expectant mother than finding herself in that condition.

She'd been screaming and crying, and she'd called her mother, not an ambulance. Then Fiona and Victor had been there and taken her to the hospital, and Gabriel showed up later.

Everything was madness and chaos that night. The fear got a hold of her, and she couldn't shake it. Her hormones were going crazy and she panicked. Then, the more afraid she got, the angrier she got.

Her mother had tried to warn her. "They're going to have to take Samuel now," she'd said. "You can't bring him into the world like this, child. You can't. You have to calm yourself. You don't understand what it will do."

Delilah's answer had been appropriate for her state of mind. "Fuck you!" she'd screamed. She screamed that phrase a lot that night. She wept, she lost it, she wanted Michael. It was the first time she'd asked to see him since she'd popped a positive pregnancy test and told him to go jump off a cliff and die. She'd never even told him she was pregnant. It didn't matter in the delivery room. She wanted him there.

Gabriel tried to find him, and because that was what Gabriel did for a living, he tracked him down a couple of hours later. But by the time Michael made it to the hospital, the doctors had already delivered Samuel while his young, scared, confused mother wept in rage and fear.

Then Delilah died.

Just for a little while. The bleed that had forced Samuel into the world a month prematurely did its level best to take his mother out of it. But the doctors fixed it. She wasn't going to have any more children, but she survived the one she did have.

Fiona had tried to warn her about that too. The women of their line got one child, and only one, to pay the bloodline forward. If they managed to survive bringing that child into the world, they'd never have another. Her mother had always advised her to choose her mate wisely because she'd only get one shot, and if the bloodline didn't approve of her choice, it would sever it—mother and child—removing the offense.

Her mother had wanted her to choose a king, a seer, someone of great blood and power themselves. Fiona made no secret that she feared her daughter would actually get knocked up at a beach party instead.

But in the end, it didn't quite go down either way. Delilah hadn't chosen a king, she'd chosen a knight—and certainly not one her mother had in mind.

Night fell on the City of Angels. The setting of the sun closed the great vault door on the energies of the day past and opened another onto the newborn dark. Spells born in the day's light retreated, and those fostered by night awakened.

Delilah awoke with an electric jolt.

Disoriented, she sucked in three sharp breaths and tried to make sense of her surroundings. The Church. She was at the Church. Laid out on the bed of the upstairs apartment. Her brother was sitting with her, kicked back in the chair across the room, smoking a cigarette.

"Shit," she grunted, wiping a cold, clammy hand across her face. She didn't need to ask what time it was. She could feel it. The sun had just set. Her throat was raw and parched, her lips papery.

"You okay, sis?" Gabriel asked. His tone was sincere.

"I'm great," Delilah croaked. She closed her eyes, pushed the little twinkles of colored lights out of her unsteady vision, and drew in a deep, slow breath. She let it out even slower.

"What happened?"

"Burned," she muttered. "Backlash. I had to throw a lot of weight around on the fly. Guess it caught up to me." Thoughts of the day trickled into the forefront like grains of sand scratching through the narrow neck of an hourglass. "Dodger fill you in?"

Gabriel gave a nod. "Yeah. As best he could. Did you say anything to Mahri?"

"Of course not," Delilah grunted. She didn't want her eyes to be open. Not yet. She wasn't numb to the memories of seeing the Doc all torn up like that. Mutilated. Animated into an abomination. Coming at her with hungry murder on its mind. Hot tears began to sting her eyes and she blinked them away. There was absolutely zero time for that shit. She was glad she didn't have to recap the gory details for her brother. Dodger had already taken care of that.

"So, what was it?" Gabriel asked at length.

Delilah forced herself into a sitting position, pressing her eyes shut against the stabs of protest that bloomed up behind her forehead. When the ice pick jabbing away inside her skull had slowed to a gentle prick, she answered.

"I don't know. Could be a spell, a curse … bad news. Whatever … it won. It got them. The Doc, Edwin." She swallowed the lump in her throat. In the end, she could only shrug.

"Dodger said somebody beat you there. Is that right?"

Delilah nodded.

"What do you think they were looking for?"

She shook her head. The Doc had been a working practitioner for sixty years. His collection of valuable relics, his catalog of the mystical and magical, couldn't easily be counted. The man had authored a dozen masterwork grimoires, scrolls, and lesser innumerable tomes. He had mastered and forgotten more disciplines than most folks would ever learn. Many of them involved carefully guarded secrets, dangerous lore, and forbidden knowledge. The only living soul who knew all of Doc's secrets was the Doc himself. And he wasn't around to answer anymore.

"Do you think that whatever attacked you was coming after the Doc and his apprentices? Coming after the Odd?"

Delilah nodded.

"So Mahri too?"

Again, she nodded. She took another deep, steadying breath, in through the nose, out through the mouth. "I think I'm on its shitlist as well. It, uh, didn't seem to appreciate me interfering in its hunt."

"Okay. So, what do we do about it?"

She didn't blame him for asking. This was her field of expertise, not his. Answering those questions was her job. She just didn't have any answers yet either. "When I figure that out, you'll be the first to know."

Her brother nodded. "Yeah, well. Better get to thinking about it. Hard. Pop wants us downstairs when you're up for it, and the king is not happy. Meaning, get the fuck up and get your shit together."

Delilah sighed. "Five minutes," she muttered, swinging her legs out of bed. She found all her joints sore and achy. She had half a dozen good, deep bruises and a goose egg behind her ear from getting tossed around at the Doc's house, and she was absolutely starving. Yeah. Life was good.

Gabriel stepped out in the hall and gave her some peace.

She peed, washed her face. Then went downstairs with her brother so they could take their beating.

20

They found their Lord Father alone in the Church's cavernous meeting hall. Once upon a time, this had been the sanctuary, where the faithful locals had gathered to worship, but long gone were the pews and the pulpit. Now, dark stained wainscoting circled the walls six feet high, and above them the plaster was painted a rich, deep red. The walls rose to an arched ceiling whereby chandeliers hung, and at either end of the great central hall tall windows rose to the roof's peak. The high windows brought a golden glow into the room by day and loomed overhead like dark portals at night. Tonight, they were purple with the hazy glow of the city sky beyond.

The center of the room was dominated by a long, polished wooden table, thick and heavy with great clawed feet. This was the Lord's Hall, the Lord's Table, and seated at the head of it sat Victor St. John in the massive old gothic chair he'd rescued from a burnt-out Cathedral in France.

The seat was huge, hand-carved and ornate. The impressive piece would likely still fetch a hefty collector's price, even scorched in spots by fire and nicked and damaged by time, simply for the stories it could tell and the intricacies and detail of its etching.

There was an ancient gouge in the wooden back just behind Victor's left shoulder. A mark left in 1807 when an axe blow had felled the bishop sitting in the chair at the time. The wood was dark, ancient and hard as stone, its burns and wounds sanded and oiled a thousand times over, but the scars remained. Above Victor's right shoulder was the Archangel Michael, sword and shield in hand, and above his left, the visage of Lucifer. At the seat's crown, a great sunburst of radiating rays and a host of lesser, nameless angels.

Carved around the base of the chair were the outstretched, desperate hands and tormented faces of those languishing in the Lake of Fire, groping up toward the unseen sky. Motionless flames carved into the face of the wood crawled up the chair, devouring them, and scattered about, fiendish devils danced on their upturned faces, hammering them back down into the Pit.

"When a CEO gets his first big gig, he buys himself a fancy desk," Victor had explained to his starry-eyed son twenty years earlier. He'd been breaking the chair out of the shipping crate in the empty meeting hall of the new Church. There'd been a cigarette dangling from the corner of his mouth and a crowbar in his hands. "That's his way of telling people, 'don't fuck with me. I'm the boss.'"

"But you got a chair?" Gabriel had asked, perplexed.

"I'm not a CEO, son. I don't sit behind a desk." Victor had smiled. "Besides, it's not a chair." Then he winked.

Gabriel had understood. CEOs sat behind desks. Kings sat on thrones.

A hemispherical tabletop liquor cabinet sat atop a claw-footed stand, holding a few glasses for service and three bottles of the Lord Crow's favorites. He'd taken a bottle of the Macallan 1939 from the tray and poured himself a three-finger taste. At his right hand was a large glass ashtray in need of emptying.

Victor lit a smoke as his children entered the meeting hall. "Close the door and have a seat."

They did as their Lord Father bade them, taking a seat to his immediate right.

When Victor was in a good mood, he'd pour them a snort from his private stock. It was the kind of gesture of paternal affection that suited him best—but he didn't so much as touch a spare glass tonight.

The three of them were alone in the meeting hall, with no other Crows attending them—not even their Lady Mother.

The silence in the room was uncomfortable at best.

Neither of them interrupted their Lord Father's quiet contemplation. Victor didn't like to be interrupted. He was the kind of man who would damn well let you know when he was ready for you to talk. Especially when his ire was up, and it most certainly was.

At length, Victor cleared his throat. "One day," he grumbled. "One day we've been on this job." He looked at his watch. "It's not even seven o'clock yet, and somehow, both of you managed to make the nightly news. In the same fucking day."

Delilah shifted in her chair and turned her eyes down. Gabriel sighed and moving to protest, began, "Hey, don't blame us. It was the Helitori who decided to go blitzkrieg apeshit out there."

Victor glowered back at him. "I'm talking. You're listening."

Gabriel didn't argue.

Victor turned his frown to Delilah. "You. You burned Doc McCoy's goddamn house down."

"I didn't have a choice," Delilah replied. She was bristling, prickly as hell, hurt and angry.

"No," Victor insisted. "You couldn't *save* the Doc. *That*, you did not have a choice about. Burning his goddamn house down along with anything in it that might have been useful to us, *that* seems like a choice."

Delilah snorted. "Yeah, well. Shit happens."

"Looked great on the SkyCam though," Victor quipped. "Burned like a merry motherfucker. Whole goddamn neighborhood came out to watch. Nothing but a crater now. Which means he's of no fucking use to us."

Delilah looked like she wanted to say something spiteful. To get some of that hurt off her chest by throwing a handful of spears at her father. But instead, she bit her tongue and looked away.

Gabriel gave her points for that. "Why don't you cut her some slack? Jesus."

Victor wasn't having any of it. "She can boo-hoo about that later. And I suggest you worry about yourself. I haven't even started to take a piece of your ass yet."

Gabriel sat back in his chair, sighing in resignation. "Well, then chew away."

Victor looked like he damn well intended to. "Let's add this shit up, shall we? We have our first run-in with the Helitori. One dead, maybe some witnesses, maybe not. Across town, we got the boogeyman who comes after Doc McCoy and one of his apprentices. Cut the guts out of one of our best chances to make some of that headway we aren't making. Literally. And what's our answer to that? Fuck the world, burn the Doc's house down. I mean, especially with the Doc gone, there can't be anything useful there, after all."

Delilah took that like a slap in the face, but she held her tongue.

"But, we did get a break, right? Mahri calls in, asking for our help. Good news, because without her, we've officially got jack and shit. She's here, so that means something must have gone right." He looked to Gabriel with a frown. "But how'd that work out again? I can catch a recap on the news tonight if you're not real sure."

All Gabriel could do was shrug. "Hey, we didn't start it."

"Hrm. So, enlighten me."

"We were in the process of picking up Mahri. She'd taken a Helitori scout prisoner. Some dude she caught trailing her through MacArthur Park."

That seemed to please Victor. "Okay. Bonus. So, we got him?"

Gabriel shook his head. "No."

"Why not?"

"Mahri killed him."

That caught Delilah's attention, shocked her out of her angry fugue.

Victor contemplated that. "You can understand my confusion as to how you let that happen, right?"

"Yeah," Gabriel grunted. It was all he had to say on the matter.

"So, the Helitori show up with a goon squad looking for their missing man?"

Gabriel nodded.

"Helluva sense of timing, don't you think?"

The thought had crossed my mind, yeah. Again, Gabriel nodded. He had an answer for that, though. Maybe it was more like an excuse. "I figure the Helitori already had eyes on the apartment building before we ever showed up. They were probably sitting on it, doing recon, trying to get a fix on their boy. But once they saw us hit the scene, they decided to make their move. Sent in the cavalry."

"And somehow that turns into a gunfight right in the middle of a neighborhood garage sale?"

"Hey, like I said. They shot first. We grabbed Mahri and split."

"Lemme do the math. That's *two* dead Helitori then, not one?" Victor seemed to accept it grudgingly. "How much of this sticks on us?"

Gabriel shrugged. "I don't know, pop. Crowded apartment building in the middle of the fucking day. Corpse in Apartment 316. Corpse in the back alley. Pretty sure none of the Helitori stuck around to give statements to the police, you know? And I don't figure they were likely to leave bodies behind."

Victor nodded. "I'm guessing us decommissioning two of their boys, that's not a secret to the Helitori right?"

"Nobody else was around when Mahri killed the kid," Gabriel replied. "But yeah. I had to do a guy in the alley, and, uh, there were Helitori witnesses."

The Lord Crow mulled that over. "Well, at least they know we mean business." He didn't sound at all pleased. Just resigned to the fact that it was done. "Fucking Helitori. See, they don't mind dropping bombs all over town because they know we'll feel the heat way more than they will. This is what happens when the out-of-towners show up and shit in your backyard. There's a life lesson there."

Neither of Victor's children could argue.

"So, tell me about the dead kid. The one Mahri took out."

Gabriel shrugged and said the only thing he could think to say, "He pissed her off. So, she stabbed him in the throat."

Victor seemed doubtful. "And you just let that happen?"

"Yeah, I fucked up."

"Didn't know murder was Mahri's speed."

"It wasn't. That's new."

"Listen, I know you got a soft spot for her, son. Now I don't know if that's in your dick or in your head, and frankly, I don't give a damn. You take care of her, and you take care of her right. Or I will."

Gabriel cocked an eyebrow. "Meaning?"

"Meaning she's a crazy bitch. She just got you and your crew dropped in the middle of a gunfight with the Helitori, making you all an accessory to murder without so much as a 'please' or 'thank you.'" His tone turned mocking "You know, because somebody pissed her off."

Gabriel nodded. "Yeah."

"Next time she gets pissed off, it might be you she's pissed at. Remember, the life you save might be your own." Victor shrugged. "In the meantime, she's the best lead we've got. And we need to know what she knows. As far as I'm concerned, she owes us that much."

"What do you want me to do with her?" Gabriel asked.

Victor looked annoyed by the question. "I want you to take her out for dinner and drinks. Maybe get your dick sucked. What the fuck do you think I want you to do with her? This ain't a goddamn charity. Mahri don't ride for free."

Gabriel nodded.

"We need to be careful," Delilah interjected. "Something was after Edwin. And it came out of nowhere and hit like a ton of bricks."

"What was it?" Victor asked.

Delilah could only shrug. "I don't know. Some god-awful spell. Some kind of curse. It's deadly. And it's extremely powerful. Chances are it's coming after Mahri too."

Victor weighed that. "Can you deal with it?"

"Once I figure out what it is, sure. Probably. Most likely."

"You don't sound sure about that."

"It's early yet," Delilah replied. "I'm pretty sure I'll get another crack at it before too long."

Gabriel noted that his sister made no mention of her belief that the curse was now after her as well. If she wasn't going to let that cat out of the bag, neither was he.

"It's safe to say we have no idea what the Doc might have told whoever did this to him," Victor noted. The Doc was their best chance at solid gold intel. And somebody had beaten them to it and left them nothing but mutilated meat. That one went up in the loss column for sure.

"The Helitori did that," Delilah grunted, anger rising up once more to take the place of shock and gruesome awe.

"Do we know that?" Gabriel asked.

"Yes," Delilah replied.

"No," Victor said. "We do not."

It was Delilah's turn to be pissy. "Well, I'm pretty sure the Doc didn't turn himself inside out. If it quacks like a duck, it's probably a fucking duck."

"Maybe," Victor conceded. "Probably even. I'm not even saying I doubt it. I've seen the Helitori do worse shit than that. What I'm saying is we don't know what we don't know. And we don't know that."

Delilah conceded, obviously in no mood to argue the point.

Victor sipped his scotch and mulled it over. "That's not the Helitori way. They don't fight black magic with black magic, so it begs the questions who, what, and why, doesn't it? Kinda reckless to assume that whoever murdered the Doc is the same people who came after his apprentices."

Gabriel and Delilah both blinked, silently. Neither one of them had really considered that.

Their Lord Father gave a single, grim chuckle. "The day's early yet. We got no idea who's turning all the screws here. Don't assume your way into an early grave, hmm?"

The younger Crows each gave a respectful nod.

"You deal with Mahri. She's your problem. I want something out of her. I want it yesterday. Mr. Washington is a very patient client. But all this noise, though, all this heat. I want to see some forward progress. This doesn't wait. Questions?"

They had none.

Victor waved toward the door with a flick of his fingers. "Go. Handle your business. I fill in the gaps at Church."

There was no argument.

21

Gabriel reached out to his sister in the hallway, but Delilah brushed him off.

"Look, I don't want to talk about it," she said. "Let's just handle our shit, okay? I'll run some interference. You just … deal with it."

He didn't push. Sometimes you just had to let the horrific shit ride, table it for another day. That was just how it went. He knew that better than most. Together, they went back to the clubhouse bar.

Gabriel watched while Delilah made her way over to Mahri and struck up a conversation. She was filling her in, mostly with bullshit, letting her know she was okay now after some rest. Delilah gave her brother a single, very discreet glance of acknowledgment and he took care of the rest.

While Delilah and Mahri caught up, Gabriel rounded up Piper and Dodger and huddled with them just outside the bar. He gave some brief instructions, then he asked Bingo to pour another of whatever Mahri was drinking. The old knight complied.

Gabriel set her drink on the corner of the bar, caught Mahri's attention, and motioned for her to come on up and join him. Delilah trailed along behind, favoring her brother with a knowing look and a little nod.

Mahri came up to the bar with the boys and tipped her drink gratefully toward Bingo. Her cheeks were rosy, her smile and eyes soft. Her sharp edges were getting all whiskey-rounded." Thanks, old man."

"My pleasure, darlin," he grumbled.

Mahri showed a faint smile as she relaxed against the bar and took in the clubhouse. "This place never changes," she quipped, sipping her drink. She laid a hand on Gabriel's arm. "Hey, I just wanted to say thank you, again. I don't know what I'd do without you guys."

Gabriel nodded. "Yeah. Well. Keep that in mind." He saw the shift in her eyes when her warning instincts fired off.

But by then it was too late.

Piper and Dodger snatched her by the arms and her drink hit the floor with a glassy crash.

"What the hell?" Mahri barked in frightened confusion as the two Crow Knights wrestled her off her bar stool and toward the basement door. "Gabriel! Dee! What the hell!"

She fought and struggled, but the two Crows held her fast.

"Just sorting some shit out," Gabriel replied. His tone was flat, sad.

"Hey! Let me go!"

"Nope," Piper said.

"Calm down, Mahri," Dodger grunted. "This is for your own good."

"Fuck you!" she replied, twisting and kicking like an angry cat. The two Crows were carrying her as much as dragging her by that point. "Gabriel! What the fuck is this? What are you doing?"

He had nothing to say.

Piper and Dodger dragged Mahri off to one of the Church's bunkers downstairs while she fought like a snared badger. Gabriel and Delilah followed. Fending off punches and claws, the Crow Knights tossed her into the protective vault and threw the door shut before she could bolt past them. Her cries of alarm and streams of profanity were silenced as the heavy, rune-scribed door slammed shut.

Piper locked up the vault. "She's loud," he noted with a grimace, wiggling a fingertip around in his ear.

"What now?" Dodger asked.

"Let her simmer for a while," Gabriel instructed. "I'll handle it from here. Everybody will be here for Church in a little bit. Let's make sure we get her some food and some water at least.

And for the love of God, nobody talk to her."

"How long you gonna let her stew?" Piper asked.

Gabriel shrugged. "I don't know. However long it takes?"

Behind him, Delilah snorted and shook her head. "I need some fresh air." She didn't linger. Breezing back up through the clubhouse bar, Delilah rounded up her shit, snatching up her jacket and her satchel. Then she left, storming out through the garage, a crackling wave of pissed off energy trailing in her wake. She'd clearly had enough of this shit for a while. It was still a couple of hours until Victor would call the table to order at Church. Everybody knew she'd be back.

When the dust settled, Gabriel went back to the bar where he found Bingo being Bingo, cleaning up the broken glass.

With Mahri safely locked away, he rounded up her backpack and dumped it onto the bar for inspection.

Inside he found a soft leather-bound journal—not a proper grimoire, but more like a notebook for keeping spells and arcane formulas—mystical short-hand. It was nearly full of Mahri's intricate notations.

There were also some stitched and laced hex bags, each one smaller than his fist, bulging with lumps of assorted contents. What was in them, and what variety of recipes and formulas, was anyone's guess.

He found a number of small vials of assorted oils and unguents, a small multi-compartment tackle box, about the size of a hardcover book, chock full of herbs, minerals, and incense. A dozen pieces of chalk, charcoals, and colored waxes. A metal vial of India ink, and a collection of stiff, fine brushes.

He checked each pouch and compartment in the bag, then turned the pack inside out for good measure. In the end, he found nothing out of the ordinary for somebody in her trade.

He didn't really find anything out of the ordinary at all. Spare socks and panties, a t-shirt and shorts; her birth control pills, wallet with her credit cards, ID, about a grand in cash. A set of keys. She had another five hundred bucks stashed away in a different pocket, and a bottle of multivitamins.

With a grunt, he stuffed everything back into her backpack where it belonged and called it good. He handed it to Bingo and asked him to stash it somewhere behind the bar for now. Then Gabriel reached over the top of the bar and secured himself a glass and a bottle. The stretch tugged at the staples in his side, and he grumbled in pain. Then he poured one for himself and one for the old knight.

"What do you say, old man?" he asked, sliding the glass Bingo's way.

His advice was straightforward as always: "Sometimes this job sucks."

Gabriel nodded. They drank to that.

Downstairs, Mahri kicked at the door and screamed at the ceiling.

Of all the pieces on the board, the Pawn has the worst lot in life. By its very nature, it's doomed from the start. Every indignity it suffers is solely to advance someone else's agenda. On the rare occasions that the pawns get to draw blood, expect them to revel in it. Because they know damn well the best they can hope for is to take somebody down with them.

22

Naomi wanted to scream. Not in pain, even though there was plenty of that, but in triumphant joy. The bit and gag in her mouth was still preventing that though—but not for much longer.

The stale darkness pressed in around her, reeking of sweat, piss, and dry, dusty rot. In the absence of sight, it was the sort of sensory immersion that became a lingering flavor. Filth and despair had a taste. But so did impending victory.

She couldn't see it in the blackness of the unlit basement, but she could feel it. She could feel everything. Where ten fingers had been zip-tied together for four days, only her thumbs still kept her fingers bound. The rat had chewed her swollen fingers bloody in the process of gnawing through the ties, but she couldn't hold it against him. It was no more than she'd asked him to do. Even as the sharp teeth nicked and nipped her brutalized flesh, she sought calmness in her connection with the little beast. He was almost done, and now she barely had control of him at all, but she couldn't risk losing him.

The impromptu familiar made his little razor blade bites at the pace of a sewing machine. Each one brought her closer to, well, whatever it was that came next. Freedom? Maybe. But, first, blood. Four days in this hole. Naked and alone. Bound and gagged. Blindfolded, beaten, and raped and strangled from her craft.

Her hunters were good. They'd kept her bound at wrist and ankle, and her fingers had been laced together, robbing her of any manual dexterity and gesture. She was stripped naked and searched top to bottom, left with nothing. Then came the blindfold and the gag, stealing her eyes and the power of her voice. Finally, she'd been chained to a dismal cellar wall without so much as a mat to sit on or a bucket to piss in. They made sure she didn't sleep, and worse yet, they had a nasty habit of letting her doze off just long enough to make her even more miserable. Brooks had made a habit of smacking her around, trying to keep her cowed. And Raider. Raider had made a habit of sneaking down on his watch for a little one-on-one time because apparently abusing a helpless woman chained to a wall got his fucking rocks off.

But two things had gone wrong.

First, Naomi was tougher than all three of her captors put together. They just didn't realize it, and she didn't advertise that there had yet to be a hard time invented that she couldn't take.

Second, they had missed something.

They should have pinned her voice box like witch hunters did in the old days. Running that long needle through her throat would have crippled her ability to make sound. But they didn't. Instead, they stole her words with the bit and gag, but they did not steal her song. It was a trick Doc McCoy had taught her. Back before she was running around behind the old man's back. Back when life was a lot simpler. And she was very good at it. Two days of work, of mesmerizing melody, hummed faintly in her throat, the lyrical tones finding their way past the muffling gag.

She found a little friend and he came to her call.

Little rat teeth sank to the bone as the last zip tie broke loose.

Naomi gasped, teetering on the edge of giggling madness. With her fingers freed, she could manage the rest, even in the pitch dark. At least one of them would be here soon to pour a bottle of water down her throat or shove a gas station sandwich in her mouth—or worse. They'd done plenty worse in the last four days.

She flexed her swollen, bloody fingers and smiled a rictus grin in the smothering darkness as she pried the gag from her mouth.

A pound of flesh wouldn't even begin to cover what they'd done to her.

But it would be a start.

23

Brooks descended the basement stairs with a bottle of water in one hand and the keys in the other. Like the rest of them, he was tired of babysitting this bitch—even if all he had to do at this point was pour a bottle of water over her head and call it even. Nobody would give a shit. She was as good as dead anyway. The reaper just hadn't caught up to her yet. But now that Hector was on his way, the reaper was back on schedule.

Brooks tucked the water bottle under his armpit, thumbed through the keys, and opened the door. Stuffing the keys in his pocket, he fired up his flashlight and stabbed the white beam across the room.

When the circle of light fell on empty shackles, and he saw the wall smeared in bloody handprints, panic jumped into his throat from the bottom of his gut.

He swept the light left. Nothing. Right. She was ten feet away, hunkered against the wall like a feral cat. Her hands were a bloody mess, and beside her, a constellation of strange runes was painted on the dirty concrete wall in her own blood.

With a shout, Brooks threw a hand under the tail of his coat, reaching for his pistol.

Then Naomi slapped her palm to the circle of runes and barked three arcane words in a raw, husky voice.

The blood circle on the wall evaporated in a burst of foul-smelling steam.

Brooks froze in his tracks, his fingers wrapped around the grip of his pistol.

"Relax," Naomi ordered, shielding her eyes from the blinding glare of the flashlight. "Hands off the gun. Put the light away. Silently. Don't make a sound."

Helpless, Brooks complied.

"Give me that," she demanded, pointing toward the water bottle. Brooks handed it over and she unscrewed the cap, leaving the white plastic smeared in blood. She took a long draw from the bottle then passed it back to him, downing the mouthful of cool water with a couple of painful swallows. "How many men do you have up there?"

"Two more," Brooks answered robotically.

Naomi nodded. She could deal with those odds. Grinding her teeth in pain and triumph, she slithered toward the slack-jawed guard on scuffed and bloodied bare feet. She moved in close, close enough to whisper in his ear.

"Do you know what the best part is?" she asked him.

"No." His face was empty, expressionless. But his eyes blazed with absolute terror.

"The best part is, I know you're in there, and I know you can see this. I know you can *feel* this." She sank her torn fingernails into his cheek until they drew blood. "And you are going to feel everything."

24

Morris and Raider were eating their supper—a bucket of fried chicken from a nearby gas station—when Brooks came back up the stairs still carrying the bottle of water.

"She not thirsty?" Morris asked as he sucked a bite of greasy meat from a chicken thigh.

Raider chuckled. Then he spotted the bloody fingernail gouges on Brooks' cheeks. "The hell happened to you?"

Brooks raised his pistol and started firing, point blank, dumping rounds into his flatfooted companions.

The steady pulse of pistol shots slapped the walls of the room with ear-splitting blasts. Morris took one in the head and pitched out of his chair to writhe on the floor. Raider made it to his feet but took a couple of rounds in the chest and then one in the neck. He staggered, rebounded off the wall and went down.

Morris sprawled nearby twitching brain shot death spasms, his bowels and bladder emptying. Raider lay on the floor in a gasping heap while blood pumped from the bullet hole in his neck. Cheek to the floor, hot and wet, he looked under the table and saw dirty, battered bare feet enter the room from the stairs.

"Guh," he managed, blood rushing up into his nose.

Then Brooks rounded the table, face slack and empty. Still holding that goddamn water bottle in his off hand, pistol in the other. And beside him came Naomi. Naked and torn and miserable and bloody. Her red hair a tangled, matted mess. Face expressionless, but eyes burning with blow torch rage.

"Gack," Raider wheezed.

"Where are we?" Naomi asked.

"An abandoned garage on the outskirts of Temecula," Brooks answered emotionlessly.

"What time is it?"

"About seven o'clock."

"Nnnh," Raider squeaked.

Naomi gave Brooks a single nod. Her meat puppet raised his pistol and put Raider's lights out for good.

25

Naomi allowed herself a few seconds to revel in the pain and death of her captors before she took a deep breath and set about making her escape a reality. Her nerves were shot, blown apart, raw. Her mind was running like a broken dump truck. Putting a series of events together that would get her out of here was extremely difficult in that state.

An abandoned garage. Okay, that computes. She was in some kind of dumpy run down kitchen or break room. Stairs to a cellar behind her. An open door out to a dark cavernous room full of junk opposite her. Another door to her right, opening into a pitch-black hallway. She could see cars through the first door, but all the cars in the bays looked like junkers—it was too dark to tell. Surely the Three Musketeers had a ride somewhere. *Probably outside,* she reasoned.

"Do you have a cell phone?" she asked Brooks.

"Yes."

"Give it to me."

Her meat puppet did as requested and Naomi stepped away and began pecking numbers into the phone with her split and scabbed thumb. Pausing, she cursed, trying to clear her head. She was a child of the twenty-first century, and somewhere in this world, she had a cell phone full of contacts. But she couldn't recall any of their telephone numbers by heart.

And calling 9-1-1 wasn't really an option.

She let out a guttural, angry growl. A number. One fucking number would do it.

Calm down. Think.

"Do you guys have a car?"

"Yes."

"Where?"

"Out front."

"Who has the keys?"

Her meat puppet pointed toward Raider's fresh, warm corpse. "Get them. Now."

Brooks did as instructed while Naomi paced like a rat and stared at the phone as if numbers would fly into it from her memory through a lightning bolt of pure will.

Wet and squelchy, Brooks had to roll Raider's bullet-riddled corpse halfway over to get to the keys from his pocket.

Suddenly, Naomi heard the scrape of a footstep on the dirty floor behind her—from the door to the pitch-black blind hallway. She spun, her heart exploding into her throat.

Hovering calmly in the shadow of the door was a man of medium height and build in a casual, open-collared gray suit. He appeared to be about fifty-something, with long brown hair combed back into a smooth ponytail, a thin goatee, and Mr. Magoo glasses that gave him the eyes of a bored owl.

His expression was neutral. The look of a man surveying the deli counter or reading the Sunday newspaper.

"Hector?" Naomi gasped, voice tight like rusted old gears.

Hector surveyed the room without expression, looking from corpse to corpse, then to Brooks as he labored to retrieve the car keys for his mistress. Finally, his stony owlish gaze settled on Naomi.

"What are you doing here?" Naomi wheezed.

Hector drew his pistol and shot Brooks in the back of the head, and with a plume of gore, Brooks collapsed into a boneless heap.

Naomi jumped and shrieked. Startled, she backpedaled, the cracked heel of her right foot slipping on the blood-spattered concrete.

Hector lowered his pistol.

"Hector... What?" she croaked, continuing her retreat, heart hammering against her ribs.

"Stop, Naomi," Hector said. He was a soft-spoken man, a voice without emotion.

Naomi whimpered, and hot tears welled up in her eyes. "You-you said you were going to help us."

"I am helping you. Now, stop. Don't make this worse. If you go out there—if you run—there's nothing I can do for you. Now, stop."

But she didn't. With a snarl of wounded rage, she spun and ran for the garage.

Hector blinked his sleepy owl-eyes twice and gave chase.

Panic drove Naomi. The same type of fear that drives the rabbit before the wolf. She kept waiting for the shots to ring out, for Hector to gun her down, but for some reason, he didn't. She didn't question why. There was no time for that. She just ran.

Pounding across the dark garage, Naomi spotted the blue glow of the nighttime world through a cracked window on a door across the bay. She ran towards it as fast as her disheveled body would carry her, dashing between hulks of scavenged cars, and ducking under a crippled lift. Halfway across the bay, she slammed her shin into something hard, metal, and immovable. The object rang like a gong, and the impact nearly took her off her feet, leaving her leg numb and her foot stupid. Blood flowed down her shin. She forced herself to keep going.

Ramming into the far exit, she smashed the bar with the palms of her hands, and the door flew open. Barefoot, she dashed out across the old broken asphalt and chipped gravel, limping and hopping on her numb, disobedient, smashed shin.

Again, Hector's eerily calm voice sounded behind her. "Naomi. Stop." But she couldn't, and she wouldn't.

The rabbit fear was in the middle of her, throwing her forward with impossible gravity, a noose around her neck dragging her like a leash and collar.

Then she saw them out of the corner of her eye.

There, not there. Gone completely when she whipped her head to the side and tried to look directly at them. Reappearing in her peripheral vision when she looked away. It wasn't her imagination. Hollow slack faces of shadowy specters watched her pass as she stomped a bloody path across the parking lot and into the scrub brush field beside the old garage. Ghostly glimpses of darksome things began trailing in her wake, giving chase and blooming up out of the ground.

Fifty yards from the garage, she felt her back begin to prickle. First, tiny little needles, like mosquito bites. Then, jolts and jabs of bee stings. They were on her, and the hooks were getting deeper. From the nighttime gloom ahead, a swarm of shapeless specters rose from the scrub, fixing her with slack-jawed stares, molten black eyes, bottomless pits—and she knew. In the corner of her vision, where she could barely see, the hungry hollow-eyed specters were multiplying, gaining, and converging. Eyes and spotlights coming into focus and zeroing in.

Whatever had been keeping them at bay, she'd left behind when she ran. And now there was no going back.

A formless shade, whispering madness flowed up out of the darkness and dragged vaporous fingers down her back. The prickling sting of the groping Misfortune nibbled at her skin. They closed in from three sides, like reef sharks on wounded prey.

With a desperate gasp, she changed course and took off to the north, forced aside by the rising spectral tide ahead and the one gaining on her from behind.

The ghostly hounds gave chase. They scuttled through the low brush like hungry spiders, slithered along a nearby creek bank, and bounded down the hillside slopes on her left and right.

More rose up before her; faint shadows of empty-eyed wraiths alive under the dim starlight. Naomi sobbed and skidded sideways, hobbling and skipping to change direction and avoid them.

She threw a desperate glance over her shoulder and saw the swarming tide closing in, the pursuit nearing its end.

Then the world fell out from under her, and there was confusion. Her stomach flew into her throat and she felt herself falling.

Then came the inevitable, terrible, body-shattering impact.

Her wind was gone. No breath. Her teeth were broken. Her body throbbed with a numb pulse, a quivering vibration in time to her heartbeat. Blood. Her mouth and nose were full of blood.

The Misfortunes had run her head-long off a low bluff and

shattered her against the rocks below—and she'd never even seen it coming. After an eternity of smothering, Naomi finally managed to suck in a wounded breath.

Her world exploded with pain. The splintered crookedness of her broken legs screamed in her body. A busted jaw left her making a wordless bawling howl. Cracked ribs fought to rob her of precious breath.

The world around her swelled in harsh, crimson light.

Then Hector was there, blinking at her with those sleepy owl-eyes from behind his coke bottle glasses. Held aloft in one hand was a stubby torch, burning with fire the color of blood. Without a word, he grabbed her by the hair and dragged her off the rocks, spilling her into the dry creek bed face down. There was too much pain to scream.

Naomi faded then—in and out, and back in again.

Hector placed a rune-scribed clay jar in the dirt a few inches from her nose.

"It wasn't time yet," he said in his eerie, calm cadence. Then he sighed, laying the blazing red torch down in the gravel at her side.

Naomi could only gasp, choke, and wheeze.

Hector stepped astride her prone form and squatted over her back. He pressed her face into the dirt restraining her with one hand. Electric pain exploded across her back, and she realized from the tug and tearing, that Hector was carving on her.

She kicked and bucked without strength. Hector held her down as his blade danced across her skin. Hisses and gags choked up out of her throat like vomit. Then the carving was complete.

Her panic spiked as Hector took a handful of her blood-matted red hair and lifted her face out of the dirt.

"Nooooouuuuhhhh!" Naomi gurgled.

Then Hector sank the blade to the hilt in the side of her neck and began to saw.

As Hector beheaded her with his knife, the hungry Misfortunes gathered around and watched with bottomless black eyes, and soundless slack jaws. All but unseen and invisible—held at bay at the edge of his blood-colored torchlight.

26

Delilah wandered down the street, scuffing her feet along the sidewalk. Angry eels roiled in her belly. Flashes of grisly imagery showed up at regular intervals to slap her in the face.

She made it as far as the pool hall at the end of the block and went inside for a drink. The place was still half-empty on a Friday night. Mostly young neighborhood bucks shooting some stick and killing time. It was early yet. Delilah breezed past the bar, ordered a margarita and two shots of tequila, and headed straight for the shit hole ladies room.

She was exhausted, mangled and directionless. Her whole body felt like half-cooked spaghetti, still dragging under the weight of all the heavy lifting she'd done at the Doc's house earlier that day.

She fried her nose with a couple lines of decent speed, and when the wiggling in her teeth slowed to a gentle vibration, she splashed some cold water on her face and called it good. *Metaphysician, heal thyself.* Her solution was a band-aid fix, and she knew it. But something was better than nothing.

By the time she got back to the bar, her drinks were ready. She fired down the tequila shooters one after another and then proceeded to nip at her margarita. Speed ants crawled up and down the back of her neck and prickled in her hairline. It wasn't good, but it was better. She wanted a cigarette, but she couldn't smoke in here. You couldn't smoke indoors anywhere in Los Angeles these days. There was the crappy little patio, but the patio was by the dumpster, and it stank like shit. She was in no mood for that, especially not with a head full of crank making her eyes bug out.

She picked at a dent in the top of the ratty wooden bar with a thumbnail, riding the obsessive intensity of someone on the leading edge of their speed. She did it until her nail was chipped and she'd gouged out a couple of fresh splinters.

She pushed her margarita back toward the bored looking bartender. "This sucks." She had a good case of tweaker manners. Straightforward and blunt.

He shrugged. "Okay."

"Just, trade it for shots, would ya?"

Frowning, he did as she asked.

"Hey, if I have a smoke, nobody's gonna mind, right?"

The bartender shook his head. "Can't smoke in here. You know that."

Delilah grunted. "Where's Fernando? He makes a better margarita. And he lets me smoke in here."

"His kid got sick. Called in."

"Who are you?"

"Miguel." He poured her shots, pitched the unwanted margarita into the bus tub behind the bar.

"Never seen you here before."

"Yeah. I'm new."

"You like it?"

Miguel the New Guy cocked an eyebrow. "Yeah. It's paradise. Eight bucks."

"Just start a tab," Delilah replied. She downed one of the two shots and sipped at the second. She could still hear Mahri screaming, cussing, panicking as Piper and Dodger dragged her away. A minute earlier they'd been hugging and mugging like besties. Then, *surprise, bitch.* It was a fine capper on an even finer day.

Delilah nipped at her tequila and looked around the old neighborhood pool hall.

She'd met Mahri here back when they were kids, and nobody made much of a fuss over what age you were as long as you were from the neighborhood. Tito owned the place back then, and he didn't mind the local kids hanging out if they had enough respect for him not to bum beers off the twenty-one and up crowd and didn't stir up any shit. That went double for the girls, who—by their very presence—had a way of stirring up shit with the low-brow male clientele. Whether they meant to or not.

Delilah remembered the night that both she and Mahri got kicked out of here—not really for anything they'd done, but rather for their own good. Some old welder dude decided to show them his dong after a few pitchers of beer. That had started some serious shit, and Tito sent the two girls packing. Then a couple of *vatos* from the neighborhood had absolutely busted that dude's shit up.

Gabriel had met Mahri here, too. He'd come looking for his little sister and wound up having a few drinks and fucking Mahri in the ladies room instead. She'd been a high school senior strutting around in her Catholic schoolgirl get-up, and Gabriel had been, well, Gabriel. He'd been just old enough to go to jail for fucking a seventeen-year-old, and Mahri had been nursing a crush on Gabriel as far back as Delilah could remember. Putting the two of them in the same room with an open bar tab and no supervision was a recipe for a bonfire.

That had been a mostly unpleasant thing for a little sister to walk in on. Her big brother and her friend fucking on the ladies room countertop. She remembered Gabriel at least had the decency to look a *little* ashamed of himself—his pants around his ankles, his dimpled ass on display. Not Mahri though. "Hey, beat it!" she'd hissed, kicking at the door with the toe of her patent leather loafer, her knees up over Gabriel's shoulders and one tit hanging out of her blouse.

Delilah had beat a swift retreat and Gabriel and Mahri had carried on with their business. Years later, it was still a punchline she and Mahri shared with a laugh. Or at least, one they had shared back when the world was still in a little better alignment—before the last half a day or so—before pitching her friend, kicking and screaming, into a cell. Before watching the animated ghoul of one friend rip another to pieces. Yeah. Nostalgia and good memories had a way of withering up and dying in the face of that shit.

This was new territory for Delilah. She wasn't real sure how to cope with it. She downed her shot. "One more," she requested, pushing the empty shot glasses toward Miguel. He obliged. She turned back on her barstool, huddled over her shot glass, and nursed it by sips. She couldn't really say how long she sat there like that, but it was long enough for the tequila in her belly to begin to cut through the speed in her nose a little bit. Her eyes were dry and she had to remind herself to blink.

She looked up into the mirror behind the bar and saw a familiar face looking back at her. It was James Finch, sorcerer and Brother Crow. He smiled at her in the reflection.

"Hi, Dee," he said, his accent very British. "You buy a handsome lad a drink?"

She couldn't help but smile, just a little bit. Finch was her best friend in the world, and he was exactly what the doctor had ordered. Which he most likely knew, which was most likely why he was here instead of down at the Church. She patted the barstool beside her. "Have a seat, Finchy. I'll fix you up."

James Finch was known affectionately by his last name as if his mother had neglected his given one at birth. He was an expatriated Brit who'd grown up a son of London's Red Stag before finding himself exiled from house and home and looking for a soft place to fall down. At the tender age of sixteen, he'd found it under the wings of the Crow, courtesy of Fiona's friends back in her native Ireland.

Finch was a fair hand in a brawl, but his real talents aligned more with Delilah's. He was a sorcerer by trade, a formally educated product of the Red Stag's reclusive White Hill Society. His specialties included Alexandrian Necromancy and a brand of metaphysical mechanical geometry that had been rebirthed by the likes of Aleister Crowley—not the Law of Thelema sideshows—the real stuff.

Finch was a rare talent, and ten years a Crow. His Four-Winged Soldier's Crow, inked on his right shoulder, sported a Blood Laurel. In his ten years of service, he'd killed for the Crow only once. No more, no less. The fact that his victim had been his own father and a warlock of the Red Stag carried the weighty respect of a mountain. Finch had earned his place in loyalty and blood, and nobody questioned it.

He wore a perpetual grin, and there was an ever-present

twinkle in his eyes as if he knew some private joke the rest of the world didn't. Maybe he did. He fancied his vintage Iron Maiden t-shirts, of which he had a closet full. He stored them in static-free, anti-lint bags like they were high dollar suits. He also liked his techno gadgets. Finch's nose was frequently buried in his phone. Witty animal memes made him very happy.

Once upon a golden summer, he and Delilah had a short-lived, but fire-hot teenage fling, back before they'd both grown up enough to realize how ridiculous they were for each other. The relationship had been based almost entirely on the fact that they both loved cool cars. That, and they still liked playing with each other's naughty bits after sacrificing their virginity to one another.

To this day, they remained the best of friends. The two of them, rolling up the coast in Finch's red 1984 Ferrari 308 GTS with the top off, laughing, joking, and passing a joint back and forth was a common enough sight. Everyone gave Finch shit about his car except Delilah. Finch had lost his shit when he'd found that thing up at auction a couple years back. His friends had questioned his life choices.

"Obviously, you've never seen Magnum P.I., mates," was all he'd said, indignantly settling the issue—at least in his mind. They'd let him have it. It was a cool car. Delilah appreciated it, and that pretty much meant everybody else could piss off.

"You're not planning on skipping Church tonight, are you?" Finch asked her after flagging down Miguel for a bottle of beer.

Delilah snorted. "And piss off the Lord Most High and Mommy Dearest? Not on your life."

"Yeah," Finch muttered. "Guess Victor's already a little pissy, isn't he?"

Delilah nodded. Her mirth cooled quickly. "Yeah, it's been a shit day."

"Gabriel filled me in," Finch said. "You want to talk about it?"

"No," Delilah said with a sour chuckle. "Do you?"

"Not really," Finch conceded. His bottle of beer arrived, and he downed half of it in a couple of swallows. "Come on. We've got a little bit of time. Let's go for a drive, get sorted out, you know?"

By that, Finch meant take a drive down to the park and burn some of that killer weed he was always packing. People liked Finch. It was hard not to like Finch. He had the best weed. That offer sounded therapeutic, medicinal. Shit, she was already buzzing two ways. A third couldn't hurt. Might even her out some.

She dropped some bills on the bar to settle the tab and took off with Finch for a little while to get her head back in the game. They drove a few blocks over to a crappy little public park and chilled. They rode the squeaking, squealing old merry-go-round together, pushing it in lazy circles while they burned through a few bowls of Finch's fine herbal remedy.

After a little of that, the world didn't seem quite so out of alignment.

By the time the hour arrived, Delilah was ready for Church.

27

Squires, probies, and prospects. Every guild, club, and organization had them. Paying your dues and working your way up the food chain was a tradition that had stood the test of time across a spectrum of cultures and cabals. For the Crow, the entry-level prospect was that of the militia.

Being militia was more than just being a friend of the family or an ally of the house. The Crow had carried an us and them mentality through its entire history. There were Crows, then there was everybody else. Once you earned a place in the militia, you could call yourself a Crow and had the right to wear the Perched Crow with pride. It was akin to being a buck private. It wasn't uncommon at all for former servicemen to find their way into this life. Being low dick on the totem pole wasn't a new concept to any of them.

A handful of Crow militia arrived that evening. They didn't have any business with the officers of the house. They were there to lend a hand, to fetch and carry, to tend to the gathering. They were paying their dues.

One of the most squared away young Crow militiamen was Twitch. He was a scrawny twenty-five-year-old kid with a crooked coppertop mop who liked novelty t-shirts, his motorcycle jacket, and his shit-kicker boots.

He'd come home from Afghanistan with a Purple Heart, checked out shortly thereafter with an honorable discharge on his DD214, and no desire to have anything more to do with the United States Army. Twitch went, he saw, he 11-Bravo'd, he got blown the fuck up, and that was plenty. He'd tell you he hated everything there was to hate about the Army, which meant he loved what he hated if you understood his meaning. He still kept a CIB stitched to the breast of his motorcycle jacket and a few photos of his old squadmates favorited in his phone.

He also had some stories of things he couldn't explain and very little desire to tell them.

Twitch had drifted until he fetched up in the right place at the right time and met the right someone. That someone had been Dodger, himself a Marine veteran with a bloody tour in early Iraq under his belt. Twitch and Dodger had shared a few drinks, a couple of war stories, and then—with a head full of vodka—Twitch shared another story. One he didn't tell very often. Because nobody believed him anyway. But Dodger did. Then Dodger gave him a phone number and instructions to call when he sobered up. So he did.

Twitch was overseeing some young militia hauling in takeout from Angelino's down the street. Pans of lasagna, tubs of salad, steaming bags of bread. Food for the Church gathering—a little hospitality put on by the Lord and Lady Crow.

Affectionately referred to as Lord of the Flies, he was the militiaman who kept the young dipshits fetching, hopping, and in check. Twitch was a solid little brother and one throwdown away from earning the Four-Winged Crow of the soldier. It wasn't a gentle lifestyle. His Crow taking flight and shaking the blood from its newly spread wings was only a matter of time. His blood or somebody else's. Often both, as Gabriel's five Ruby Crosses, soon to be six, and Dodger's seven could attest. You only got your Blood Laurel once—the first time you killed for the Family. But every time you bled for the Crow yourself, they honored it.

Dodger asked him how he felt about that once. That being a Crow meant he might have to get on the trigger again, or that he might get bloodied up himself, neither of which had happened since Afghanistan.

Twitch had shrugged and answered honestly. "I figure with the bill I already got racked up, a little more blood ain't gonna make a big difference either way."

It was a good answer.

Twitch and the other young militia tended the ranking

Crows as they gathered and made ready for Church. Victor sent Twitch himself with his black Caddy to pick up Lady Fiona, and Twitch got her to the Church johnny-on-the-spot by ten to eight.

"Everything set?" Victor asked the young militiaman.

"Food's hot, food's here," Twitch assured the Lord and Lady Crow. "Everybody's present and accounted for."

Victor nodded. "Good. Eat, drink, and be merry," he called out to the crowd, hooking a thumb toward their dining hall. "Because we got some serious shit to talk about."

28

They ate, they drank, they caught up, and before long, they gathered behind closed doors at Victor's table for Church. It was their time to meet, to have their voices heard, and for their Lord Crow to lay down the law.

These were Victor and Fiona's knights and champions. Gabriel, their captain. Piper, Dodger, and Bingo, respected knights. Delilah and Finch, chiefs of their arcane talent. Anna, healing hands who stood between them and death.

There were dozens who wore Victor's Crow, scattered across Greater Los Angeles and into the desert, but these were the full-timers, the ranking Crows who had a voice in Church and a seat at the Lord's table.

Victor waved his hand at the table. "Sit."

Then Victor, Fiona, and Gabriel laid it all out, and the Crows paid heed.

There was the formal request by Dante Washington for the services of the Crow to clean up his mounting mess. His missing and ailing men. The unknown and arcane shadow hanging over his house and all of his holdings. The mounting misfortunes. All of it harm done by an enemy yet unknown and unseen. There were big numbers being talked about at the table, a serious payday with a righteous return. Dante Washington's enterprise represented an arrow of sustainable business to add to the quiver and a powerful ally on the street. It was a big deal if they pulled it off right.

But there were also big risks. Taking on Washington's business was tantamount to going to war with an enemy they hadn't even identified yet, sight unseen. There was no guarantee they could defeat that mystery enemy or make peace with them if they proved too hot to handle. It was a huge roll of the dice.

The Lord Crow and the Bingo were of similar mind on that thought. Fortune favors the bold and they got no argument from the table. To a man, they all had bills to pay, and for those accustomed to it, living like a gangland rockstar didn't come cheap. Ditch diggers dig ditches, and they had their shovels ready.

The events of the day were laid out. Gabriel had gone to fetch Mahri from her hideout in Koreatown and had stepped on a land mine instead. They still didn't know where and how that was all going to land. Mahri was now safely in their care, and there were two Helitori hunters dead on the ground. The Helitori would lay both of those bodies right at the Crow's feet.

The Odd's place in this whole mess, spearheaded by Mahri, was thrown out on the table. Washington's woes were believed, in part, to be their fault, and they were friends of the Crow. That complicated matters, both personally and professionally. Those otherwise-peaceful part-timers had cut a deep wound into Dante Washington's house, and they'd evoked the ire of the Helitori in the process. There were a lot of people out on the street looking to collect heads and pounds of flesh to settle up those debts.

"With the Doc gone, what's Mahri say about this shit?" Dodger asked, looking to Gabriel.

"Nothing so far," Gabriel replied. "I haven't really had a chance to press her yet, and she hasn't volunteered anything."

"I'm sure she'll be a little more conversational and cooperative after she's had a chance to cool off in the basement for a while," Victor said. His tone suggested he expected it, whether she actually was or not. "She's here now. She's got a target on her back. And we're gonna look after her. She's the best lead we got."

Discussion of it clearly made both Gabriel and Delilah uncomfortable.

Piper, not so much. "You know, I don't get it. If this is gonna be an issue, then why don't we just round up what's left of the Odd and dump 'em in a ditch. Solves Washington's problem and tells the Helitori to get the fuck outta town. What am I missing here?"

"They're our friends," Delilah replied.

"Your friends. Not my friends. I don't drink beer with these people or hang out at their family picnics and fuck their moms." He looked to the Lord Crow. "Why should I care?"

Victor remained stone-faced. Piper had a point.

But Gabriel bristled. "You're being shitty about this, Piper."

"And you can eat me," Delilah added, raising her middle finger.

"I ain't man enough, darlin, but I'll give it a try," Piper quipped with a smirk, flicking the tip of his tongue like a snake.

"Stop acting like children," Fiona scolded. "This is serious business." When the Lady Crow spoke, the table respectfully settled.

It was Dodger who spoke up first, calm and orderly. He looked over to Gabriel. "Piper's not wrong. I mean, sure, you used to bang boots with Mahri, and Dee does bad movie night with them, or whatever but beyond Doc McCoy, what's The Odd done for us lately? They're grown-ups. They got themselves into this shit. This ain't exactly a consequence-free lifestyle."

"That's what I'm saying," Piper echoed, rapping his ring-laden knuckles on the table.

Dodger shrugged. "Don't get me wrong. Yeah, the Doc especially, he was a friend. I'm all for some payback. We don't let that slide. But, business is business. We better figure out who owes that tab, settle it up, and then get back to work. If Washington is the job, and Washington wants Mahri, well, what then?"

"Let's think about that," Bingo said, his voice a low grumble. Then he proceeded to lick his fingertips and roll a joint while the table waited on him to continue. No one rushed him. He lit up, took a couple of good puffs, and passed it to his son on his right, who took a hit and passed it to Gabriel who kept the chain going.

"Lotta scratch laying on the table with this one. And not a dollar of it for bringing the heads of the Odd to Dante Washington. Now, I don't kill nobody for free unless it's personal. I sure as shit ain't doing Washington no favors outta the kindness of my heart. And I ain't interested right now in taking his blood money. I've known a couple of those kids since they were in grade school, including that kid we threw in the basement tonight. We flip on the Odd, people get the idea that being a friend of the Crow is hazardous to your health."

In the wake of Frankie Pallone's recent retirement, that resonated. Painfully. When Bingo turned his faded denim blue gaze on Gabriel, the Captain Crow knew he meant that for him.

Bingo stroked his beard and shook his head. "If Washington wants to settle that score, he can go settle it. We got no business settling it for him. But we also got no business getting in his way either. Mahri and those kids didn't do nothing to us. That ain't about the Crow. But they did make their beds. They're gonna have to lie in 'em at some point." Bingo shrugged. "Hell, maybe they can make it right. Get their tit out of the ringer."

Victor was interested. "Keep talking, old man."

"They're gonna want to fix this. What's left of 'em. Get those crosshairs off their backs. Why don't we help them help us? Then we can talk about settling up those other debts. We don't shit on our friends. And we sure pay it back if somebody does. The Doc's gone. Edwin's gone. Can't help that now. But, we got Mahri. Felipe, Alex, and Naomi are still out there somewhere. We probably ought to do something about that."

Delilah tossed a little mocking sneer toward Piper. "See? Now that's what *I'm* talking about."

"You're so cute when you're indignant. Your eye, it twitches just a little bit." Piper was unfazed. "And when Mr. Washington asks us to hand them over as a sign of professional loyalty?"

"Guess we cross that bridge when we get to it," Bingo conceded. "But if we don't wrangle up these fuckwits with a quickness, somebody is going to. And that means the Helitori is probably going to kill 'em. It doesn't help us in any way to let the Helitori get their hands on these kids."

"As of today, it's the only advantage we have," Anna said, supporting her father's theory. "Daddy's right. Tomorrow might be another story. But today? Well. It's a start. Everybody and their dog is gunning for them so it must mean they're worth something."

Victor contemplated it, looked to his son and the captain of his Crows.

"We're not gonna feel right about this, just letting the wolves eat them," Gabriel said. He looked at Piper and chuckled. "Well, most of us, anyway."

Piper blew him a brotherly kiss. Gabriel continued. "They're the best chance we have of doing this the easy way. They've got all the insider knowledge of what we're up against. Of what went wrong, and more importantly why."

Victor looked to Piper. Piper shrugged and settled back in his chair. He said nothing for a very long time. Then, "Yeah, fuck. It's a good idea."

Lastly, Victor looked to Fiona, his Lady Wife.

Fiona nodded. "If they can prove their worth, then they're worth our effort and protection. If they can't, or won't, then we can't afford to risk blood and treasure on them just for the sake of old friendships." She looked to her children and sighed. "Sorry loves, that's truth."

"Anybody else?" Victor asked. But no one had anything more to say on the matter that hadn't already been said. He gave the table a full thirty seconds to speak up. Their silence was considered their acceptance. Then he laid down the law.

"This is what happens," Victor St. John said, his tone one of long-standing authority. "We start chasing down the rest of Mahri's little dipshits. Now, we certainly don't owe them any favors, but if they want our help, they gotta pay the toll. That means they come with us, cooperate with us, and do what we say. They give it up—all of it—no bullshit." Victor looked hard at his son. "That means Mahri too. She ponies up pronto, or she gets a bus ticket and takes her chances. No more fucking around."

Reluctantly, Gabriel nodded.

"As far as the Helitori, they can go fuck themselves. This is Crowtown, and we need to be damned sure they know who runs shit around here. And it ain't them. If we don't stop this now, they'll get the idea that it's okay and they'll just get bolder.

You punch a schoolyard bully in the throat. And that's what they are. Well, this is my schoolyard. We make sure the Helitori gets the message."

No one argued.

"Mr. Washington's business, and his cash, is our primary concern. You don't take a shit without considering how it impacts our relationship with him. Got it? If Washington and Mahri's crew can't work out their beef, I'll handle shit from there. That ain't on any of you."

Delilah looked like she might object.

"And it ain't up for debate," Victor said. "Anybody got a problem with that?"

Everyone held their tongues, but a couple of expressions around the table suggested otherwise.

"Okay. You all make whatever arrangements you need to make with your daytime lives. As of tonight, this shit is on. We're gonna find out what Mr. Washington's losing sleep over, and we're gonna send it kicking and screaming back to Hell. Any questions?"

"Can I get paid in Asian Lady-Boys?" Piper asked without missing a beat.

Victor chuckled. "Fuck off."

The room chuckled with him.

"Questions?" the Lord Crow asked.

There were none.

"Okay. Drink and be merry then get acquainted with the job." He looked pointedly at Gabriel then. That iron glower said results were expected—and soon. "When something breaks, we'll move." He struck up a cigarette. "That's all, folks."

29

Gabriel found Twitch sitting guard duty on Mahri's cell himself. He'd brought a stool down from the clubhouse bar and was propped up against the wall thumbing through an old issue of *Maxim* magazine.

"You don't have to camp on her. She ain't going anywhere," Gabriel remarked.

Twitch rolled up his magazine and tapped it against his knee. "Bingo told me to."

Gabriel chuckled. "Oh. Well, you better do it then."

"You going in?"

"Yeah. Open it up."

Twitch did.

The vault was about twelve feet square and unfurnished except for the porta-potty stuck in the corner. It was the bedside commode-type used in hospitals—running plumbing into the vault would have negated its purpose. Water was both a grounding agent and conductor when it came to the metaphysical and this vault was designed to keep energies in and out. All it would take for something to slip past those defenses was a steady drip of water. Just venting air into the vault was risky enough, but like a hamster in a shoebox, if you didn't poke some air holes, you wouldn't have to worry about the hamster for very long.

Interlocking circles of runes covered the floor, walls, and ceiling. A special collage of protective symbols spanned the door and parted only when the plane of the closed door was opened. The protection spells restraining this vault were the product of a dozen disciplines. The work of Fiona, Delilah, and Finch.

There was the faint smell of piss in the air from the bucket, and Mahri was seated against the back wall with her knees pulled up to her chest, her eyes hot and angry. She looked haggard and exhausted.

"Damn," Twitch muttered when he caught sight of the angry witch in the cage.

"Go get her something to eat and drink," Gabriel instructed. "I got this. Button it up." The young militiaman pulled the door shut and locked it. When the plane of the door was again flush in the jamb, Gabriel felt the weight of the runic protections take hold.

The spells inked into his skin faltered and fizzled, their energy strangled away. It was an unpleasant feeling as if he'd suddenly lost half his muscle tone. He could have sworn his skin was sagging like an old man if he couldn't see otherwise with his own eyes. He could only imagine how this vault made Mahri feel—naked, helpless, alone.

"I'm sorry about this," he said honestly.

Mahri scowled and looked away.

"It's for your protection, as much as ours."

"Get fucked."

Gabriel accepted that in the spirit in which it was given. "You want a cigarette?"

"Get fucked."

He nodded. "Hungry? I'm sure you're thirsty, right?"

Mahri glowered at him, crossed her legs, put her hands on her knees, and leaned forward. "Get. Fucked."

Gabriel rubbed his forehead. "Yeah, you mentioned that already." He tucked his hands in his pockets and leaned against the wall beside the door. "Mahri, I don't have time for games or bullshit."

She grunted, angry. "Coulda fooled me. Oh. Wait. You did."

Gabriel took a deep breath then exhaled his irritation out with it. "I'm guessing Delilah never had a chance to tell you what happened today. Did she?"

"No. She didn't. Do I give a fuck?"

Gabriel nodded, his expression grew serious. "Doc McCoy's gone, Mahri. Edwin too. Somebody killed them."

Mahri blinked. A grimace of pain slashed across her face, but she wrangled it under control. "Somebody? If they're dead, then the Helitori killed them."

"Maybe," Gabriel allowed. "But maybe not. You've made some serious enemies, kiddo."

She glowered at him but offered no reply.

"Dante Washington. You were working for him, and something went south," he said. It was a statement, not a question.

"Says who?"

"Says Dante Washington. Now, I've got it on good authority that he isn't the one gunning for you. Yet. But somebody or something is, and it's not just the Helitori. What happened to Doc McCoy and Edwin, that's something different. And I bet you can tell me what it is. Can't you?"

Mahri looked away.

"I need to know what's going on, Mahri. I can help you. But you gotta tell me what's up."

She stewed in stubborn silence.

"Look, I know what I know. You were working for Dante Washington. I know that. The Helitori knows that. By now the Watch knows that. So, let's just chalk that up as a given and move on. Okay?"

Mahri shrugged. It was all the consent she was going to give.

"Where does Doc McCoy figure in?"

Mahri closed her eyes and shook her head.

"Whatever it is, it got him killed, Mahri. Edwin too."

"And you think that's on me?" she snapped.

Gabriel shrugged. He lit up a cigarette. "I don't know. Is it?"

She offered no response.

"Okay. Let's talk about something else. What went wrong?"

"What do you mean?"

"Dante Washington's losing street soldiers and pretty much says the cloud of doom is hanging over his head like a Bugs Bunny cartoon. He blames you. Says it's blowback for some tangle you got into."

She chewed her lip and held her tongue.

"I can't do anything for you if you won't talk to me," Gabriel said. He paused and let her simmer for a little while. "Let's start somewhere simple. How'd you get hooked up with Dante Washington to begin with? He's a real warlord, kiddo. His outfit ain't no joke. That's not your speed and never was."

She sighed and nodded. "Althea Gentles. Washington's resident priestess."

Gabriel cocked an eyebrow. He hadn't uncovered much about Miss Althea yet, but his experience so far was that she rated true hardcore. Mahri was good, but she wasn't on Miss Althea's level for sure. The priestess's order for the Vert Grimoire of Jean-Francois Mercier told him that much. It made him wonder what sort of work Miss Althea preferred to outsource rather than dirty her own hands with. "So, Miss Althea recruited you for a job?"

Mahri shrugged. "Something like that."

Gabriel was skeptical. "I don't imagine the Doc wanting anything to do with Dante Washington's outfit. My guess is, he didn't. Yeah?"

Mahri nodded. "It wasn't exactly official coven business."

"Meaning you were doing work for Washington on the side against the Doc's wishes."

"Me and Felipe," Mahri admitted reluctantly.

"What kind of work?"

"Nothing heavy. Just, being good neighbors. Miss Althea was new to town, we were helping her get to know some of the local wildlife. You know the drill."

"And everything was cool? Until what?"

"Something went missing."

"What was that?"

The corner of Mahri's mouth curled up in a faint, rueful smile. "Thirty-four million dollars."

Gabriel already knew the answer, but it still punched him in the jimmy every time he heard it. He whistled through his teeth. "That'll ruin a guy's mood. Where's the Odd figure in?"

"The Odd's specialty—you lose it, we find it."

"So why you? He's got pros that work for him. Mercs. P.I.s. He's got some cops. Why not find his shit the old-fashioned way?"

"Because they tried, and they couldn't. Like you said, mercs, P.I.s, cops. Even Miss Althea. But no luck. The cash fell off the face of the earth along with the fucker who took it."

"And Miss Althea thought you could do better?"

Mahri shook her head. "No. She wanted Doc McCoy. He turned her down."

Gabriel pondered that, and it computed. "But you didn't, huh?"

She shrugged. "I figured Doc was just being Doc. He's gotten really skittish, you know, over the last few years."

"Well, he's mostly retired, right?" Gabriel replied. "Was, I mean."

Mahri nodded. "Yeah. But I'm not."

"And the kids sided with you over the Doc? Why?"

"I dangled a bunch of money in front of them."

"So, naturally, you figured the Doc couldn't possibly know better, so you rolled the dice and took your chances?"

"Hey, for a six-figure finder's fee on the missing cash? You bet your ass."

"And the ducklings just fell in behind you?"

She shrugged. "Naomi needed some cash bad and fast. She had her own issues. Alex wasn't gonna pass up an opportunity to get his mom out of some of her bad debt, and Edwin was Edwin—he wanted a pile of hundred dollar bills to jerk off into." She sighed. "You have to understand, Gabriel. The Doc was getting out. Winding down. Retiring. The rest of us, we have to move on, you know?"

Gabriel nodded. He could appreciate that. "So what didn't work out?"

At length, Mahri spoke. "You're working for Washington too, right? So you know the score. Failure is not an option."

Gabriel nodded.

"He hired us to find his money and the fools who ripped him off. His priestess couldn't do it. Doc McCoy wouldn't do it. And I blew it. I couldn't pull it off either."

"And Washington wouldn't let you walk away from that? He's out nothing, he goes and finds somebody else and tries again. Shit, he might have come to us next. We get along pretty good with him. What am I missing here?"

"Yeah. Well. Let's just say, maybe I didn't know when to quit."

"Meaning you got greedy."

Mahri blinked, looked away. "I guess if you want to see it that way."

"I don't think I'm seeing it any way. It's just how it is."

She didn't argue. "I had to get creative. Had to make it happen."

Gabriel could sympathize, but only to a point. Rolling hard, running with the big dogs, meant knowing when to say when. Meant learning how to avoid writing checks your ass couldn't cash. Mahri had failed that lesson the very hard way. "What did you do?"

"I pushed, and I pushed some more," she said with a distant smile. "Be careful what you wish for, right?"

Gabriel thought she looked very scared and more than a little guilty. Something wasn't adding up. "You, uh, didn't mention Felipe when you were trotting out everybody's reasons for siding with you over the Doc."

Mahri looked at the floor.

"You know who ripped off Washington, don't you?"

"Yeah," she said quietly. "I found the money. Well, at least the *puto* who took it."

Gabriel waited not so patiently for the rest of the story.

Mahri took a deep breath and let it out slow. "Felipe ripped off Dante Washington. It's my fault. And I am completely fucked."

30

A t last, Mahri spilled the beans and Gabriel listened. "Felipe had been scamming the Doc's work for a very long time," she said.

"How long?"

She shrugged. "Long enough to have gotten his hands on all kinds of stuff he shouldn't have been messing with."

"And you knew?"

"I suspected. But I didn't know. Not until things went off the rails with Washington. I don't know. I guess maybe Felipe had been setting us up for quite a while. And then boom."

"And you didn't do anything about it?"

"What was I going to do? Felipe and I were already scamming the Doc on this thing with Washington as it was. By the time I figured out Felipe had his own fucked up plans, it was already over and done. And I'd been helping him by keeping the Doc out of the way."

"I'm guessing you haven't shared any of this with Washington yet, huh?"

Mahri scoffed. "I'm pretty sure 'I didn't do it, it was all Felipe' isn't going to fly with him. I like my head attached to my shoulders."

Gabriel was at a loss. "You said Felipe's been scamming the Doc's work behind his back. That he rolled you and the other Oddies under the bus." He shook his head in confusion. "You're telling me he ripped off a big-time L.A. kingpin for thirty-four million in street cash, wiped out a warehouse full of his men, and left you and your crew to hang for it? We talking about the same Felipe Ortiz here? What am I missing?"

Mahri looked more than a little scared.

Gabriel felt a chill slither up his spine. "What did Felipe get himself into?"

She swallowed the lump in her throat before responding. "Felipe's been whispering into the Outer Darkness, *papi*. It whispered back."

The Outer Darkness was oblivion. The lightless, empty canvas upon which existence was painted with stars and dust. Alien. Strange. Hungry. It was the *absence of*. The Devourer. The Void. It was an expanse of reality incompatible with the mortal mind.

The vastness of the heavens, where stars burned and worlds turned, left mortals in fear and awe. The emptiness behind them brought only madness. It rubbed up against the mortal world where light was absent. The roots of the earth. The cold depths of the sea. Those forces could be called to in the darkness between the stars.

The nameless things that prowled the Outer Darkness were chaos and hunger incarnate. Their true and complete nature beyond the ability of mortal kind to perceive. Mortals could only postulate and theorize about those impossible intellects that dwelt in the Void. Were it not for their hungry insistence, their endless desire to bleed into the mortal world, to eat and drink and drag it back to nothingness with them, they'd be no more than myth at all.

It was beyond the known power of any mortal discipline to reach beyond the Veil into the Outer Darkness. Such doors were one-way portals. Mortals did not go without. The Outer Darkness intruded within. But the doors were infinite, and in the form of ancient spell and ritual, we possessed many of the keys to open them. We only had to be willing to try, competent and bold enough to turn the keys, and from there, to call to them. *Come in, come in. The way is open.*

If one's power to work the locks was great enough, one's voice strong enough to be heard, their will resilient enough to hold the way open, they could allow them through. The things that dwelt in the Void would open long-sleeping eyes. And they would come.

Violating the Outer Darkness was considered anathema to peaceful practitioners of the Art. It was reckless, dangerous, beyond hope of control. There were no bargains to be struck or deals to be made with the things that dwelt beyond the gates. There were no trades, no exchanges, no secret power to be brokered. Invoking them, opening the Ways, was like tapping into a force of nature. Wind for the metaphysical sails.

Their passing, their presence, was like harnessing the power of the atom. It was fickle and dangerous, on the razor edge of disaster even under the best of circumstances. Teasing, tempting lore existed, about those horrid few who had managed to capture that lightning in a bottle. To turn the swell of power, the touch of woeful wills as they crept across the passages, to a desired purpose. That which leaked through the fabric of existence became fuel for their fires.

All those tales, predictably, came to bad ends.

Madness, woe, despair, destruction, and atrocity on horrific scale. But they were also lessons about practitioners who had accomplished great things. Before the rug was pulled out from underneath them anyway in the blackest oblivion.

Touching the Outer Darkness was the last hope of the desperate. It was putting the pistol to your head and squeezing the trigger to see what came next. Tremendous cost with no guarantee of payback, or even what form the return would take. It was everything peaceful practitioners usually avoided.

"Jesus, Mahri," Gabriel said. "Felipe? Really?"

She nodded.

"And he turned it on Washington?"

She nodded again.

The light bulb went off. "Is that why the Helitori is here?"

For the first time, she looked very small and very frightened. She nodded, slowly, reluctantly. "Yeah," was all she had to say about that.

PART FOUR

Abyss

When I whispered into the Outer Darkness, I became all things in it, and it all things in me. I became its mother. I nursed it. I became its lover. I fucked it. I was conduit. Lightning rod. Portal. Window. Door. I became its eyes where it could not see, ears where it could not hear. Priestess. Prophet. Healer. Destroyer. I am Whore of Shadow. Eater of Kings. Turner of the Key. Daughter of the Endless Night. Kill me. You can't. I dare you.
Please.
Make it stop.
Kill me.

Oksana Kozlov
Last words and testimony prior to her execution by
The Watch
Leningrad, 1953

31

Gabriel wanted to rail on her. To chew her ass, say something hateful. *You stupid, greedy bitch. What were you thinking?* But he didn't. Instead, he took a deep breath and said, "Mahri. Look at me."

She did.

"You're gonna have to talk to my mom and my sister."

Mahri squirmed. "I'd rather just talk to Delilah. She'd understand."

Gabriel snorted. "Oh, don't worry. My mom's gonna 'understand' all right."

Mahri scrambled to her feet, crossed the chamber frantically and quickly enough that Gabriel's guard came up. But she wasn't attacking him. She grabbed both of his hands and squeezed.

"Come on, *papi*," she said, her voice pleading. "Don't do this to me. Your mother hates me. I mean, she really hates me."

Gabriel got it. Mahri was terrified of Fiona. To be fair, anybody with any sense at all was afraid of her. "Cooperate with her, then."

"I am cooperating!" Mahri replied, her tone sharp, frightened. "She's never going to believe me. But you do, right?"

Gabriel was not quick to answer.

"Come on, Gabriel. You do. Right?"

"What happened at Doc McCoy's place today?"

Mahri's eyes flicked left, then right. Then she shook her head. "I don't know."

"You're lying to me," Gabriel said. "You don't tell me, I can't help you."

She looked wounded. The next word looked like it hurt to say out loud. "Felipe."

"You sure about that?"

She shrugged. "He really jammed us, man. When I figured out what he was up to and what he'd done. I guess I—" Tears welled up in her large, dark eyes. "I guess I didn't realize how bad. Until now. I thought he was just trying to scare us off. It must have caught up to Eddie at the Doc's place. I don't know what happened to the Doc, though. I swear."

"Do you think Felipe could have done that to the Doc?" Gabriel asked. "Drunk on power and wanting the old man to give up all the goodies?"

Mahri looked positively miserable. "I never would have thought he'd turn on us. Not like this. I guess he could have done it, yeah. It'd make sense."

"When you found out what Felipe was up to, did you warn the Doc?"

Mahri shook her head. "I thought I could get it under control."

"Meaning you thought getting the Doc involved would fuck up your payday."

She didn't respond to that.

"So, he probably had no idea what was coming? Probably invited Felipe right on in for a little student-teacher pep talk. And then Felipe crucified him. Turned him inside out. Peeled the skin off him."

Mahri's jaw flexed, and her nostrils flared. She scrubbed the butt of her hand against her cheek, grinding the tears away as they finally fell. "I get it, okay? Enough. You don't have to keep rubbing it in."

"I haven't even begun to rub it in," Gabriel replied.

"Fuck this," Mahri snorted and turned away as if she had anywhere to go in the little cell.

Gabriel caught her by the elbow. "No more games and no more bullshit. You had your chance, and you blew it. Now it's my turn. Got it?"

At reluctant length, Mahri nodded.

Gabriel let her go. "Do you know where Felipe is now?"

She shook her head. "I don't know."

"Mahri…"

"I don't know!" She threw up her hands in frustration. "Jesus, I'd tell you if I did!"

Gabriel chewed on it, aggravated. Being aggravated wasn't helping. What was done was done. Bullets couldn't be taken back. "Okay, change gears. If you were Felipe, and you're in deep shit, where do you go first?"

She puzzled through it, and Gabriel gave her a chance to work it out. "He'd go to the Doc, but..."

"Then where?"

"He can't go back to Washington. Not now. Washington doesn't know it was Felipe that hit him. Yet. But if he starts sniffing around back there, he'd sure as shit figure it out."

"You don't think he'd turn right around and sell you out to Washington? Pin the whole thing on you? Even if it just bought him a few days to work on his out, that's all he needs."

Mahri looked a little queasy. Like maybe she hadn't thought about that yet.

If Felipe boomeranged back to Washington and sold his version of events, that opened up a whole new, and awful, can of worms. Gabriel tabled it. "Damn it, Mahri. Why didn't you come to us for help sooner? Why did you let this get so out of control?"

Mahri snorted, scrubbing a fresh tear from her cheek. "You know how it is. In this business, you handle your own, right? Besides, don't act like the Crow is some kind of charity or something."

"I would have helped you. Delilah would have helped you."

"Yeah, well, that's great. But Victor and Fiona run the show. Would they have helped me? I already got one bill I can't pay. Didn't need one from them too."

"Out of options now, though, huh?"

Mahri sniffled, rubbed the heal of her hand against her forehead. "Yeah. I guess I am." Her breathing hitched, and the fear bubbled up again. The more upset she got, the more she tended to talk with her hands. Now was no exception. "Washington's gonna have my head, *papi*. If not him, then the Helitori is gonna kill me. And if not them... Felipe..." Mahri's voice was thin and jittery. Her hands trembled.

"Okay, stay with me. Where else? Felipe needs an out more than he needs anything else. He's got plenty of cash. Way too much to just walk out of town with a suitcase. Who does he trust that's higher up the food chain than he is, but that's outside his usual circles?"

Mahri seized on that idea. "Jimmy Torres."

Gabriel tried that on for size and nodded. Yeah. That added up, maybe. "Okay. We'll talk to Jimmy Torres then. See if Felipe's been barking up his tree."

Mahri nodded, working hard to bottle up her fear. "I fucked this up so bad."

"Yeah, well. You're here now. You aren't alone. We'll figure it out."

Mahri tried to laugh, and it came out a single sob. But she managed a strained smile. She leaned in and laid her head on Gabriel's chest, curled up tight against him and wrapped her arms around him. The gash in his side wasn't so numb anymore. The fresh wound complained, as did his budding crop of knots and bruises. But it didn't matter. Something about Mahri's surrender took all the fire out of his aggravation.

There was a beat of hesitation, then he wrapped his arms around her in return.

A decade of history and nostalgia rolled over him like a warm ocean wave—like the surf going over his head on a sunny tropical beach—she still smelled right, felt right. Sounded right. Looked right. Even though she was twisted up like a knot of barbed wire. Being too close to Felipe's bad juju had wreaked some havoc on her head, but it was still Mahri.

Feeling the shape of her up against him—her curves, soft and firm; her hair, like warm black silk—started putting thoughts in his head that had no business being there.

He remembered when she ran away from home. She'd been a senior in high school. She was eighteen by then, so their little flings were mostly legit by that point.

Her older brother Anthony had started bringing home some bad shit from the neighborhood. His new main man Luis was sweet on her, but Mahri wasn't sweet on Luis and their pops sure as hell wasn't cool with it.

There had been a fight, and Luis put their dad in the hospital for disrespecting him. Anthony tried to cover it up, to stay cool with his crew. Their mom was a wreck, everything was sideways, so Mahri freaked out and just split.

Anthony tracked her down and tried to get her to come home. Then Luis tracked Anthony down, and there'd been another fight. Anthony was a tough kid, but Luis was hardcore. He made Anthony his little bitch in the alley behind the Fast Trip—beat him bloody and made him kiss his boots. Mahri jumped in between them and Luis flipped.

He'd busted Mahri up pretty good for it. He bloodied her nose and mouth and left her with a black eye and fat lip. She's skinned up her hands and knees when he'd dragged her across the pavement and tossed her out of the end of the alley, warning her to never get between him and his business ever again.

Her friend Paulina tried to take her home, but Mahri wouldn't go. Ditto for the hospital. Instead, Mahri got angry. She went and saw Gabriel and *his* friends, and Gabriel asked her one question. "Who did this to you?"

She told him.

Two nights later, Luis was on his way home from a dog fight. He was two blocks from the house the last time anybody could account for him. But he never arrived, and nobody ever saw his fool ass again.

Only Luis Aceveda and the people who disappeared him knew what happened that night. No one else. Not even Mahri.

Gabriel had killed before that night. His first was when a witchhunter from Texas had left him no choice. He'd sent that bastard's head back to Austin in a box. His worst, the retaliation against a rival sorceress who'd been stupid enough to muscle in on Crow territory. One long, bloody night later, he and his brothers had put nine bodies on the ground, and the rival sorceress was no longer a concern. Both incidents had been hot-blooded. Business.

But that's not how things were at all when they took Luis Aceveda out to the desert. Piper had put the pistol in his hand and said simply, "Your call, little brother."

Gabriel had never killed a man in cold blood. Never even

CLAY SANGER

really thought about it. But there was Luis, kneeling, bleeding from a beating, hands tied behind his back, pleading for his life, praying and begging God and his mother to save him, and forgive him. *I'm sorry. I'm sorry.* It was what they all said. All these tough motherfuckers were suddenly so very sorry when they found themselves on their knees in the dirt staring down a pistol.

Gabriel put two in his head. *Boom-boom.*

Then he and his Brother Crows buried him in a shallow, unmarked grave at the forgotten end of a dirt road and afterward Piper explained: "This wasn't business; it was personal, and you can trust me when I say your old man isn't cool with personal shit being done behind his back. Not even by you. So this never happened." They never talked about it again. For some reason, he thought about that night a lot. He thought about it now, standing there, holding Mahri while she shivered against him.

"I'm sorry I flipped out before," Mahri said. "I'm just so scared."

"I know," Gabriel said, running a soothing hand over her hair. "We're gonna figure it out. Okay?"

"Okay," Mahri breathed. Her head tilted up, just a little, and Gabriel felt the tip of her nose nuzzle ever so lightly against his Adam's apple.

She paused there, frozen, waiting.

Gabriel closed his eyes and swallowed.

Mahri Took a deep breath, then pulled away, laying her forehead back against his chest. She let the breath out with a long, tired sigh.

Yeah. Both of them knew damn well that wasn't the answer right now. It kind of seemed like it might be. But it wasn't.

About that time, Twitch popped open the vault and came in with a tray of food and drink.

Saved by the bell.

"Oh," Twitch said when he opened the door and saw the two of them standing there in a very quiet, very intimate embrace. "I can come back," he suggested, already beginning to retreat.

Both Gabriel and Mahri laughed and said, "No," almost simultaneously. Reluctantly, they separated.

Mahri wiped the tears from her cheeks and made an effort to put on a more pleasant façade. "Hey, is that for me?" she asked, nodding toward Twitch's tray, summoning up a faint smile, tucking her hands into the back pockets of her shorts.

"I don't think so," Twitch replied suspiciously. "This was for a mean Mexican girl. Where'd she go?"

Gabriel gave him the stink eye, but Mahri laughed. She glanced at Gabriel. "Leave him alone. He's cute."

Twitch grinned and gave a cocky shrug. "Eh."

Gabriel let off a single sour grunt of a laugh. "You can't handle her, Twitchy. Trust me." Gabriel glanced down at the food tray. "Take that back upstairs."

Twitch didn't look so cocky then. He looked confused. "Really?"

Mahri looked equally taken aback.

"Yeah. Really. This is fucking stupid," Gabriel replied, gesturing around the vault. A little part of him hoped he didn't have that turned around backwards. Only one way to find out. He turned back to Mahri. "Take the apartment. Clean up, whatever. We'll get you some fresh clothes." He looked to Twitch. "Put her food wherever she tells you to."

"You sure about this?" Mahri asked. Obviously, she was concerned that Gabriel's fellow Crows might not feel as comfortable with her running around the joint as he was.

He nodded. "Yeah. Don't leave the Church without me. Don't tell anybody you're here. And if something gets scary, you head down here and shut this door. Okay?"

She nodded. "Yeah. Okay, *papi*."

"Have a bite to eat. Get yourself together. We'll talk to Jimmy Torres. You and me. I'll call Jimmy and work it out. See where that leads. Twitch, get some wheels. You're coming along too. Backup."

The young militiaman nodded. "Roger that."

Mahri gave Gabriel's arm a grateful squeeze, then she turned to Twitch. "I guess just, put it on the bar for me, and I'll be down for it after I get cleaned up."

Twitch nodded, but he didn't move.

Gabriel gestured toward the vault door. "Ladies first."

With that, Mahri gathered herself up and stepped out of the vault, heading back upstairs.

Twitch was confused. "Uh…"

"You have a new mission in life, Twitchy," Gabriel said, steering him toward the vault door. "First, you keep an eye on her. Twenty-four hours a day, seven days a week, until I say otherwise. If you have to take a piss, you make sure somebody is covering for you. Got it?"

"Yeah. Got it."

"If she needs something, handle it. Take care of it for her. Do not let her leave unless she's leaving with me. If something isn't right, call me. If something *really* isn't right, put her ass back in the box."

"Is Victor gonna—"

"Victor is going to take it up with me, not you," Gabriel assured him, placing a hand on his shoulder.

"Okay, yeah, got it," Twitch said. "Uh, you said first. Does that mean there's a second?"

"Yeah," Gabriel replied. He fished a cigarette out of his jacket and struck it up. "Don't fuck her and definitely don't piss her off."

Twitch chuckled nervously. "Heh, you'd kill me, right?"

Gabriel shook his head. "No. But she might."

32

Once they were back upstairs, they encountered Victor coming down the hallway. Mahri did her best to keep walking and look humble while Twitch did everything in his power to skate right on past the Lord Crow without having to explain.

Victor let Mahri pass, but he grabbed Twitch by the sleeve of his jacket and stopped him in his tracks. He didn't say a word. All he did was arch one eyebrow and fix Twitch with that granite glare.

"Gabriel told me to," he said by way of explanation.

Victor released him with a grunt. "Go. Do your shit."

Twitch didn't squander the opportunity to escape.

As Gabriel came up behind them, Victor held his hands out wide. "What the fuck is this shit?"

"It's handled," Gabriel assured him with a dismissive wave. "She gave it up. The whole sad ass story."

Victor contemplated that. "And you believe her?"

Gabriel shrugged. "Well, I don't disbelieve her." He pulled his Lord Father aside into the nearest doorway and lowered his voice. "It was Felipe. He's been playing this dirty from both ends the whole time. He's into some bad shit, pop. I'll fill you in a little later. We're about to go chase a lead."

Victor looked perplexed. "Felipe Ortiz ripped off Dante Washington? The same Felipe who likes yoga, granola, and pretty white boys?"

"It's fucked up," Gabriel agreed. "And it's complicated. I'm gonna need about a minute to sort it out. Okay?"

"Hrm," Victor grunted. "Well, we got other problems."

Gabriel felt his blood pressure go up by a couple of points. "Of course we do. Like what?"

"I just got an emergency call from Jonathan Markus. Washington's security chief. One of Washington's street captains just hit the floor. Babbling and screaming like his head's gonna spin around and he's gonna start puking pea soup."

"You're shitting me."

"Nope," Victor replied. "So, if Felipe is our boy, then he just sucker punched Dante Washington right in the eye. While we've spent the day jerking off. We have to fix this. Now."

Gabriel couldn't argue. He fell in with his Lord Father and followed him at an urgent march downstairs.

Victor broke the news with a simple, "Drop whatever you're doing."

Considering most of his Crows were in a holding pattern for the night, catching up, getting up to speed on the intel, drinking, joking, and smoking, the hall came to order pretty quick. Victor pulled his people together in the clubhouse bar and filled them in.

One of Washington's street captains had just hit the deck screaming and crying with a real desire to pull his insides onto the outside. That was bad. It was clearly an attack. What kind remained to be seen. He deferred to Gabriel then to share the intel he'd gotten from Mahri.

Mention of the Outer Darkness left the room quiet as a tomb.

Bringing up Felipe's connection to it all elicited an "I told you so," from Piper.

With that, the Captain Crow could not disagree.

"What do we do?" Delilah asked.

"You take the talent on hand, you and Finch, and go deal with Washington's red alert," Victor decreed.

She nodded. "What about Washington's talent? Miss Althea?"

"She'll be waiting for you," Victor said. Then he gave her an address. It gave all of them a reason to pause. Baldwin-Crenshaw, down in the infamous Jungles. The epitome of the dark heart of L.A. Gangland. Not exactly an outsider-friendly neighborhood.

"You sure?" Delilah asked, cocking a dubious eyebrow. Finch's doubt mirrored her own.

Victor nodded. "Consider yourselves invited guests of Mr. Dante Washington. But don't get too comfortable. Follow?"

They did.

Gabriel took the lead. "Dodger, Piper. You go with them. Back them up."

"On it," Dodger replied without missing a beat. "What's your angle tonight?"

"I got a lead from Mahri," Gabriel replied. "I'm gonna chase the rabbit. See where it goes."

Piper balked. "So, if we're riding shotgun for Delilah and Finchy, who's backing you up?"

Gabriel shook his head, dismissing Piper's concern. "I'll take Twitch with me. Mahri too. I'm not planning on starting any trouble."

Dodger chuckled grimly. "Never are. You sure, brother?"

Gabriel nodded. "Yeah. Just remember what happened at Washington's cash depot. If the boogeyman hit one of his captains, you guys are going to the place that's most likely to get out of hand. If shit gets ugly, you get Dee and Finchy, and you get the fuck out of there. Don't let the ceiling fall in on you."

"Yeah, back at ya," Piper grunted. It was clear that nobody liked splitting up the team like this, but circumstances dictated otherwise. Dodger and Piper followed their Captain's orders and went to gear up for the run to the Jungles.

The machine started to move.

Delilah pulled Gabriel aside. "What lead?" she asked.

"Jimmy Torres," Gabriel replied. "Mahri's best guess where Felipe might have gone looking for help."

"If half of what Mahri claims is true, Jimmy's not going to help him."

Gabriel nodded. "Yeah, I know. But even if Jimmy slammed the door in Felipe's face, it's the best place I've got to start. Hell. It's the only place I've got to start."

Delilah wasn't sober, but she looked serious as a heart attack. "Do you believe her?" She didn't have all the details on his heart-to-heart with Mahri yet, but she had enough. Delilah looked less than convinced.

Gabriel told her the same thing he'd told their Lord Father. "No reason not to. Yet."

Delilah snorted. "Do you trust her?"

"No."

She grinned, a lopsided, humorless smirk. "Yeah. Right."

Gabriel lit a smoke and shook his head. "Okay. I get it. I'll be careful. Quit hassling me and go handle your shit."

"Aye-aye, cap'n," Delilah replied with a smart-ass little salute.

"And sober up," Gabriel chided. "This is serious shit."

But Delilah only laughed, a sour chortle. "Don't I know it."

Then she was gone.

33

The Crows on duty made ready for their late night house calls. That meant different things to different Crows.

Delilah and Finch put their pointy little heads together and mapped out what assorted paraphernalia they might want for the night. Which meant suiting up for any eventuality they could think of because they had not the first clue what they were getting themselves into. Only that it was bad. Then Delilah pulled Finch aside in the kitchen and cut out a couple lines of speed to rev the engines. "Take your vitamins," she insisted, offering the second rail to Finch after she'd vacuumed up the first. He didn't argue.

Dodger grabbed radios for the two crews while Piper and Twitch squared away the wheels. The gunslingers strapped vests on under their shirts and armed up like they expected a fight with gun, blade, or claw. They grabbed some M4 carbines out of the Church's hidey holes and piled them up with loaded plate carriers in the trunks of their respective work cars. The plate carriers were outerwear vests, heavy body armor with ballistic plates, carrying loaded mags totaling one hundred and eighty rounds a piece for the M4's. Just in case. They were on the clock now, and shit had a way of changing with a quickness.

"We're good to go," Dodger reported shortly thereafter. "Want us to wait on you?"

Gabriel shook his head. "No. You guys roll on. I gotta make phone calls first."

Dodger nodded and turned to head out.

"Hey, Dodger," Gabriel called.

The big man turned back.

"How you feeling about it?"

Dodger had come by his nickname honestly. He was just one of those guys with an almost supernatural sense for when the shit was about to hit the fan. And he was better than most at zigging when others were zagging. His brother Crows relied on that instinct like radar.

"Fifty-fifty," he reported with a shrug.

"Yeah? Any idea which fifty?" Gabriel asked.

"Nope," Dodger replied. Then he was gone.

Once Gabriel had checked and stowed his gear, he washed a couple of pain pills down with a mouthful of scotch to take the grinding edge off his aches. Time might heal all wounds eventually, but in the short term, time made all wounds hurt like a bastard. Once he had some medicine in him, he went to handle his business.

First, he called Jimmy Torres. He got one of Jimmy's shop assistants and waited patiently for her to put the man on the phone.

Jimmy Torres ran an herbal health dispensary down in Boyle Heights—that was a fancy name for a weed shop. He was almost entirely legit, too. The weed that went out his front door was all legal dispensary business, and anything that went out his back door wasn't on the list of California or Federally controlled substances. That was all foo-foo herbalism shit that no cops, legislators, or average citizens took seriously. Just as well for Jimmy.

Jimmy cultivated fine weed and finer alchemical remedies for anything that ailed you. He could get an elephant's limp trunk hard as a rock or send you on a trip Hunter S. Thompson wouldn't even be able to describe. Jimmy Torres cooked a mean brew, and he'd make almost anything to order—for the right price. Alchemy was generally a hell of a lot more expensive than chemistry, but, oh, the results.

Once upon a time, he'd been a foot soldier for the House Del Torro. They were a rival of the Crow, but a friendly one rather than a bloody one. Jimmy's days of being a Bull wore out some time ago, and he moved on to other pursuits. He was the kind of guy that had friends here, there, and everywhere, who seemed to know just about everybody—the kind of guy you went to if you were in deep shit and needed a favor.

"How's tricks, Jimmy?" Gabriel asked when Jimmy answered the phone.

"Gabriel the Crow," Jimmy Torres said with a smile in his voice. "No complaints. How's it with you?"

"Eh, I got this thing I need to talk to you about."

"Yeah?"

"Yeah. Felipe Ortiz. Ring a bell?"

Jimmy didn't miss a beat. "Yup. He came to see me. I'm not real surprised to be hearing from you, either."

Gabriel puzzled at that. "You're not?"

"Nope. Felipe was working for Dante Washington. Now he's not. Now, word is that you're working for Dante Washington. So... Well. Seemed likely you'd show up."

"Who says I'm on the job for Dante Washington?" Gabriel asked.

Jimmy chuckled. "Mr. Dante Washington does. And the two assholes who already came in here looking for Felipe this morning."

"What two assholes?"

"You want my best guess? Helitori, that's who."

"You're a popular guy, Jimmy."

"Yeah, well, I try."

"Problems?" Gabriel asked.

"Nope. I sent Felipe and *his* problems packing about five minutes after he showed up. So they didn't become *my* problems."

Gabriel could appreciate that. "What did Felipe want from you?"

"He wanted me to put him together with The Bull. He had a case to make, wares to sell, and needed a ticket off the planet."

"And what did you do?"

"Told him to go piss up a rope. He looks real bad, man. Twitchy as hell. Got a storm cloud following him like that donkey from Winnie the Pooh. Besides, the math ain't hard."

"Yeah?"

"He won't say so, but he's on the run from Dante Washington, and word on the street is Dante Washington is light a whole lot of cash. I try to steer clear of the guys that are running away from the dumpster fire, you know?"

Gabriel chuckled. "I heard that. So, did you throw him a bone or anything?"

Jimmy was slow to answer.

"Come on, Jimmy. Help me out. I'm not gonna hurt him. But you want me to find him before anybody else does. Don't you?"

It got quieter on Jimmy's end of the conversation. Like maybe he'd stepped in the back away from the hubbub of his storefront for some privacy. "Yeah. Okay," he said at last. "Felipe used to be a pretty good kid, you know?"

"I do," Gabriel conceded.

"I might have told him that the Couatl was more the speed he needs," Jimmy said. "You know, if I was to have given him any advice, that is. Which I didn't."

"Of course you didn't," Gabriel replied.

"I'd consider it a favor if it happened to come up, that you made sure Mr. Dante Washington knew that too."

"I can do that," Gabriel replied. "So. You said there's word on the street about Washington. What are you hearing?"

"Not much," Jimmy replied, and Gabriel could hear his shrug through the phone. "Just that something big went down and it cost him a pile of cash. That's one bad guy to have pissed off at you." Jimmy cleared his throat. "Consider that some advice too. If I was giving any. Which I am not."

Gabriel computed that. "Thanks, Jimmy."

Then he was gone.

He went upstairs and rounded up Mahri. She was fresh from the shower, hair still damp, wearing some spare clothes Delilah had kicked her way. Gabriel hadn't returned her backpack and workings yet. They were still downstairs behind the bar in Bingo's care.

"I talked to Jimmy," he said.

"Yeah?" She plopped down on the edge of the bed to tie her shoes.

Gabriel nodded. "Yeah. He says Couatl's where to start looking for Felipe."

Mahri paused. Gave that its due. Then she went back to tying her shoes. "That's not good news."

"Nope."

"But we're going?"

"Yup."

"When?"

"Now. Meet me downstairs when you're ready."

Gabriel didn't linger, and Mahri didn't argue.

They linked up with Twitch and the red Tahoe. Gabriel did the driving. Mahri rode beside him in the passenger seat, and Twitch rode in the backseat with a rifle a short grab away in the cargo hatch behind him. They rolled out under a purple dome of Los Angeles sky, bound for Westlake Diamond Street turf to seek the Couatl.

It was fifty-six degrees and hazy, and Jimi Hendrix's *Voodoo Child* was on the radio.

Magic is magical. Redundant, yes? Not when you consider what magic is not. Physics. Chemistry. Engineering. Mathematics. Magic may be instructed by these things, woven in tandem with them. But it's ruled by a different set of laws, and those laws were made to be bent and broken. Magic is Art. Mutable. Changeable. Endlessly varied. Defiant even of its own boundaries. Begging to be modified, to be altered, manipulated. By its very nature, the magical exists to be fundamentally transformed by sheer will. Not so much for gravity, light, the atom, and two-plus-two.

To learn magic is to understand its boundaries. To practice magic is to break through them. The Art is always shadowed by a component of the unknown. Ignorance can be deadly. Push the boundaries hard enough and the Art becomes a bomb. One strapped to your back with unbreakable chains, counting down on a burning fuse you can't see and can't stop.

34

Delilah's crew had an address and a time. Around eleven o'clock they came rolling into the neighborhood, creeping up on the back streets of the Jungles in a pair of discreet work cars.

Big public displays of affection like Gabriel and Delilah had encountered earlier in the day were off the menu. They were strangers in a strange land here. They didn't blend in. People would see and remember them. No one who ran the streets here had any reason to protect them. And that was a bad time to leave a smoking crater behind. The order of the hour was *be cool.*

The caravan of Crows navigated their way through a dark labyrinth of alleys and back streets. Their route was lined with parked cars crowded against the curbs, numbered garage bays with dented doors, and dumpsters tagged with graffiti. Two and three story row apartments crowded every block. Clusters of ancient palms leaned over the rooftops like crooked watchtowers. It was the sort of neighborhood where you saw a lot of bars on windows and could find a slick, tricked out Benz parked next to a ratty old pedophile van on any given block.

On their way in, they passed a constellation of whirling blue and red, a dazzling light show thrown off by half a dozen LAPD cruisers. Two kids in red bandannas were getting hooked up by four officers, while eight more stood watch over the scene, keeping the looky-loos at bay. The commotion had drawn a crowd, and it wasn't an overly friendly or welcoming one at that. L.A.'s Finest had their reasons for not coming down here light on manpower.

The Jungles was action-central for the Jungle Stones, Black

P Stone Nation. The neighborhood was the epitome of the way the climate had shifted across L.A.'s gangland. Over the last ten years, it had rained indictments and injunctions on the Jungle Stones until it poured. Despite the pressure, they'd weathered the storm and evolved. The streets were quieter, but they'd never been tougher, and the Jungle Stones and the other sets that worked the hood were a reflection of their streets, leaner and meaner. This was unfriendly country if you didn't live or have business here.

The Crow's intel said that Mr. Washington had come up Red, a Blood in his youth, Jungle Stone, and he still had friends with the Jungle and City Stones, Rollin' 20s, Fruit Town Brims, and other sets. He did business with them on multiple fronts. If the word on the backside of the street could be believed, he also helped bangers who wanted to get out of the life, get out. Apparently, Dante Washington was a complex man.

Their route came to an end in the back lot behind a squat, aging, three-story apartment building. The place had a certain *open for business* look about it. Nothing too over the top and obvious. It was just a little more active than its neighbors, a degree or two more hoppin' even for a Friday night. There were a few residents laughing, joking, and cutting up in the parking lot and many more in the little courtyard beyond the spiked iron gate. All young for the most part. There was music playing, thumping and bumping from somewhere inside the yard. Loud enough, but not so loud as to rile up the neighbors too much. On the side of the building above the back gate, there was a large decorative splash of cut-out wooden letters, painted white, bolted to the rust red stucco that read *The Hyde.*

The place looked more like the peak hours of a Friday night block party than a gangland headquarters—which was exactly how these folks wanted it.

Washington's management crew down in the Jungles used the backstreet apartment complex as a base of operations and safe house. The boys on this block took pains to blend in and do their business, keeping it tight with the other neighborhood sets. Quiet and cool.

There were a handful of young men manning the back

gate, displaying their Red, smoking and shooting the shit. The arrival of the Crows certainly caught their attention. Theirs and everyone else. Carefully navigating the wandering pedestrians, the Crows parked on the near side of the lot, right next to two big SUVs that sported ballistic glass and run-flat tires.

Acting like they belonged there, because putting any other foot forward might invite a challenge, the Crows dismounted their vehicles. Delilah led the way to the gate, leaving a streamer of blue cigarette smoke in her wake as she walked. The Crows fell in behind her and headed up the sidewalk.

"Miss Althea Gentles is expecting us," Delilah told the men at the gate.

They looked the crew of Crows up and down, and the man in charge gave a nod. "Yeah. Okay. Go on in. Across the yard. Middle row. Number six."

The Crows took their invitation inside.

The scent of old concrete and trampled yard dirt mingled with cigarette smoke, beer, and a hint of weed. Music pulsed, the boys were hanging out, mackin on the ladies, the girls were flirting with the boys. Everyone was sipping on bottles, or toting red plastic cups, and passing the occasional joint. Here and there, young men with neighborhood style and hard faces kept watch among the sheep.

Curious eyes followed the Crows through the crowd, across the courtyard, and into the underbelly of the middle building. As they crossed out of the courtyard, into the yawning central breezeway, the dimly lit corridor swallowed them.

A dark, echoing stairwell loomed overhead, sloping upward in right-angle switchbacks to the second and third floors. Cigarette butts, broken glass, and the occasional beer can littered the edges of the corridor. Penthouses were for pampered princes. Ground floor digs with lots of escape routes were for people who worked for a living. This apartment complex was a beehive. A dozen ways in and out, perfect should the quail ever have to scatter.

Delilah rang the bell for Number Six.

An athletically fit young black man dressed in casual khakis and black polo shirt answered the door. He wasn't much taller than she was but looked like he was assembled out of spring steel. Beyond, the apartment was orderly and quiet. No music playing. Nobody hanging around smokin' and jokin' and no gangster's paradise sensibility about it. It was a big place, but discreet from the outside. Several units had been joined into one without fanfare.

"Miss St. John?"

Delilah nodded. "We have an appointment with Althea Gentles."

The man stepped aside, motioning for Delilah and her crew to come on in. Delilah stepped over the threshold and felt the faint pressure of well-laid wards. It was a coolness, a cleanliness. An inexplicable sensation of fresher air. A filtering of the metaphysical noise that echoed in myriad layered waves in the outside world. Not a tingle or a prickle but just the opposite. The absence of that. Like suddenly becoming aware of how warm the sunshine had been after a cloud moves across it overhead.

Delilah scanned the interior of the apartment and saw nothing out of the ordinary for this neck of the woods. Nothing to draw attention or pique curiosity. The appliances of the wards were out of sight and well-hidden. Only tinfoil hat loonies carved their wards into the walls for everybody and their dog to see. This work was clean, professional. There was security and comfort here. But not complacency. The doorman was packing a pistol tucked into a waistband holster at the small of his back which he made no effort to conceal.

As he welcomed them inside, Jonathan Markus, Mr. Washington's chief of security, entered the room and gave a friendly smile.

Delilah shook his hand and one by one, introduced the Crows in attendance for the evening. Markus was the sort of man that marked and measured each of them in turn.

"Miss Gentles is waiting for you. This way."

The Crows let Markus take the lead, following him into the kitchen. Delilah pondered why Mr. Washington's chief of security would be here in the middle of the night. Perhaps he was tasked with escorting Miss Althea. Ahead, a tea kettle began to whistle.

They met Miss Althea Gentles at the stove, tending a pot of tea.

She was a stunning woman. Liquid grace. Serenity in motion. Nothing hurried, a monument of calm. Her vibe was unmistakably bohemian. Delilah guessed she was in her thirties but couldn't be sure. She was reminiscent of her mother in that way, seemingly ageless. Not old, not young, and hauntingly beautiful.

"Miss Althea," Markus said respectfully and nodded toward their guests. "The Crows are here."

She continued preparing her pot of tea. She favored the newcomers with a glance and a soft smile. "Welcome."

As they entered the kitchen, they were hit by a warm wave of fragrant spices on the air. Delilah recognized the aroma of freshly ground and brewed medicinal herbs. While they waited, the priestess went about her business, mixing a potent tea, a thin long-handled spoon tinkling brightly against the porcelain lip of the teapot as she slowly stirred in a pinch of this and a dash of that. Delilah could see her lips moving, could just hear the soft breath of speech, but she couldn't make out the incantation.

The tea made, she placed it and a cup and saucer on a tray and turned toward the hallway beyond. "Thank you, Jonathan. I'll take them from here." The chief of security stepped aside. Miss Althea turned to the Crows. "Would you come with me, please?"

With a nod, Delilah motioned for her crew to follow the priestess's lead. "Piper, would you stay with Mr. Markus?"

Piper nodded and took up his watch.

Miss Althea led them down a long hall beyond a number of closed doors, and at the end, they reached a master suite. One of Markus' men stood guard outside the door and opened it at the approach of the priestess.

Behind the door, Delilah was quite surprised to find Mr. Washington himself. He was perched quietly in a chair beside the bed. Beneath the covers, a middle-aged black man slept, and Mr. Washington sat with him in silence like a visitor in the ICU.

The sleeping man's mouth hung open, dry and pale. His breathing was slow and deep, his body deflated, the sleep of pure exhaustion. A long garland of meticulously woven greenery hung over the headboard from the wall, its tail draping down to wrap the full distance around each post, forming a closed square around the bed. At the bedside table, a cone of incense expelled a thin ribbon of blue-gray smoke into the dim lamplight like a tiny volcano.

The room had a feeling of sickness to it that no herbs or incense could keep fully at bay. It was a confined stuffiness more than an odor. A staleness of the air. Oppressive. Still. Like the dead air in a musty basement. The claustrophobic closeness of a closed casket. None of the priestess's efforts seemed to brighten it.

The bed-ridden man was battered and scarred. Old wounds. Old gang tats. There was a little bit of gray at his temples. He was shirtless, and the covers were pulled down to his belly, revealing the battle-scarred chest of a man lucky to be alive several times over. A garland of woven greenery similar to the one that encircled his sick bed was draped around his neck, spilling over his bare chest.

The Crows stepped inside, and Delilah motioned for them to hang back, to keep a respectful distance. Hovering near the door, they waited and watched as the priestess continued on.

"He's sleeping," Mr. Washington noted when Althea arrived at the bedside.

The priestess nodded. "Good." She set the tray down on the nightstand and poured a cup, offering it to Mr. Washington. He accepted it with a distracted smile and took a small sip, cradling the warm vessel in both hands.

Miss Althea turned to the bed then and laid a gentle hand on the stricken man's brow. She closed her eyes and for several long seconds seemed to measure him in silent concentration.

Mr. Washington looked tired, nearly as haggard and worn as the poor man laid out in the sickbed. His face was hard and stoic, but his eyes showed his fatigue and concern. Delilah got the picture. Mr. Washington and this man had a long history. One didn't rise to the ranks of O.G. and beyond with very many friends from back-in-the-day who were still drawing breath. The bullet points of that story were written on Dante Washington's face as he sat quietly at his friend's bedside.

Not exactly what Delilah had been expecting.

Business was business, but the scene before her left no doubt that this business was also very personal for Mr. Washington. That was a customer not likely to be tolerant of fuck ups.

At length, Mr. Washington set his teacup aside and took a break from his vigil while Althea tended to his friend. He introduced himself to the newcomers.

There was something peculiar about a man who was a giant in reputation and small in stature. Dante Washington stood no taller than five-foot-seven and was slight and slim. But he had eyes like chips of coal and the wordless confidence of an emperor. You didn't butt heads with a man like Dante Washington. His crown was made of iron, not gold. With street kings, you either got onboard, got out the way, or you got bloody. There wasn't anything else. Beyond the Rolex, the expensive suit, and the man's education, he was still all street.

"Welcome," Mr. Washington said, shaking hands and making the rounds. He had a grip like a machine, and when Dante Washington shook your hand, he looked you in the eye.

Once introductions were made, Delilah nodded toward the sick bed where Miss Althea tended the fallen captain. "What am I looking at here?"

Mr. Washington considered his answer. When he spoke, he smiled, but there was no humor in his voice or adamantine eyes. "Evil, Miss St. John. Do you believe in evil?"

Delilah nodded. "I do."

The details would come, but Delilah got the picture. She motioned for her partner to come up and join her. "Finch, let's see what we've got here."

The experts stepped in, and the Crows got down to business.

35

Delilah asked Miss Althea Gentles the million-dollar question. "What do you think this is?"

Her response was not encouraging. "I don't know."

That caught Delilah off guard. She'd helped secure the Vert Grimoire of Jean Francois Mercier for the priestess. It was a master-work of the Merovingian Discipline, and it was unlikely that Miss Althea would have placed an order for such a product if she wasn't a master of the discipline herself. The Merovingian way had always eluded Delilah. So structured, so precise. She didn't have the right mind for it. But Miss Althea clearly did, all of which meant she was certainly no dabbler or petty amateur. She was the real thing yet even she had no idea what was going down here.

Delilah nodded. She could deal with the hand she'd been dealt. One person's *I don't know* was another person's paycheck, after all. The Crow wasn't here to knit a scarf.

"May I?" she asked, nodding toward the stricken man.

Miss Althea looked to Mr. Washington who gave his approval with a single nod.

Setting her satchel aside but within reach, Delilah moved to the man's bedside and motioned for Finch to take up a position opposite her. "What's his name?"

"Maurice," Mr. Washington replied, then he chuckled. "Silver Dollar."

It was pretty clear that just saying the man's street name brought back a lot of memories for the gangland king. Delilah could relate. At last, she looked to Finch and gave a nod. Taking their time, they began a cautious examination. First of the ward of garland greenery surrounding the bed and then of the man himself.

Silver Dollar was cool to the touch, not feverish. He displayed no fresh wounds, or strange boils or sores. His breath was stale but otherwise unremarkable. Hands and fingers were scarred and tattooed, but otherwise normal. No strange discoloration to his nails, no peculiar marks in his palms. The man was out so deep he was practically comatose. Delilah shined a penlight in each ear, gingerly peeled back each eyelid and inspected each eye, figuring that would wake the man, but it didn't.

His pupils slammed shut against the offending light like bear traps. Delilah wondered if there might have been something behind them that disliked the light. His eyes gave her pause.

His breath was deep and steady, his body limp in exhausted unconsciousness.

Tucking her little penlight away, Delilah turned to her satchel on the bedside table and began to sort through the contents. First, she took out a small vial of water and uncorked it.

"This might be... uncomfortable," she cautioned, turning to Mr. Washington and Miss Althea. Then she dripped a few drops of purified water on Silver Dollar's forehead and lips.

Nothing.

Delilah corked the vial and put it back in her satchel.

Her face contemplative, she sorted through her bag once more and produced a small silver talisman. It looked like an ancient pitted coin, irregular in shape, the markings on its face worn smooth with centuries. With caution, she pressed the coin to the man's forehead.

Nothing.

Placing the coin back into the satchel she withdrew two other items. One was a bracelet of a dozen assorted rune-graven charms. A knot of gold. A circle of silver. A tiny death's head carved from yellowed ivory. A square sliver of old bone etched with blood-red runes. Others. More. She fastened it around her wrist.

The other item was a three-foot-long length of delicate silver chain. She looped that into a coil and handed it to Finch. "Just in case."

Finch gave a crooked smile. "Got it."

"What do you think?" she asked her partner bluntly.

Finch shrugged. "Not Infernal." Unconsciously, he worked the coil of fine silver chain between his thumb and forefinger like a penitent man saying a Rosary. He looked to Miss Althea. "How long ago did this happen?"

"About three hours ago."

Finch nodded then looked to Delilah.

Delilah plucked at the garland of woven greenery. "You work fast."

"I was prepared," Miss Althea replied.

I'm sure you were, Delilah thought but kept it to herself. The priestess had ordered the Vert Grimoire of Jean Francois Mercier because she'd been expecting an attack. Delilah wondered just how much of that concern she'd actually shared with her boss.

"Does he ever wake up?" Delilah asked.

"On occasion."

"What does he do when he's awake?"

"Laughs, cries, mutters and swears. Marginally responsive. It's difficult to be certain if he's even aware that anyone is in the room with him. Like a man dreaming."

"He sounds like a schizophrenic strung out on dust," Mr. Washington said, his tone blunt.

Delilah asked the indelicate question. "Is he?"

"No. He doesn't even drink anymore."

Delilah tugged at the blessed garland of woven greenery, motioned toward the incense. That was not the Merovingian Way. That work had elder Pagan roots. Much older, much simpler, but no less powerful. Lavender, Artemisia, Goldenrod, and Sage. Root of Rue and Fox Grape. Meticulously and beautifully woven on a braid of hempen twine. Stitched into the garland at irregular but obviously calculated intervals were raw chips of sparkling quartz. Miss Althea was a practitioner of many disciplines, it seemed. And she was damn good. "Has any of this helped?"

The priestess was honest. "No."

Delilah looked to Finch, but he was at a loss. His eyes told her what she needed to know. There was no smoking gun here.

No flashing neon sign. This could be any of a thousand possible awful things. They were going to have to push.

Thoughts of the intel they'd gotten from Mahri about Felipe and his dabbling in the Outer Darkness pinged across Delilah's radar. If that was true, then the potential horrors at work here were a bottomless abyss. And the edge was fickle and slippery.

"Bear with me," Delilah requested. Then she removed a single slender tallow candle and simple candle holder from the satchel. The candle was old, and hand carved with a hundred tiny suns.

She pulled a matchbox out of her satchel and struck up a single wooden match. She touched the pale flame to the candle wick, and for five seconds, it refused to light. She whispered to it, a gentle pyromantic charm, coaxed it, encouraged it. Then, smoldering with a faint, pulsing ember, the flame took to the wick. "Close the door, please."

Once Miss Althea did, Delilah moved around the other side of the bed and pulled the curtains closed as tightly as she could overlap them, shutting out the purple city glow. She teamed up with Finch, and they went to each window and repeated this process. Then she returned to the bedside, inspecting the candle which was now burning, but just barely.

Satisfied, she turned out the bedside lamp, plunging the room into darkness.

The only light came from the small, pale candle flame.

As the darkness deepened, the light of the candle flame grew. A barely smoldering ember rose to a birthday candle glimmer. Then rose to the height and brilliance of a lantern wick.

Stark shadows slanted across the room—and across Silver Dollar—monochrome and sharp.

Delilah moved back to the bedside and leaned over the man, placing a hand on his brow and inspecting his face once more in the granite edges of the eerie candlelight.

For a full minute, there was nothing.

Then Silver Dollar's eyes popped open. They flooded with inky blackness.

"Shit," Delilah muttered.

Shadows, lightless black, exploded from Silver Dollar like a grenade blast.

36

The man let out an inhuman howl and sprang off the bed, defying gravity. He lurched forward in a swarm of ropey shadows. Strong hands grabbed Delilah by the face and tendrils of living shadow enveloped her. In a spinning heap, Delilah and Silver Dollar went crashing to the floor. Clawing at her face and body, Silver Dollar and his hungry shadow aura washed over her like the smothering tentacles of a kraken.

"Maglo et tun'y-eth," Silver Dollar snarled, nose to nose with her in the nimbus of writhing shadows. *"Maglo ar khun!"*

With silken, oily pressure, the shadow tendrils probed at every orifice. Mouth, ears, nose, slithering up between her legs and down the crack of her ass. Groping and twisting, looking for a way in. They pressed painfully against old scars. They pried on her teeth like rubbery fingers.

"Maglo kath ruun. Huath un dir, fingrab naglo carcureth," Silver Dollar's lips brushed her cheek as he whispered alien nonsense. *"Maglo et tun'y-eth."*

Delilah St. John was no easy prey. The wards inked into her skin tightened and stung. One of the charms on her wrist began to smolder like a red coal, nipping her in hot little bites. The metaphysical pressure of her defenses kept the violating tendrils at bay. For the moment.

The bedroom door shivered, and the windows rattled in their frames as some unseen force slammed against them.

Dodger and Finch sprang to Delilah's aid with shouts of alarm. The writhing halo of shadowy tendrils swelled and reared up at their approach like a nest of angry serpents. It whipped and snapped, hammering each of them back with wounded grunts.

Miss Althea pressed herself between Dante Washington and the howling, thrashing entity, wide-eyed, raising a warding hand before her.

Desperate, fighting, choking, gagging, Delilah pressed her will against the candle.

The flame screamed to welding arc brilliance. The swell of shimmering light gave off an audible crystalline whine.

Silver Dollar shrieked and scampered aside like a frantic crab, reeling and dodging away from the blinding aura of light as it burned through the room. The writhing man-thing roared a high-pitched wail, and slammed into the darkened corner, cratering the drywall. His writhing nest of shadow tendrils shrank and climbed into the darkness toward the ceiling, building, rebounding, dragging the man's flailing body up the wall like a puppet on gruesome strings.

"Get out!" Delilah shouted, taking the momentary respite to roll the opposite direction and stagger to her feet. No one listened. Dodger sprang forward again, and Finch uncoiled the silver chain, repeating Delilah's warning to run to Mr. Washington and his priestess.

Mr. Washington grabbed the door handle while Miss Althea stood between him and the roaring shadow-thing. The door didn't budge. On the far side, Mr. Washington's security team could be heard, shouting, hammering, pounding. But the door was sealed shut.

The shadowy fiend boiling from Silver Dollar's flesh howled an alien, unearthly roar.

Dodger threw himself between Delilah and Silver Dollar as she back peddled and retreated. Shadows coiling, massing, Silver Dollar leaped from the corner like a hungry spider, the writhing black aura exploding to massive proportions. The swell of power drove the burning light back, whittling it down to a pale silver glow. With whipping tendrils and fists, the thing blew through Dodger in a blink, pitching him aside like a ragdoll.

Frantic, Delilah dove across the bed and snatched the candle from the end table, hitting the floor on the far side in an awkward roll.

Silver Dollar cleared the bed in a single bound and bore down on her, halo of snapping black tentacles whipping the room like a tornado.

Brandishing the blazing candle before herself like a sword, Delilah squeezed her eyes shut and barked a staccato phrase of command. A bomb blast of white light filled the room with an audible clap, a sound loud enough in the confines of the bedroom to leave ears ringing like a gunshot. The brilliant peal cracked the nearest window above Delilah's head.

The blast sheared the writhing shadow mass from Silver Dollar's form and sent the man crumpling to the floor in a boneless heap. The snarling shadowy specter scuttled away, up the walls, onto the ceiling like an octopus in manic escape.

Delilah's hand was numb from the power of the blast. Spots danced before her eyes. Her ears were ringing. The shadowy thing hissed and snarled and darted along the ceiling with the liquid grace of flames and the speed of a great scuttling spider.

Like a black arrow, it tore loose from the ceiling and speared its way back into Silver Dollar's body, burrowing down his throat, peeling through the scars on his bare back with vicious speed. Inky black tendrils wriggled their way into his nose, his mouth, his ears, through his skin, up his ass. They drew no blood, but it certainly couldn't be said they caused no harm.

The man screamed, a wail of fear and pain. His body convulsed in electric jolts.

By degrees, the clinging shadow disappeared. In five seconds of raping violation, it vanished entirely, a final tendril snaking its way down Silver Dollar's throat and out of sight.

The possessed man gave off a hungry growl and pushed himself up to his hands and knees. His eyes had gone eight-ball-black, and the oily living shadow was wriggling from his eye sockets like worms made of molten tar.

Finch sprang forward, long silver chain in hand. Sliding on his knees to Silver Dollar's side, he grabbed the man by the hair, yanked his head back, and hastily looped the chain around his neck like a cowboy roping a calf. As he twined the chain around the stricken man's neck, an incantation of binding flew from his lips in a hurried growl, rising in a crescendo as the chain began to tighten of its own accord. *"Hannatu uatae, hannatu uatae. Kempoi e'calovistae. Hannatu. Hannatu..."*

Silver Dollar bucked and kicked, snarling and gnashing his teeth like an animal, but Finch held on, the intonation of his spell carrying through at a deliberate and methodical pace. An inhuman growl of protest rumbled deep and alien from somewhere in Silver Dollar's chest. Then it was silent. The man's body went slack, he sagged, crumpling to the floor. The brilliance of the candle flame dimmed from welding arc white to pale yellow once more. Finch released his grip on the tail of the chain and fell back on his ass with a relieved sigh.

The room was stunned silence. Finch let out a chuckle. Then a great tendril of shadow erupted from Silver Dollar's back, snatching Finch around the shoulders like a cracking whip. With a jerk, it heaved him across the room. He bounced off the floor and rebounded into the wall with a windless whiplash grunt.

"Finch!" Delilah screamed.

Silver Dollar exploded from the floor and clung to the ceiling like a bug. His neck took on a boneless quality and his head twisted around like the head of an owl. The silver collar around his neck hissed and burned, blistering his flesh. Inky tendrils tried to escape his throat, to blossom and take form beyond his body, but they were restrained, writhing madly in his mouth, lashing out in ones and twos from his torso. The chain stretched and strained with an audible high-pitched keening.

Then Miss Althea interceded.

"Stop!" she commanded in a booming voice, firm and authoritative.

Silver Dollar hissed and growled at her, scuttling backward along the ceiling, his joints hinging and unhinging grotesquely. It made him look like a gargantuan insect. A nest of oily black tendrils quivered in his throat and mouth as he hissed, joining their thin, papery voices with the hellish chorus.

There was a little silver knife in Miss Althea's left hand, and with a quick stroke, she slashed it across her right palm. Clenching her bloodied hand into a fist, she began shaking it in broad strokes at the ghoulish man-thing crawling along the ceiling. Her blood flew in tiny crimson droplets, like casting holy water from an aspergillum at Mass.

The beast flinched and roared.

The chain binding it continued to stretch and burn.

"Back!" Miss Althea commanded. "Back! Back! Back!" With each word, she blessed the creature in her own life's blood and with each red slash, it retreated with a pained flinch. Stroke by stroke, Miss Althea drove the thing down the wall, joints hinging and unhinging, head lolling sickeningly.

With a final chorus of snarls, Silver Dollar crawled back into bed, a surreal sight like watching the whole event unfold in reverse. The hissing tendrils retreated down his throat. He laid down.

"*Maglo. Maglo imbabue. Maglo ar khun,*" he whispered. Then closed his eyes. He was still. The binding chain stopped sizzling against his flesh, and at last, it went slack around his neck.

Miss Althea's legs wobbled under the strain, and she sank to her knees, clinging to the footboard of the bed to keep from collapsing entirely. Her slashed palm left a red smear on the comforter.

The room was silent, lit only by the faint flickering of Delilah's ceremonial candle.

"Jesus Christ!" Finch coughed, fighting to get his wind back.

"Are you okay?" Delilah asked, feeling a little stunned.

Finch nodded but decided the floor was a fine place to be for the time being.

She looked to the shivering priestess. "You?"

Miss Althea nodded.

Shaken and bell-rung, Delilah leaned back against the wall and let out a quivering breath. "Well shit," she muttered. "Way to go, A-team." To her left, Dodger was in the process of scooping his ass up off the floor. "You okay?"

He grunted an affirmative response. Like Finch, he was gonna feel that in the morning.

Wide-eyed and mesmerized, Mr. Washington huddled against the wall by the door.

The entity's hold on the door failed then, and the security team came shattering through in a clatter. Markus and two of his men burst into the room, guns drawn, faces taut, and Piper was right on their heels. Dim light spilled in with them from the hallway beyond. Miss Althea raised a bloodied hand, shaking her head, staying them.

With vibrating hands, Delilah fished a pack of smokes from her jacket pocket and tried to regain her composure. Sticking the butt in her mouth, she lit it with the pale flame of the still burning candle. When the cherry glowed, she took a drag and blew the candle out.

Delilah looked up at the confused security chief and his men. "Do you, uh, wanna get the lights?"

Then she sat there and smoked her cigarette.

Mute confusion came into the room with the growing crowd. Nobody knew what to say. No one except for Mr. Washington, that was.

He cleared his throat, straightened his jacket and gave a single nod. "Thank you."

Anytime, Delilah thought grimly. Then she tested the strange word on her own tongue, a soft, reverent whisper. *"Maglo."* It didn't mean anything to her ... yet. But it would. *Holy shit, what have we gotten ourselves into here?*

37

Gabriel parked the big red Tahoe at the curb on Bixel Street off Temple, not far from where the 101 and the 110 slammed together west of Downtown. The trio dismounted and headed south on foot and Gabriel and Twitch each had a smoke while they walked. Gabriel was in the lead, Twitch brought up the rear, and Mahri was between them.

The block was mostly squatty apartment buildings and raggedy duplexes with bars on the windows. The sidewalks were narrow and lined with wrought iron fences. Ill-kept hedges and wiry palm brush overhung them in stretches, leaning into the path. Working street lamps were few and far between, so darkness magnified the threatening claustrophobia of the brushy sidewalks and crowded curbs. Empty parking spaces along the street were rare, each gap sticking out like a missing tooth.

At the bottom of Bixel and Court, they passed a neighborhood mural on the wall of a local market. The north half of the mural was Aztec-inspired: pyramids, figures in traditional dress, and a prominently displayed blue diamond bigger than a basketball. The artist's nod to being on Diamond Street turf. The south half of the mural was all mariachis and villagers, dancing and celebrating. Our Lady of Guadalupe, life-sized and center stage, divided the two eras in peaceful prayer.

Across the street was a neighborhood basketball goal, and industrious kids kept court lines chalked onto the asphalt beneath it—but nobody was on the street shooting hoops at this hour.

They crossed Court Street, turned for a block, and then

ducked down a long, narrow alley. The walls on either side were tagged with Diamond Street *placas*. Up ahead were lights, and rapper Big Pun could be heard knocking out beats through a car stereo.

"You don't wander off," Gabriel warned, throwing a glance back at Twitch.

"Roger that," Twitch replied. No doubt, he understood this was a bad place for a random ginger-headed white kid to get lost.

The alley opened up at the cul-de-sac parking lot of an old apartment building, and the lot was hopping. Music was thumping, and there were neighborhood locals everywhere. It was a straight-up *cholo* block party, and the Crows weren't invited. Their arrival drew some attention.

One young man, perched on the bumper of a nearby lowrider Ranchero, waved them down. He was short and stout and covered in jailhouse ink. He smiled like he was happy to see them and called out to Gabriel over the music. "You get lost, *ese?*"

The little raven-haired *chica* on his hip laughed.

Gabriel said nothing. Instead, he noticed an older man across the way look up and shake his head at the young buck. *Leave that one alone,* the gesture said. Gabriel didn't recognize him, but the man recognized Gabriel. It was enough for them to pass in peace into the old apartment building. From there they went through the breezeway, and into the center yard where the Couatl was keeping court for the night.

Once upon a time, some fool had dug a pool in back there. But that was long filled in, and now, it was more like a garden. Palms and brush, crabgrass, sandy turf, and chipped concrete. Here and there, huge flowers bloomed burgundy and gold, hanging heavy on fibrous vines.

Seated at the far end of the small brushy courtyard on a concrete throne was the Couatl; a jaguar, big, lean, and strong, lounged at her bare feet, as if that sort of thing were normal for the rough side of a bad neighborhood in L.A. The cat watched with intelligent emerald eyes as the Crows approached. She was attended by twenty retainers, most of them young and male. Torches burned in the yard, rather than lamps or lights, throwing long shadows that swayed and stretched as the night breeze stirred the vines and palm brush.

The Couatl was petite and bronze-skinned, with long, braided hair the color of blood. Shimmering feathers of red and gold were woven into her braid. Turquoise and gold circled her wrists and long, graceful neck. She wore an ankle-length mink coat, cut-off jean shorts—and nothing else. Her bare midriff could be seen between the furry lapels of the coat along with a large diamond stud in her belly button and the faintest curve of her bare breasts. However, the big, audacious coat left most of her to the imagination, and none of that was by accident. The Couatl was notorious for toying with what she considered men's poor little pea-brains, and nothing derailed the average goon faster than showing a little skin.

Gabriel, with no desire to become dinner, and the good sense to know better, was not so easily derailed. Even after she'd suggestively uncrossed her legs and leaned forward, allowing the turquoise necklace to slide down her cleavage like a silky blue landslide. In the torchlight, her skin had the faintest golden sheen, like head-to-toe body glitter, both gossamer and fine.

"Gabriel the Crow," the Couatl purred. Her accent was definitely south of the border with a hint of L.A. street.

Gabriel inclined his head in a respectful bow.

The Couatl got right down to business. "What tribute do you bring me?"

Gabriel reached a hand into his jacket and produced two items in offering: a single gold coin and a cigarette. She motioned for him to come forward. The big cat at her right hand watched him intently but didn't lift its head as he approached her throne.

He bent low and lit the cigarette for her, then passed her the gold coin. Once she'd taken both the coin and the first drag from her smoke, Gabriel withdrew to a respectful distance.

With small, graceful fingers, she turned the coin, face and tail, inspecting it, then it disappeared up her sleeve with the barest of gestures.

"Why does the Crow speak to me tonight?" she asked.

Gabriel didn't mince words. "I'm looking for Felipe Ortiz. And word is, he came to you."

The Couatl reclined on her throne a hand wandering down to scratch her big cat between the ears while she considered that. "Why are you looking for Felipe?" she asked.

"Business," Gabriel replied.

The Couatl nodded and looked past Gabriel's shoulder to his other companions. "I don't know you," she said, her gaze flickering dismissively over Twitch before moving on.

To his credit, the young militiaman gave a respectful nod and held his tongue.

"You, however," the Couatl said, her dark eyes fixing on Mahri. "Miss Mahri Ramirez, yes?"

Mahri offered a short, courteous bow. "Yes."

The Couatl cocked a slender blood-red eyebrow. "Interesting. Very interesting." But she didn't elaborate. She motioned to one of her retainers—a pretty young man in casual street clothes. He wore a large opal ring on his right hand, and his hair was pulled back in a meticulously combed black ponytail—he came to his queen's side and bent in low so she could speak to him in confidence.

Then he took off into the decrepit old apartment building, stepping with urgency.

The Couatl smiled but said nothing. She wasn't big on small talk.

Was that good or bad? Gabriel couldn't tell, and the Couatl wasn't likely to let on. A long, tense minute or so later, her retainer returned with another handsome young man trailing behind him.

Felipe Ortiz was just pulling on his jacket as he rounded the corner into the garden courtyard.

He saw Gabriel and his companions at the same instant they saw him. Everyone froze.

"Felipe paid me one hundred thousand dollars—cash—for a safe place to catch his breath," the Couatl explained while the man stood, slack-jawed, not twenty feet away. His eyes widened in shock, darting around the confined courtyard like a mouse desperate to evade the cat. She turned to Gabriel. "Is he worth more than that to you?"

Gabriel didn't hesitate to answer. He grinned, a wolfish, predatory expression reminiscent of his father. "You bet. And I pay in gold." He knew what the lady liked.

The Couatl's ruby lips twisted into a mischievous smile. "*Orale.*"

"Shit," Felipe wheezed. Then he threw up his hand and slashed it across the air while Gabriel went for his gun.

38

Everything happened in about two seconds.

The air around Felipe's slashing hand bent with a light-less shimmer, like ripples in a pond. When his hand cut back the other way, it was clutching a dagger-like shard of jagged, pitted iron.

Gabriel's Sig broke clear of its holster and came up in both hands, its muzzle tracking for Felipe.

Felipe barked out a commanding cry as he thrust the shimmering ancient dagger shard out before him. *"Maglo Ar Khun!"*

The lightless aura exploded into a soundless shockwave.

Ripples ran over the gathered retainers, kicking up dust, slapping the palms, and sending them swaying and snapping. Some of the retainers staggered, others fell.

The shockwave reached Gabriel a split second before his muzzle found Felipe.

Then the world turned upside down, and Gabriel found himself wallowing in the crabgrass and dirt, with the defensive wards of his tattoos burning and numb.

His ringing ears flooded with a thousand corrupt whispers. *Maglo... Maglo... Maglo et tun'y-eth...*

He pushed the slithering noise out of his head and dragged himself to his hands and knees with a growl, looking across the courtyard, searching for Felipe. His vision threatened to somersault, but he kept it together long enough to see the little shit sprinting away, retreating back through the apartment building.

Gabriel lurched to his feet, grinding his teeth against the

disorientation and creeping numbness of the phantom whispers. He raised his gun in his shaky hands, but there was no shot as Felipe disappeared around the corner into the gloom.

All around Gabriel, the Couatl's retainers were stumbling, staggering, crawling. The Couatl herself, however, remained anchored to her throne, unmoved. Her eyes were closed, her face set as if willing away an unpleasant thought or bad dream.

With Felipe escaping, Gabriel spun to check on his companions.

Mahri was on her knees, holding a hand to the side of her head as if she'd taken a bell-ringing blow and young Twitch was out cold in the dirt along with half of the Couatl's retainers. Mahri knelt beside him, a hand on his shoulder, trying to steady herself as much as him.

Then, more of the Couatl's men were coming into the courtyard, drawn by the commotion, and one of them had a gun.

One of the Couatl's retainers let out a blood-curdling, maniacal shriek, *"MAGLO AR KHUN!"* His fingernails dug furrows down his own cheeks, and with a snarl, he leaped toward the newcomer who held the pistol.

There were screams, shouts, and the crazed man was snarling and howling, fighting like a rabid baboon while groping for the gun. Four of the Couatl's men piled on him, trying to wrangle him under control. He was all they could handle.

Then a second retainer began to shriek. *"Maglo!"* he cried. *"Maglo et tun'y-eth!"*

The Couatl's eyes snapped open, freeing herself from the meditation she'd been under as protection from Felipe's spell. She had the emerald eyes of a serpent. Or perhaps, a dragon.

While half a dozen of the Couatl's men battled with the first spell-struck madman, the second waded into the screaming mosh pit from behind. The knife from his belt was now in his hand, and he went straight to using it.

His sliver of white steel slashed and jabbed and people began to cry out as they were cut.

Then a single gunshot barked from the dogpile, and a man howled in pain as an accidental discharge sent a slug through his ankle. Things were getting out of hand, fast.

Furious, the Couatl barked orders to her jaguar, and like a light switch, it went from sleepy to on the prowl, taking off in a blur of gold and black after Felipe.

By then, the Couatl was on her feet, her serpent's eyes blazing with anger. A spell flew from her lips at a commanding pace as she raised her arms and bent her will against the mess Felipe had left behind. As her hands rose overhead, the red and gold feathers in her braid prickled and flared out, like an enraged tropical bird on an angry strut. Matching feathers slid from beneath her bronze skin to encircle her wrists and her waist, drawing up her bare midriff in a line.

Twitch, stunned, opened his eyes. "What the fuck?" he snorted in amazement.

Another scream and more chaos as other retainers tried to wrestle the knife-wielding maniac under control. Shoving, pushing, cussing, screaming. Men piling on top of each other.

The jaguar disappeared down the breezeway and into the darkness.

Gabriel had a choice to make. So he made it.

"Get out of here! Now!" he barked at his stricken companions. Then he took off in the direction in which he'd seen Felipe and the jaguar disappear.

Ten flying paces and the darkness beyond the outer breezeway swallowed him.

He ran past a row of garbage cans and spilled out into a high, narrow alley between rows of apartment buildings where the only light came from the windows above and the purple sky overhead.

He caught sight of the big cat as it loped ahead and disappeared around a darkened corner. With no time to hesitate or think too much about it, he followed at a sprint with gun in hand.

Just before he reached the corner, there was a flash of eldritch light and a sharp electric crackle like a transformer overloading. It was followed by a howl—an inhuman feline scream of pain—the great cat crying out as though something had hurt it badly.

Then the alley plunged back into darkness.

That slowed Gabriel's roll.

He fetched up short of the corner, and his pistol came up. His pulse hammered in his ears. The adrenaline gave him tunnel vision but made his night eyes sharp.

He took a breath…two…then he cut the corner and cleared it into the next alley. His muzzle scanned left and right and found a dead end. No doors. Just barred windows about a foot above head level and three-story rooftops.

A naked young man was fetched up against the back wall of the dead-end alley, quivering, clutching his belly with bloody forearms. While Gabriel watched, the last few inches of the jaguar's tail melted away into coccyx.

His eyes had blown from their sockets, and as the seconds passed, fresh wounds bloomed black beneath his skin and began weeping blood. Whatever spell had felled him, it left him in broken ruins. He moaned and coughed up gore while gray ropes of intestines pressed through his bloody embrace with the pressure of his hacking.

Nothing else. No Felipe in sight.

Gabriel didn't buy it. Cautiously, he backed away from the dead-end alley, eyes scanning. "You still here, Felipe?" Gabriel whispered.

Nothing.

"Come on," Gabriel taunted in a low, drawn-out tone. "Let's see what you got. Poke your head out. Take your best shot. Let's see who's faster." The wreckage of the mutilated shifter was a grim warning, but Gabriel wasn't easy prey. He'd take his chances in a head-to-head brawl with the likes of Felipe Ortiz.

A few heartbeats later, the gutted shifter fell silent and died, wheezing a final, blood-soaked exhalation.

A garbage can banged ten feet to Gabriel's left making his attention snap that way on instinct.

Then something fast and invisible blew past him on his right, darting into the open alley once more, taking advantage of the split-second distraction.

Gabriel spun back around to the right, tracking the invisible presence, content in that moment to fan a mag down the empty alley and hope for the best.

"Felipe, stop!" he shouted. But nothing. No response. Gabriel was a half second away from opening fire when there was a scrape in the dead-end alley behind him. He turned back, just in time to see the dead shifter rising drunkenly to its feet.

"Shit," Gabriel grunted.

The shifter looked up, and its empty eye sockets lit with pale, hungry white light—a cold, merciless radiance like stars in a black sky.

It worked its mouth, slurping blood. *"Maglo et tun'y-eth,"* it gurgled.

Then it charged, lurching forward.

Gabriel back-pedaled and lined up two shots: *Boom-Boom.* The muzzle strobed like a camera flash in the dark alley; the reports flat and hard. The first round hit the thing in the forehead, the second in the cheek, but it didn't even break stride.

Now it really had Gabriel's attention. Fading back towards the Couatl's compound, he retreated, skipping fast, to put space between him and the lumbering creature. His pistol went back in the holster, but his knife came out, and his trot turned into a run as the creature with the glowing white eyes picked up the pace and gained on him.

Gabriel managed to keep the thing at a distance while he prepared his workings. His mind was moving fast, and his body tried to keep up. The creature was closing in, picking up speed.

Knife in hand, Gabriel pulled the flask from his breast pocket and poured honey-thick oil over the blade. He screwed the cap back on the flask, dropped it back in his pocket, switched his knife into his other hand, and drew his cigarette lighter. Then he stopped, held his ground, lit it, and whispered a pyromantic charm as the flames licked the dripping oil.

The oil caught, lighting the blade with a brilliant golden radiance, swelling and redoubling until it blazed in Gabriel's hand like a torch.

The creature paused, cocked its head to the side. A disturbingly curious expression for a mangled corpse with burning white eyes.

"Yeah," Gabriel grunted, bringing the blazing knife to bear, lips peeling back from his teeth in a Viking snarl. "Come on, motherfucker."

Then they bore down on each other, twisting and battling down the narrow alley. The creature swiped and clawed at Gabriel like an enraged zombie. Gabriel ducked and dodged and slashed back with his flaming blade. Lighting jolts of pain flashed through his wounded side with every jerk and movement. Adrenaline and old-fashioned toughness blurred the fish hook sting of it. For now.

When he cut the creature, it burned, and the flames caught in its flesh with the unnatural hunger of his spell.

But, when the creature hit him in return, it fucking hurt, too.

Once the creature was burning from half a dozen good cuts, the alley began to fill with the sweet stench of charred meat.

Twisting and shoving, Gabriel lunged in for the kill—and he missed—the thing caught him by the throat instead, slamming him up against the alley wall with supernatural strength. The impact and the pressure on his throat nearly put his lights out.

Gabriel was only dimly aware of the burning blade slipping from his fingers and clattering to the alley. The creature punched him in the gut, driving the wind from his lungs and kept him pinned to the wall with not an inch to budge.

Then, a nest of oily and awful tentacles wormed up through the skin of the creature's forearm, groping at Gabriel's face.

That slapped Gabriel back to his senses like a bucket of cold water.

Tugging and pulling helplessly at the tentacle-wreathed arm, Gabriel fought. He fought for air, to get blood past the vice-like grip and into his brain, and he fought for his life. He snarled and he kicked—first one foot, then the other, but he couldn't dislodge the creature.

He tried to break the stranglehold, but even when Gabriel heard the creature's bones crack, the pressure didn't lessen. There was something beneath the flesh that was driving the thing. Something that wasn't dependent on muscle and bone. The tentacles wormed and prodded, pushing against his lips, coiling around his neck like a noose.

The creature began lifting him off his feet. Gabriel felt the weight lightening under his heels, even as the edges of his vision began to turn red, then black.

The creature smiled at him, and its bloody mouth was full of tentacles, writhing and rasping.

For Gabriel, sound went first, replaced by his own pulse pounding in his ears. Then went the lights; the last thing Gabriel saw in the collapsing darkness was the white fire of the creature's burning, hungry eyes.

Then he was falling, and in the numbness of his mind, he realized it didn't have a hold of him anymore. He hit the ground with a windless grunt, and blue-white light exploded through his skull.

For a second, everything turned black. Then his head nearly popped off his shoulders once the blood and air started flowing again. With the rushing return of consciousness came the fiery vengeance of his various injuries. The gash in his side was wet and warm beneath the bandages and the staples bit at him like tiny fangs.

He gasped and sputtered and recognized Mahri's voice above the shrieking howls of the burning corpse-thing.

Commanding, demanding, Mahri fought like hell, hexing the creature back, down, and away from Gabriel. Her hands slashed at the air as she pulled on the invisible threads of her spell. The creature retreated, bucking and writhing like a puppet fighting for control of its own strings.

Mahri did not relent; in just a few seconds, she was as much in control of the thing's body as it was.

It twisted and collapsed to its hand and knees, dragging itself towards a nearby storm drain.

Punchdrunk, but seizing the moment, Gabriel scooped up the burning knife, lurched to his feet, and bore down on the creature while Mahri could still hold it – to finish it off before it could escape.

Mahri heaved, and the thing rose up, trying to stand so it could fling itself closer to the drain. She wrenched it back like yanking on the reins of a horse, holding it for one last second.

Gabriel lunged past, flaming blade leading the way like a

plunging comet and with a furious cry, he buried the knife to the hilt between the creature's shoulder blades.

Its body went as stiff as a board, and something in the spell that held it together broke under Gabriel's willful, fiery strike.

There was no blood, just a burst of cold, white fire mixed with the hot, golden flame. Then a flood of black ooze spilled out of the wound, promptly igniting, and it began to burn away in greasy, foul tar smoke.

Gabriel kicked and shoved and wrenched the withering, blackened knife from the creature's back, the spellfire on his blade exhausted. Its knees unhinged, and as it collapsed, its host body ignited like a flash of gunpowder. The entire thing vaporized into swirling ash before it hit the ground.

The fires flared and went out, plunging the alley back into darkness, awash in dying eddies of fading orange embers.

Gabriel looked to Mahri and found her as wide-eyed and awe-struck as he was himself.

Twitch, urgent, hurried, broke the silence. "Cops, cops!" he hissed.

No time to celebrate, to debrief or to go back and make peace with the Couatl.

They split, dodging the cops and the Couatl's wrath.

39

Twitch drove while Gabriel got his head screwed back on straight. They got on the freeway, blended into the late night traffic, and rolled casually down the highway. Gabriel dropped the ruins of his knife into a plastic zipper bag and tossed the divination crystal from his visit to the busted up cash depot in with it. He was pretty certain all that nasty mojo would lead right back to the same smoking gun—the sliver of jagged iron he'd seen in Felipe Ortiz's hand.

Wrapping up the baggie, Gabriel tucked it into his breast pocket. He was still catching his breath when Delilah rang him up.

"We got problems," she said.

He grunted. "Yeah, no shit. What do you got?"

Delilah laid it for him, and he paid close attention.

"All right. Stay put. I'll be there right now." With a tired sigh, Gabriel hung up.

"What's going on?" Mahri asked, reaching up from the back seat to lay a hand on Gabriel's arm.

"Lots of shit," he replied with a grim frown, but he didn't elaborate.

"Where are we headed now?" Twitch asked.

"*You* are going to take her back to the Church," Gabriel instructed Twitch. Mahri looked like she might protest, but Gabriel waved it down. "I've gotta roll for Washington Enterprises, ground zero. There's a clusterfuck we gotta sort out. We do *not* want Washington's people to know we've got you just yet. Right?"

Reluctantly, Mahri nodded.

"It's bad enough that Felipe knows, and he got away. Best thing you can do is go back to the Church and lay low until we figure out what happens next."

Mahri didn't argue.

Gabriel turned to Twitch. "Drop me off up here. I'll take a cab. I don't want her anywhere near Washington's crew just yet."

Twitch hesitated. "And leave you, captain-my-captain? You said nobody rides alone. You gonna make me explain that to Dodger?"

"Yeah, well. Do as I say, not as I do. I'll be fine. You worry about your own ass. Why don't you call Gator? Get him up to the Church to back you up."

"Oh. Gator got stabbed by his old lady a couple days ago."

Gabriel cocked an eyebrow. "Stabbed dead?"

"No. Stabbed in the ass. They made up. They're fine. But he's face down for a few days."

Gabriel nodded. "Good to know. Grizz, then?"

"Yeah. I'll call him." Twitch was quiet until they caught an exit and he pulled into a gas station. "You sure you're okay alone? Because Dodger's gonna whip my ass for it."

"Hey, I run this show. It's my call. I'll be at the Church in the morning taking care of business. Beat it, little brother. I'll be fine." He looked over his shoulder at Mahri. "Take her home."

Twitch accepted his marching orders and nodded as Gabriel turned to exit the car with a pained wince. Everything hurt. Again.

Mahri grabbed his hand before he could get out.

"Be careful," she said, fixing Gabriel with a worried and exhausted expression of her own.

"You too," Gabriel said. "And ... thanks." She'd saved his ass back there when she should have been running away. It gave a guy a lot to think about.

To that, Mahri only nodded in silence.

Then they went their separate ways for the night.

40

Gabriel arrived at The Hyde around one in the morning, and there, he circled his Crows around Washington's table for some executive decision making.

First was security. Miss Althea and talent on loan from the Crow would stay with Silver Dollar in shifts of two around the clock. He was never to be left alone without one of them nearby. There were a lot of awful, hateful things that touched the mortal world, and his condition was still more mystery than managed. Even after that gruesome display, they still had more questions than answers—but one thing was for certain—if he got out of hand like that again, none of Mr. Washington's street soldiers or security contractors would be able to stop him.

Silver Dollar was a ticking time bomb. It wasn't a matter of if, but when, and the only answer was to exorcise whatever the hell had infested him and send it back where it belonged.

All things in due time.

"So, he was attacked then?" Mr. Washington asked, but it was more statement than question.

"No," Delilah replied, drawing a host of curious stares, Miss Althea included. She shrugged. "He wasn't attacked. He's... *stained*. He got too close to something awful and got a little on him. More like an infection."

"Attacked, infected, stained. Is there a difference?" Mr. Washington asked.

"Yeah," Delilah replied simply.

"How do you know that?" Miss Althea asked, cradling her freshly bandaged hand in her lap.

Delilah deferred to her captain before answering, and

Gabriel nodded his consent. "It's like this. Even people without talent, they've got natural metaphysical defenses. They just don't know it. Like an immune system. The mind and the spirit aren't just wide open. When people are the targets of a metaphysical attack, that immune system reacts. It bristles up and stays bristly. You can feel it on them. It's like armor, needles." She glanced at Finch, and a single nod from him said he agreed. "Whatever happened to your boy in there, he didn't fight it. He's soft as silk."

That went over like a lead balloon at Washington's table.

"I've known that man in there for twenty-five years," Mr. Washington said. "He is not inclined to fuck me. I promise you that."

Delilah held up her hands, not wanting to piss on the boss-man's shoes. "Hey, I'm just telling you what I found. It doesn't *mean* anything. On the flip side, that same immune system that didn't react to the intrusion is now fighting like a bastard against the infection. He's feverish as a bonfire, in a metaphysical sense."

"But?" Mr. Washington asked.

Delilah cleared her throat. "Well. He must have trusted whoever did this to him. He let them in. Now whether or not he was a willing accomplice or got played for a fool, I can't tell you. But if he ever wakes up, you might want to ask him where he's been spending his nights. And maybe if he knows where your money is."

Mr. Washington contemplated that, stretched it, tested it. Clearly, whether he liked it or not didn't affect if he found it plausible. A solemn nod said that he did indeed.

"Are we any closer to understanding who hit my depot?" Mr. Washington asked.

Gabriel gave a bone. "Yeah, we are. Felipe Ortiz."

Mr. Washington cocked a curious eyebrow. "You sound very certain."

"That's because I am. Ninety-nine percent anyway." He wasn't completely though; not yet; but they needed a win. It was the only one he had. It was nothing he couldn't smooth over with a bald-faced lie or two if it turned out being wrong.

Mr. Washington gave a nod. "I'd like to say I'm surprised,

but I'm not. What about the rest of his crew? Mahri, Alex. There was a surfer boy and a little redheaded professional cocksucker too."

"Still working on it," Gabriel reported, and it was mostly true. "Right now, the safe bet is that they're spooked and on the run because their boy Felipe went nuclear. They're scared of him, and they're scared of you. Everything so far points to Felipe being a one-man show, or if he had help, it probably wasn't from his coven."

"What about their master? Doctor Angus McCoy," Washington asked.

"He's dead," Delilah said. "Somebody caught up to him in the last day or two and tortured him to death."

"You'll excuse me if I don't assume that was a coincidence," Mr. Washington replied.

Gabriel nodded. "No, it's related. We just don't know how yet."

"Find out," Mr. Washington said, and it didn't sound like a suggestion.

"So, what is... this?" Miss Althea asked at length, nodding back down the hall toward Silver Dollar's sick room.

Delilah licked her lips and answered honestly. "Stain of the Outer Darkness. It's what the Helitori is hunting for. And they're not wrong. You're gonna have problems with them that aren't going away."

"We'll handle that," Markus assured her.

"I want this cleaned up," Mr. Washington ordered, his tone quiet, but firm.

"We can do it," Delilah assured the group. "But it's going to take some time to put it together. We don't know enough yet. And that's a good way to get killed."

"Or worse," Miss Althea added with a nod of agreement.

"How much time do you need?" Mr. Washington asked.

Delilah bit her lip. "Until we run out of it? I've got some ideas, but we need to get closer to a solution. And that's just going to take some time."

Mr. Washington looked to his priestess. Her stoic expression and a nod indicated that it was a reasonable answer.

"We can rotate out with some of your boys," Piper suggested, gesturing around the table to himself, Dodger, and Gabriel. "Keep an eye on things. Plus up the security around here. Our guys have seen some of this stuff before. Your guys, maybe not so much."

Gabriel deferred to Mr. Washington, who looked to his chief of security, Jonathan Markus. The suggestion received his consent.

"One thing though," Delilah said, speaking up. "He can't stay here. That shit in his head is contagious, and there's gotta be a thousand civilians on this block. Last thing you need is one of them catching the demon clap and going axe murderer in the middle of the street. Or twenty of them."

"What do you suggest?" Markus asked.

"Somewhere remote," Delilah replied. "Nobody around except your people. Somewhere you can control who comes and goes and who passes by. Do you have any dogs?"

"Dogs?" Markus asked, cocking an eyebrow.

"Or cats. Cats are even better. Canary in a cage," Delilah explained. Then she smirked. "Kinda like earthquakes, they usually spot this kind of trouble coming before we do. If something gets out of hand and he starts slipping through our containment, the animals will go apeshit."

"I'll see what I can do," Markus replied. He looked to his boss. "Sweet Valley?"

Mr. Washington nodded.

"What's Sweet Valley?" Gabriel asked.

"A ranch property of mine out in Ravenna," Mr. Washington replied. "Nearest neighbor is two mile sections over, and they're in the Philippines six months out of the year."

"That would do it," Delilah said.

"What happens if Silver Dollar... expires?" Washington asked, tone suggesting he was contemplating unnatural causes.

"Nothing good," Gabriel replied, thinking of the star-eyed corpse that had tried to pull him apart like a fly earlier that night. If he was catching his sister's drift, that freakshow from the alley in Diamond Street didn't have shit on the nuclear bomb laying in the other room.

Delilah shook her head vehemently. "The only thing keeping him contained right now is about ten percent our effort and about ninety percent him not wanting to be turned inside out. He dies, we lose that natural containment and chances are, that thing in him is on the loose in its brand new meat suit."

"Nothing's simple," Mr. Washington remarked, his iron expression unreadable.

"Can you move him?" Delilah asked. "Now?"

Mr. Washington waved his hand and gave Markus a nod. It was a done deal.

Gabriel spoke up. "Piper, Finch. You two stay with Miss Althea, first watch. Help her get Silver Dollar relocated. I'll get some relief rounded up for you in the morning."

"On it. Miss me while I'm gone," Piper replied. He turned to Miss Althea. "You guys got satellite out at the rancho deluxe?"

The priestess cracked a little smile and nodded.

Piper gave his crewmates a shrug. "Take your time."

"In the meantime, the rest of us chase leads," Gabriel said. And there were certainly plenty of them to chase. That was their cue to get back on the road. The hour was late, and before long, it'd be early and time to hit the bricks all over again. This wasn't the kind of job that would wait. The roundtable broke up, and the various gears began to turn.

Delilah grabbed her jacket and huddled briefly with Finch. "You good?"

"I got this," he assured her with a wink.

Delilah gave a grateful smirk, then her expression grew serious. "You be careful."

Finch nodded and sketched a little salute. "Yes, ma'am."

As they gathered up to leave, Mr. Washington handed Gabriel one of his business cards. "My direct dial is on there. Keep me informed of your progress."

The Captain Crow nodded and shook the man's hand, then they headed out. Piper and Finch escorted them to the parking lot.

When they reached the cars, Gabriel struck up a fresh cigarette with a tired sigh. He looked to the talent. "Any advice for the night watch?"

"Don't poke the bear," Delilah replied.

"What do you mean?" Finch asked.

Delilah shrugged. "Just a feeling. Didn't you notice it? The more chaotic everything got, the stronger that thing inside Silver Dollar seemed to get."

Finch inspected the fresh goose egg on the back of his head with his fingertips and winced. Yeah, he got the point. Going head to head with the thing had just about resulted in catastrophe. "So, keep things calm?"

"If we can," Delilah said with a nod. "Use your inside voices, you know?"

They got it.

Gabriel favored Finch with a concerned frown. He looked a little gimpy on his right leg. "You gonna be okay there, Finchy?"

"I'll feel it in the morning," the young sorcerer replied, but he smiled. "I'm good, boss."

Gabriel gestured to Finch and Piper. "Okay, you two keep things locked down here. Wherever Silver Dollar goes, you go. I'll get on the horn in the morning and get some bodies coming in to rotate out." He looked at Finch. "Sure as I leave you here, Pop's gonna want to rally the talent. I need somebody to sit watch on Silver Dollar when you're gone. Izzie?"

Finch nodded. "Yeah, Izzie's good. This is right up her alley."

"All right. It's late, and it's been a very long fucking day. Anyone who isn't staying, go home. Get some rest. Tomorrow will be here before you know it, and there's plenty to do. Questions?" There were none. "Okay, I'm done. Look out for each other tonight."

Piper grinned and pinched Finch on the ass—hard. "I'll make sure nobody breaks his heart, big daddy."

Finch flinched but otherwise took it without expression or reaction. "You got problems, mate."

Gabriel turned to Delilah. "I've got something for you."

"A little piece of Felipe? Because that would be great."

"Next best thing. Well. Things, plural," Gabriel replied. Then he produced his Ziploc baggie full of bad mojo. "A little hair o' the dog. Twice."

She snorted. "And it's not even my birthday."

"Do what you can," Gabriel replied. "Mom can help. And Finchy too when I get him back to you. I need to be able to find the fucker on the other end of this, and he's probably not going to make it easy." He jiggled the baggie. "Chances are all this static points right back toward Felipe. We cannot let him get away."

"I'll get started on it first thing in the morning," Delilah assured him, taking possession of the two nasty relics. Two points of reference was good. Three would be better, but beggars couldn't be choosers. She'd work with what she had.

"Come on," Dodger offered. "I'll give you a ride home, little sister. We'll pick it up after some shut eye."

Gabriel exhaled a plume of smoke through his nostrils with a tired sigh. "All right. That's it. Go home."

And that was that. Finch and Piper went back to Number Six to man the night watch and help collect Silver Dollar as the rest of the Crows rolled out.

41

A head full of speed combined with flashbacks of the day had kept Delilah from getting any real sleep. Dancing with the devil at Dante Washington's safe house hadn't helped matters any. That corruption, that taint, that malevolent darkness, it had a way of sticking to you until the sun came up and chased it away. She couldn't even pee without feeling it shoving its way between her legs or take a sip of water without the sensation of it trying to burrow down her throat. It would pass, she knew, when the sun came up. The other ghosts of the day though... those were going to be a lot harder to lay to rest.

Two of her friends had died, and she'd watched it happen from front row center. She and her brother had talked about that before. The way the weight of that just sort of sits in the middle of your belly and never seems to go away. How the memories of fighting for your life would creep up on you without warning, grab you by the back of the hair, and send your heart galloping all over again. Talking about it hadn't really prepared her for when her turn finally came though. The life and death reality of the day hit her like a ton of bricks anyway. That night she found herself tearing up a couple of times, but couldn't say she was feeling any sort of emotion at all really. Just numb. She supposed that was normal.

All things being equal, it'd been a right shitty week.

Her father's slogan came to mind: *If it was easy, anybody could do it.*

Sleep was hard to come by, but she didn't even really try.

Not for Dodger, though. He crashed in her spare bedroom

and slept like the dead. That gnarly Marine could sleep anywhere, any time.

Sleep being stubborn, and the night full of phantoms, Delilah embraced the tweaker stereotype and cleaned. It was cathartic, and frankly, her house was a wreck. It needed it.

She had a lot to think about. The puzzle in front of her was big, full of those tiny, shitty little pieces, and she was still missing about half of them.

The Helitori's accusations were real. She'd seen the stain of the Outer Darkness on Silver Dollar with her own eyes, and the man hadn't fought it until it had shoved a black tentacle up his ass and turned him into a finger puppet. Whether he'd been a willing disciple or a dumb ass rube remained to be seen. Either way, he was a fucking idiot for playing with the plutonium.

Maglo.

The word crawled back and forth across her brain with the lacy legs of a spider. Left and right. Forward and back. There was something familiar about it. But she couldn't put her finger on it.

She and Gabriel hadn't had much of an opportunity to debrief, but what'd she'd gotten so far added to that hollow ball in the bottom of her stomach. Grief? Is that what it was? She didn't know. All the wounds were still so fresh, and honestly, she didn't know how she was supposed to feel about all of this. She scrubbed the sink and didn't dwell on it.

Felipe was heartbreaking news. Mahri's account of Felipe flipping his wig and turning his back on everyone was just that—Mahri's version of events—and Delilah had no doubt that any version of events Mahri proposed was going to be prone to exaggeration and include whatever it took to make herself look like less of a backstabbing bitch. But Gabriel had backed it up. Felipe had tried to kill him. The bad mojo he'd been slinging stank of the same stain that was on Silver Dollar. She didn't need to work the leavings Gabriel had brought her to know that. The echoes from the busted up cash depot; the leftovers from Felipe's attacks on Gabriel; the stench on Silver Dollar. They were all dots on the same map. Like metaphysical bomb residue and now it was time to connect the dots.

Delilah plopped down on the bed in a mountain of socks and proceeded to fold—she had lots of socks—epic amounts of socks. Ones and twos. One right after another. Tight little tweaker balls.

Maglo.

While balling up a pair of thigh-length stockings that had little cartoon panda faces all over them, her mind seized on the word. This time it froze there. This time it caught. The light bulb went off.

She jumped up off the bed, sending socks flying, and dashed into her den. She began to peel notebooks and grimoires from the shelves, thumbing through them with speed-fueled impatience. Failing to find what she was after, she stacked each of them aside, one by one, until a pile was spilling across her worktable.

Then she found what she was looking for: a journal of notes she'd made years ago, bullet points of a discussion with the Doc about entities and intellects of the Outer Darkness.

Maglo.

She peeled through the pages, making the paper snap.

Maglo.

Page, skim. No. *Snap.* Next.

Page, skim. No. *Snap.* Next.

Page, skim. No. *Snap.* Next.

Then, in the last few pages of the notebook, enumerated in the Ptolemaic, were representations, known names, of an entity they had discussed—an entity known by many names:

The Watcher Behind the Way Shut.

The Dreamer of the Cold Fire.

Whisperer of Many Eyes.

Eater of Dust.

The Fifth Horror.

Maglo.

A dreamer in the Outer Darkness, great and old. The mad devourer. Blackness of mind and soul. Entropy and horror. Nothing less than a god.

"Jesus," Delilah muttered, closing the notebook.

The Doc had never given her much on the subject of the Dreamers in the Outer Darkness, the Nine Horrors. Myth and legend but very little substance. He played every truth he knew about the Outer Darkness close to the vest—because the truth was dangerous. Dangerous to know or to even think about. She ran her fingertips over the cover of the book. "Maglo," she whispered, and a shiver crawled up her spine.

There was very little inherent to the Art that had frightened Doc McCoy. He'd treated with demons and devils and the ghosts of tyrants and madmen. He'd walked beyond The Veil, into the Wild Fey and back again. He had born witness to the sunrise in the west and the sunset in the east. A lifetime of wonders and horrors, both strange and sublime, but even he drew a line at the Outer Darkness.

"The Way should be shut," he would say when pressed too hard on the topic. That and nothing more.

But the Way was not shut. Not now. Not here.

Morning—it would have to wait until daylight when the Eyes of those things which dwelt in the Outer Darkness were on the far side of the world. There was a lot to learn and little time to learn it—but it would have to wait until the safety of daylight.

Somewhere in the last violet hours of the night, she'd finally sweated enough of the heebie-jeebies and speed from her system to stop moving. She sat down in her big comfy living room chair, stared at the blank television screen, and once her eyes closed, they slammed shut like tomb doors.

42

It was nearly dawn by the time Hector got the mess cleaned up and got back to his motel. The place was a sleeping ghost town as he marched across the parking lot, rune-scribed clay jar tucked under his arm. Stepping into his room, he hung the *do not disturb* sign, and locked and chained the door. He set the ancient clay jar aside on the nightstand and then turned on a single lamp. He turned on the bedside clock radio, tuned it to the first station that came in, and cranked up the volume.

Then he drew the curtains tight and pulled a suitcase out from underneath his bed. Deliberate and methodical, he laid out his workings. One of the items was a small silver flask adorned with strange runes. He unscrewed the stopper of the flask and took a long swig of the bitter licorice-smelling liquid. It burned his tongue and throat, and its gritty texture coated his teeth like sand. Best to get it on board first. It would take some time to work.

Then Hector stripped naked, carefully folding his clothes and laying them out neatly on the foot of the bed. From his prepared workings, he rolled a metal studded mat onto the floor. It was reminiscent of a prayer rug, with dime-sized metal studs sewn into it every square inch or so, blunted and pyramidal in shape.

Setting his workings on the floor beside the mat, and the clay jar at its head, Hector slowly lowered himself and knelt in the center of the rug. The metal studs pressed painfully into his shins and knees.

From his workings, he then chose an ordinary ball clamp. Nothing special about it. Just some mail order cock-and-ball torture device from a smutty sex shop. He clamped the device around his testicles and tightened the screws until his stomach began to cramp. He drank in the pain and centered himself on it. The mat was a start, but this was much better.

Pushing through the pain, his knees aching, his balls throbbing, Hector carried on with his ritual. He lit a candle and set it beside the clay jar. It gave off a thin ribbon of greenish smoke that smelled like rotted meat. He waited—with the studs biting into his knees, and his balls turning purple in the clamp. He stared at the candle flame with unblinking, unflinching eyes.

After a few minutes, the candle flame began to bleed, slowly, through a spectrum of colors—pale orange, mint green, purple—then the candle itself appeared to soften, to twitch, to wiggle and squirm like a restless tentacle.

Hector looked around the room and noticed that the walls and the ceiling were beginning to ... to breathe, to expand and contract. And the shadows had taken on a three-dimensional depth.

The potion was taking hold; it was time.

His hands felt large ... numb ...clumsy, but he didn't let it stop him. Reaching down to his prepared workings, he picked up the cat-o'-nine-tails and like a flagellant monk, he began to whip himself, slashing the whip over his shoulder and across his back. The leather straps snapped and popped, and welts rose, but to Hector, it was nothing. His back was a nest of scars and torn tattoos. Old Aryan Brotherhood ink dominated his mutilated back; a torn shamrock and swastika; SS lightning bolts framed a Death's Head, and the words *100% TEXAS PECKERWOOD* were stenciled across the nape of his neck. A different Hector. A different life.

His balls screamed, and his knees howled, but he whipped himself until blood began to weep freely through the welts.

Snap. Crack. Pop.

His back was burning with pain and Hector drove himself to the brink of madness with trembling hands. He began to flinch with each strike and to whimper, but still, he kept cracking that whip. He could still take more, so he did.

His breath came in ragged gasps.

Snap. Crack. Pop.

He yelped with each slap of the knotted whip, and sweat flowed down his back, mixing with the watery blood from the weeping welts. It tricked down his ass crack, dripped onto his heels. The song on the radio drowned out the lashing of the whip and covered his barks and cries.

Snap. Crack. Pop.

The last strike took the whip involuntarily from his hand, pure reflex. His body gave up. That was the wall, and Hector broke through it.

Collapsing forward on hands and knees, gasping, grunting and shivering in pain, Hector wrenched the lid from the ancient clay jar. He pressed his sweaty cheek to the lip of the opening and peered inside.

Naomi's severed head stewed in the tacky gore at the bottom of the jar—bloody and torn—her red hair a ratted mop of black blood. Her freckles standing out like pinpricks on her pale, bloodless skin.

"Show me!" Hector demanded, his voice quivering with pain but cracking with authority.

Naomi's dead eyes snapped open. Her jaw worked, lips squirmed. A wheezy, wet sound escaped her bloody mouth.

In a broken rasp from Beyond the Veil, she spoke in many voices, some of them not her own.

And Hector listened to it all.

PART FIVE

Blood and Fire, Flesh and Bone

All concerns of men go wrong when they wish to cure evil with evil.

Sophocles

43

Home for Gabriel St. John was a 2004 Ocean Alexander 61 Pilothouse in Marina Del Rey. He had grand plans for himself and that boat. The kind of plans that were probably never going to come together. That didn't really matter though. The possibility was enough. Besides, for Gabriel's tastes, it beat a condo or an apartment and sure as hell beat living inland, which was not where he wanted to be. He hadn't bankrolled enough in his working life to finance a hillside pad in Malibu like his mother and father. But all in due time.

The boat had practical applications as well. Natural, flowing water had a powerful grounding effect on the magical and mystical—even more effective than any defensive ward or device, and in his line of work, a houseboat was a good as a portable nuke shelter.

Failing all else, he could always sail the son of a bitch up to Vancouver or down to Old Mexico and see what happened next. All things being equal, Gabriel considered that as Plan B.

He was dreaming about dogs while his neighbor's outbound morning wake gently lapped the hull of his boat with a soft *thunk-thunk-thunk-thunk*. It was enough to wake him up at half-past eight. Tomorrow was already here, and there was no hiding from it.

Forcing his eyes open, Gabriel rolled over and sat up, swinging his feet painfully over the side of the bed. He cleared his throat, had a good smoker's coughing fit, and scrubbed a hand over his exhausted face. He grunted, realizing he was sore. Sore all over. He'd had a full fight card with a pair of Helitori assholes at midday, and then at midnight, he'd gotten his ass kicked by Felipe's creature down on Diamond Street. His back was as tight as a bowstring, he was covered in knots and bruises. He had ligature marks around his neck better suited to a dead hooker at the bottom of a dumpster. The stapled gash in his side throbbed like it was alive—and he'd managed to catch just enough sleep to stiffen up like a board. He sighed. Oh yeah. Today was going to be grand.

Crawling out of bed bare-assed and black-and-blue, he pulled on some sweatpants and a t-shirt and choked down a cocktail of horse pills with a swig of orange juice. Then he scrounged up his cigarettes and his phone and made his way to the aft deck for some sunshine and a smoke. Bleary-eyed, with a head full of cobwebs, Gabriel kicked back in a deck chair and drank in the morning sun. Finished with his cigarette, he waited for the pain pills to take the edge off the hurt.

Then he called Celeste, and he had no real idea why. To his surprise, she answered.

"Mr. St. John. How lovely it is to hear from you."

For a moment, Gabriel was mute. "Yeah. Hi."

She chuckled. Celeste had a musical laugh. "Well, hi. And what can I help you with?"

Gabriel was silent. He wasn't really sure. It took him a good long while to think of something worth saying. At length, a thought struck him. "What, um, what do you do? When you're not working, I mean."

She chuckled. "Well, now. That's a very personal question, isn't it Mr. St. John?"

"I suppose so. Humor me. One thing. One thing you like to do when you're not working. Not, like, pick up the dry cleaning or go to the store. Something special. Something that matters."

She gave a light laugh. A very soft one. But she answered. "Aerial dance. Aerial silks, to be specific."

Gabriel chuckled. Her one little laugh had pushed a brick off his load. "I don't even know what that is."

"Well. Google it," Celeste suggested.

He thought he could hear her smile through the phone. "Yeah. I'll do that."

"Okay, it's only fair," she replied. "What do *you* do when you're not working?"

Gabriel wasn't even sure how to respond. He never really thought about it. "I don't know," he said.

"Oh, come on. That's not how this game is played. What was your request? One thing? Something that matters? Tell me one thing, Mr. St. John."

"Gabriel. Please. Mr. St. John is my father."

"Gabriel," she said, her tone soft and playful as if she were testing the word.

Imagined or real, Gabriel heard a radiant smile on the other end of the phone. He thought about it. Tried to conjure images of something he enjoyed rather than something he just did. "Riding. I like to ride my bike. Especially up in the mountains."

"Cycling?"

Gabriel was the one who laughed this time. "No. Motorcycle. That kind of bike."

"I see. Do you ride a lot?"

"No. I don't really. But I love it. The rumble of the pipes. The wind. The faster you ride, the less you have time to think about anything else. It just kind of takes over."

"Why don't you do it more often?"

"I don't know. Work I suppose. Do you, uh, aerial dance a lot?" Gabriel couldn't help but think how awkward and juvenile that sounded, but the bullet was fired.

"Yes, I do. You know, I believe you can't find time for the things you love, Gabriel. You have to make it."

He could agree with that.

"So," she said, her tone turning to an inviting purr. "I have reservations at the Intercontinental tonight and some unexpected availability in my schedule. Can I interest you in a cocktail and some company? You sound like you could use a little unwinding."

The Intercontinental down on Avenue of the Stars. That seemed, somehow perfect. Whitebread, Century City tourist L.A. and the company of an intelligent, beautiful woman versus, well, what amounted to his normal daily life.

Gabriel was tempted. Tempted wasn't even the word for it.

"You are a helluva saleswoman, Celeste. But I don't know if I can tonight."

"Raincheck then," she offered, and he could still hear the smile in her voice, real or not. "Hopefully it's one of those things you love that you never get to make time for that's keeping you busy tonight, Gabriel."

He laughed. "Yeah, hardly. Just work. But, yeah, we'll see. Maybe."

"I'd like that," she replied. The smile was back.

"Me too. Thanks for taking my call. I appreciate it."

"My pleasure, Gabriel. I don't expect I'll fill that appointment tonight, so if you wind up with some time, give me a call, and we'll redeem that raincheck."

"I'll do that."

Again, that sunshine smile seeped through the phone, real or not. "I look forward to it." Then she was gone.

Gabriel discovered a lump in his throat and swallowed it. That was new—and different.

He had another smoke and waited until numbness of the pain pills spread to his fingertips. Then he went back below deck.

Gabriel hit the shower, got his head screwed on straight, and started making calls.

Saturday was in full swing.

44

Delilah's doorbell rang at half-past ten, her eyes springing open like scratchy red trap doors. It took her a second to get oriented, to remember where she was and why she was there. Home. She was home, crashed out in her easy chair and her ass was numb. Dodger was sitting barefoot and shirtless at her kitchen table, eating a ham sandwich.

He snorted in the direction of the front door. "Want me to get it?" he asked, standing up and tucking his pistol into the waistband of his jeans.

The doorbell rang again. She could feel it, even through the wards on her threshold. The caller needed no introduction. And to her displeasure, he was alone.

"Nah," she muttered with a scowl, straightening herself up. "I got it."

Delilah opened the front door, unsurprised to see Michael LeMay standing there with a very mild, very mirthless grin on his face.

"Your timing is perfect," she muttered sarcastically.

"Yeah, I sort of guessed that," he replied. He looked her up and down with a frown.

She realized then that she must have looked as spun-out and hard-crashed as she actually felt. Two days of drinking, smoking, tweaking, and throwing around hard magic like it was free had that effect on a person. Her eyes were red and bleary, her cheeks hollow and sunken, her snowy white hair a lumpy mess, and she'd slept in her clothes ... again. She'd had about four or five hours of shitty sleep in the last three days, so yeah, it probably showed.

Michael, however, kept his observations to himself. He reached into his jacket pocket and produced a small zipper-top plastic baggie with what appeared to be a chunk of charred wood about the size of a deck of playing cards inside. Some of the bright red paint from the Doc's siding was still visible on the burnt piece of wood.

She chuckled. "Hmm. Yeah. That figures."

"You want to explain it me? Or do you want me to assume the worst? And do you want to do it on the front porch or inside?" He pointedly made no move to cross her threshold without her invitation.

Delilah contemplated those options in silence for a very long time. "Come on in," she said at last.

Once inside, Michael spotted Dodger straight away. Not that the hulking, shirtless, barefoot, bearded, tattooed biker was hard to miss. "Dodger," he said with a nod and that same mild, smart-ass grin. "Is this where you're spending your nights these days?"

Dodger didn't dignify it with a response. Instead, he looked to Delilah.

"We're fine," she replied, giving him a grateful nod. "Can you give us a minute?"

Scowling, but making nothing of it, Dodger left them alone and went to sit on the back patio.

"How's Samuel?" Delilah asked once they were alone.

"He's good," Michael replied, taking off his sunglasses. "We've been doing the pre-school thing since January."

Delilah perked up. "Yeah? He like it okay?"

Michael nodded. "Loves it. They do music and art and all kinds of stuff there. He's reading."

Delilah smiled. Thoughts of her snowy haired baby boy hit her especially hard right then. Exhausted and worn raw she felt her eyes start to sting and looked away, banishing those demons for another day.

"So, you want to tell me what happened with Doc McCoy?" Michael asked.

There was no sense in denying it. All burned bridges and scar tissue being taken into consideration, the two of them still had a painfully intimate connection. Michael would have known the scent of her spellfire as surely as she would have known the smell of his aftershave. That was never going to change. No matter how much both of them might want it to.

"Yeah," she said. "I burned his house down. Not really on purpose. It just sort of happened that way. Do you want to know why?"

Michael nodded. "I do."

She bought herself some time to think by scrounging up a cigarette. She lit one and pondered her options.

Delilah gave Michael the cliff's notes version and nothing more. Having the Watch balls-deep in their asses was pretty undesirable, and she didn't want to be responsible for wiping off the lube any more than she already was.

She told him she'd found Doc McCoy dead, murdered, and mutilated and that his place had been ransacked. She blamed the Helitori.

"Lot of blame flying around these days," Michael replied. "I'll ask you the same thing we asked the Helitori. Got any proof?"

Delilah blinked, incredulous. "Other than Doc McCoy managed to live a happy and healthy seventy years or so until the Helitori showed up in town?"

"Yeah. Other than that."

"No." Delilah felt his doubt and his scorn. Michael was good at that. It was one of the reasons why they never worked—because that shit pissed her off. "I know what I know."

"It's not what you know. It's what you can prove. And you fire washed the scene, so…"

She snorted. "Give me a fucking break." She wondered how many times that little factoid was going to turn around to bite her in the taint. "Let me guess, they deny it?"

Michael shrugged. "Don't know, haven't asked them yet."

"You planning on it?"

He nodded. Then, "What else happened?"

Delilah treaded over that ground with great care. She told the truth about Edwin. How they'd found him there at the Doc's house, sitting on the grisly scene, stunned and speechless. She warned Michael about the curse, the swarm of malevolent spirits, the thing that had possessed the Doc's mutilated corpse. She let him know he could cross Edwin off his list of Circle Odd refugees. By then she was working on her second cigarette.

"Damn," Michael offered with sincerity. "There's still Mahri, Felipe, Naomi, and Alex."

Delilah nodded, played her poker face straight as a razor, giving up nothing about Mahri or Felipe.

"We can help them, Dee. We can help them in ways you can't."

Delilah scoffed. "Tough sell, Michael."

He persisted. "If we help them, it doesn't start a war. If you help them, you're getting between the Helitori and their sworn prey."

"Is that how wearing the white hat works?" Delilah asked with a snide smirk. "You boys just sit back and have a self-righteous circle jerk while you let the bloodthirsty witch hunters do your dirty work for you?"

Michael shrugged. "If they play by the rules and their prey doesn't? Yeah. Maybe. You hear from the Odd, the smart move is to make them our problem, not yours."

She nodded. "I'll take it under advisement."

"So, what about the Helitori? Crow's working for Dante Washington, right?"

Delilah scoffed. "Says who?"

Michael only shrugged. "Eh, that's what I heard. Dante Washington's on their shit list too. You rubbing off on each other yet?"

She shrugged. "Haven't heard a peep. They're probably too busy torturing harmless old men to death." Like the rest of her family, she was a professional liar.

"What's your next move?" Michael seemed like he actually expected an answer.

Delilah shrugged. "Get my nails done." Michael didn't look irritated. He never looked irritated. But she knew he was, nonetheless.

"I'm trying to help you," he said.

She managed a smile. "No you're not, doll."

"So that's how it is?"

Delilah nodded. "Today? Yeah."

"Suggestions?"

"Try again tomorrow." Delilah knew he wouldn't give up. But he would back off and regroup. Go bark up another tree until he came up with something better to come at her with. Anything she could do to buy a little breathing room between the Crow's business with Dante Washington and the interference of the Watch was gravy. But she had no doubt that boomerang would be coming back around again—and probably soon.

Michael stood up and put his sunglasses on. "You think of something you want to talk about, you call me. Day or night. Any time."

Delilah gave a single noncommittal nod. "Where's Samuel?"

"Where he ought to be," Michael replied. Then he left.

45

Victor St. John started off the day by making a few calls of his own. While he was going down the list, he dialed up Herbert J. Wortzworg. There was the sound of power tools and machinery in the background. A grinder. An impact wrench. Wortzworg Collision and Auto, and it sounded like business was good.

"I'd like to buy you lunch," the Lord Crow offered.

"That's unusual," Wortzworg replied. He had a nasty, unpleasant voice. The kind of voice associated with sleazy New Jersey pimps, child molesters, and slimy men who might throttle their elderly mothers in their sleep for the insurance money. "To what do I owe the pleasure?"

"Business."

Wortzworg gave a rotten chuckle. "I'm all about the business, Mr. St. John. Reuben Deli. I like lunch by eleven. Pick me up a pastrami brown bag. I'll be in my office all day."

The Reuben Deli lunch counter was already packed shoulder to shoulder heading into the lunch hour, so Victor's quest for Wortzworg's pastrami brown bag special took some time and patience. Greasy lunch sack finally in hand, Victor made the trip around the block to Wortzy's garage.

The place stank of grease, oil, and sour body odor. As per usual. The ugliest woman in the southwestern United States manned the front desk. She sort of snorted at Victor when he pushed through the greasy front door.

"I'm here to see Wortzy," he said.

"Appointment?" the woman asked in a voice that sounded like the product of eating lit cigarettes as much as smoking them.

Victor waggled the greasy brown paper sack. "Lunch date."
She hooked a fat crooked thumb over her shoulder and went back to her issue of *Vogue.*

Victor let himself into the garage through the side door.
The garage was buzzing with thick, squat men. Hairy and in a variety of shades from dark to light, they were all just as ugly as the lady at the front desk. Some were short and stooped, but one slope-browed fella was damn near seven feet tall and built like a potato with arms and legs. These guys were sweaty, swarthy, and they stank up the garage like a locker room trash can.

They didn't seem to be speaking much English either. Or Spanish.

"St. John!" a squat, hairy, balding man called out from the loft office at the back of the shop. He was painfully reminiscent of Danny DeVito from his days in the cast of *Taxi.* "You got my sandwich?" The illustrious Herbert J. Wortzworg.

Victor raised his hand and showed the sack.

The tall slope-browed potato man leaned in for a sniff.

"Ay, fuck you, Leo!" Wortzworg bellowed. "That's mine. You little couch-fucking piece of shit."

Leo seemed to take the hint. He picked up a couple of wrenches with an acidic frown and got back to work.

Victor went up to the office loft for his lunch meeting.

"How's the good life, Wortzy?" Victor asked, dropping the greasy brown bag on the boss-man's cluttered desk. Herbert Wortzworg's desktop looked like the aftermath washed in by a tsunami. Wadded up papers. Discarded food wrappers in varying states of age and decay. An overflowing ashtray filled with butts crushed and flattened to the extreme by an anxious smoker. A worn-out issue of some twenty-year-old German fetish porn magazine. Half a dozen putrid old paper coffee cups. An invoice for repairs showing a balance due, spattered conspicuously with crusty red-brown stains—probably somebody who learned the hard way what comes from stiffing the likes of Herbert Wortzworg.

"I'm a very busy man, St. John," Wortzworg snorted, feigning impatience. "Whaddya need?"

Victor nodded toward the greasy lunch sack. "Little something extra in there for you."

Wortzworg cocked a bristly eyebrow and peeled open the sack. Looking inside, he licked his thick lips in anticipation. Upending the sack on his desk, he poured out the contents. Each piece seemed to garner his equal admiration and attention.

Big fat pastrami on rye, wrapped up in grease-stained wax paper.

Baggie of hand-cut chips, all crispy, freshly-fried, leaking through their wrapper.

Dill pickle spear.

Two stacks of banded hundred dollar bills, totaling twenty-grand.

Wortzworg chomped down the pickle spear like a billy goat and nodded his approval. "Very thoughtful of you."

Victor shrugged. "Eh, you know how it is. A little tribute. Just a reminder that we're friends."

Wortzworg laughed, going about tearing into the sandwich and chips with eager hands. "Is that what we're calling it today?" He picked up the sandwich and shoved it into his big mouth all the way to the back of his throat, taking an enormous bite. He chewed and smacked, little bits tumbling from his lips to his shirt. He didn't seem to care. With a gulp, he swallowed and chased the massive bite down with a swig of cold coffee. "So, what can this friend do for you today? Grab a seat."

Sitting down anywhere in Herbert Wortzworg's office wasn't high on Victor's list of things he wanted to do, but he humored the nasty little man and took a seat across the desk. It was definitely the sort of place that made you want to wash your hands and get your shots up to date.

"I got a problem," Victor said.

"What sort of problem?"

"The extended family kind."

Wortzworg snorted. "You stupid goddamn Micks. You're as bad as the goddamned Guineas with this family shit. Only thing worse than both of youse is gen-yoo-wine Irish. 'Cause half of them think they got family and God both on their side. But of course, you married one of them, so who am I talkin' to?"

Victor cocked an eyebrow. "Careful, Wortzy. We're friends, remember?" No one disrespected Victor's queen—not even in jest—except for maybe Wortzworg, because he just didn't give a shit.

"I hear your kids got a little off the leash yesterday."

Victor cocked an eyebrow. "Heard what from who?"

Wortzworg only smiled, an awful, putrid expression. "Hearing things is my business, St. John. Information just has a way of finding its way from God's lips to my ears."

"I think you got that idiom backward, boss-man."

Wortzworg ignored the barb. "I don't understand why you don't just put the law into their thick skulls with the back a ya hand. Do you run this show or dontcha?"

Victor didn't take the bait. "Obviously, you don't have children."

Wortzworg snorted dismissively and gave his crotch a grab. "I got plenty of children. They damn sure know who the boss is."

Victor shook his head. Wortzworg had a way of wandering off topic. Not because he was scatter-brained, though he'd swear that was the case if you called him on it. Wortzy was an information broker, and he was always fishing. If you followed the little shit down the rabbit hole, you'd be telling him the color of your momma's panties in five minutes. His gift of gab was equally a gift of grab and Victor wasn't biting. "Stay on topic, huh?"

Wortzworg shrugged. "I'm just sayin. So, if this family business isn't about the antics of your offspring, what is it about?"

"Uh-huh. I got a problem."

"You mentioned that," Wortzworg noted, then he inhaled another bite of sandwich.

Victor nodded toward the pile of cash and potato chips. "Twenty-grand says you already know what my problem is."

Wortzworg contemplated that while he chewed. He nodded. "There's a crew of Helitori headhunters in town, and they got a bone to pick. With anybody who gets in their way."

Victor wasn't shocked, but he was annoyed. "So you already

knew that, and you don't bother to give a guy a call?"

"Hey, do I owe you any favors?" Another huge bite and the heaping sandwich was almost gone.

"I suppose not," Victor conceded. "But let's call that a sizeable down payment on 'you owe me some shit now,' shall we?"

Wortzy eyeballed the stacks of cash. "How big of a down payment?"

"Don't get greedy," Victor cautioned. "Looks like the Helitori are here and planning on a lengthy stay. I need to put a pin in the map where these cockroaches are setting up shop. Like, yesterday."

Wortzworg mulled it over as he finished off his sandwich. At last, he nodded. "That can be arranged. Might take a day or two."

Victor scowled but knew Wortzy wasn't likely to give up anything he already knew without making a show of it. The little shit lived by the motto of never making it look easy.

"I'm also looking for Doc McCoy's kids from the Circle Odd. They're in some real deep shit and are probably running, hiding, or both. I need to find them. You get me a line on one of them, I'll make you a happy son of a bitch."

"I like being happy," Wortzworg replied. "I'll see what I can dig up."

"One more thing," Victor said.

Wortzworg grunted. "Now who's getting greedy?"

"Dante Washington. He's got some problems of his own that we're helping him sort out. You hear something on the street with his name on it, you let me know about it."

Wortzworg grunted. It seemed like agreement.

"Get me what you can get me, pronto. We can fill in the blanks as we go along."

Wortzworg flipped through the stacks of cash with greasy fingers. "Might take a little more gas in the tank than this, though."

Victor stood up and smiled. "You can bill me. I'm good for it."

"Yes, you are," Wortzworg conceded. "I'll be calling."

"Looking forward to it." Victor rose, fighting the urge to dust off his ass.

"Oh hey, one thing does come to mind," Wortzworg said, chewing through a mouthful of chips. He gave it some drama as if the thought had just been sent to him via lightning bolt from the gods above.

"I bet it does," Victor muttered. "What's that?"

Wortzworg's beady eyes twinkled. "The Watch is in town too. I got it on good authority that the old Turk himself came in through LAX a couple of days ago."

Victor processed that but said nothing.

"Helitori in town on a witch hunt. The Watch creeping up everybody's six o'clock." Wortzworg gave an awful smile. "Something slip through, Vic? Something creeping around out there that we should all be concerned about? I dunno. Smells like a pretty big deal."

Victor smiled, cold and wolfish. "If you can answer any of those questions, you let me know, would ya? I'll make it worth your while."

Wortzworg chuckled. "Yeah. I bet you will."

With that, Victor took his leave, exiting through the garage amidst the clank and hammer of power tools and the guttural grunts of a language rarely heard outside Wortzworg's walls.

46

Gabriel spent his morning rallying the troops. Professional hard-asses who wore the Four-Winged Crow of the soldier. Muscle. Manpower. A little plus-up in the push-and-shove column. The Captain Crow started putting the troops on standby, letting them know that shit was on and he might need to drop a metric ton of whoop-ass on something on short notice. Until they heard otherwise though, everybody was supposed to be extra cool.

He also checked on his people in the field, making sure everybody was still good to go come the hard light of day.

The first thing he did was call Piper to check in. Piper was wide awake, and his voice was a little raw like he'd been up yammering all night. Probably had a nose full of speed, keeping the engines hot. Piper fancied the occasional crystal breakfast.

"How's things at the ranch?" Gabriel asked.

"All quiet on the western front," Piper quipped. "We're good. Got Silver Dollar moved without much trouble. Around dawn, he woke up for about thirty seconds and started screaming. Then he was out. Nice digs, Sweet Valley Ranch. There's horses and shit."

"Okay. Well, hang loose until we get some relief vectored your way. Might take a minute."

"Can do, boss."

Then Dodger reported that Delilah had rattled around the house like an alley cat all night and she was crashed out. Considering the events of the day before, none of that surprised Gabriel. Dodger was going to give her a little more time to sleep it off before bugging her too bad. Other than that, they were straight.

Gabriel called in Izzie too, to bring more talent to the spookshow. She was a little artsy, a little butch, and she was a killer bassist who thumped strings in a local metal band as well as a couple of jazz ensembles. She had high-value expertise in possessions and hauntings, and the two of them were pretty tight. Her sorceress's Crow flew on her right shoulder blade, and it sported a Blood Laurel. Izzie had killed in a nasty scrape once and saved Gabriel from getting blindsided in the back of the skull, so she never paid for drinks when the Captain Crow was around.

She met Gabriel at the Church late that morning, and there were some smiles and hugs. They hadn't seen each other in a while, but not much had changed except her hair, which had gone from blond pigtails to a cherry-red crop—which suited her.

They hung out in the clubhouse bar with Bingo, who was mixing bloody mary's for brunch and having a little hair of the dog that bit him. Sometime in the small hours, a very well-medicated Bingo had curled up behind the bar to sleep it off, and he now stood not ten feet from that spot mashing a celery stalk in the bottom of his glass.

"Y'all motherfuckers be quiet," he grumbled when Gabriel and Izzie got a little too rambunctious for his hungover tastes. They sipped their beer and caught up, obliging the old knight with a reasonable volume.

Anna showed up around lunchtime and Gabriel balked when she prepared to give him a check-up, but Anna stood her ground.

"Doctor's orders," she insisted and corralled him in the Church's infirmary. The Captain Crow complied, tossing his shirt over the chair with a sigh. He let her check and re-dress his wounded chest and poke at his bruises.

"Well, you've already torn your staples," Anna murmured, inspecting the purple gash across his ribs. Some of the staples had held, and some hadn't. He had a fair number of fresh bumps and bruises too. "A little worse for wear since I saw you last night." With a frown, she inspected the ligature marks around his neck. "Rough date?"

Gabriel shrugged. "Eh, had better." After yesterday's events, Gabriel looked like a man who'd wandered away battered from a car accident. Or maybe a man who'd slipped his noose and escaped the gallows on his way to the car accident.

Anna chuckled. "You and my brother—human punching bags."

"Well, at least it's an honest living."

"He in as rough a shape as you?"

"We're fine. Mint condition."

She pinched at the stapled gash across his chest, and Gabriel sucked in a sharp breath. "Big baby. Mint, huh? Well, somebody definitely opened the package and played with you. Your collector's price is going down."

"Ha-ha."

She put him back together as best she could and replaced the dressings with fresh ones. "You really ought to think about a vacation when this job is done. Take a little time off and let some of this heal up the right way."

Gabriel nodded. "Oh, hell yeah. As soon as this shit's over, I'm going to Costa Rica and getting stoned for a month. Pay pretty senoritas to feed me grapes."

With a rueful smile, Anna pitched her gloves into the wastebasket and washed up. Gabriel chuckled too because they both knew he was full of shit. The job would end. Then it'd be time for the next one. And the next one after that. Hopefully though, the next few would be a little easier on the heavy lifting than this one had been. This one was turning into the job from Planet Motherfucker.

"Hey boss," Twitch said, poking his head into the infirmary. "Victor's here. He wants a minute with you."

"You link up with Grizz?"

"Yeah. We're good."

"What's Mahri's story?"

"She just woke up, dude. Asked for a bagel, wanted to know if I had any weed, then went to the shower."

Gabriel chuckled. "Thanks. Tell the big man I'll be out in five."

Twitch nodded and took his leave.

While Anna finished up, Gabriel threw his shirt back on and got himself together.

"You look a little better today," she said.

"Yeah. A little sleep will do that for you." Grinning, he thanked her for checking up on him. Then Gabriel went to see the Lord Crow.

He found his father alone in the meeting hall, seated at the head of his table in his massive old throne. The Lord's Hall looked much different by day. It was much less imposing when filled with white sunlight; much more empty and cavernous. Victor lit a smoke when his son entered the meeting hall. He'd already poured himself a snort of scotch. "Close the door and have a seat."

Gabriel did as asked then took a seat to his father's immediate right.

The Lord Crow plucked a crystalline tumbler from the service and poured his son a couple fingers of the good stuff. He reached across the table and planted it in front of Gabriel with a weighty *thunk*. "You know, I was all prepared to come in here this morning and break my foot off in your ass—tell you to get your head in the game. Ask you what's been eating you."

Gabriel eyeballed the scotch glass, then his father. He picked it up and took a sip. "But?"

Victor shrugged. "But now I come in and see everything running like a well-oiled machine."

It was a rare compliment, and Gabriel managed a small smile. "Yeah, well, sometimes it's as if we knew what we were doing. Yesterday was a sucker punch. Just needed to get our feet on the ground, that's all."

Victor took a long drag off his cigarette, exhaled, and sipped his scotch. "So. What *has* been you eating you, son?"

Gabriel shook his head. "I don't know. Nothing, I guess. Just … busy."

"Yeah." Victor didn't sound so convinced. Gabriel couldn't blame him. "Been a messy couple of days, huh?"

Gabriel conceded that. "It's been better."

Victor was quiet for a long while, and when he spoke, he sounded as sincere as Gabriel could ever remember. "You know this is all just business, right?"

Gabriel nodded.

"You can't let the business stuff get personal. You can't do this work with your heart. Business has got to stay up here," Victor said, tapping his temple. "We got plenty of personal irons in the fire—like this thing with the kids from the Odd."

Gabriel leaned back in his chair, studying the contents of his glass rather than looking at his father. He didn't want to talk about the intersection of business and personal feelings. It had been a bad week for that.

Victor must have sensed it. "You gonna pretend like we ain't talking about it?"

Gabriel shrugged. "About what?"

"About that messy shit with Frankie Pallone, getting the book back. This thing with Mahri and the kids from the Odd. Business, son. Not personal. Do you understand?"

"I do."

"This work … it's hard, and it'll eat you up if you don't keep that straight." Victor was stern, serious. "And the others see it."

Gabriel cocked an eyebrow.

"Bingo said something to me," Victor explained with a shrug. "He thinks you're a little burned out."

"I'm fine," Gabriel insisted. It was almost true. Though hearing that the old knight thought otherwise amped up his doubt a notch or two.

"Do you know why I run this outfit the way I do?" Victor asked.

Gabriel rolled his eyes. "Jesus. We don't have to have this conversation."

"Yeah. We do," Victor replied, jabbing the tip of his finger against the tabletop for emphasis. "One time, son."

"One time, what?" Gabriel asked.

"You let one of these motherfuckers get over on us one time, and everything we got is gone. Everything people did time for. Woke up in the hospital all busted up for. Spilled blood for. It's all gone. That shit is contagious. Take your Uncle fuckin' Frankie and everybody like him who thought they could get one over on us because we're good to them, and if you don't squash that shit it's *all gone*. If you let one go, one time, you're gonna have to face them all."

Gabriel took a sip from his glass. "You talking about Mahri?"

"I'm talking about all of it," Victor replied. "Business—not personal. You can't get those mixed up. Yeah?"

It took a while, but at last, Gabriel nodded.

Victor was quiet for a while. "I know I put a lot on you, son. Do you know why?"

Gabriel had his theories, but he held his tongue. The smirk in his eyes did not go unnoticed.

"Yeah, I see what you're thinking there. But you're wrong." Victor wasn't angry. Just matter-of-fact. "I do it because you're good. You're the best I got. And that's saying something in this company."

The Lord Crow rarely handed out pats on the back. It made Gabriel a little uncomfortable in his own skin. He turned his gaze back down to the golden liquor in his glass and was quiet.

"Some guys are loyal, some guys are talented, others are smart, tough. Solid when the shit goes down. And some are just hell on wheels, but they're your hell on wheels." Victor fixed his son with those granite eyes. "Ain't very many guys are all of the above. You get me?"

Gabriel nodded. He got it. For right or wrong, he got it. "So, what's with the pep talk?"

"Just a reminder. Of how much this family needs you. Needs you keeping your head and your heart straight. And how much they need to *see* that. *Captain*."

Gabriel got the point. "I'm good, pop."

"You sure about that?"

"Yes, sir."

"Okay," Victor replied with a nod. He said no more on the matter. Instead, he smiled. "What you need is a good night out. Nothing more therapeutic than going downtown in a high-dollar suit to get your dick sucked by a mid-grade broad in a low-rent bathroom."

Gabriel chuckled. His father, ever the eloquent blue-collar New York Irish kid at heart. "Yeah, I'll take it under advisement."

Victor switched gears. "Okay, so fill me in about last night."

Gabriel reported the events that took place at The Hyde with Silver Dollar and Felipe slithering out his fingers like a greased pig at the Couatl's.

"So Mahri's story checked out?" Victor noted.

"So far, yeah."

"Does Washington know you got that close to Felipe?"

"No. And I don't plan on telling him either."

Victor chuckled. "That would be wise."

He told Victor about the jagged sliver of iron that Felipe had wielded like a wand, and how Felipe's newly acquired mojo seemed to be fueled by it, like a token of vicious power. The Lord Crow got a greedy twinkle in his eye. Everything had a price tag, and whatever that relic was, it was likely worth a fortune. *But.* Gabriel wasn't so certain. There was a fine line between dealing in dangerous artifacts and taking a bite of the poison apple. Some things were better left at the bottom of a hole because you can't spend the money when you're dead— or worse. Gabriel didn't take it as a positive sign that Felipe's whole world appeared to be circling the drain. He managed to sidestep discussion of the relic, for the most part, tabling it for later. They'd cross that bridge when they reached it. First things first. Like seeing if Fiona could identify it. Then they could revisit it.

He laid out his plan for the day, the muscle and talent he was putting on task.

"Right now, we're still juggling chainsaws. Delilah, Finch, and Izzie can hopefully get a handle on whatever's crawling around inside Silver Dollar. That will make the customer happy. At least for now. Buy us a little good will to work out the rest of this mess."

"I don't like the things we don't know here," Victor said. "Lot of blind corners."

"Washington had a crew of mercs sitting on the safehouse where they're keeping Silver Dollar. Pros—not neighborhood bangers."

Victor cocked an eyebrow.

"Shit got wild last night, and they got a little bug-eyed, but they didn't run screaming."

Victor processed that. "So, that kind of pro?"

"Maybe. Their security chief, Markus, definitely."

Victor nodded. "I'll look into it and see what talent Mr. Washington's got on his payroll that he's not telling us about. I got Wortzy kicking over rocks. One more rock ain't gonna break the bank."

"What about the other kids from the Odd?"

"Nets are out," Victor replied. "We'll see if we catch something. If Wortzy doesn't turn something up on one of them, then they've already split town for Katmandu. You bumped up against Felipe. You get us anything we can work with?"

Gabriel nodded. "Yeah. Sis is gonna get to work on it as soon as she gets going today."

The Lord Crow nodded. "She'll need your mother's help. Need to get Finchy back in here too. We need to find Felipe, fast, before he either splits town with the cash or comes back swinging."

"Then what?" Gabriel asked. But he already knew the answer.

"Get paid and put him out of our misery." Victor downed the last swallow in his glass.

That was going to be the outcome, and there wasn't any sense in pretending otherwise. If Mahri's story was on the up-and-up, Felipe had made his coffin, and he needed to have the decency to lie down in it.

"Felipe's new toy," Victor said, looking very serious. "That stays between us. You don't tell Washington and his crew about it. Savvy? We'll see what happens with it."

Gabriel nodded, rising from his seat. "I got it. I'm going to get back to work. Thanks for the snort, pop."

That was as close as Gabriel came to saying thank you to his father for acting like a dad. It didn't happen very often. He stepped out and Saturday kept rolling.

47

Alonzo Baker arrived at Hector's motel in Anaheim in the mid-afternoon, having fought the freeway for two hours. The traffic—even on a Saturday—he fucking hated Los Angeles. Alonzo was tall, forty, and built like a hunting cat. He favored nondescript threads because, like most people in his profession, he didn't want to stand out in a crowd. As he headed across the sunny parking lot toward Hector's room, he pocketed his sunglasses, revealing a cut beside his swollen left eye. Bullet fragments. A memento from yesterday's gunfight with the Crow. A stark reminder of just how close he'd come to having his head blown off by Gabriel St. John.

Two of his boys, Toby and Waits, hadn't been so lucky. They were propping up shallow graves in a forgotten corner of California desert. There were no hero's funerals in this line of work. Toby was new, but he'd been a good kid, and Alonzo hated to lose him; Waits on the other hand ... they'd worked together for six years, faced some truly awful shit together on three different continents. And Gabriel St. John had cut him open like a pig in some shitty back alley in L.A. That score was going to get settled—whether here and now, or somewhere else, later didn't matter—only the certainty of it.

He stepped inside Hector's motel room and snorted at the lingering stench. It was a cross between spoiled milk and rotten meat. "Smells like something died in here."

Hector was not alone. He was attended by a lanky white man with a careless mop of blonde hair and a very small, petite woman with dark hair and a pale, pretty face.

The man leaned against the far wall, arms crossed, one

foot on the baseboard and one on the floor. Like a bored pimp holding down a street corner. That was Reinhardt, a foot soldier from a cell of Brother Knights in Seattle.

The woman, sitting in a chair in the far corner of the room, flipping through a magazine, was Amelia, a sister of the same outfit. It looked like Hector was calling in some backup, and Alonzo didn't like that. This was their hunt. Their blood and honor on the altar. Outside muscle need not apply. And Amelia … well. But Alonzo knew now wasn't the time or place to argue about it, and in the end, all the Brothers and Sisters were sworn to the same cause. He'd let it ride. For now.

Hector stood by the window and blinked, expressionless, gazing out across the parking lot. "Close the door."

Alonzo did as ordered, then Hector pulled the blinds shut.

"You look like hell," Alonzo said, noting the hunter's drawn, exhausted expression. "Hot date, late night?"

"Something like that," Hector replied. Once the blinds were drawn, Hector turned back to the room. But rather than strike up a conversation, he wandered the floor and seemed to lose himself in the cheap, generic flower print hanging on the wall above the rickety little motel room table. He was quiet for a very long time.

Alonzo took in the rest of the room. There was a large ancient-looking clay jar sitting on the table beneath the flower print. It appeared to be a handmade canopic funerary piece, dug up out of some crypt a couple thousand years after it was originally interred. It was smeared and spattered with black stains. Dried blood. A large sleeping bag was laid out on the bed, unzipped and open, like a shabby comforter. The jar was old business. The sleeping bag, new business.

"How are our new accommodations coming?" Hector asked.

"We're set," Alonzo replied. After the dust-up with the Crow and evacuating their wounded, Hector had given orders to relocate and set up shop somewhere new. Surest way to keep the sky from falling in was to not stay in any one place too long—especially once you were made.

"Good."

"How'd things work out with Naomi?"

Hector inclined his head toward the ancient clay jar. "Be my guest."

Alonzo was willing to take the bait. He walked across the room and tugged the lid off the vessel. It was still a little tacky with old black blood around the rim. He looked inside, took three long slow breaths, then put the lid back on the jar. "One down," he grunted, swallowing the nasty taste in the back of his throat. "She give you guys any trouble? How'd the prospects do?"

"I told them she needed to be broken," Hector explained. "These idiots thought broken meant beaten, raped, and chained to a wall. She was made of steel. They didn't break her. They just bent her a little and pissed her off. She killed all of them for it."

Both Alonzo and Reinhardt were quiet.

Not Amelia though. She snorted out a single bark of grim laughter, then turned the page in her magazine.

Hector, still studying the cheap floral print on the wall, reached up and scraped a fly-spot off the glass with his thumbnail. "No one understands how dangerous these people are. Not until it's too late. A word of advice, gentlemen—don't underestimate them. Any of them. Not even the least of them."

"Did you get anything from her?" Alonzo asked.

"It was a waste. A senseless waste. That girl was a professional liar even in death."

"So, where does that leave us?"

"We try again."

Reinhardt chuckled at Hector's take on the four little part-time amateurs from the Odd. "You have a surprising amount of respect for this little coven, yah?" His accent was decidedly German, but his English was flawless.

"Yes. Because I understand what they are."

"Yah? What is that?"

Hector was suddenly less philosophical and more serious. "Do you realize what it takes to do what they've done? It's one thing to be seduced by the infernal, whispering promises and passion in your ear. It's beautiful, sublime, and seductive. But it's another matter entirely to look into the Outer Darkness without flinching. It doesn't hide what it is. You have to look at it, and you have to *see* it. Its giggling madness, its agony, its oblivion."

He picked at another spot on the glass. "Any lucky idiot can accidentally lasso a tornado, but it takes a real champion to hang on to the rope."

"Well, when you put it that way..." Reinhardt quipped.

"Yes."

"You feel that same way about the Crow?" Reinhardt asked, and Alonzo bristled. As far as he was concerned, breaking the Crow wasn't up for debate. It was absolute. It was going to happen, if he had to stay here and do it on his own.

"You mean how do we handle them?" Hector asked.

Reinhardt nodded.

Hector's answer was straightforward. "The Crow is Dante Washington's hired gun. And they're professional predators. Man-eaters. You put down man-eaters when they get in your way."

Alonzo liked that answer.

Reinhardt seemed less sure. "And the Odd?"

"Their potential notwithstanding, baby birds with broken wings," Hector said. "You put *them* out of their misery."

Reinhardt harrumphed.

"I'm sorry, what is it exactly that you're doing here?" Alonzo asked, eyeballing Reinhardt.

"It wasn't his decision," Hector said. "Or mine. It's decided. It's done."

From her seat, Amelia grinned like the cat that ate the canary but offered nothing.

Neither Alonzo nor Reinhardt continued in their grousing. But it didn't make the two men like each other anymore. They'd gotten off on the wrong foot and were probably going to stay there.

The sound of a car pulling into the motel lot and up to Hector's door caught their attention. Hector moved to the window, pulled the curtain back an inch, and took a look outside. He nodded to his companions. The new business they were meeting to handle had arrived.

There was a knock on the door, and Hector cracked it open, leaving the chain fastened while he looked the newcomer up and down.

Alonzo could just see past his shoulder through the crack. Their visitor was a tall, willowy, shy-looking black kid. His eyes were hollow with exhaustion—Alex of the Circle Odd.

"Are you Hector?" Alex asked, his voice jangled and nervous.

"Yes." Hector unlatched the chain and motioned for Alex to come inside.

Ducking in like he was running from the mob, the kid hustled through the door.

"Check him," Hector instructed, gesturing toward Alonzo.

He stepped in as ordered and gave Alex a good pat down.

"There's a gun," Alex warned, his tone abrupt, tense. "In my back pocket. Sorry. I didn't know what to do with it."

"Yeah, don't sweat it, kid," Alonzo said, finishing his pat down. He filched the gun—a little Taurus .380—out of his back pocket. The kid had probably picked it up on the street for pocket change. Alonzo cleared it and then dropped it on the table next to the grisly clay jar. "He's clean."

Alex's eyes followed his pistol until it wound up on the table. Then they seized on the jar. He looked away immediately.

Alonzo shook his head. *Yeah, that's exactly what you think it is, kid.*

"Please," Hector said, gesturing toward the foot of the bed. "Have a seat."

Alex did as instructed and picked nervously at the hem of his shorts, scraping at it with his thumbnail. "So, how does this work? What do we do now?"

Reinhardt detached from the wall and cleared the distance in two long-legged strides, then he snapped a loop of metal links over Alex's head, his attack a fluid blur.

The lash looked like a pronged choke collar for a dog, the forward section of the loop attached to either end of an engraved silver bit. Rather than wrap it around Alex's neck like a garrote, he yanked it tight, twisting and turning, digging it into Alex's face. Like wrestling a horse under control by its bridle. Reinhardt jerked the bit back into Alex's molars. The prongs on the wicked leash burrowed into his cheeks, tearing gouges into his face.

Alex tried to scream and was silenced into a gagging wheeze as the bit buried into his mouth. The bigger man overpowered him like a child and dragged him back onto the bed while he kicked and clawed in panic. Then Reinhardt grunted a short string of guttural alien commands and Alex's body jerked as if tasered.

He thrashed, his muscles locking in agony. A tooth broke against the silver bit with a bright *crack* as his teeth clamped down.

"Hold his legs," Hector instructed calmly, motioning for Alonzo to jump in.

Alonzo did, and together, he and Reinhardt wrangled Alex under control. As the two men wrestled with Alex, Hector went to his suitcase and rifled among his things. He produced a loaded syringe, plucking the cap off with his fingertips and priming the needle with a few flicks of his fingernail.

With each passing second, Alex's control over his body, along with his ability to protest, waned. His whimpers and strangled cries tapered off to a soft, toneless wheezing, his muscles, locked tight, stopped responding, and his whole body spasmed like a giant cramp. Alex was paralyzed. Frozen. His eyes were wild, like a panicked horse, but he was unable to scream or speak. He could barely even breathe.

Hector came to the bedside and plunged the needle into Alex's neck.

A few seconds later his eyes fluttered shut and his body went slack.

Reinhardt re-secured the bit in Alex's mouth, cinching it off tight, prongs digging raw holes into the boy's torn cheeks and he locked it in place with a clasp at the back of his head.

Through the whole thing, Amelia had never even set her magazine aside.

"Wrap him up," Hector instructed. "Reinhardt, when you're done, back the car up to the door. We're leaving."

Alonzo went with the flow, helping Reinhardt manhandle Alex until they could zip him up in the sleeping bag. Once cocooned, Reinhardt took up the car keys and disappeared outside.

Alonzo tucked his shirttail back into place and straightened his jacket. There was a momentary pang of conscience, a little nip of guilt. By all accounts, Alex had the cleanest hands out of anyone in the Circle Odd. Just like Naomi, he'd taken the bait to come in peacefully so they could *help* him hook, line, and sinker. There was something dissatisfying about that, but Alonzo buried it. Sometimes the mission demanded that you do ugly shit, and that was just how it was.

Hector policed up his suitcase. "You help Reinhardt load him in the trunk." That quick, he looked like he was ready to walk out the door.

Reinhardt brought the car around, popped the trunk, and came inside. He pitched Hector's suitcase in the back seat and came back for Alex.

"Cameras?" Alonzo asked.

"Already handled," Reinhardt replied. He watched to make sure the coast was clear, and then they loaded the lumpy sleeping bag into the trunk of the car without fanfare. Once that was done, he passed the keys back to Hector. "Now we work on the kid, yah?"

"No," Hector replied, nodding toward Amelia. "*We* do. You hold up *your* end of the bargain. You drive her around."

Once more, all Amelia did was grin. That quick, Hector made it very clear what Reinhardt's place in the pecking order was—he was the visitor, the backup, second string, just the stone-hauler—and he best tread lightly. Amelia was the talent and his only reason for being included at all. Reinhardt looked perturbed, but he didn't argue.

Hector nodded. "Alonzo, make sure he's got the address."

"Anything else?" Reinhardt asked. He'd developed a little chip on his shoulder at being put in his place, and it was showing.

Hector hooked a thumb toward the jar. "Get rid of that." Then he headed toward the exit without missing a beat.

Reinhardt blinked. "Any particular instructions for that?"

Amelia turned another page in her magazine. "There's a dumpster outside."

"Really?" Reinhardt asked.

Hector nodded in agreement, then left.

Alonzo smiled and patted Reinhardt on the shoulder. "See you tonight, hotshot. Thanks for all your help." Then he put on his sunglasses and followed Hector, leaving Reinhardt behind to clean up the mess while Amelia finished reading her article.

48

Delilah and Dodger arrived at the Church after midday, then Dodger teamed up with Izzie and headed out for Sweet Valley Ranch to relieve Finch and Piper. Once that was squared away, Delilah poked her head in on her brother. He was alone at the clubhouse bar, peeling the label off a bottle of beer. Bingo had retired for a little midday siesta, leaving the bar in amateur hands.

"You look like hell," Gabriel quipped, but he managed a grin.

"Back at ya," Delilah replied. "Michael came to see me."

Gabriel frowned. "What'd he want?"

"The usual. Wanted to know why I was burning shit down, and to know if I knew why the Helitori was trying to kill my friends. He wanted to offer his 'help.'"

"What did you tell him?"

"To piss off, for the most part."

"So now the Watch is all up in our shit?"

"They're working on it, yeah," Delilah conceded. "Anything new?"

Gabriel shook his head. "Not yet. Wortzy's hitting the streets though, so we'll see if something shakes loose. You ready to get to work?"

"Yup," Delilah replied, feigning cheerfulness. "Fasting and sober and all that shit." Tonight, she'd work a divination to try and find Felipe one more time. Fasting was part of preparing herself for the ride and staying sober was just to keep her head clear. Though to be honest, she could use a bowl or two of Finchy's good herbal medicine to help even out the rough spots. She was on the bottom slump of last night's tweaker binge, which meant she pretty much felt like shit. "I'll be working downstairs."

Gabriel nodded. "Have you thought about asking Mahri for her help? She's closer to Felipe than any of us."

"Yes, I have," Delilah replied. "And no, we're not going to do that."

Gabriel looked like he expected an explanation.

"She's a wild card. I don't need a wild card right now."

"She saved my ass last night," Gabriel said.

"Good."

"She wants to help."

"Then she can help by staying out of the way."

Gabriel just shrugged and shook his head.

That was enough to irritate Delilah, who was already plenty irritable at being hungry and sober. "Look. You're not gonna make me spell this out, are you? *Fine.* Yeah. She's Mahri. I love her. *But,* Doc McCoy's dead, and she's as responsible for that as anybody. So you'll excuse me for feeling a little conflicted about that, okay?"

Gabriel raised his hands in surrender, not wanting to pick a fight. "I get it, kiddo."

"Do you?" Delilah didn't sound convinced.

"I do."

She sighed. "I'm sorry, but I don't trust her. You might. I don't. You say she's on our side, fine, that's your call, and I trust you on that. But I don't want Mahri around when I'm sticking my neck out. You may have a selective memory on this, Gabriel, but she has a bad habit of cutting and running when shit gets tough, and I can't afford that."

Gabriel grunted a single, sour chuckle.

"Neither can you," Delilah cautioned. Then she shrugged, not knowing what else to say on the matter. "Just... Be careful, okay?"

Gabriel nodded. "Yeah." He changed gears. "You let me know if you guys need anything for tonight."

Delilah smiled. "I got this." She flicked her fingers toward the door. "Go. Do Gabriel shit. If you just sit around here all day, you're gonna get on my nerves."

Gabriel smiled too. "Maybe I'll go get a bacon cheeseburger." He only said it to needle her. He knew she was starving.

"Butthole," she muttered and then headed off into the bowels of the Church.

49

Gabriel went for a drive to clear his head and stopped off around four o'clock for a cup of coffee and a cheeseburger at a little dive down by the Forum. The afternoon had turned hazy, warm, and golden.

When he was done, he perched on the trunk of his car and had a smoke while he decided what to do next, but he was in no hurry. Wortzworg and his little minions were crawling the streets, and that net was cast. If there was something to shake out, they were likely to find it fast, and his own people were just a phone call away and keeping their eyes and ears peeled as well. If any Crow in Los Angeles caught a whiff of something worth talking about, his phone would ring.

He thought about making a trip to Sweet Valley, to check up on things with Silver Dollar. But he dismissed that notion. It was handled, the right people were on it, and he didn't need to hover like a fidgety helicopter mom on the playground.

God, Mahri ... what the hell was he going to do with her? The answer, for the time being, was nothing. Not until Delilah, Fiona, and Finch gave him a direction they could jump. And that was going to be a while. He needed to get his head straight about her and put some mental distance there before he did something stupid, though.

He finished his cigarette, put it out in the last swallow of his coffee cup. He'd just dismounted his bumper and dropped the cup in the nearby trash can when his phone started to buzz. The caller ID showing it was Jimmy Torres.

Gabriel answered though he was kind of dreading the conversation. "What's happening, Jimmy?"

"Bad news travels fast," Jimmy complained. "I point you toward the Couatl, and you go piss in her Cheerios?"

"Eh, blame Felipe," Gabriel replied.

"Yeah, well, thankfully she does. Mostly. You do realize, as far as she's concerned, she gave him to you. She expects whatever ransom you offered her paid."

"Yeah, well, I'll sort that out. She's gonna have to take a number, though." Gabriel frowned and struck up another smoke. "That's not why you called, though, is it?"

"No, it is not," Jimmy confirmed. "So, you know how I told you Felipe wanted me to put him together with the Bull, but I refused?"

"Yeah."

"Well, karma comes full circle. The Bull asked me to get him a sit-down with *you.*"

Pepe Ramos, the Bull of Los Angeles. Chief emissary of the Queen of House Del Torro in Southern California. A street captain extraordinaire, like Gabriel himself.

"What does he want?"

"Well, like I said. Bad news travels fast. He's got an interest in Felipe, and he wants to talk about it with you."

Gabriel didn't hesitate. A meeting with the Bull might be exactly what he needed. If they could shake hands on Felipe Ortiz being a common enemy, it could add some wagons to the circle. Every safe harbor Gabriel could deny the little shit brought them that much closer to nailing him. "Okay. I'm in. When and where?"

"He's back in town tonight. *La Campeche* at eight?"

Gabriel nodded. "Yeah, I can do that."

"Okay. I'll pass the word."

"Thanks, Jimmy."

Jimmy balked. "Don't thank me until you see how it turns out. I don't make any promises. My sway with the Bull ain't what it used to be."

"I'll keep that in mind," Gabriel said. Then they hung up.

50

Finch and Piper returned to the Church around four o'clock and Fiona wasn't far behind. Their update was less than encouraging. "Things were stable until midday," Finch reported. "Then, transition, and now that things are sliding toward night..." He shook his head. "There's a very real sense that we aren't doing well. Izzie's holding down the fort, and Miss Althea went to get something to help us contain the problem for as long as we can."

Delilah cocked a pale eyebrow. "Like what?"

"She said she was coming back with a casket. And the Vert Grimoire of Jean Francois Mercier." He shook his head, not sure what the priestess plan was, nor had he been able to get her to elaborate. "But yeah, you can feel it. The worm is definitely starting to turn."

"Anything in particular?" Delilah asked.

"Birds," Finch replied. "Starlings to be exact. Thousands of them. Starting to gather all over the ranch. They clearly know something we don't."

That wasn't creepy or anything. Delilah sighed and nodded. "Okay, Finchy."

Finding Felipe was still a top priority for the talent, so they fell in with Delilah in the basement laboratory and got straight to work preparing the night's divination. This would be nothing so simple and sloppy as a by-the-seat-of-the-pants Red Dream. Felipe was too powerful a target for that. This divination would have structure and safeguards, and great caution would be exercised. The risks of jumping in after him with both feet were just too high. Besides, the going assumption was that Felipe would not want to be found and that made things exponentially more difficult. Delilah, Finch, and Fiona worked diligently, chasing the setting sun.

"Where do we even begin?" Finch asked without looking up from his task. He was slowly walking the floor of the Church laboratory, inspecting the runes laid out for the night's divination—the ones that would conceal their prying eyes from detection. "I mean, honestly. One of the Nine Horrors. We're not even talking theoretical at this point, are we? This is something we're going to *have to* deal with."

Fiona offered no reply. She walked the opposite side of their spell circle performing the same inspection.

Finch looked up to Delilah, who was toweling off her hair. She was barefoot and naked except for her bathrobe. She'd just finished a long, quiet, meditative bath under a cool shower to ground away the metaphysical noise of the day. God knew there had been more than plenty of that. She pulled the towel away from her head and her snowy white hair feathered down to frame her face, curling up and sticking out at the ends. She blinked. "What? Are you talking to me?"

"Yeah, I'm talking to you," Finch replied. When she continued to give him a puzzled look, he recapped. "The Elder Thing that's bouncing around inside Silver Dollar's head? If we want to get paid—and who doesn't want to get paid—we're going to be expected to deal with it, right?"

"Yes," Fiona replied curtly. "Now pay attention to your work, James." Fiona never called anyone by their nicknames or their surnames. Always their given names. No matter how strange it sounded to everyone else.

"Work's done," Finch answered with a dismissive flap of his hand. Then he turned back to Delilah. "Tell me you've got an idea about that."

Delilah shrugged. "A couple. Maybe. I don't know, Finchy. It's all kind of new information."

"One thing at a time, children," Fiona scolded. "Here and now, we're divining the location of Felipe Miguel Ortiz. Which, need I remind you, is not a game." The Lady Crow finished her inspection of the protective circle and gave a nod.

"I'm just thinking we might consider renegotiating the price is all," Finch said. "Things being what they are."

"Victor's decision," Fiona reminded him. "And he will decide soon enough."

Delilah didn't throw gas on the fire by jumping into the conversation. Her mother was right. It didn't matter right now. They had other work to concentrate on first.

For reasons unknown, Delilah was feeling antsy. That wasn't good, considering the ride she was about to take. She needed to be calm, centered, level. She didn't need to take anything into the divination with her that might skew the results. In all fairness, being clear-headed and sober tended to *make* her a little antsy, and she'd been in that condition all goddamn day. But her mother would frown upon her and Finch stepping outside for some self-medication right before the big show—and she'd be right to do so. Delilah didn't need to be euphoric and cotton-headed any more than she needed to be antsy.

Level. Neutral. A blank canvas ready to receive. Her metaphysical footprint had to be light as a feather. She couldn't allow noise from her anxiety or big puffy white clouds of her serenity to enter with her. This was the black mage, tainted by the Outer Darkness she was spying on. Not some off-the-cuff Red Dream she was riding for a white trash shifter pack.

By the time the sun slipped below the horizon, and the great energetic tides of the mortal world rolled over from day to night, they were prepared.

After one more walk-through, Finch looked up at his cohorts. "Are we ready to do this?" He looked to Fiona first, who nodded her consent, then they both looked to Delilah.

Her nerves remained unsettled, and she couldn't quite bottle them. But it didn't matter anymore. The sun was down, and the clock was ticking. She nodded towards Finch. "Bring the bucket, would you?"

Finch brought her a blue plastic pail full of a warm salty brine, and her mother lit a long narrow taper that bloomed up a pale yellow flame. She set about the inner and outer circles of the prepared ritual area and one by one lit all twenty-one candles that joined the two rings.

While Fiona worked her slow and methodical way through the entwined circles, Delilah brought her focus on task. This was delicate, meticulous, precise work. She sought to take nothing into the Divination that might distort her vision. She sought to be an empty canvas. An invisible window. She looked around the spell circles, cast now in the flickering halos of candlelight. She looked to her mother. "Ready?"

Fiona gave a single nod.

Delilah removed her robe and tossed it aside, well away from the circle. Being naked as the day she was born in front of Finch and her mother was no cause for self-consciousness or embarrassment. As with every other aspect of this divination, she could take nothing into the circle with her that might distort her reading or increase her metaphysical footprint.

She took a deep breath, gave Finch a final nod, and closed her eyes.

He upended the lukewarm bucket of briny water over her head, and as it washed over her, it was just cool enough to take her breath away—it was one last rinse to ground out the energies collecting outside the confines of the circle. They would have been clinging to her like static during the time she was waiting.

She ran a hand down her face, brushing the salty water from her eyes before it could sting them too badly. She smoothed back her hair and then shook the excess from her hands and feet as best she could. It made her feel a little awkward, like a stork dancing in a rain puddle. She caught Finch trying to suppress a grin. "Don't you laugh at me," she muttered.

Finch sketched a simple salute and stepped away.

Delilah took three deep, centering breaths and watched the salty water circle down the drain in the laboratory floor.

She strode forward across the lab and stepped inside the circle. Moving with calm deliberateness, she knelt at its center. Soft candlelight sparkled off her water-dappled skin and reflected in her violet eyes. She inhaled, and the dampness opened up her nose. She gave her mother a nod to continue with the ritual and timed her own breathing into a gentle, steady, fluid rhythm until, degree by degree, Delilah was calmed and centered.

She let the rest of the room fade away into insignificance. She was safe. Finchy and her mother would be there to pull her out if something went wrong. There was nothing to fear. Fear was a distraction. Fear was poison. Fear was the screaming red madness in her aura that would announce her presence to the very prey from which she sought to remain hidden.

She waited, quiet and still in the dim candlelight as her mother did her workings at the simple wooden altar that stood at the edge of the circle.

Fiona placed a small earthenware bowl, enameled in a rich olive green, on the altar before her. On her right was a gooseneck silver decanter of hot, purified water. Laid out upon a pristine cloth, to her left and cleansed in smoke was the knife Gabriel had used to slay Felipe's creature in the alleyway. Beside the knife was the divination crystal Gabriel brought back from the plundered cash depot. Both had seen the shadow and stain of Felipe's magic. They would anchor the night's divination back to their master.

Fiona began to intone an incantation in a low, gentle voice, but Delilah put the words of the spell out of her mind lest they take root there and create undesirable noise. As the Lady Crow spoke her spell, she took up the silver decanter. Steam rose from its neck as if from a warm teapot. With her other hand, Fiona took up the charred knife and laid its bloodied blade across the earthenware bowl. Then, weaving the steaming stream from the gooseneck spout back and forth, she poured the pure water across the blade.

Steaming water rolled over the blackened steel and in the candlelight ruby droplets rained into the waiting bowl beneath. Once the blade had been sampled, Fiona set it aside and repeated the process with the smoky crystal.

When she was finished, she set the decanter aside and raised the bowl in both hands and approached the circle.

Stepping carefully through the opening she had left in the circle, Fiona presented Delilah with the steaming bowl. Delilah accepted it with a reverent nod.

Retracing her footsteps with equal caution, Fiona withdrew from the circle. Once beyond the outermost ring of runes, Fiona bent down and retrieved one of the candles, lit but not yet in position.

With a final parting nod of confidence to her daughter, Fiona placed the candle within its warding glyph and sealed the circle.

Delilah felt the world beyond the circle drift away into a darkened, silent fog. Only the dancing candlelight, the runes about her, and the smooth concrete floor within the circle remained. A sense of weightlessness, of neutral buoyancy, settled over her. Prickling energy passed along the lines of the runes and up her body. It was a peculiar mix of sensations, a cross between playful flicks of a lover's tongue and the marching crawl of ants. She kept the sensation contained. Too easy now, wrapped in the protections of the spell circle, to just drift away carelessly.

She closed her eyes and inhaled the steam rising from the pink-stained water in the bowl. The vapor had a peculiar weight, a density. She raised the bowl to her lips and sipped the blood tea.

Then she took three deep breaths.

Delilah opened her eyes.

And once more, the world rushed away into the crimson fog of a Red Dream.

51

The fall down the crimson rabbit hole was long, dizzying, and deep.

At several points along the downward spiral, faces drifted out of the bloody gloom, but Delilah was unable to capture them. Noise. Insignificant people. No one that had mattered to the man she sought.

This wasn't where she wanted to be, floating along in the crimson maelstrom. She focused, probed, dug deeper.

She knew the Red Dream could only show her that which she brought into it, what the tokens Gabriel collected had to offer. But those would be enough to put her on the scent of Felipe's workings, and from there, she'd do the rest.

There was so much noise. A thousand little echoes from all the people Felipe's power had recently touched. People whose life trajectories had been altered one way or another by crossing Felipe's path. There was a bottom to this well. A place that divided everything before, and everything after.

The place where Felipe first whispered into the Outer Darkness for the power to kill, and it whispered back, granting his request.

Delilah dove down deep, seeking it out, putting the extraneous noise out of her mind.

There she found Felipe, or more precisely, the memory of him.

It was night shrouded in the crimson fog of lost memory, chill and rainy. Those were few and far enough between in Los Angeles that it marked the place and time for Delilah well. She was with Felipe's memory, at the time and place that Dante Washington's cash depot was robbed.

Felipe stood alone in the rain, facing the depot from the parking lot, his back to her. In his right hand, he clutched a great tall staff of writhing, monstrous shadows. Within the aura of miserable hunger, Delilah could see that what he really held was a sliver of pitted iron, jagged, slender, and dagger-like. As he clutched the token in his fist, shadows, blacker than black, wormed their way in and out of his flesh, crawling up and down his arm. They passed in through his chest and came out through his mouth with his breath like steam. The shadows swarmed around him like a nest of hungry eels, sliding in an out of his body, passing back and forth between Felipe and the jagged iron bit in his hand.

Felipe pointed the relic toward the depot doors at the top of the loading dock. Up and down the block, the power went out, and the writhing darkness that took on the form of a great staff in Delilah's vision exploded, rocketing toward the door like a black lightning bolt.

The door shivered, then slowly swung open.

Felipe called to Maglo, the Fifth Horror, for madness—and madness came. The cloud of ink black phantom eels surrounding Felipe swarmed into the cash depot through the open door. In the Red Dream, the screaming and dying began.

Delilah could feel an echo of the memory as the power flooded through Felipe. It was like having a back-bending orgasm while the person fucking you shotgunned a toot of coke up your nose. It was bulletproof invincibility. It was gold and God, a font of power without end. An ever-flowing tap of mutilation and ecstasy.

The sense of it almost overwhelmed her, nearly cast her out of the Red Dream gasping for breath. And for her, it was nothing but a distant memory. What that must have felt like to Felipe in the moment would have been beyond addictive. Beyond power. Beyond joy or euphoria.

It would have driven him fucking mad.

And he kept doing it. Over and over and over again.

Creeping like a cat in the wake of memories past, Delilah followed Felipe into the bloody dark as he whipped and battered the cash depot with the vicious madness of Maglo.

Delilah crossed the threshold with him, and the world turned, folding in on itself.

When it righted again, they were no longer at the plundered cash depot.

She was running through the red dark from a great golden cat with the face of a beautiful young boy. She turned a corner, raising the shadowy mass in her right hand, snarling and triumphant. The great cat rounded the corner, and she destroyed it—its guts ruptured, its bones snapped, its lungs turned to pulp, and its eyes exploded.

Then, while it lay there, torn and dying, she violated it with the essence of Maglo—and breathed black life into its agonizing death.

Her hunters pursued her, but she wasted no more time on them. She left her awful golem, alive with Maglo's malice, to deal with them.

But it wasn't good enough. That was last night when Felipe had tried to kill Gabriel. It did her no good to know where he'd been. She needed to know where he was *now*. Cautious, knowing she was dangerously pressing the boundary that separated the memory of Felipe's workings from his waking mind, she drove on.

Again, the world flipped and turned, and when it righted once more, she was in a city of rust and steel. She had a sudden sense of being apart from Felipe's memories. Something had turned. Something was wrong.

She was busted.

She was eye-to-eye with Felipe at the edge of his mind, met by him at the gates of his castle of rust. Too deep. Too far. One echo of memory too many and Felipe saw her. His eyes blazed white with Maglo's hate, and he strode forward to meet her, writhing blackness shrouding the iron bit in his right hand.

It was time to leave.

Withdrawing, Delilah cloaked herself in the haze of lost memories, creating a blinding fog between her and Felipe's will to pursue. She began to force her way back through the Red Dream. Like a swimmer in deep water fighting their way upward toward the surface with smooth, solid strokes, back toward the conscious mind. *Calm,* she told herself. *Back out calmly. Thrashing will only make you even more visible.*

From the depths below, she heard Felipe scream with Maglo's thunderous thousand voices. Then something grabbed her, and all sense of calm flew out the window as the red world around her flooded black with hungry shadows.

Delilah screamed as dark specters swarmed up out of the crimson depths, sinking their putrid claws and teeth into her spirit. She had wandered too far, taken a great risk in following Felipe's thread all the way to the edge of his waking mind and he'd lashed back at her with everything he had.

Clinging, vile specters sliced her to the spiritual bone.

She was naked in here, adrift in the crimson fog, kept safe only by the armor of protective incantations she had prepared with Finch and Fiona. The phantoms chewed and tore, ripped and screamed, worming their way into every chink, every tiny gap.

One of the foul specters hooked her deep, a feeling like talons burying into her belly, trying to pull her guts out through her asshole.

Screaming, grinding her teeth against the agony, Delilah kept driving upward through the fog. Her only hope was if she could drag the hungry predators back into the confines of the ritual's gateway—then, she would have power—then, her mother and Finch would be waiting to help her.

The evil specters hauled against her, trying to drag her down, and the tug of war continued.

In a fighting, clawing, kicking clinch, they spiraled upward through the endless red gloom. The specters clung to her like lampreys, gnawing, raking, biting, and shrieking.

All Delilah could do was scream and keep driving on.

52

Within the ritual circle, Delilah suddenly shrieked, and Finch and Fiona both jumped with a start.

Delilah was dragged from her knees down to all fours by an unseen force that. It snagged a hold of her and pulled her face to the floor. Delilah struggled against the invisible attacker to no avail. Unseen hands pulled at her hair. Phantom fingers left divots in her skin as they closed over her wrists and ankles. Bruised red welts appeared along her bare back as something tried to tear into her from behind.

"Fiona!" Finch shouted, pointing at the apex of the ritual circle. "Open it!"

"Wait!" Fiona warned.

But Finch was having none of it. He rounded the circle at a sprint. "Open it. Now!"

Hissing under her breath, Fiona tore the candle from the apex of the circle. Without slowing, Finch dove inside, scrambled around behind Delilah, and snagged her under the arms. Then he heaved with all his strength, but she didn't budge. Not an inch. It was like trying to lift Thor's hammer.

"Fiona!" Finch called, straining. "Help!"

Fiona began to intone a spell, words flying from her lips at a machine gun pace. In the circle, Finch struggled, feeling the corruption of the putrid, malicious things that were attacking his friend.

He held on for dear life while Lady Crow tried to save them both.

53

L ike a missile on a manic ride toward the moon, Delilah
rocketed out of the depths of the Red Dream. And the parasites ripping her apart held fast.

They assailed her with horrific images that were as real-
istic as the sensations she was feeling. In her mind's eye, they
gnawed her tongue out. Gouged her eyes. Split her open from
belly button to asshole. Bit nipples off in bloody tears. Ripped
her hair from her scalp. Pried on her fingers until the bones
snapped and even pulled teeth from her mouth.

Then, Felipe's leering face floated up out of the writhing
blackness, and he surged forward through the lamprey swarm
and latched his hand on her throat.

Delilah screamed in fury and drove her bony little fist
into Felipe's phantom face. Once. Twice. Three times for good
measure. Then she buried her thumb in his right eye.

Spectral blood flowed, and Felipe screamed, letting her
go—because as juiced up as he was, he had forgotten just who
he was fucking with. He disappeared into the murk below as
she rocketed upward through the Red Dream.

Then there was a calamitous golden flash of light and
sound.

The pain, the grotesque injuries, they faded into vibrating
numbness, and the attacking specters began to lose their grip.

She was close. Real world sensations flooded in and
joined with the experience of the Red Dream. Something else,
someone else had a hold of her. Pulling her away from the
vicious beasts now nipping at her heels, kicking and stomping

down at them along with her as she rushed upward.

With a triumphant cry, Delilah erupted back into the waking world.

She and Finch went flipping over backward, twisting around to pile up on the floor in a heap.

Delilah looked between their tangled feet, and she actually saw the translucent image of three grotesque apparitions as they flooded into the circle with them.

Finch let out a scream as one of them sank its translucent claws into his groin and leg. He slid out of Delilah's embrace and was dragged back toward the center of the circle.

A second phantom joined in the vicious grapple, and Finch began to buck and kick in wailing agony.

"No!" Delilah screamed, diving forward and grabbing Finch by both wrists. She dragged him toward the circle's edge while the specters tried to pull him toward the center. "Finch! Help me!"

Grinding his teeth, Finch finally got his heel anchored against the floor, and he shoved, twisting like a gazelle caught in the jaws of a crocodile.

For a split second, he broke free of the groping specters and managed to lurch halfway to his feet.

Scrambling, dragging, heaving, and gasping, Finch and Delilah collapsed outside the circle. They managed to fall all over themselves without dislodging any of the candles.

"Close it!" Finch shouted to Fiona.

The Lady Crow jammed the candle back into its warding glyph at the apex of the circle even as the ghostly specters launched themselves at the gap. The candle slammed home. There was a loud *slap* of noise and spectral wind. All twenty-one candles in the circle huffed out in a hiss ... and the snarling specters vanished.

Delilah and Finch were sprawled on the laboratory floor in a breathless tangle. Finch was still wincing in pain.

"You okay?" Delilah asked.

"Other than feeling like I got my tenders ripped off?" Finch replied. He sighed. "Yeah. You?"

"I'm okay." She sat up and pulled her knees up to her chest.

She was still very much naked, wet, skinny, and starting to shiver. "Mom?"

Fiona nodded. "I'm fine." She was glowering at the dark, empty circle. Then she glowered at Delilah instead. "What was that?"

Delilah shook her head and shrugged. "I might have zigged when I should have zagged."

It could have been worse. The burn of the Red Dream, which had left her so shaken the night out in the desert with the Godfather and his pack, was little more than an annoying itch this time around. The perks of riding a Red Dream with the proper caution and preparations first. Exiting the circle had stripped most of the lingering effects of the Red Dream from her. Which was good, because she'd been treated to all sorts of feelings, sights, and sensations that she never wanted to have or see again.

Finch handed her the towel and the bathrobe. He was still gimping on that right leg from the night before. This hadn't done him any favors.

"Thanks," Delilah said, slipping the robe on. "You sure you're okay, Finchy?"

"In perfect order," he replied with a lopsided grin as he helped her to her feet.

"I take it you got caught?" Fiona asked with a disapproving frown.

Delilah sighed. That was her mother. Always easy to please and sympathetic in the extreme. "Something like that. But, not before I filled my data banks with nightmare fuel."

She shrugged into the robe and wiped her face with a sigh. A wicked little smirk twisted her lips at the memory of stomping Felipe right back down into his nasty little rabbit hole. *That's right, you motherfucker.* It was never wise, no matter how big the stick you were swinging, to follow Delilah St. John down the dark alley of her own Red Dream.

She could feel the pieces of her Red Dream coming together, like a line of dots connecting in blood. She looked to her Lady Mother as Fiona inspected the workings on their altar. "How'd we do?"

After a moment, Fiona held up the little divination crystal for her to see.

It had turned blood red.

Delilah smiled. "Gotcha, asshole."

54

In his castle of rusted steel, Felipe Ortiz fell to his hands and knees, clutching his head. He screamed. "You bitch! You fucking bitch!" Lights danced behind his eyes while the ice pick dug around in his skull. A parting gift from Delilah St. John.

He shrieked. Wept. Laughed. He wailed at the darkness with only the shadows and the Will of Maglo to hear him. He didn't need anything else, and he didn't *want* anything else.

They would be coming. Soon. And that would be good. That would be just fucking fine. He willed them to come for him. Dared them.

"Fuck you!" he screamed, thrashing in the dark. "Fuck you!"

A hundred rats had gathered around to watch him with small black eyes in the dusty dark. Something wicked, something foul, something almost electric had drawn them, and while they watched with their small black eyes, they pondered with small black minds.

Felipe squeezed the jagged sliver of iron in his right hand and pounded his fist into the dirty floor until both his knuckles and palm were bloody.

The Fang of Maglo bit deep into his hand. It drank.

In a tantrum of rage, Felipe jabbed the Fang into the floor point-first, and it bit into the old concrete like soft wood. A metallic shriek echoed through the dusty darkness like a peal of thunder.

Every rat fell dead. They tipped over without a twitch—even dropping from the rafters and girders above to hit the floor in furry wet plops. *Plop. Plop. Plop.*

Felipe Ortiz sat in the shadows, screaming, giggling,

and crying like a madman. "Gonna have me some fun," he whispered between screams, grinding the tip of the Fang in the concrete. "Gonna have me some fun..."

55

Gabriel rolled Downtown at eight o'clock and cashed in his appointment with Pepe Ramos at *La Campeche*. The ropes were up on the sidewalk, but the line was empty. No eager club-goers were waiting to get in yet, but they'd start assembling soon enough. *Campeche* didn't open for another couple of hours, but when it did, it would party all night. Until then, the place was very private.

"I have an appointment with Pepe," Gabriel told the well-dressed no-neck at the door.

The man let Gabriel pass with a simple nod.

The Bull of Los Angeles was seated at a prominent VIP booth at the back of the cavernous dance floor sipping a cocktail. He was attended by four hard-looking house soldiers and to his left sat two stylishly dressed young men. One of them wore a straw-colored cowboy hat. To his right sat a little boy—small and slender, dressed in a dark suit as if on his way to a wedding. Or maybe a funeral. His dark hair was meticulously combed, but there was something alien in his posture—it was too still, too straight. As Gabriel approached, the little boy's gaze tracked him the way a praying mantis tracks a fly.

Other than Pepe and his entourage, the plush club hall of *La Campeche* was deserted.

Pepe rose as Gabriel climbed the steps to the booth and extended his hand in greeting. The Bull of Los Angeles was fifty-something, of modest height and build, sharply dressed in a dark suit and a striped shirt, with not a sliver of gray yet showing in his black hair and thick mustache.

Pepe's soldiers kept a respectful distance while the players met at the table.

"Welcome, welcome. Can I offer you anything?" Pepe the Bull asked as he shook Gabriel's hand.

"No, thank you."

"Please, sit with me." Pepe gestured toward the table, and Gabriel pulled up a seat.

He studied the Bull and his guests. The young man in the cowboy hat wore a diamond-encrusted gold watch—the precious stones catching the light, throwing off a dozen tiny rainbows. Designer boots. Designer jeans. Designer cowboy shirt. On his right hand was a three-piece ring set, one each adorning his index, middle, and ring fingers, and each digit sported a leering skull—*Tres Muertes*—cartel enforcers from down south. Mexico's most ruthless were in the house tonight.

That wasn't particularly comforting.

Neither was the little boy, who continued to study Gabriel with his emotionless insect-like stare, unmoving in his smart little suit.

Gabriel cleared his throat and got down to business. "So, Jimmy Torres tells me we have something in common. Felipe Ortiz."

Pepe gave a slight nod. "I think we may have several things in common, *carnal*." He produced a cigar from his jacket, taking one for himself and offering one to his guest.

Gabriel declined.

Pepe seasoned the end of his cigar by rolling it in the pale flame of a wooden match until it was glowing merrily." The *Videntes del Toro* had a vision," he said at length.

"Is that so?" Gabriel asked. "And what did the old gals see?"

Pepe nodded, cigar smoke swirling around his head. "They saw a red-eyed crow pecking black maggots from the eyes of a dead horse. What do you suppose that means?"

Gabriel chuckled. "I don't know, Pepe. Maybe it means that we're about to make a killing on the ponies. Why the sudden interest in crows and maggots and crazy old oracles?"

For those gifted with it, old age and clarity of the Sight rarely went together. Each Look eroded the mind, stretched the

Eye wider and wider. Years of burning the Sight made a seer eccentric. *Decades* of it made them nutty as a shithouse rat, with Eyes stretched so wide it was hard to predict what they might see and harder still to understand what they saw. Such a fate was in his sister's future if she wasn't careful with her gifts.

Gabriel could see Pepe counting the chits, doing the mental math. It set him on edge.

Finally, the del Torro captain spoke." This is Alejandro Castillo," Pepe explained, nodding toward his guest in the cowboy hat. "He represents the interests of friends who are very dear to *La Reina del Torro.* His people are not pleased. So my queen is not pleased."

The cartel enforcer tipped a finger to the brim of his hat in a curt nod.

"A pleasure," Gabriel replied. He inclined his head toward the creepy little boy. "And who's he?"

"My nephew," Pepe said, making no effort to sound sincere. "Little Juan Carlos."

Gabriel grunted out a single chuckle and tried not to let his rising paranoia show.

"I've been hearing things, *carnal*," Pepe said.

"Busy streets out there," Gabriel replied with a shrug. "Like what?"

Pepe continued. "You know, the Bull and Crow been at peace for a long time. Everyone making friends. Everyone making money. I would hope if something were threatening to change that, and you knew something about it, we might be able to sit down and discuss it. Before things got out of hand."

A warning chill crawled up Gabriel's spine. His voice got low and his demeanor deadly serious. "What aren't here to talk about Felipe Ortiz, are we Pepe?"

Pepe shook his head.

Every instinct Gabriel had acquired from a life on the street told him to haul ass. This was not going according to plan, and things that didn't go according to plan got you killed—but, so did being a skittish punk when you ought to be cool. Being skittish made you look guilty and weak, and those were two things you couldn't afford when you were in the shark tank.

Gabriel kept rolling the dice. "Then what *are* we here to talk about?"

The Bull of Los Angeles took a long pull from his cigar, savored it, then blew it out. "Thirty-four million dollars in missing cash."

Gabriel's stomach sank to the floor as he connected the dots. Dante Washington, one of Southern California's biggest money launderers. Thirty-four million in cash missing from one of his depots. And not only did Pepe Ramos, the Bull of Los Angeles, know all about it, but he was sitting here with a cartel enforcer who was pissed off over it too.

Which could only mean one thing.

The thirty-four million wasn't Dante Washington's money. It was the cartel's.

Gabriel took a deep breath. "Where's this going, Pepe?"

Pepe gave a solemn shrug. "I told you I was hearing things, *carnal*."

"Such as?"

"Who took the money."

Gabriel didn't like the look in Pepe's dark eyes. "Yeah?"

Pepe nodded. "Word is, the Crow got paid."

The adrenaline started to flow as the cartel enforcer's ring-laden hand slipped discreetly beneath the table into his lap. "You don't believe that, do you?" Gabriel asked.

"It's not what I believe," Pepe said, almost apologetically. "It's what I'm obligated to prove. And I owe it to my queen and the friends of my house to find out."

Gabriel nodded, his pulse beginning to race in his ears while his hand inched toward his own pistol. The whole room tightened up like an over-wound guitar string. Four of Pepe's soldiers. Two cartel *sicarios*. And the child of the corn. The odds. They were terrible.

Pepe shrugged. "Business, *carnal*."

"Yeah," Gabriel replied.

Then everything went to shit.

56

Everyone moved at once. Everyone but Pepe Ramos. He didn't move at all.

Gabriel and the two *sicarios* sprang to their feet. Pistols came out in a blur. Pepe's Bulls began to move.

It was little Juan Carlos who decided things though. His alien stillness broke, his jaw unhinged, and his mouth opened with a roaring hiss. A swarm of swirling shadows burst from his gaping maw like the dark breath of an angry dragon.

The swarm swept over Gabriel, heaving him backward off his feet. He bounced across the polished dance floor, skidding and sliding.

The shadowy mass coiled around him, cold and suffocating. His warding tattoos burned and tightened, trying to fend off the fiendish attack. As the shadows twisted and turned, they coalesced into a vaguely recognizable form—spiders—hundreds of them in an unstoppable host of scuttling darkness.

The mass of spectral arachnids spread over Gabriel from head to toe, spilling across the floor as he kicked, thrashed, and scraped.

Their little clawing legs pried at his eyelids, pressed between his lips, and wiggled into his nose and ears.

Gabriel screamed, a roar of primal terror, then barked an arcane command. *"Eladris-akai!"*

His right shoulder and upper arm blazed with agony as the warding spell tattooed there flashed to life. The skin bruised and wept blood. There was a flash of brilliant sapphire light and a peal of whip-crack noise.

The swarm of spectral spiders disintegrated in the blast,

retreating from their victim and attempting to flee as the counter-spell consumed them.

By the time Gabriel got his bearings and started scrambling to his feet, little Juan Carlos was already on the move.

The nasty little thing cleared the table in a leap and hit the floor on all fours. There, in a grotesque posture somewhere between ape and spider, he rushed at Gabriel. An inhuman, high-pitched and blood-curdling shriek boiled out of his gaping jaws.

Gabriel stood, his Sig came up, and he dumped a mag into little Juan Carlos as the rest of the players in the room ducked and scattered for cover. Several rounds ripped the boy's flesh, stabbed holes in his body, spattering unwholesome black goo. The creature snarled in pain but didn't even slow down.

Frantically, Gabriel began to backpedal as he swapped magazines.

Juan Carlos rushed on and just kept coming.

Gabriel rammed the second mag home. Juan Carlos jumped. Gabriel reared back and planted a kick right in the middle of the little creature's sternum. That sent the boy reeling, bouncing and sliding across the dance floor, limbs flailing for purchase.

Gabriel kept moving while his thumb came down on the slide release of his weapon and the slide snapped forward, chambering a fresh round.

Then he fanned the second mag toward the watching gallery consisting of Pepe Ramos, his four Bulls, and the two *sicarios*. That ratcheted up the chaos. Gabriel kept dashing toward the doors, popping rounds at Pepe, his crew, and his guests.

The return fire began instantaneously. Bullets hissed and screamed. The room filled with the back and forth bark of gunfire and the bright strobes of muzzle flashes.

Little Juan Carlos flipped back to his scrambling hands and feet and came rushing back into the fray.

An incoming pistol round punched Gabriel in the right side of his chest, slamming into his vest, hot and painful. It staggered him, but he was barely aware of it in the rush of adrenaline and the buzzing numbness of the fading counter-spell. A hot lance of pain grazed across the knuckles of his gun hand from another incoming round.

Gunshots echoed and clashed as combatants ducked and dodged. A chaotic gangster's melee gone off the rails.

Juan Carlos closed. Fast.

Gabriel rammed a hand into his jacket pocket as his pistol ran dry a second time. He ripped one of the rune-engraved sticks from his pocket. *"Arkath!"* he barked, dropping to a knee, tucking his head. The runes along the six-inch length of ash wood sparked into a fitful orange glow.

Juan Carlos leaped like a springing tiger. A nimbus of swarming spectral darkness exploded around him, hungry and hateful. It began to rain phantom spiders.

Gabriel shoved the glowing rod above his head in a clenched fist, trailing embers. *"Infernus,"* he whispered, and the rune-engraved rod detonated like a bomb in a halo of green flame.

A shock wave radiated from the blast, blowing the windows out of La Campeche, setting off car alarms up and down the crowded Downtown street. Pedestrians on the sidewalk were sent reeling, running, and screaming.

The blast shredded little Juan Carlos's hellish form, driving his shadowy wreckage before it like leaves in a storm. The raining hail of spectral spiders was vaporized.

Pepe and his gallery dropped, covering up from the tidal wave of green flames, knocked senseless by the blast. They were too far away to be burned, but the shockwave flattened them.

Gabriel was unharmed. Untouched.

His sister Delilah had crafted those rune sticks just for him, painstakingly attuned them to the wards in his tattoos. The blast washed over him like wind, whipping his coat tails, flattening his hair. The rod disintegrated to ash and crumbled in his hand.

By the time Pepe and his gallery regained their senses and got back on their feet, Gabriel was gone, and *La Campeche* was on fire.

57

Herbert J. Wortzworg waddled into the Lord Crow's hall, tugging at the crotch of his pants like his dick itched. "Fix me up there, Vic," he said, flicking a gesture toward the Lord Crow's tableside service.

Cocking an eyebrow, but issuing no complaint, Victor poured Wortzworg a drink.

The nasty little man plopped down in the chair at Victor's immediate left and scooped up the glass. He took a sip, approved of it with a grunt, then finished it in a single gulp.

"So," Wortzworg said with an unpleasant snort as he motioned for Victor to set him up again. "A couple of things stand out here that aren't the usual shit."

"You gonna tell me?" Victor asked as he poured.

"Miss Althea Gentles," Wortzworg said. "She's got the kind of reputation I'm not used to seeing."

"Yeah, and what's that?"

"She doesn't have one. Nobody knows who she is, and I mean nobody."

"What?"

"I'm telling ya, there's nobody walking around town with the kinda horsepower you say she's got, and I don't know about it. I don't know what to say, Vic. She's not on my radar. And I don't know where she came from."

"Okay. You got a line on any of Mahri's kids?"

"Well, Edwin's dead and gone. So's Doc McCoy, but, you already knew that. My understanding is that *you* have Mahri, but you're not going to confirm or deny that, so moving on. Alex is in the wind, no idea where he's at. But best sources think

Naomi got snatched up by the Helitori before you were even on the case, and they already disposed of her. So, maybe Alex and Mahri are still out there. But the rest of the Odd, they're retired. No helping it now."

"You didn't mention Felipe Ortiz," Victor said.

Wortzworg grinned. "Noticed that, did ya?"

Victor nodded.

"Lots of people asking around about Felipe Ortiz, Vic. What'd he do?"

Victor shrugged. "If you don't know, I don't know. What am I paying you for again?"

Wortzworg chuckled. "Lots of high-quality shit. Anyway, near as I can tell, Felipe Ortiz is still alive and kicking. Blew out of the Couatl's little Diamond Street sex dungeon last night like his ass was on fire. With your captain hot on his heels."

"High-quality shit, huh? I'm paying you to tell me stuff I *don't* know." Victor scowled. "Don't make me play Go Fish here, Wortzy put your cards on the table. You ain't earned your pay yet."

The foul little man grunted a laugh. "Heh. So, Jonathan Markus. Washington's mercenary-in-chief, you know where he was before Washington hired him? Jersey. You know what he did?"

Victor shook his head.

"He hunted down Anton Trotsky for the Gambali Family."

The Lord Crow cocked an eyebrow. Trotsky was a warlock and hell-on-wheels at that. An independent operator who didn't take shit from anybody. He'd gotten on the wrong side of a Jersey Mafia family in a heist gone wrong. The whole thing had been a setup from the start, with Trotsky offering the Gambali's one free sample of his work to prove that his brand of spooky was the real deal. But then Trotsky double-crossed the job, took the heist for himself, and left an inconvenient body count behind for his co-conspirators.

When it was over, Trotsky went ghost, and nobody had been able to touch him since he dropped off the radar—until Jonathan Markus apparently.

"So, I suppose we talk about Anton Trotsky in the past-tense now, right?" Victor asked.

Wortzy nodded and finished his second glass of Victor's good stuff. "That's tasty."

"What about the rest of Markus's crew?" Victor asked.

"Eh, they're pro's but not that kind. Markus is the real talent. He's a newcomer on the scene, but his resume is solid. Not quite sure where he got into spooky work yet, but I'll find out."

Victor mulled it over and poured a snort for himself. "So, what part are you hanging on to for a bonus?"

Wortzy smiled. "Now, would I do that to you, Vic?"

"Every time," the Lord Crow assured him.

Wortzworg gave in. "Okay, first, I know why Dante Washington's got a bee in his little bonnet. There's a truckload of cash, literally, somewhere out there in the wild, and it's got his name all over it. Something along the lines of thirty-four mill. Losing track of that will ruin a man's attitude. Explains all the hustle and bustle in Washington's playground lately, don't it?"

"Hrm," Victor grunted, unimpressed. "You're behind the times, Wortzy. I already know about the cash. He hired Mahri and the kids from the Odd to find it. They couldn't, they got their asses in deep shit, and now, it's time for the grown-ups to clean up the mess. I'm already on that. What else you got?"

The unpleasant smile that stretched across Herbert J. Wortzworg's face gave Victor pause. "I know who took the money," he said.

Victor paused. "Who?"

"Word on the street? *You*."

58

The revelation landed like a punch to the gut. Wortzworg laid out what he knew, and Victor's blood pressure steadily rose until the vein in his forehead was pulsing merrily and his teeth were grinding.

Dante Washington was going to have a motherfucking aneurysm when he got wind of it.

It was a lie, a fish story fantasy most likely ginned up by Felipe to get the Crow off his back. But there might not be any convincing a man like Dante Washington of that before shit reached critical mass.

He poured himself a drink, and another for Wortzworg and lit a cigarette.

His phone rang sixty seconds later. It was Gabriel.

His son talked, and the Lord Crow listened. "Are you okay, son?" he asked at length. On the other end, Gabriel answered. "Get back here. Now," Victor ordered. Then he hung up the phone.

Victor St. John was still and quiet for so long that Wortzworg helped himself to another slug from Victor's bottle.

"So? What's eating you?" Wortzy asked with a smart-assed snort. The little bastard thought he already knew the answer, but he was only partially correct.

Victor glowered at the nasty little man, his face expressionless, his eyes chips of granite. "It's not Dante Washington's money," he said grimly.

Wortzworg stopped mid-swig. "Come again?"

Victor laid out the connection to the cartel, and when he was done filling in the gaps, Wortzy pushed back his chair and climbed slowly to his feet. "Where are you going?" Victor grunted.

Wortzworg shrugged. "Nowhere. Just figured I'd stand up first if I was gonna shit my pants."

Yeah. That pretty much summed it up.

Victor pushed his glass aside without finishing the last swallow. His expression more dark and brooding than usual.

"You uh, want we should tell the lady of the house?" Wortzworg asked.

Victor shook his head. "Not now. She's busy." He was thoughtful and quiet for a while. "I may need a couple of sizable favors from you real soon, Wortzy."

"Favors?" Wortzworg snorted. "I don't do favors."

Victor waved his hand dismissively, "You know what I mean."

Wortzworg grunted a laugh, "It'll cost you."

"Oh, I'm sure. What'd you have in mind?"

"Dinner," Wortzworg replied.

Victor looked puzzled. "Dinner?"

"Yeah. Somewheres fancy. Somewheres you wouldn't normally be seen with the likes of me."

Victor chuckled, "Yeah. That could be arranged."

Wortzy seemed pleased by that. "In the meantime, what would you like to do now?"

The Lord Crow contemplated that for a good long while, then he rose slowly from his throne, tall and straight. He set the good bottle of Macallan in front of Wortzworg with his silent blessing and said, "You get back out there on the street. I'll let you know when I figure the rest out." Then he picked up his own glass and walked silently from the Lord's Hall.

Wortzworg took the bottle and his leave.

59

Gabriel was shirtless, sitting on a bar stool in the clubhouse while Anna put him back together. Again. That had become a habit over the last couple of days. She'd tried to wrangle him back to the infirmary, but he'd made it as far as the clubhouse bar before pulling up a stool and a bottle and saying, simply, "Fuck it." Then he poured a drink for her and a drink for himself.

She'd grabbed her crash bag and worked on him right there while Bingo played nursemaid.

His right upper arm looked like it had been whipped with a flog until it wept blood. The price paid for forcing all that horsepower through the dispelling glyph tattooed there

The right side of his chest, just below his nipple looked like a black-and-blue bull's eye from the pistol shot he'd taken in the vest from one of the visiting *Tres Muertes sicarios*. That'd be the size of a dinner plate by morning and was going to hurt like a son of a bitch. It already felt pretty beastly.

Anna was cleaning up his bullet-grazed knuckles, commenting on how lucky he was to still have a functioning hand when fellow Crows began piling in on him.

Piper wandered in first and laughed when he got a good look at his captain. "Oh, damn. Ouch," he said, trying to contain his chuckling fit.

"Give me a fucking cigarette," Gabriel grunted. "Any word from Dodger and Izzie?"

Piper handed over a smoke and nodded. "Yeah. Talked to them about thirty minutes ago. They're all good in the hood, but they say nighttime ain't the right time. Silver Dollar's starting to get twitchy. And the birds." He leaned in and lit his captain's smoke.

Gabriel frowned. "What birds?"

"'Eh, some shit happened while you were gone."

Gabriel shook his head. First things first. "It'll keep. Mahri behaving herself?"

"Yeah. She hasn't made a peep since."

"Twitch keeping a close eye on her?"

"If it was any closer he'd be getting peed on. Which, I guess might be one of his things. Who knows."

"Nice," Anna murmured. She bandaged up Gabriel's bloodied knuckles.

The flapping stride of bare feet came rushing down the hallway in a hurry. Then Delilah burst into the clubhouse bar dressed in a damp bathrobe. The look on her face was deathly concern. She looked her big brother up and down and blinked. "Piper said you got shot." She seemed a little confused.

"Well, he did," Piper replied with a chortle.

Gabriel turned a little so she could see the fresh tie-dye job spreading out on his right side.

"Ewww," Delilah muttered, the worry easing out of her expression by a couple of degrees. Then she saw his arm. "Jesus, Gabriel, what did you do?"

"There were a lot of spiders," he replied and took a drag off his smoke.

Delilah came over and inspected his shoulder. She shook her head and sighed, "You've really got to learn better control over this."

"There were a lot of spiders," Gabriel repeated. "When will I be able to use it again?"

"Uh, not sure? I never expected you to mangle it up like this. Probably not until it heals. Maybe longer."

He nodded. That would have to do.

News of Gabriel coming home all banged up brought in the rest of his family not long after that. Fiona had the least to say but looked the most concerned. She didn't take well to seeing her kids torn up. Part of the job or not, Gabriel knew it scared her. It scared her every day. He gave her a wink, letting her know that he was okay.

As always, Fiona was cool, calm, and composed. But she didn't look the slightest bit relieved.

Gabriel couldn't blame her. If Pepe Ramos and his cartel friends had been out to kill him, he would have been dead. He had walked flat-footed into an ambush with pros thinking he was meeting friends. That kind of thing made for good television, but that was exactly how you ended up in a body bag on the street. The only reason he was still breathing was because they'd wanted to take him alive. He knew it, and so did everybody else.

Fiona squeezed his hand, kissed his scruffy cheek, and said no more.

When Anna had put Humpty Dumpty back together again, Victor ordered everybody to report to the team room. He also called out to Twitch because he wanted Mahri there, too.

Gabriel raised an eyebrow to that. "You sure?"

"Yup," was all the Lord Crow would say on the matter.

Then down the hall to the team room they went.

60

The bulk of the Crows had military or mercenary-trained backgrounds on their resumes, and the team room was a reflection of that. The walls were pin-up bulletin boards, dry-erase whiteboards, and a projector and screen with an accompanying laptop. Along the walls were a number of large reference maps—city, state, and beyond. There were ranks of chairs and a couple of old well broken-in sofas. Several long narrow tables ran the length of the room.

Dead space on the walls was filled in with pin-up girls, some assorted flags the boys had collected around the world, and an Alfred E. Neuman poster sporting the iconic "*What... Me worry?*" slogan. At some point in its history, a bored Crow had drawn a mustache and a dick picture on that poster.

On the whiteboard, written in a stern blocky hand was "*Swampthing - pay your fucking child support.*" It was signed by Victor. Below that, in a chicken-scratch scrawl was added: "*And stop knocking up fat chicks!*" It was signed with a smiley face and a crude drawing of a very round curvy woman. It looked a little like a poorly rendered prehistoric fertility idol. She was being rear-ended by a scrawny stick figure with a crooked pecker.

Victor leaned against the wall and waited as his Crows filed in. He caught Twitch at the door and had him wait just outside with Mahri.

When the house was in order, Victor spoke. His mood was solemn, no bravado, no bullshit. Just the facts.

"So, we have some developments," Victor announced. "For those of you who don't already know, here's what's up. The money we're chasing for Dante Washington. It's not his money.

It's Mexican cartel cash. One of the customers his organization launders for."

That had a chilling effect on the entire room.

"To make matters worse, word on the street is that we're the ones who stole it."

"You gotta be shitting me," Piper groaned. "Felipe?"

Victor held up a hand and gave a sympathetic shrug. It seemed likely, but he couldn't answer that yea or nay. "Right now, we got bigger issues."

"Such as?" Bingo asked.

"The cartel's heard the word on the street about us and the money," Victor replied. "Gabriel tried to go have a sit down with Del Torro tonight, but Pepe Ramos and his cartel buddies tried to scoop him up."

Gabriel cleared his throat. "So, we're somewhere between 'deep shit' and 'open season' with the cartel."

"Then we better hurry up and fix that," Piper said. "What about Washington? We on his shit-list now too?"

"I don't know," Gabriel replied with a shake of his head.

"But we're gonna find out," Victor assured everyone. "I haven't made that call yet. I wanted to talk to *my* people first. Here's the deal. The way I figure it, Washington knows damn well we didn't knock over his depot. With the insider info he's got, that just won't add up."

"For what it's worth," Gabriel said, "It didn't seem like Pepe Ramos much believed it either, but, business is business."

"That means we have to decide which way we jump," Victor said. "Right here. Right now. The payday is Dante Washington. The alternative is going straight to the cartel and trying to make peace."

Bingo chuckled. "I don't imagine us saying 'hey, we didn't do it' is gonna be very convincing."

Victor nodded. "Nope, probably not, which means, either way, we have to find the money." He gave his talent a nod. "Which we have not done yet, but we are getting closer, right?"

Delilah nodded. "Yeah, we're definitely getting closer."

"Washington lied to us," Piper grunted. "Fuck him and the mustache he rode in on. Why don't we just cut him out of the loop, track down the money and the dumb motherfucker who stole it, and go straight to the cartel? If we come up with a thief *and* their cash, we still have a pretty good chance of getting right *and* getting paid."

Victor nodded. "We do. Only problem there is that Dante Washington isn't likely to take too kindly to being cut out. Especially if we embarrass him in front of the cartel. It's our best bet of settling the beef with the cartel before it gets out of hand, but you can guarantee we make an enemy out of Washington in the process."

The room was quiet.

"Either way we go, it's a risk," Gabriel said. He took a deep breath and gave his two cents. "The safer play is stick with Washington."

"How you figure?" Piper asked.

"We've got some leverage over Washington. *Some.* We got nothing on the cartel. And they've got enough muscle and manpower to roll us under twenty times over. It isn't like *Washington* didn't know who the money belonged to. That means he's desperate. He's got to make this right. If not, he's got a war with the cartel and every partner he's got starts wondering if he can keep their money safe." Gabriel looked to his Lord Father. "We're his ticket to do that. Without us and without the Odd, he starts over from scratch. And things get ugly for him in a hurry."

Anna cleared her throat, "All of that assumes Washington isn't about to roll in here guns blazing and feed us to the cartel to cover his own ass. Right?"

Bingo grunted. "She's got a point there, slick."

"It's a card, but I don't think he'll play it," Gabriel replied. "Burning us as a scapegoat might buy him a day or two, but it doesn't actually get him any closer to the money. No money, no win. And I don't think he'd want to run the risk of putting us together with the cartel—not knowing what we know."

The part Gabriel didn't voice was his concern that if they were missing something here, then they were fucked, likely in the worst possible way. Being an outlaw meant making life-and-death decisions based on the information you had. What-ifs and maybes would drive you mad. You could second guess yourself into total paralysis. His Lord Father had taught him that.

All he could do was look at Anna and Bingo and shrug apologetically. Because they certainly weren't wrong. "I don't have a better answer."

The room fell quiet again.

Victor tilted his head toward his talent, Delilah, Fiona, and Finch. "I need to know—yes or no. Knowing what you know now, can you handle what's coming down the pike?" He counted them off on his fingers one by one. "Can you find Felipe? Can we find the money? And can we handle this shit with Silver Dollar?"

The three practitioners exchanged glances that looked less than absolutely certain, but in the end, they were in agreement. Yes, they could.

"All right," Victor said at last. "Then it's a question of do we hang with the job *and* Washington, or do we break off and go straight to the cartel." He scanned the faces around him. "Anybody got anything else they want to have heard?"

When no one did, Victor turned to Bingo. "What do you say, old man?"

Bingo was contemplative, quiet, and then he nodded. "World ain't big enough to run and hide from the cartel. Especially not with Del Torro in their corner. We stick with Washington. We finish the job."

The Lord Crow looked to Anna.

"Yeah, okay," she said reluctantly, siding with her father.

"Dodger's not here. What do you think your brother would say?" Victor asked.

Anna didn't hesitate with that answer. "He'd say go for it."

"Piper?" Victor asked.

"Yeah. Fuck it. Let's get that paycheck."

He looked to his talent. "You sure?"

They gave a collective nod.

Then he turned to Gabriel, prince of his house and Captain of his Crows.

Gabriel shrugged and managed a thin, flat smile. "If it was easy, anybody could do it, right?"

Victor took it all in, and he was not quick to respond. He looked one more time to his Lady Wife, and Gabriel could tell that both of them had their doubts.

The Lord Crow went to the door and opened it onto the hallway where Twitch and Mahri were waiting. "Come on in," he said, gesturing for them to enter.

Mahri looked uncharacteristically sheepish and fragile. Gabriel wasn't used to seeing her like that. She was always swagger and attitude. But not tonight. Not anymore.

When Victor approached her, she cast her eyes down, obviously intimidated by the shitty position she found herself in.

"You been a friend of this family a long time," Victor said gently. His tone was almost paternal. "Mistakes have been made. It is what it is. Those can't be taken back now. All we can do is move forward. Yeah?"

Mahri nodded.

"What I need to know is, are you with us, all the way, whatever it takes?"

The Lord Crow's statement hung in the air, unflinching and absolute.

Mahri swallowed the lump in her throat and replied simply, "Yes."

Victor placed his scarred hands gently on either side of Mahri's face and kissed her on the forehead. "Good girl."

"What about Washington? I—"

He shook his head, matter-of-fact. "You're with us. I'll make sure he understands that."

Mahri nodded her gratitude.

Then the Lord Crow stepped aside and lit a smoke. He surveyed the faces of his Crows—his family—one by one. Then he nodded. "I'll give Washington the call."

61

Victor made his way back to the Lord's Hall, sat upon his throne, and took out his phone.

Mr. Dante Washington answered on the third ring. "Good evening, Mr. St. John. What news do you have for me?"

Victor couldn't help but chuckle. "Oh, I got lots of news. How about you?"

"I have some, yes," Washington replied. "Such as that the word on the street is that you know where my thirty-four million dollars is."

Victor was prepared for that. He laughed. "Yeah, well, you and I both know that's bullshit, don't we?"

"I suppose so," Washington conceded.

"Here's what's not bullshit though. That thirty-four million. It ain't yours. That was cartel cash on the way to the laundromat."

A long pause. "And where did you hear that?"

"Heard it when some cartel goons tried to nab my son looking to get to the bottom of it. I'm sure they had a real swell time planned for him too."

"No point in denying it then, is there?"

"No, not so much."

"So where do you suppose that leaves us, Mr. St. John?"

"I'm not real sure. Why don't you tell me."

"I think it means we are most definitely in this together. For better or worse. Wouldn't you agree?"

"I'm going to need some convincing."

"As you said, word on the street is that the Crow stole the money. I have yet to hear *my* name. That puts you in a pretty uncomfortable place. I can protect you from the cartel, at least until this matter is resolved, then everyone can be friends again. You get paid, the cartel gets soothed and compensated, and business returns to normal."

Victor chuckled. "Yeah? And while you're protecting me from the cartel, who's gonna be protecting you?"

Washington was too slow to answer.

"Uh-huh," Victor grunted. "That's the thing, ain't it? If we walk, you're fucked."

"I don't think I see it that way," Washington replied.

"I do, and who knows ... maybe you and I go our separate ways, and we track down the cartel's cash ourselves. Make one hell of a peace offering to them, wouldn't it?"

"But not with me," Washington warned.

"Eh, I think you'll be pretty busy keeping the cartel off your back. Won't have time to mess with the little ol' Crow, will ya? Particularly after we make the cartel our new best friend."

Washington was quiet for a good long while. Then he began to chuckle.

Victor did not take that as a good sign.

"Not bad, Mr. St. John," Washington replied. "But here's the thing. I think if you were so sure about that outcome, we wouldn't be talking right now. You'd have already thrown in on the side of the cartel and lost my number. But you don't know if you can make out clean with the cartel, and you *definitely* don't know if you can scoot past me. Sound about right?"

Victor held his poker face. But Washington's assessment was on point. "Hrm. Well, maybe you're right, Mr. Washington. Maybe we are in this together."

"That was my thought, yes," Washington agreed. "Neither one of us closes this deal unless we do it together."

"Fair enough," Victor said. "Then before we go any further, we need to talk about price. As in, it just went up."

There was a long pause on Washington's end. "That's an odd position to take for a man who just agreed he can't do this without me."

"And it's a bad time for a man who just agreed he can't do this without *me* to get cheap," Victor warned. "This is how it is. You kept some pretty damn important information from me, and in doing so, you fucked us both. Now I have to clean it up, so we either settle on this, or you're on your own, and I'll take my chances with the cartel. Contrary to what you might believe, I kinda like my chances."

"What are you proposing?"

"I want you to take that original offer of yours, five percent, and I want you to double it. Then I want you to cash half of that out up front, and I want that on the table in front of me tonight. Then, we fix what you've already fucked up, cure what ails you, and we get you that money back before the cartel starts filling garbage sacks with heads."

Washington was silent.

"There is no other play here," Victor said. "You know it, and I know it. It's either this or we're not friends anymore, and you know where that goes. What's it gonna be, Mr. Washington? Stay? Or go?"

At length, Mr. Dante Washington gave Victor his answer.

62

Victor's Crows waited in somber silence for his return. Their usual mirth had all but bled out of the room. They were painted into the coffin corner, all of them knew it, and like surviving an ambush, the only way out was to fight their way through it.

That point of no return had arrived at last—with teeth.

It was a long fifteen minutes.

Victor returned to the team room at a quarter past ten. His expression was unreadable.

"Washington's on board," Victor announced. "Game on."

However, not all was sunshine and roses in the arrangements made between Mr. Dante Washington and the Lord Crow. There were some notable caveats.

First was *time*. Washington was willing to pay the Crow's price and do anything in his considerable power to facilitate the effort, but it had to happen now. Not later.

"Where's Felipe?" Victor asked, looking to his talent.

Delilah spoke up. "There's an abandoned scrap yard on the west side of Compton. Used to be King Salvage. He's there."

"How sure are you?" the Lord Crow asked.

"Hundred percent," she replied.

"If he runs, can you find him?"

Delilah nodded confidently. "I've got him until the sun comes up, and he's not getting away." The expression on her face said her connection with him was ugly, unpleasant, but solid as a rock.

Victor looked to his Captain Crow.

"We don't wait then," Gabriel said with a nod. "We know

where he is, and we hit him while he's standing still. Every hour we give this little fucker, the stronger he gets. We don't need him alive to find the money. All we need is his head."

"Fuckin' A," Piper grunted, echoing his enthusiasm.

That part was decided, but Victor looked more grim about the next piece of business. "They want us to move on Silver Dollar," he said.

"When?" Fiona asked.

"Now."

That brought a quiet chill over the room.

Delilah's jaw dropped. "Tonight? Are you serious?" She exchanged shocked looks with Finch and her Lady Mother. "We weren't expecting to do this on the fly, Dad. With everything else going on, we've had, like, an hour to talk about it. It's not the sort of thing you just—"

"It's decided," Victor said gently but firmly, cutting her off short.

"Victor," Fiona said with a single shake of her head. "This is not a good idea."

"It wasn't negotiable," the Lord Crow explained. "If you haven't noticed, things haven't exactly been going smooth on this job. Washington's confidence in us is at an all-time low, and one of his terms was to put our money where our mouth is. I can't say he's wrong, either. We bring back the head of the shit sack who stole the cartel cash, we clean house, and we do it tonight—that's how it's gotta be."

There were grumbles and half-hearted protests, but it was Gabriel who shut them down.

"He's right," the Captain Crow said, backing his Lord Father. "After everything that went down tonight, we don't want to still be on the wrong side of the Cartel come tomorrow. We don't get a second chance. We get this done. Now."

"Well," Finch said, clearing his throat nervously. "I'm excited to be a part of it. How about you?" He wasn't speaking to anyone in particular. "Speaking of confidence being at an all-time low, how are we feeling about Mr. Washington these days? Where's our piece of the pie?"

"I made him double the payout. How's that?" Victor replied.

Finch blinked. "Oh."

That got everybody's attention. Money talked.

Piper cut to the chase, no taste for bullshit. He looked to his captain, "So, how do we hit Felipe?"

"We don't," Gabriel replied, shaking his head. "You're not going."

"Whoa, whoa, whoa," Piper said in protest. "No way you go alone, boss. I'll go with you."

"Me too," Twitch offered.

But Gabriel held up his hand. "I appreciate it guys. I do. But I've seen what Felipe's capable of, and chances are he's even stronger now than he was twenty-four hours ago. You guys just aren't equipped to deal with him, and there's no time to do anything about it." He looked over at his Lord Father. "Besides, I probably won't be alone, yeah?"

Victor nodded. "Washington wants Markus in on whatever goes down with Felipe."

Piper snorted a sour laugh. "So, you're 'not gonna be alone' with Washington's all-star mercenary hit squad."

Gabriel shrugged. "I'll worry about me. I need you to look out for *them*." He nodded toward the talent, Delilah and Finch. "They're gonna be driving fast and taking all the chances tonight. If something goes wrong, if Silver Dollar gets loose..."

Piper frowned, but he nodded. "I got it, cap'n."

He gave Piper a crooked smile. "Don't worry about Felipe. I bumped heads with him once, and he ain't all that. I'll handle it."

"I'll go with you." After Mahri spoke up, you could have heard a pin drop

Every eye in the room turned her way, most of them dubious and doubtful.

"What?" she asked, looking a little self-conscious.

Gabriel's face was grim. "You understand what's gonna happen out there tonight, right? And even if it goes well, it puts you back on Washington's radar."

She nodded, scared, but resolved. "I said I was in. All the way."

Gabriel nodded, and for the first time in all this mess, he

looked like he might have been a little proud of her. "Yeah, you did."

That seemed to bolster Mahri's confidence. Just a touch. She nodded. "You won't be alone. Me either, right?"

Gabriel nodded.

The team room was quiet as a tomb.

"Anything else? Victor asked.

No one spoke up.

"That's it then," he announced. His tone had the finality of a coffin lid slamming shut. "Let's move like we got a purpose."

There was no more discussion to be had.

The Crows went to work.

63

Alex's interrogation by the Helitori was more terrifying than brutal. They understood that once you started hurting somebody, they'd say almost anything to get you to stop. Hector wasn't interested in being told just anything. He wanted the truth. And apparently, Alex was both ready to talk and had truth to tell.

The subbasement was light-less, windowless. Pitch black. Hector flipped on the lights, and Alex flinched against his bonds, his eyes pressing into pained slits as he cowered back against the wall. Hector watched as Alex struggled to make out the newcomers to his cell through the whitewashed blinded haze.

Slowly, Hector approached. Alonzo, Reinhardt, and Amelia followed at his shoulder. "You know," Hector said, inspecting the bonds that tied Alex to the wall, "Your coven mate, Naomi, met her end in very much the same way."

It was a true statement. Alex was naked, shivering, bruised, and chained to the wall in a dark, pitiless hole. The young warlock began to shake.

"I have questions for you," Hector said. "Do you want to answer them?"

"Yes," Alex replied quietly.

"Do you want to die?" Hector asked.

"No."

"Good. All you have to do if you want to stay alive is tell me the truth. Can you do that?"

"Yes." Alex licked his lips. His eyes were open a little wider now, adjusting to the glare of the naked bulb. "If I answer your questions, will you let me go?"

"Not yet, but soon."

Whether Alex liked the answer or not, he had no choice but to accept it.

"I've done my homework on you. You seem like a nice, bright young man. A man with a future ahead of you. Decent family, some education and scholarships. A very talented musician. Very different than your coven mates.

"Naomi. She was a professional whore, third generation white trash, probably soon to spawn the fourth. Edwin was a spoiled rich boy who had neither the intelligence nor the ambition to amount to much of anything. Mahri, she has talent, doesn't she? But she's just some scheming little wetback who's reach exceeds her grasp. She just hasn't figured it out yet. Felipe, a little fag with delusions of grandeur. But not you, Alex. You're very different. What happened to you?"

"I... I don't know."

Hector wasn't convinced. "You don't? Here I thought you were ready to talk to me. But that's not getting us off on the right foot, is it?"

"No, I guess not."

"That's okay, son. I'll give you that one. Let's try it again, shall we? How did a good young man like you get mixed up with those awful people? Love and sex, maybe? You were infatuated with one of them? One thing led to another, then...?" Hector shrugged. "It happens. A lot more than you might think, really. Even very good people will follow their hearts, or their loins, into the worst kinds of trouble."

"It's not like that," Alex insisted. "I was just trying to help my mom. She's sick. Cancer. I just wanted to help cover some of the bills. That's all."

"Ah," Hector replied. "And how did you meet the Circle Odd?"

"Doctor McCoy," Alex replied, and his tone was sad. "He found me. Said I had a lot of talent. And that I could probably do a lot of good with it."

"Have you ever heard the phrase 'fruit of the poison tree?'" Hector asked.

"Yeah."

"Nothing you gain by these means will help anyone, Alex."

"The Doctor wasn't like that," Alex replied.

Hector nodded. "But Mahri was. Wasn't she? And Felipe. Oh, Felipe..." Alex hesitated, and Hector shrugged. "If you're not ready to talk to me, I can always come back when you are. Maybe tomorrow. Or the next day. How *is* your mother doing, by the way?"

Alex shook his head. He didn't want to be left alone again, down there in the dark. There were *things* down here. Noises and sounds ... whispers ... eyes. He wasn't alone down here. He was terrified of being left alone in the dark again. Amelia's work, but *he* didn't know that. "I said I'd talk to you, and I will. It's just—"

"Difficult," Hector supplied. "I know. You thought these people were your friends. You considered the doctor a mentor." Hector placed a gentle hand on Alex's torn cheek and nudged him until the young man met his owlish gaze. "But where are they now?"

Alex looked away.

"They left you. They abandoned you. They bid you good luck and left you to take your chances on your own." Hector patted him on the shoulder. "And so here we are."

"Yeah."

"I need to know you're telling me the truth, Alex. Your friend Naomi tried to lie to me, even in death. And I want to believe you."

"I already said I'm out. I'm done. I'll tell you whatever you want to know."

"I know you will," Hector replied. "I believe you because you want to go home. You do want to go home, right? You don't want to be left down here."

Alex nodded fervently.

"Okay," Hector said calmly, offering a reassuring smile. "Then talk."

So Alex did, and Hector listened. At first, it was business as usual, much of what Hector already knew or already suspected. But then Alex had things to say that Hector had *not* anticipated. And what he heard changed everything.

Hector was patient. He listened to it all, his expression giving away nothing.

From Alex, he finally got a name. Confirmation. *Maglo*.

By then, Alex was in tears, mentally broken by exhaustion and grief. A scared kid confessing his crimes no matter the consequences. Just needing to be free of the weight of them, to get them off his conscience.

"Where is it?" Hector asked, wiping a gentle thumb across the boy's scabbed, tear-stained cheek. "Where is Maglo?"

Alex sniffed and shook his head. "I don't know."

Hector was sincere. "I believe you."

Alex sighed. It was good to be believed.

Hector turned to Amelia. "Find it."

Then he walked away with Alonzo and Reinhardt, leaving Alex alone with her in the dank little basement.

Amelia smiled and raised a hand. Extending her index finger, she touched the tip of her long nail to the curve of the naked light bulb.

Tink.

At her touch, the filament began to fade. Harsh white. Hot orange. Dull amber.

As the light bled out of the room, Amelia's face began to melt, twisting while Alex watched into something feral, hungry, and vicious.

Alex began to scream.

Darkness swallowed the room.

In the blood, all the truth came out.

64

Gabriel tracked Mahri down in the upstairs apartment. She'd wandered off once the Crows started gearing up to go to war. She was sitting on the bed, staring at the window without actually looking at anything. She startled a little when he opened the door.

He leaned against the edge of the door and offered her a smile. "You doing okay?"

"Mm-hmm," Mahri replied with a nod. It was all less than convincing.

Gabriel stepped inside and closed the door behind him. He was carrying her backpack full of workings in his left hand and a black tactical vest in his right. It was bulkier than the usual soft body armor the Crow wore on the street.

"You're gonna need this," he said, setting the backpack beside her on the foot of the bed. Then he held up the vest. He was wearing one as well under his jacket. "I want you to put this on," he said, and then he passed the vest to Mahri.

She nodded and accepted it, giving it a once over. "It's stiff."

"Yeah," Gabriel replied, wrapping his knuckles against the sternum of his own vest. It made a rigid thumping sound. "Plates. They'll stop rifle rounds."

"Oh," Mahri said sheepishly. Then she laid the vest down on the bed and looked at the floor. "I hadn't really thought about ... I mean ..." She paused, took a deep breath. "I think I'm gonna be sick."

Gabriel looked toward the bathroom. "Do you, uh, need me to get you a trash can?"

Mahri shook her head. Her hands were trembling. "It's just. I don't *do* this kind of stuff. You know?"

Gabriel nodded. "I know."

Mahri was the hot-blooded, fiery temper type. And yeah, maybe she had a screw or two loose as well from getting too close to the bad mojo. She'd stab a son of a bitch in the throat in the heat of the moment—which she had demonstrated to Gabriel's ultimate shock and surprise—but this was different. There was a lot of time to think about the things that were about to happen, and a lot of time to wonder *what if?*

The next event in her life was going to be a straight up ruthless witch hunt. The premeditated homicide of a lost friend. There could be witnesses. There could be casualties. People on the street were going to know about this. If somebody *ever* talked …

And that vest sitting there was a stark reminder that there were probably going to be bullets flying around. Possibly one with her name on it.

"I'm really scared, *papi*," she said and sniffed back the tears.

"I know," was all Gabriel could think to say. That fact gave him some hope that maybe Mahri was a little more … *Mahri*, and a little less the twisted up witch-on-the-run he'd dragged out of Koreatown earlier. "Me too, kiddo."

She smiled. It was a tiny, fragile expression.

He took her by the hand and gently pulled her to her feet. When he helped her don the vest, they were very much in each other's personal space, and the urge to do something about it was strong. They knew *where* all the parts fit and liked *how* they fit; it just felt natural after their ten years of practice with each other—but it just wasn't the time, for either one of them.

But, she did hug him, pressing up on her tiptoes so she could press her cheek to his. "I'm so sorry for all of this, *papi*."

He hugged her back, reluctantly at first, but then beyond the ability to turn her away. "I miss you, kiddo. All the time."

"Me too, *papi*."

Gabriel felt a hot tear roll down her cheek and onto his.

"I don't know what I'm going to do," Mahri whispered.

"When all this is over. I've fucked this up so bad. And the Helitori—"

"I'm gonna put you on a plane," Gabriel replied, matter-of-fact. "And you're gonna go somewhere else, and you're gonna start over. And we're gonna help you do that. We got friends all over the world. You're gonna be fine. Okay?"

Mahri nodded in silence.

They didn't love each other. Not really. But what they had was more than just history. It was *something*, and that something was *real*. *Real* was enough.

He held her out to arm's length, wiped the tear from her cheek, and smiled. "Let's go handle our business. Yeah?"

"Okay. Can you give me just a minute to get my shit straightened out?" she asked, holding up her backpack.

"Sure," Gabriel said with a nod and headed downstairs. She wasn't long behind him.

In the team room and clubhouse bar, the mood was very sober. Delilah and Finch were in a rush. They needed to get rolling pronto. The guardian angels, Piper, Twitch, and Grizz, were left standing around trying to keep their nerves under control.

"How you feeling, Twitchy?" Gabriel asked with a lopsided grin.

Twitch was leaning against the bar, a ready, loaded plate carrier and his M4 beside him, just in case. The young militiaman flashed a thumb and forefinger in a hanging loose gesture. "Feeling fine, boss," he said with a smile.

"You got my wheels ready?" Gabriel would take a work vehicle, one of the burly SUVs, and leave his POV and most of his own workings at the Church.

Twitch nodded and handed him the keys. "Yup. Hardware's in the back seat floorboard if you need it."

"Thanks, Twitchy," Gabriel said.

Then he looked Twitch and Grizz up and down. They were the backup, on call, quick reaction force. Big ol' Grizz was more of a ditch digger than a fighter, but he was as trustworthy as it got—you could count on him. And Twitch was Twitch—a lover, a fighter, a runner and a gunner.

"You guys are coming with me," Gabriel decided.

Twitch and Grizz blinked at each other. "We are?" the big man asked.

Gabriel nodded. "Back up. I mean *way* back." Gabriel started thumbing his phone, looking at a map. "Here." There was a twenty-four-hour McDonalds several blocks away from the old King Salvage yard. "You guys park it here and be cool. Don't draw attention to yourselves. Don't roam around. Get a Big Mac and sit tight. If I need you, I'll call you."

Twitchy thumped Grizz on his meaty chest. "Get the wheels, dude." They were moving.

Gabriel and Piper exchanged a brief hug and pats on the back.

"It's all good, brother," Piper assured his captain. "I got *this*. You handle *that*."

"Status updates," Gabriel reminded the Sweet Valley crew. "I want to hear from you guys every fifteen minutes or less. Otherwise, I'm gonna have to send Bingo after you."

The old biker chuckled and gave them all the bird with his knobby middle finger. "I been drinking," he reminded them. "So don't fuck this up."

Victor gave reassuring nods to both Gabriel and Mahri as they passed through. His face was calm, stoic, unconcerned, and confident. Whether he actually *was* or not remained a mystery.

Fiona stepped forward and hugged her son. She kissed him on the cheek and laid a gentle hand to the side of his head. "Careful now, son," she said quietly. "Whole and safe. Do you hear me?"

"Yes, ma'am," Gabriel replied and hugged her back hard until his cuts and bruises twinged.

He led Mahri out into the Church garage and made a quick check of his gear load-out in the backseat floorboards. Then they climbed aboard.

Delilah caught them as the garage door was rolling up. "Not gonna stop and say good-bye?" she quipped as she bounced up to Gabriel's window.

He grinned. "You were busy."

"Yeah, well, I needed to bum some cigarettes." She smiled. It was her way of shrugging off the tension, her form of swagger. Gabriel gave her the unopened pack in his jacket without complaint. "You and Finch ready to roll?"

Delilah nodded. "We're heading out right behind you guys."

"Good. Don't let Washington's amateurs fuck this up," he pleaded.

Delilah winked. "I got it." Her bravado faltered a little, and the worry showed through on her face. She reached into her pocket and produced the divination crystal Gabriel had brought her back from the plundered cash depot. It was still affixed to its leather lash, but the translucent white crystal had taken on the hue of frozen blood. She passed it to her brother. "Just in case Felipe bolts on you. A little something to help track him down. It'll burn out when the sun comes up, so don't drag your feet."

Gabriel smiled and nodded gratefully, sticking the token in his breast pocket.

Delilah's tone turned grim. "He knows I saw him. He knows I can find him. Why isn't he running?"

Gabriel didn't dwell on it. "I guess he's not afraid of us anymore, kiddo."

"Be careful," she said.

"Yeah. You too."

Delilah looked at Mahri then and said, "You take care of him, and he'll take care of you. I mean it."

Mahri nodded. Delilah turned to leave then, but Mahri called out to her. "Hey, I uh. I'm just—"

Delilah shook her head. "Yeah. I know." Then she headed back in to tend to her business.

Gabriel and Mahri rolled south for the meet with Markus, Twitch and Grizz trailing ten minutes behind. They rode mostly in silence. The hunt was on, and there wasn't much left to talk about.

Shortly thereafter, Delilah and her caravan headed north, bound for Sweet Valley Ranch and the exorcism of Silver Dollar. Their ride was a quiet one as well.

Night stood, dark and deep, over the City of Angels.

65

The industrial ass-crack of Compton wasn't exactly a welcoming beacon of the community. The defunct remains of King Salvage sprawled through the middle of the hood like the ruins of some rusted alien city. There were tall girders and a squatty, broken down crane. Mountains of scrap and crushed cars stacked up like cordwood through the yard. Cavernous tin-sided buildings lined the property providing the lot with privacy, and a tall razor-wire topped fence surrounded the rest of it, providing security—except for the main gate that was. It was wide open. There was something decidedly ominous about that.

The opposite corner of the block was dominated by a massive shipping container farm. Apparently, a place where forty-foot shipping crates went to die by the acre. There were two liquor stores and a busy bus stop around the corner, both of them lit up like dirty ports in a sprawling industrial storm. Densely packed residential neighborhoods spread out to the east, more tangled industrial district rolled away to the west.

Gabriel made a couple of orbits, getting his bearings and becoming familiar with the locale before committing.

On his second trip around the block, he took the crystal pendant from his pocket and gave it a test. The pendulum seemed to move of its own accord. A slight tug in the direction of its target that was too faint for Gabriel too see, but he could sense when holding it.

"So, this is really it, huh?" Mahri asked.

Gabriel mulled it over. Good escape routes. Freeway access. Shit hole side of a bad neighborhood. Lots of cover and plenty of privacy. Smack dab in the middle of urban wasteland. "Yeah," he said grimly.

Then he made one more orbit, killing the last couple minutes of the time they had left. After that, he made a right turn, cruised by the liquor store, and down the dark block until he reached the appointed meeting place—a scabby, forgotten park a few blocks from the scrap yard. Once there'd been a swing set and a merry-go-round here, but now there was just an empty lot, some rusty metal bolted to broken concrete, and truckloads of trash. A broken down old sofa. A dented up refrigerator with bullet holes in it. Not all of Los Angeles was experiencing gentrification after all. Some of the forgotten corners of old Southland were still rotting away merrily.

It was a staging area, a rally point where they would link up with Markus and his crew. And then they'd go hunting.

As they waited, it was quiet except for a status check text message from Delilah and the Sweet Valley crew. They had most of an hour of drive time ahead of them, and they were still en route. Gabriel replied with an acknowledgment and clear status check on his end.

"I'm still shaking," Mahri whispered after a while.

"That's okay," Gabriel assured her, his voice also a low whisper. It seemed appropriate for the reclusive dark. He could feel the buzz of nervous tension in his own hands as well. "So am I. That's how this works, kiddo."

She didn't seem to take much comfort in that.

While they waited, Gabriel held the divining crystal in his hand and studied it in silence. It pulsed like a beating heart. Faster when they'd been nearer to Felipe's hideout, slower and more faint now that they were further away. It continued to pull in the direction of its target.

It was thirty minutes later when Markus rolled up in a heavyweight security SUV, like the kind he'd last seen when they'd met at the plundered cash depot: Ballistic glass, run-flat tires, upgraded suspension, armored body and engine compartment.

By all appearances, it was just Markus and his driver.

The two captains dismounted their vehicles and met in the middle for a handshake.

"Mr. St. John. Good to see you again," Markus said.

As they shook, Gabriel took note of the radio bud in Markus's ear.

Markus looked past Gabriel's shoulder, and his smile softened into something like relief. "Miss Ramirez. Good to see you again as well. We were beginning to worry about you."

"Yeah, hi," Mahri replied quietly as she exited the vehicle, her backpack clutched tightly in her hands. She was understandably nervous. Victor had promised to square things with Washington on her behalf, but no one yet knew how that would play out. There was no time to dwell on it.

Markus turned to Gabriel. "So, how would you like to play this?"

"Carefully," Gabriel replied. "I don't think I have to tell you the risks of bumping up against Felipe. Not now. Just being in the same room with him is hazardous to your health."

Markus nodded. "I appreciate that, but it's handled. Courtesy of Miss Althea. Me and my boys are bulletproof against Felipe's voodoo bullshit until the sun comes up."

Gabriel pondered that. That was a level of confidence that was admirable, but potentially misplaced. Thoughts of the Vert Grimoire of Jean Francois Mercier came to mind, and he could only hope Miss Althea had done her homework well. "Okay, then. What did *you* have in mind?"

Markus smiled. "We're going in through the front door."

"Oh yeah? Markus, this ain't a bank robbery."

"I know that." There was a menacing glint in Markus's eye. "Come here. Let me show you something." He led the way to the hatchback of his security SUV. He popped the door, tore a canvas tarp off the cargo, and let Gabriel connect the dots for himself.

Beneath the tarp was a handsome young man, bound and gagged, and beaten black and blue. He was blonde-headed, slender as a reed, blue-eyed, and stripped down to his t-shirt, underwear, and bare feet.

Mahri gasped.

Gabriel knew the kid. His name was Jamie, and he and Felipe were a known item.

"Christ, Markus. He's a civilian," Gabriel said.

Markus was unmoved. "And I don't give a fuck. I am done chasing this motherfucker's fruity little ass. I want him alive. I *need* him alive. There is shit on the line we *both* need him for before we put him in the dirt."

Gabriel balked. "What are you talking about? Nobody said anything about taking him alive." He wasn't fond of this change in plans. Not fond of it at all.

"Do you know what he's worth if we bring him into the Cartel alive?"

Ah. That. Gabriel had a good idea.

"Amnesty. Debt settled. Back to business as usual." Markus tilted his head, leaning toward Gabriel in a conspiratorial fashion. "For *both* of us."

"Jesus," Gabriel grunted, looking away, unsure. "You understand, Felipe ain't a house pet anymore, right? You get how dangerous he is?"

Markus shrugged. "What can I say. Plans change. I got my marching orders." He favored Gabriel with a confident look. "I've got a cleanup crew around the block. This doesn't go right, they land on him like Hiroshima, and the job gets settled anyway."

Gabriel snorted. "Lotta good that does you and me. If that's how it goes, it's because we're coming out of there in bags."

Markus smoothed down the edges of his goatee with his fingertips. "Look, you want to keep your people whole, right? So do I. Cat's outta the bag. This business with the Cartel ain't no joke. You get it? If you're on their shit list, they say 'jump,' and you say, 'how high.' They want Felipe Ortiz alive? I'm gonna give him to them. Now … do you want to be part of that win, or do you want to go home empty-handed? Because I don't give a fuck either way. You choose."

Plans change, Gabriel thought. Changes in plans made him suspicious. Downright jumpy, even. Gabriel put on his best poker face and nodded. "Yeah. Okay. Let's do it." He looked down at the poor kid hogtied in the back of the SUV. "Tough break, Jamie."

Making an omelet meant breaking eggs. He filed it away as something he could worry about feeling guilty for later. Right now, it was show time.

And the warning bells were ringing like mad behind his stone-chiseled poker face, screaming that he couldn't trust Markus any farther than he could throw him.

The kid strained against his gag, trying to speak, panic and tears filling his eyes. He was pleading, Gabriel realized. Begging for his life.

Markus was one ruthless son of a bitch. All he did was shrug. "I'm gonna take loverboy in there, and we're gonna see if Felipe wants to make a trade. Or at least, if he'll poke his head out long enough for us to drag him out by the throat."

Gabriel issued one final warning, "Felipe knows he's made and he ain't running. What does that tell you?" It was a rhetorical question.

With a frown, Markus slammed the cargo hatch shut. "We gonna do this or we gonna stand here and stare at each other?"

Gabriel swallowed the sour taste in the back of his throat and gave a single nod. "Let's go. You're driving."

66

Felipe had left the door open for them. That was unsettling enough as it was.

Markus had his driver pull up across the street from the main gate and park at the curb. The hour was late, the surrounding blocks shabby industrial. There was no one around. Even the street lamps were few and far between on this street—fitting, somehow.

Gabriel threaded a suppressor onto the muzzle of his Sig while Markus checked his own weapon and re-situated the Velcro shoulder straps of the body armor under his jacket.

Markus tilted his head toward Gabriel. "You ready?"

Gabriel nodded.

Markus looked to Mahri. "How about you?"

She nodded, clutching her backpack close.

The mercenary captain winked. "Let's go do some business together." Then he stepped out into the street, leaving his driver with the parting instruction of, "Sit tight."

Gabriel swung his long legs out of the back seat and helped Markus haul Jamie from the back. With one of them on each arm, they marched the weeping kid across the street and toward the main gate, Mahri following close behind.

Gabriel could feel the crystal pendant pulsing in his pocket, its heartbeat growing more insistent with each step, like a galloping horse on the run.

The old scrap yard was lightless, no lampposts, nothing. Just the purple dome of the city sky overhead and maze-like walls of crushed cars and unrecognizable masses of twisted metal.

They passed through the main gate, moving down the wide central alley.

With a startling rattle, the heavy metal gates swung shut behind them, squealing and coming together with a jarring slam. The security bar rammed shut, and six feet of chain clattered and tied itself up in a knot, binding the two sides of the gate together.

Then it was deathly quiet.

Markus, his expression mild, even bored, put his pistol to Jamie's head and called out to the ominous dark, "So, I suppose that means we have your attention."

Indeed, it appeared they did as Felipe walked out without fanfare or coaxing, emerging from the shadows ahead like a Great White Shark swimming into view out of the hazy depths.

Jesus. He looked terrible. Felipe had always been handsome and smooth, but now his clothes were a baggy, dirty mess. His face was drawn and haggard, his dark eyes hollow and wild. Whatever power was on his side, it was eating him whole at an exponential rate. In twenty-four hours he'd gone from none-too-worse for wear, to a vacant-eyed ghoul.

Gabriel noticed Markus swap his pistol from one hand to the other. Then his free hand slipped discreetly into his jacket pocket.

"How we been, dog?" Markus taunted. "Eating your vegetables? Getting your rest?"

Felipe blinked, taking on a slow, insectoid expression. The jagged iron dagger was in his right hand, clutched tight in his bloody-knuckled fist. "Are you okay, Jamie?" he croaked as if remembering how to speak was an effort.

Jamie wept silently. He was not up for this.

"It's okay, baby," Felipe said in a soft voice, drained with exhaustion. "It's all gonna be over in a minute."

"This is how its gonna work," Markus said. "You drop that pig-sticker on the ground, *you* come with me, and I let him go. Everybody will go home when this is over. You have my word. But, if you fuck with me, you have my word that I will kill you both."

"Your word is shit," Felipe grunted, and, blinking again,

he looked each of them over, one by one. First Markus, then Gabriel, then Mahri, and when he was done, he looked at Jamie. "You're a real son of a bitch, Markus." He sounded too tired to be grieved. Too tired to be afraid.

Gabriel got the message that there was some bad blood, between Markus and Felipe that he didn't know about, and standing there in the shark tank that greatly concerned him.

Markus pressed the pistol to the side of Jamie's head to illustrate his point. "Limited time offer, Felipe. Clock starts now."

Felipe didn't even balk. Didn't stall for so much as a second. "Okay," he said, relenting, defeated. "Whatever it takes."

The ugly little worm of suspicion, of outlaw instinct, turned over in Gabriel's belly.

Something wasn't right.

The hackles rose on the back of Gabriel's neck, and he brought his pistol up.

As fast as he was, Felipe, filled with the Essence of the Fifth Horror, was faster.

The jagged iron spur slashed the air, erupting in an explosion of dead-black shadows. For all the protections inked into Gabriel's skin—a decade's worth of the finest ward-work money and favors could buy—Felipe bitch slapped him and Mahri both like children, sending them sprawling and stunned to the deck with a thought. Before they could begin to recover, Felipe pinned them to the spot under the crushing weight of an unseen force.

In contrast, Markus weathered the attack well and stood his ground. He turned with the invisible blow like a fighter pivoting off a shield, keeping his feet underneath him. Miss Althea's work paid off indeed.

As he spun back around, his off hand came out of his pocket clutching a glass vial filled with sapphire blue liquid swirling with dark specks.

Markus raised the vial overhead and barked three words of an ugly counter-spell. He intoned the arcane syllables with confidence, but awkwardly and with little art. The vial lit with a watery eldritch radiance and Markus heaved it toward Felipe like a grenade. It exploded in midflight, showering Felipe with a nimbus of ghostly blue light.

The glowing tendrils slithered around Felipe like a net to trap and ensnare. But wherever they touched him, they burned away like steam, setting off an audible screech like metal on metal.

Felipe smiled, the attempt to hex him down rolling off his back like water. Then he jabbed the dagger toward Markus, and a twisting lance of ink-black lightning issued forth. It struck the mercenary captain in the center of his chest, buzzing like a band saw. Felipe grabbed Markus with it like a lasso and whipped him aside, throwing him off his feet and onto the muddy ground where, stunned and breathless, Markus lay gasping for air.

Felipe stalked forward like a hungry lion.

When Gabriel grunted and began to find the strength to move, Felipe pressed his will over him and pinned him back to the ground. "Stay down," he warned. "I'll get to you in a minute, Crow."

Jamie remained untouched, still standing in the middle of all the mayhem, shivering and weeping into his gag.

Felipe came forward and wrapped an arm around him, hugging him close. He kissed his cheek and made gentle, soothing sounds. "I need your help with something," he said.

Then he rammed the twisted shard of iron into Jamie's heart.

White fire burned through the wound, boiling up out of his mouth, out of his eyes, bright and hot, bathing the lot in a flare of sharp monochrome shadows. Then the flames withdrew, like pulling the fire back in reverse, rewinding it. It turned cold and black.

The oily essence flowed into the blade, into Felipe.

If Jamie could have screamed, he would have. Instead, he died.

Five seconds of otherworldly agony and Felipe tossed Jamie's spent corpse aside.

Then he turned to Markus, and pointing the jagged iron bit at him gracefully, like a conductor with his baton, he let the corruption flow. Slow and hungry, it coiled out of the blade in half a dozen tendrils of creeping shadow, sniffing up and down

Markus, probing, tasting, and teasing.

Markus let out a wounded gasp, and his body stiffened and quivered as the corruption toyed with him.

"You feel that?" Felipe asked. "That's blackest black, man. That's better than coke and sex and money, all in one." Felipe pressed harder, and Markus screamed. "Don't fight it," he said. "It's easier if you don't fight it. All you're gonna do is make it hurt more." He smiled a horrible, rotten grin. Felipe's head was full of grinding gears and broken things. And it showed in his corpse-like smile. "We're gonna have us some fun."

For a few seconds, Felipe was wholly focused on tormenting Markus—like a cat zeroed in on toying with a mouse. His concentration for anything else lapsed, just for a second, and in that moment, Mahri slipped loose of Felipe's invisible shackles by a hair.

Her own effort strong, lyrical and precise, she lashed out a counter-spell of her own. Not at Felipe. He was too strong, armored in the madness of a hungry god-thing, fueled by a fresh kill. Rather, she struck against the ragged binding spell that held her and Gabriel captive, shattering the invisible chains that rooted them to the ground like a hammer coming down on glass.

Felipe spun, dagger coming around, igniting with a lightless black halo—a promise of murder hissed in the writhing shadows. Felipe raised the dagger to strike.

Gabriel's pistol barked twice from where he was sprawled on the deck.

The first shot hit Felipe high in the chest. The second in the side of the neck. He staggered. The black aura surrounding the wicked relic evaporated in an empty flash.

Gabriel dumped five more shots into Felipe's chest. *Pop. Pop. Pop. Pop. Pop.* The suppressor didn't make the shots quiet, but it did make them sound more like a hammer banging on a metal plate than gunshots. It did its job.

Felipe's legs unhinged as Gabriel stabbed forty-five caliber holes through his chest. He collapsed, landing flat on his back.

By then, Gabriel was on his feet and advancing, muzzle pinned on Felipe.

The stricken warlock reached up with a trembling, blood-spattered hand. His mouth working silently, breathlessly, he met Gabriel's gaze.

Then the Captain Crow shot him in the face.

Felipe deflated and was still.

Wincing and shaken, Markus struggled to pull himself up into a sitting position.

Gabriel stabbed him with a look of contempt. "Fucking amateur." Then he went to Mahri, helping her to her feet. "You okay?"

She nodded.

"Nice home run," he said, giving her a squeeze on the shoulder.

Mahri was still too stunned to say much more than, "Yeah."

Trying his legs on for size, Markus found his way to his feet and cued up his radio, calling in the hounds to rally on his position. Then, still wincing in pain, holding his side, he policed up his dropped pistol and looked down at Felipe's body. "Shit."

"I told you," Gabriel said.

To that, Markus could only nod. He worked on regaining his composure while his men vectored in from around the block. Making himself useful, he went and unlocked the gate.

"You sure you're okay?" Gabriel asked, looking to Mahri.

"I'm fine, *papi*," she replied. "You?"

He nodded reluctantly. Then he looked at the twisted, jagged length of pitted iron lying in the mud beside Felipe's bloody hand. "What is that?"

"I don't know," Mahri replied with a shake of her head.

Sixty seconds later two more big security SUVs trundled into the lot, pulling up alongside their position and parking in a line.

As Markus's men dismounted, the intel and orders began to flow.

"Cops?" Gabriel asked, assuming they were monitoring the airwaves.

"Nothing yet," Markus confirmed. He gestured toward the trailing SUV and Felipe's bloody body. "We need to get him loaded up. If I don't have him alive, I sure as fuck need him dead."

"Hmph. Consolation prize," Gabriel grunted. Two more of Markus's men dismounted. They had their rifles in hand. That gave Gabriel pause. "What now?" he asked.

Markus shrugged and wiped his hand off on the hem of his jacket. "Well. Like I said. Plans change."

Then he turned on Gabriel like a dog, his pistol coming up.

67

The two captains moved like striking snakes. Fast, steady, and sure.

Gabriel was just a hair faster.

Rather than fire and find himself in the middle of a mercenary shooting gallery, he sprang forward instead, pistol whipping Markus across the face. In the same instant, his right hand clamped down on Markus's wrist, taking control of the gun.

The blow staggered Markus, broke his rhythm, and Gabriel used that instant to haul him in, spin him around, and strip the pistol from him, sending it into the mud.

When the two men quit turning, Markus had a bloody nose, and Gabriel was using the mercenary captain as a human shield with a gun to his head.

Dragging Markus along, Gabriel put his back to the nearest SUV.

Every gun in the yard snapped in his direction. Including however many Markus had out there that he *couldn't* see.

Fuck, fuck, fuck, fuck! Gabriel pulled himself in tight and small behind Markus. His heart rate ran off the rails, and the adrenaline bloomed like ice water in his veins. The fear hit him, counting the last moments of his life in feathery heartbeats and panicked seconds.

Markus was still coughing and blinking spots out of his eyes from getting jacked in the middle of the face. Two of Markus's men were shouting, giving Gabriel commands to drop the gun and let him go.

Then Markus howled with excitement. The sound of a man who's just been thrown off a roller-coaster ride only to find he has somehow survived. "Woo! You slack-jawed motherfuckers see that shit?"

"Drop it! Drop it!" Markus's men ordered in tones that suggested they expected to be obeyed.

Markus moved to wipe his bloody nose, but Gabriel twisted the muzzle of the pistol against the back of his head. "Don't," he warned in a low, quiet growl.

Markus complied, his hands frozen in plain sight. "You got mad skills, son. You looking for a new job?"

"Shut up," Gabriel grunted. There were a lot of assault rifles pointed at him right then, and he was in no mood for Markus's bid to distract him. "Back the fuck up!" Gabriel ordered with a commanding shout, bending Markus's head forward with the pressure of the gun muzzle.

"You all gonna let this motherfucker kill me?" Markus asked. There was a smug smile in his tone.

Gabriel gave him an ultra-quick three second pat down and ran his off hand through a couple of pockets. He took Markus's cell phone.

"Drop the gun and let him go!" barked one of the mercs.

Gabriel's mind ran on broken train tracks at the speed of sound. When the shit hit the fan, sometimes it hit so fast you didn't even have time to *blink*, let alone *think*. He turned to Markus's nearest driver and SUV. "You. Put your weapon down. Open the driver's side door. Start the truck. *Do not* get in."

The driver looked to Markus over the sights of his rifle.

"Better do what he says," Markus agreed.

The driver slowly put his rifle on the deck then raised his hands and made his way to the driver's side door of the SUV.

"Very slowly, chief," Gabriel warned.

Moving with extreme caution, the merc opened the door and did as ordered.

"Headlights on. Unlock all the doors," Gabriel said. "Now, get the fuck back. Leave the door open."

The driver did as he was ordered and backed off. Gabriel began to slide down the side of the first SUV, Markus in tow, heading toward the one that was ready to run.

"You better think about what you're doing, son," Markus

said. "These are some hard motherfuckers standing here in front of you. You think they're just going to let you drive out of here with me? How far do you think you're going to get?"

"I don't have to get very far," Gabriel replied as he began to slide down the side of the running SUV. "I just have to get off this lot."

Markus's security SUVs were a lot more hardened than the nondescript work car Gabriel and Mahri had shown up in. It might be enough to keep some ballsy shooter from taking his head off during the breakout. Surely, the vehicle could be tracked, but he didn't need it for very long—just long enough. One hurdle at a time.

Markus laughed. He didn't sound quite as amused as he had a moment earlier. "Okay, so what do you want it to say on your tombstone? Because it's about to say 'dumb motherfucker' on it."

"Zip it," Gabriel ordered. "Mahri, get in the car. You're gonna drive." He was flying by the seat of his pants. He spared half a glance in Mahri's direction to make sure she was moving and that nobody was in her way. She was all clear and heading toward the car.

Aggravation began to replace Markus's bravado. "Son, I am in the business of bringing you in alive. But you keep this up, and I will change my business, do you understand? You are *not* winning."

But that was more bullshit than confidence. Unless the twitchy mercs were willing to go through their boss to get to him, he was five seconds from being home free. Mahri climbed into the driver's seat and set her backpack aside. She was shaking like a leaf. *Good girl. Just keep moving.*

Gabriel reached back and popped open the rear driver's side door, sliding his hip into the seat, bracing his foot against the floorboard. He made ready to pull Markus in with him and yank the armored door shut.

Then they were going to drive right out through the front gate. If anybody had the guts to take a pot shot at them with their boss on board, hopefully the up-armored security vehicle would hold them off for the few seconds they needed to get away.

"Get in here, asshole," Gabriel growled in Markus's ear. He sank his fingers like vice grips into a pressure point beside the mercenary captain's throat. Markus made a pained choking sound and buckled toward that side, forced by physiology to comply. Wincing and grunting in pain, Markus backed up into the SUV as Gabriel hauled him in like a bowling ball.

He dumped Markus into the seat. Before the mercenary captain could shake it off, Gabriel planted a knee against his groin and an elbow deep into his neck at the corner of his jaw, pinning him like a bug to a mat. Then he leaned across him and hauled the heavy armored door shut as fast he could. It took two seconds, and nobody took a shot at him.

The door slammed shut with a heavy thud and rush of air, sealing them inside the bullet resistant cabin.

Gabriel's voice was a harsh, excited rush. "Okay, Mahri. Drive—"

Then white light and pain exploded behind his eyes.

68

Gabriel was face down in the dirt, his head throbbing like a thumb that had been smashed under a hammer. The world was awash in the harsh white haze of vehicle headlights. He could taste blood in his mouth and had grit in his nose and eye. He tried to raise a hand to wipe it away, but he found himself almost entirely paralyzed.

He struggled against the sensation of paralysis and his warding tattoos buzzed faintly. Then hooks of pain slammed into him with a vengeance. He let out a winded yelp as if he'd taken a boot to the skull and balls simultaneously—which was pretty much what it felt like.

"Don't struggle," Mahri said, her tone pained, her voice weak, without any conviction or authority.

"Mahri," he managed to grunt, his voice a ragged clot in his half-paralyzed throat.

Then Markus slammed a kick into his gut, taking the wind out of him.

"Hey!" Mahri shouted tearfully. "Don't hurt him. That was the deal."

"Bitch, please," Markus cawed. "Don't you have any sympathy for this motherfucker. You think he came here tonight to play Scrabble? He was gonna give you up. Just like the rest of them."

"That wasn't—" Mahri protested.

But Markus cut her off. "I know, that wasn't the plan. Well what do you think he would have said if I'd told him, 'well, shit, plan's changed, guess maybe my boss wants her head on a platter after all?'" He paused as if waiting for an answer, but

Mahri didn't offer one. "He'd have said, 'whatever saves my ass, sounds good to me!' Or maybe just 'tough luck, bitch.'"

"You said you wouldn't hurt him," Mahri said.

"I said I would take him *softly*," Markus replied. Then he picked his pistol up out of the dirt, squatted down and pressed it to Gabriel's temple. Mahri flinched and held her breath. "Since I could be blowing his goddamn brains out, I'd say this counts as taking him *softly*." Markus turned to his crew. "Get him up."

Two mercs came forward, slung their rifles, and hauled Gabriel to his feet.

His warding tattoos buzzed in time with his heartbeat, but they did him no good. Something had cut right through them, and it was firmly in control.

Markus holstered his pistol, wiped the blood from his nose onto his sleeve, and proceeded to give Gabriel a nice hard-knuckled shot to the face. Gabriel's head snapped bonelessly to the side and sagged slowly back to center. "About five of those and I might feel like we're even," Markus grunted. "Come on. Pat him down."

Gabriel tried to get some sense of his predicament as the mercs came forward to search him and turn out his pockets. It was difficult because neither his head nor his eyes wanted to cooperate, but he thought there might be eight of them. Seven mercs plus their boss.

One of the mercs produced a large leather bag, hand-stitched, dyed in purples and greens. It was about the size of a ten-pound potato sack, adorned with glyphs in silver and turquoise. As they confiscated Gabriel's things, they dumped them into the holding bag.

One of the mercs stripped his little Ruger .22 out of his shoulder rig and held it up, questioning if it went in the bag too.

"Everything," Markus replied. "Every goddamn thing. You find a used rubber in his pocket, put it in the bag. I mean it. You check in his mouth. You check his dick. Don't leave this slick motherfucker *nothing*."

There was nothing Gabriel could do to resist them. If they released their hold on him, he'd just fold up on the ground, and he knew it.

They took everything. His Sig. 45, spare mags, his smokes and lighter, cell phone. They even took his belt. Then they stripped him of his oil flask and his binding lash.

Markus chuckled as the braided leather lash came out. "You're certainly into some different shit, aren't ya?"

They took his blasting rod—the *one* they found in his jacket pocket. *One.* The merc holding it eyeballed it funny. "Is that a cigar?" he asked.

"Put it in the fucking bag," Markus said. "Shoes. Get the goddamn shoes. Don't want no shoe-bomber on the ride home."

So they stripped him of his shoes, took his jacket, and yanked off his bulletproof vest in a loud tearing of velcro. Everything hurt. The pain in his stapled side chewed through the paralysis and adrenaline buzz with sharp little teeth. A dozen accumulated hurts throbbed in a respiratory pulse, like the slow red blinking of the lights on a radio tower.

When they were done, he sagged between two mercs, beaten and bloodied in his shirt sleeves and sock feet.

"He's clean," one of the mercs announced.

Mahri was standing off to the side, crying silently. In her hands, she held one of her small leather hex bags, and she was slowly working it around and around between her fingers like a baker kneading a small chunk of bread dough. The rhythm of the action was steady, deliberate, and focused as a monk with his prayer beads. She was clearly struggling to maintain her concentration.

"You wanna give him a kiss before we go?" Markus asked.

She just glowered at him and shook her head, continuing to work the hex bag through her fingers.

Then Markus stepped up, got a handful of Gabriel's coal-black hair, and yanked his head back so he could look him in the eye. "You know, I've been doing my homework on you for a long time. And you know what? Everywhere I go, people are scared of you. You and your whole freaky ass family. Hell, son, *I'm* scared of you. Look at the fucking trouble we're going to here just to make sure you don't hassle us."

Gabriel tried to speak, and it came out a croak. "Get. Fucked."

"Yeah, I know," Markus said with a sigh. "I bet you'd

love to break it off in my ass right now, huh? Yeah. You are a serious piece of work, Mr. St. John. A real killa, no doubt." The mercenary captain smiled a bright, high-dollar grin. "I bet if I had her let you go right now, you'd let me meet the monster. Wouldn't you?"

Gabriel managed a stiff, disjointed nod, barely a movement at all. He grunted and said something indecipherable. "...*kath.*"

Markus was still smiling when his right jacket pocket lit up with a warm orange glow. Memories of Gabriel's hand in that pocket flashed across his widening eyes.

"*Infernus,*" Gabriel croaked.

The world disappeared in an exploding halo of screaming green fire.

69

The boomstick Gabriel had stuffed in Markus's pocket cooked off at its master's command. The boiling green flame and telekinetic blast washed over Gabriel like wind.

The nine other people surrounding him in close proximity, seven mercs, their captain, and the traitorous witch, weren't so lucky.

Gabriel lost sight of Mahri as she sensed the swell of eldritch energy and tried to fling herself behind some cover an instant before the blast.

Markus was blown right out of his own shoes. The rune bracelet on his wrist shielded him from enough of the blast to keep him from being pulped into hamburger, but it still dropped him burnt and stunned to the dirt.

Mercs were flung back by the blast as the wave of burning force slammed into them. Some of them cratered into the surrounding SUVs. The armored security vehicles rocked on their suspensions as the shockwave and bodies collided with them. Others were flung away into the yard, bouncing in broken heaps on the ground in a twenty-foot radius. A couple more staggered away and collapsed, their clothing on fire. Everyone was burnt, stunned, and cold-cocked.

Gabriel collapsed to the deck as the two mercs holding him were sent flying in the blast. A second later the spell restraining him popped like a soap bubble. Mahri had lost her concentration on maintaining the foul little hex.

For two heartbeats, Gabriel lay face down in the dirt, panting, trying to catch his breath while fireworks of pain exploded behind his eyes.

Fear burned away.

Rage, black and absolute, took over in its place and stole the edge from the pain.

While the mercenaries around him screamed and flailed—some burning, some trying to regain their senses, and still others waylaid completely—Gabriel clawed his way painfully back to his feet.

His face twisted into a sinister mask of murderous fury.

He scooped up the nearest rifle, press checked it to make sure it was loaded and ready, then, teeth bared like a wolf, he waded in.

Markus struggled in front of him, trying to make sense of the world, trying to get his pistol hand under control. Gabriel dumped two shots into the mercenary captain's pelvis. Then another one up into his gut under his body armor as he lay stunned on the ground. Markus jerked and spasmed as bullets shattered bone. Brass shell casings spun away through the headlight-washed darkness as the hammering crack of rifle fire echoed over the neighborhood. Gabriel kicked Markus's pistol away while the man lay there deflating.

Then there were seven.

Gabriel turned to the right where a merc lay shivering and stunned on the ground, his face half burned away. He put two bullets in his skull, sheering his head apart.

Then there were six.

He squatted over the corpse and peeled an extra magazine from the man's plate carrier, stuffing it into his pocket before moving on.

Next was a merc who was crawling away on hands and knees, dragging his rifle along by the sling. Again, Gabriel targeted his unarmored lower body and laced shots through his legs and pelvis, sending him to the ground. Then he put one in the back of his head.

Then there were five.

He finished off another helpless merc.

Then there were four.

He wheeled the rifle around to another who was pulling himself up on the side of an SUV, staggering painfully back to his feet. He lit him up too.

Then there were three.

A pistol popped, a round buzzed past. Gabriel dropped to a knee, spun, and locked in on a mercenary who'd managed to get back into a sitting position twenty feet away. He dumped rounds into his plate carrier and then one into his face and the merc folded up into a pile.

Then there were two.

Gabriel swapped the nearly expended magazine for a fresh one.

One of the wounded mercs had crawled some distance away. His leg was still on fire. Gabriel lined up on him and put a single round through the top of his head, setting off a gory pink plume. The merc collapsed.

Then there was one.

Gabriel scanned the battlefield and spotted a pair of legs sticking out from behind the rear bumper of the trailing security SUV. Rifle shouldered and ready, Gabriel moved quickly, slicing around the corner of the vehicle.

There he found the last merc. The poor bastard was flat on his ass, shivering from shock and his burns. His rifle was splayed at an awkward angle between his legs. He was groping at it with blistered, sloughing meat hook hands, burned too badly to handle his weapon. The back of his jacket was burned away, charred skin and cloth indistinguishable.

When Gabriel rounded the vehicle, the merc froze. He looked up in wide-eyed shock. Weakly, he shook his head. "No," he wheezed.

Gabriel finished it. *Boom.* The spent shell casing clattered away.

Then, it was quiet.

The feral rage slowly bled out of Gabriel's face. What was left behind was an empty mask and glacial blue eyes that had turned to frozen stone.

Gabriel stepped over the wreckage of the merc he'd bunkered and began marching toward Markus like the Angel of Death. Along the way, he scooped up a discarded pistol from the ground and slung the rifle across his back.

Markus was still laying there in a spreading pool of his own blood. Burnt, half blind, shot to pieces, leaking piss and shit. The bracelet on his wrist had swallowed so much energy that it had burned him to the bone, sloughing the skin back along his arm a good six inches revealing pink meat. It was still hot and cooking, molten and misshapen.

Gabriel loomed over him, tall and terrifying.

Markus looked up at him with his one good eye and gasped like a fish out of water.

Gabriel spotted the jagged iron blade tucked into Markus's belt. With a scowl, he knelt and took it from him. "You said you wanted to meet the monster," Gabriel said. "The monster's here now."

Gabriel stood, raised the pistol, and shot Markus in the throat.

Then he left him there to die. Slowly.

He scanned the scene for Mahri and found her on hands and knees between the security SUVs, tucked up like a kid from an old Cold War duck-and-cover drill. She was sobbing.

The hex bag and her backpack full of workings lay in the dirt beside her, completely forgotten. She knelt there shivering in shock.

"Look at me," Gabriel growled quietly.

She sobbed louder.

"Look at me."

She did then, her whole body trembling. Her eyes were huge and bright, her expression one of absolute mortal terror. Fight or flight had broken down. She was simply frozen.

Gabriel raised the pistol.

"Oh, God, no, please, please!" she bawled, turning her terrified gaze away to stare bug-eyed at the dirt six inches from her nose. "No. No..."

"I trusted you," Gabriel said.

Mahri fell silent, into total vapor lock, waiting to die.

Gabriel was no less numb himself. Stunned. Heartbroken. None of it made any sense. The gears in his mind ground to a halt trying to compute what Mahri had done. He just *couldn't.*

He lowered the gun and brandished the jagged blade in front of her face. "Is *this thing* what this shit is all about?" he demanded.

The only answer Mahri could muster was weeping.

He scooped up the little hex bag and ripped out its stitches. Inside he found all sorts of assorted samples—no doubt taken from him for a very long time—hair, small bits of cloth, and a couple of the curated pieces were even fresh. Trimmings from Mahri's shirt from the day they'd scrapped with the Helitori in Koreatown. Little strips of cloth spotted with his fresh blood to tie it all together. He'd left the bitch unattended with her workings for five minutes, and she'd fucked him.

By the looks of it, fucking him had been part of her plan for quite a while now—before they ever crossed paths in Koreatown. She'd been collecting little bits of insurance on him for God knew how long. It was all a con. The whole thing.

And then he just couldn't look at her anymore.

What was left of the rage evaporated. It left only numbness behind.

He picked up her backpack and tossed it and the vile little hex bag into the front seat of SUV he'd tried to hijack. He pitched the rifle he'd been using in on top of it.

He rounded up the discarded holding bag the mercs had stuffed his gear into. He didn't have time to hang around and inventory it because he was sure every cop in Compton would be there in a few minutes.

He retrieved his lighter and his oil flask from the sack and drizzled the backpack, the hex bag, and the front seats of the SUV with the honey-thick fluid. Then he struck up his lighter and lit it. Hungry blue flames spread quickly through the oil and in seconds flared to brilliant, spell-fanned golden heights.

As the vehicle fire flared into life, Gabriel scooped his bulletproof vest up off the ground, slipped an arm through it, and dropped it over his head, letting it flop loose over his shoulders. The act of raising his arm like that sent a lightning bolt of pain through his wounded side that nearly upended his stomach. He choked it back down.

Gabriel left Mahri crying and shivering in the dirt to whatever fate awaited her. He didn't have it in him to finish it. Not her. The monster was already gone.

She may have sensed the change in her fortunes. She called

out to him, pleading. "Gabriel, please."

But he didn't look back.

Sack in one hand, pistol in the other, SUV burning brightly behind him, Gabriel walked away in his sock feet, his steps heavy, still punch-drunk from the burn of Mahri's vicious little hex. Still hunched and hobbled in pain.

He rounded a tall stack of flattened cars, blundering into the open.

He came face to face with a wide-eyed merc and the muzzle of the man's rifle. The driver Markus had left across the street. Gabriel had forgotten all about him. And now he was there, twenty yards down the lane, rifle at the ready.

Gabriel had a split second, long enough to realize he was a dead man.

Then the shot rang out. *Boom.*

The gunman's head unzipped in a plume of gore and he dropped to the ground in a boneless heap.

There was Twitch, hugging the cover, rifle to his shoulder, finger on the trigger, defending his Captain. As the driver went down, Twitch advanced, his head on a swivel. When he reached the downed merc, he dead-checked the son of a bitch with a double-tap. Muzzle flashes strobed bright in the gritty dark.

Then it was quiet again.

"Jesus," Twitch wheezed. "What the fuck happened?" His rifle was still at the ready, his eyes scanning the ominous dark.

"I'll explain later," Gabriel replied in a raw, husky voice. Then he started walking, plodding along as fast as his shaky legs would carry him.

Twitch fell in behind him, keeping nervous track over their six as they fled the yard through a gated side entrance. Once they were clear, he sent a text to Grizz to come pick them up.

Sixty seconds later, the burly militiaman and the work vehicle came zipping around the corner. Gabriel and Twitch piled aboard without missing a beat before the wheels quit turning. Then, they were underway, listening to the radios as the cops vectored in.

Gabriel got out his cell phone and began pecking at it with his thumb.

"Where are we going?" Twitch asked.

"Get me back to my ride," Gabriel growled. He tried to call his sister. She didn't answer. He tried Piper, Dodger, Izzie, Finch. Nothing. No one home. He moved then to call his Lord Father, but warning instincts stopped him mid-dial. Probably should have stopped him several calls ago. That burner phone was done. "Grizz," he said quietly without looking up. "Drive faster."

They got Gabriel back to his work car and set to go their separate ways. The radio scanner, alive with the chatter of thirty cops zeroing in on a Compton warzone, made it a short goodbye.

"You want us to go back to the Church?" Twitch asked.

"No, I do not," Gabriel replied. "You scatter. You don't go home. You don't go back to the Church. You don't call anyone, not even your mama. That goes for every swinging dick Crow you might cross paths with."

That scared Twitch, it was plain on his face. "You got it, boss."

The first whirling halos of arriving blue and red zipped past the next block over. Tactical Response Teams and air support would be hot on their heels if they weren't here already. The cordon would set in, and *nothing* would move for blocks. And it was all going to happen very, very fast. "Go. Get the fuck outta here. Don't do anything until I call you."

"Where are *you* going?" Twitch asked.

Gabriel's reply was a growl. "Washington's ranch."

70

There were birds. Thousands of them. Tens of thousands. So many that the power lines hung low under their weight. Limbs sagged in the sparse trees as their numbers grew. The foul presence held captive at Sweet Valley Ranch drew them like moths to the flame. That many birds should have been restless and fluttering, noisy and raucous, even at night. But they weren't. They were all but still and silent.

Why they were here, what they were waiting for, and what they were going to do, was anybody's guess.

"I've seen this movie already. It doesn't end well," Piper grunted as they rolled down the long dusty drive past dark trees laden with starlings. Black wings. Black eyes. Black night. He had the noids. Delilah could sense it.

"Problem?" she asked quietly over her shoulder. "Other than the obvious, I mean."

"I'll let you know," Piper replied calmly. He looked out the window and scanned the trees. "Why are they here?"

"I have no idea," Delilah replied.

"Whose side are they on?" Finch wondered aloud.

Delilah couldn't answer that one either.

They pulled into the circle drive in front of the massive ranch house and parked. Even the peaks of the ranch house roof and the rooflines of the surrounding stables, barns, and outbuildings were lined with starlings. There were a couple of Markus's mercenaries holding down the front porch. Dodger was with them.

"Evening kids," the big biker said, walking into the yard to meet them as they exited their ride. "One of you got a smoke?"

They got the message. He wanted to have a chat. They slowed

their approach, and the four Crows huddled in the yard just out of earshot of the two guards.

"Everything still good?" Piper asked, filching a cigarette out of his jacket for Dodger.

"Yeah," Dodger said, taking it and sticking the butt in the corner of his mouth. He didn't sound so sure though. "Lot of security just showed up."

"How much?" Delilah asked.

"Plus four of Markus's mercs." Dodger was being very casual and very discreet. "They came in, checked in with the security detail, and then they all went upstairs. That makes eight. Four on the first floor. Four somewhere upstairs."

"What else?" Piper asked.

"Not sure," Dodger conceded. "Some neighborhood homies showed up about an hour ago. Half a dozen of them. Some of Silver Dollar's boys from back in the hood. Showed up with a van full of groceries and then just stayed."

Delilah grunted. "So much for keeping the exposure to Silver Dollar small and under control." She sighed. No helping it now. "Please tell me Miss Althea came back."

Dodger nodded. "Same time the homies rolled in. Miss Althea showed up, and they rolled a coffin in off that white panel van out there."

"A coffin?" Piper asked.

"Yup, no shit. Miss Althea's been in the back working on it ever since."

"Did you get much of a look at it?" Delilah asked.

Dodger shook his head. "Nah, not really. Miss Althea's doing her thing and is not to be disturbed. But Izzie got a good look at it."

That would work. The whole situation had Delilah feeling impatient. "Okay, well, I'm sure they're wondering what we're standing here talking about, so finish your smoke and let's get in there."

"Copy that," Dodger said simply. He nodded toward Finch's vintage 1983 Iron Maiden *World Peace Tour* t-shirt, the white one with The Trooper on the front. It was in damn fine condition. "Nice one, dude."

Finch smiled that lopsided grin. "Thanks, mate." Then, retaining his crooked grin, he leaned toward Delilah. "You feel that?"

She nodded. You'd have to be dead not feel it.

This place was rotting. Festering.

Their feeble attempts to contain the corruption of the entity inside Silver Dollar were deteriorating rapidly. It was an order of magnitude worse now than it had been twenty-four hours earlier.

"Was it this bad when you were here earlier?" she asked.

Finch shook his head. "Nope. Not at all."

But then night had fallen again, and things began to change. She patted Finch on the arm. "We're running out of time."

They went on inside.

The whole damned placed seemed to have a putrid heartbeat. Delilah wondered if she viewed the building from a helicopter above if she'd spot it breathing. In and out. Swollen and foul.

She accepted the fact that she was orders of magnitude more sensitive to the vibe running through the bones of this place than the average bear. But there was certainly no denying it, not even for the mundane mortals who were here. This had become the sort of place you wanted to get away from and couldn't really explain why.

We're losing him, Delilah thought grimly, casting an uneasy glance down the hallway toward the chamber where Silver Dollar was being kept. Doing this at dawn would be infinitely better. But Delilah didn't think the containments would hold through the night. Not at this rate.

She waited with her companions in the cavernous living room as patiently as she could muster. It was hard to just lounge placidly in a pool when there was a shark tied up at the other end. One held in place by a fraying piece of dental floss.

She noted that Dodger took up a position near the hallway door and Piper posted up not far from the front entrance. Both of them had a view into the kitchen. Those were the ways in and out of the room. They were paranoid.

God, you should be, she thought.

Izzie came out from Silver Dollar's room a few minutes later, running a hand nervously through her short-cropped cherry red hair. There were some quick hellos then she gave everyone the low down.

"Here's the plan," she explained, grabbing herself a bottle of water and taking a seat on the arm of the sofa. "Miss Althea's written a Merovingian Noose into that coffin. We just got done moving him into it. If something goes wrong, we shut it, we lock it. We pray for sunrise."

Delilah had to give credit where credit was due. "That's smart. Miss Althea's play?"

Izzie nodded.

Finch's eyebrow arched. "She did that in an hour? You certain?"

Izzie nodded again. "The Merovingian isn't my chief discipline, but it looked pretty solid from what I could tell."

"Where'd she get the Noose?" he asked.

Delilah gave off a single chuckle. "The Vert Grimoire of Jean-Francois Mercier."

Finch looked impressed. "Right. She's a quick study, isn't she?"

Izzie snorted and took a swig of her water. "She's a Merovingian Master is what she is."

"Wonder if she's looking for a new place to work?" Finch pondered.

Delilah gave him the stink eye.

"What? She looks damn good in that little bohemian getup, doesn't she?"

She flicked him in the middle of the forehead. *Flick.* "Focus."

"So, we're never going to get that *thing* to crawl out of Silver Dollar by asking it nicely. Got a plan?" Izzie asked.

"Yeah. I do," Delilah said. She produced her notebook from her ever-present black satchel, opened it to her most recent work, and passed it to Izzie.

Izzie inspected the formulae, stretched across the pages in Delilah's chicken scratch scrawl. "Reaving of the Seven?"

Delilah nodded. "Giovanni Bellini specifically used it to exorcise the stain of Azgrubel, the Eighth Horror, from Treviso in the spring of 1450." Delilah's doubt got the better of her for a moment, and it showed on her face. "With the time we have to work with, it's all I've got."

"What does that mean?" Izzie asked.

Delilah tried to recover her bravado. "It means we're going to make it work."

There was no argument. The Crow talent trusted her, and they trusted Fiona. And this was the best the two Lady Crows could come up with on the fly. It would have to do.

"And I assume it's gonna take all of us to manage it?" Izzie asked.

"The more, the merrier, certainly. The Reaving takes at least three. So, guess that means the three of us do the deed and Miss Althea bats clean up if we fuck it up." Delilah shrugged. "Probably for the best anyway. That's her bomb shelter in there, not ours. Best if she mans the gates, huh?"

No one disagreed.

"Okay," Piper said, taking a peek behind the front curtains into the front yard and driveway beyond. "Where does that put the rest of us?"

"Muscle," Delilah said. "Let Washington's people do the fetch-and-carry work. You guys know how to use binding lashes, and you won't go buggy and run away screaming if the time comes and you've got to."

Piper and Dodger nodded.

Dodger's gaze turned down the long dark hallway, then back again. "Heads up, they're coming out," he said softly.

Delilah caught it. Something was bothering the big man. His radar was going off. She could see it on his face.

A few beats later Miss Althea came into the living room attended by a pair of mercenary guards. She looked very relieved to see her guests. "I'm so glad you could be here on such short notice," she said, giving Delilah and her companions a respectful tilt of her head.

Delilah turned and took another uneasy look down the hallway herself. "How long until we're ready to do this. If you can't tell, the sand is really starting to move through the hourglass."

"For certain," Miss Althea replied. Two more mercs came down from upstairs to join them. "It's almost time."

Three of Silver Dollar's neighborhood crew came in through the kitchen. They were nervous, and it showed.

Then one of the mercs put a pistol to the back of Piper's head.

Around the room, the guns came out, and that quick, the five Crows were surrounded at gunpoint.

Piper looked over his shoulder and fixed the merc with a deadpan expression. "Hope that thing tastes good. Because you're about to eat it."

"Easy, Piper," Dodger cautioned in a calm, steady voice. The room was full of hair-trigger nerves. That, and guns. "Everybody just be *very* cool."

Delilah looked to Miss Althea. She should have been shocked, but somehow, she wasn't. Just stunned, really. A great, universal *are you fucking kidding me* moment. "Really?"

"Afraid so," the priestess replied.

71

The mercs moved in, patting down and disarming the Crows. They stripped them of weapons, workings, and their phones—pretty much robbed them of everything they carried, right down to their billfolds and pocket clutter. Then they lined them up on their knees and trussed them up in plastic flex cuffs.

"You," one of the mercs warned as he zipped Delilah's wrists behind her back. "You or any of your other *talent* here so much as bats an eye or whispers a word, and not only will I shove a bit-and-gag down your throat, I will personally kick the teeth out of your mouth. Is that understood?" He made damn sure the zipper cuffs bit into her wrists.

Delilah winced. "Easy there, big boy. Buy a lady a drink or pull my hair first, would ya?" She was showing bluff and bravado, but inside, her heart was hammering away, the adrenaline was flowing, and her stomach was doing flip-flops. "Althea," she said, ignoring the mercenaries. "Listen to me. Whatever this is, why don't we talk about it? Work something out."

"I'm sorry, dear girl," Miss Althea replied. "It's not up for negotiation."

Of course it's not, Delilah thought, her mind racing. If Miss Althea wasn't in a negotiating mood, then that meant it was time to move on to Plan B. Whatever *that* was going to be.

Miss Althea took Delilah's ever-present black satchel of workings for herself and hooked it over her shoulder. The mercs rounded up the Crows weapons and made off with them at once. Credit had to be given where credit was due. These guys were pros, and they moved like they'd taken prisoners a time or two.

One of the mercs produced a canvas sports bag, and it was filled with drawstring sacks made of dark cloth. One by one, they pulled them down like hoods over the Crow's heads and tied them off.

Delilah felt a pang of claustrophobic stress when it came her turn, and then a stab of near-panic when she felt the binding lash loop around her neck. It took effort not to struggle or try to bolt. The lash was rough, braided leather and chips of quartz. The merc looped and fastened it around her neck with fast hands, leaving a raw burn line across her throat.

When the loop closed, her body weight seemed to double. Her limbs felt suddenly heavy. Her muscles slack and weak. Where she normally felt full of air and energy, her center suddenly felt drained and empty. The enchanted lash grounded out her inner power, cut her off from the forces around her, and left her feeling numb and shaky.

Then the mercs and homeboys hauled them to their feet and ushered them down the hall, somewhere toward the back of the house. Being held under the sway of the binding lash and blinded by the hood was disorienting for Delilah. She lost all sense of direction. She was marched forward, around a turn, and then deposited roughly into a cushioned seat. A couch, she thought. Maybe in some side den.

"Hey, you forgot to jiggle my balls," Piper grunted at his captor as he was dumped on the couch beside her. She could just make out the faint silhouette of the guard through her hood. Then there was a slap. Piper laughed at the blow. "Real tough guy, right? That's okay. I'll remember you. You're the one who hits like a little pussy."

"Shut your mouth, fool," the guard snapped. He didn't sound as cool and collected as the mercs. Must have been one of Silver Dollar's homeboys.

"Enough," one of the mercs said calmly.

But the guard slapped Piper upside the head again. "I'll beat your ass," he drawled confidently.

Piper laughed. "Shit, I take that back. You hit like *half* a little pussy."

"Go," the merc ordered. Delilah lost sight of the guard's

vague outline through the hood, and for a moment there was peace again.

There was quite a bit of commotion through the room. A lot of folks moving here and there with obvious purpose. She got the impression that not only were the mercs talking to each other, but they were also chattering on their radios. Then came the squeak and clack of the casket-laden gurney coming down the hallway.

It got louder and then rolled right on by and a door opened, squeaking on its hinges. The air shifted in the room, and Delilah realized the door was just ahead of her at her twelve o'clock. She could smell gas and motor oil, the scent of dry cut grass. A garage, out through a side entrance maybe.

They were wheeling Silver Dollar and his brand new shipping container right out the door.

So what are they going to do with us, she wondered. It was anybody's guess at that point. They might load them up too. Or make a clean getaway and leave them here. Hell, the possibility existed that once Silver Dollar was safely away, they might just shoot all of them where they sat.

That thought had a very sobering effect.

Then another one hit her. *What were they going to do with* him?

"Where are you guys taking him," Delilah asked through her hood. "Do you realize what you're messing with there? I mean, for real?"

"Shut up, bitch," one of the guards muttered.

"Hey, Dodger," Piper called out.

"Yeah?" Dodger replied. He was in front of them and to the left. The door was to the right.

"What do think they're gonna do to us?"

Dodger grunted. "I dunno. Maybe that one with the little pussy hands can come over here and suck my dick."

Jesus, Delilah thought, her stomach clenching up. They were baiting, stalling, throwing up a distraction. Which meant that something bad and something violent was probably right around the corner.

"Would you all shut the fuck up?" a homeboy said from somewhere near the door. That wasn't little pussy hands. That was somebody else.

"Why?" Dodger asked. "What are *you* gonna do, short stuff? Suck my dick too?"

"Man, fuck you and your dick."

Piper laughed. "Hey, Finchy, you okay?"

"I'm good," Finch replied. His voice was not entirely steady.

"Izzie, how about you, sister?"

"Yeah. Good."

Piper leaned to his left and bumped his shoulder against Delilah. "Dee? That you?"

"Uh-huh, yeah," Delilah replied. *Shit. They're trying to map the room, figure out where everybody is.* She took a deep breath and just tried to play it cool. There were still a lot of people coming and going. Too many, she thought. Her doubt and fear were starting to climb.

The gurney moved outside and very quickly the room became much less hectic.

"You don't take your eyes off them until I get back," a merc ordered.

"Yeah," the homeboy by the door replied.

The door closed. For a few seconds, Delilah could hear the loaded gurney trundling away, clicking and clacking while it rolled across what might have been brick pavers. Then it got very quiet in the room.

And Piper kept right on jabbering. "Hey, Dodger. Knock-knock."

"Who's there?"

"Howie."

"Howie who?"

"How we gonna hide all these bodies?" Piper laughed.

Dodger gave a grim chuckle. "Okay, I got one." Delilah heard Dodger craning around in his seat. "Hey, little pussy hands. Knock-knock."

Silence.

"Come on, man, knock-knock."

"Shut your little two-tone mouth, bitch," the homeboy replied.

Dodger chuckled. "Dude. Did you just call me an oreo?"

"Yeah, and a bitch."

Dodger paused. "Well, okay, then. So. Knock-knock."

Delilah tried to dial in her ears, to chase away the nervous butterflies. She realized then that the room count was five Crows and two homeboys. And the door was closed.

"He can't answer you, dude," Piper quipped. "Not with all that dick stuffed in his little faggoty-ass bitch-nigga mouth."

And that sent a spike of rage through the room.

Just as Piper intended.

Delilah heard some expletives. Some shuffling of feet. Fast movement. She saw a silhouette blur across her dim view through the sack over her head. One of the homeboys barreled in on Piper.

Then the couch cushion bucked, and Piper was on his feet in the blink of an eye.

A muffled scream. Choking, gagging sounds.

Hot, wet blood. A struggle, kicking feet.

A shout of alarm. An end table went over with a thud. Then that voice was crushed out in the sudden silence of a winded gasp. Frantic struggling. Grunting.

Delilah tucked her feet up and tried to pull away from the violence. Finding herself blind and bound in the middle of fight sent a surge of fear through her.

There was muted chaos around her. Piper and the guard he was wrangling heaved sideways on the couch and fell half on top of her. She heard an awful, wet slurping sound, and more hot blood spilled across the top of her leg. Then Piper yanked the guard away, and she lost track of them as they hit the floor.

Then it was over.

Bloody hands untied the binding lash from around her neck and pulled the sack off her head. Her hair blurred around her face in a static-frizzed halo for a second before settling.

Jesus.

There was blood everywhere.

On the floor in front her was one of the homeboys. His throat was sawed open and still pumping blood.

Piper put a hand on her shoulder, still clutching the slender little hold-out knife he kept stashed in the back of his belt band. "You okay?"

She nodded and choked down the lump in her throat. The guard on the floor in front of her wasn't much more than a kid. Twenty years old, maybe. His mouth was moving like a fish gulping air. His eyes were wide and staring at nothing while his fingertips still groped weakly at the bloody carpet.

Across the way, Dodger was finishing his own grisly business, his face still hidden beneath his hood. Where Piper had sawed his way out of his restraints, Dodger had used technique and old-fashioned horsepower. He'd skinned his wrists bloody in the process, but it got his hands free in time for him to get a hold of the second guard as he'd rushed in to help the first.

And once Dodger got his hands on somebody, their chances of coming out ahead fell through the floor.

The big biker had hauled the second guard in tight and hooked one of those long arms around his neck like a muscled noose. The guard's tongue and eyeballs were bulging out grotesquely, and his entire head had turned purple. There was no more fight or life left in him.

Dodger pitched the smaller man aside like a broken doll and ripped the hood from his own head. It left his hair and beard a wiry wild tangle.

"Hurry," Piper ordered, urging Dodger toward the other two Crows who were still hooded and bound. His bloody knife slipped down between Delilah's wrists and popped her restraints. "Get up, sis. We gotta move. Now."

"My bag," Delilah said, rubbing at her chafed wrists and looking around frantically as she lurched to her feet.

"Gone," Piper replied. "Went out the door with Miss Althea."

Dodger freed Izzie and Piper went to work on Finch.

While Piper was finishing up freeing their fellow Crows, Dodger stripped the two dead guards of their weapons. Each of them was sporting a pistol. Only one of them bothered to pack a spare mag. Dodger kept the forty-five with the spare mag and tossed the nine mil to Piper.

Delilah looked around, trying to get a sense of where they were. Some kind of den or game room. There was a pool table and a big screen television at the far end of the room.

The interior hallway door opened, and a third homeboy

popped into the room. He was carrying a backpack in one hand, and a bottle of sports drink in the other.

He froze. His eyes flew wide.

Dodger and Piper sprang on the poor kid before he could so much as twitch.

What happened next looked like an old-fashioned prison yard shivving, and Delilah looked away until it was over.

"Come on!" Piper hissed in a low, urgent voice, motioning for everyone to fall in with him and Dodger.

Delilah, Finch, and Izzie followed suit, and they had to step over the still gasping, blank-eyed form of the mortally wounded homie sprawled bloody in the hallway.

Quickly, they filed in. Dodger took the lead, and Piper brought up the rear. Going out the exterior door wasn't an option. That way led to the remaining homeboys and Markus's mercs. So down the interior hall they'd have to go until they found another exit.

"C'mon, c'mon, c'mon," Piper whispered as he shuttled the Crow talent past him and into the hallway.

Then the exterior door popped open, and two more homeboys froze in their tracks at the sight of the carnage in the game room. Their eyes flashed from their buddies, bloody and dead on the floor, to the fleeing Crows.

Busted.

Piper didn't hesitate.

Before the two new arrivals could so much as squeak, he raised his stolen pistol and opened fire, sending them flailing and scurrying for cover back out into the breezeway.

"That's right!" Piper shouted with grim glee. "Everybody wants to be a gangster until it comes time to do gangster shit!"

"Go!" Dodger barked, spurring the gaggle into motion.

Piper fired a couple more ear-splitting parting shots at the open door as they withdrew.

A beat later, the world *outside* erupted in a barking hail of gunfire.

The Crows instinctively dropped and got low in the hallway, hunkering down against the walls, covering up as best they could. Rifle rounds pecked and popped as they cut through the walls. High. Low. Nowhere in particular.

It took a few seconds for it to sink in.

That gunfire. It wasn't somebody shooting at *them.*

It was something outside, shooting at Washington's mercs.

There was no time to sort it all out. The roaring exchange of gunfire mounted wildly as opposing assault rifles began to bark back and forth.

Sweet Valley Ranch lit up like a Third World war zone.

"Go! Fucking go!" Piper shouted, shoving the line from behind.

They went.

72

Delilah's world turned into a disjointed blur of gunfight adrenaline.

Outside, the courtyard echoed with the rising exchange of gunfire. Men were shouting, screaming. The dark hallways raced by as they stomped along, twisting and turning and bolting through the back rooms of the sprawling ranch estate.

They slammed up against a door and Dodger grabbed the handle.

A tickle of foul, black decay slithered up Delilah's spine.

"No," she hissed, reaching out toward Dodger. "Wait."

Then a ragged fist burst through the door, sending splinters of wood flying. Groping, it latched onto the sleeve of Dodger's leather jacket.

"Jesus!" Dodger shouted and tried to pull away.

The groping hand held him fast with unnatural strength.

The big biker planted his boot against the wall and heaved, popping the heavy stitches in the shoulder of his jacket before he finally broke free of the vice-like grip.

Then the door shuddered under another blow and swung broken into the hallway.

The Crows retreated back the way they'd come, and a figure shoved its way into the hall with them. He was still dressed in his raggedy, torn, filthy street clothes. His dark skin had gone chalky and sallow. He was covered in filth and a number of small wounds, all caked over and dry. Hair that had once been in neat cornrows was now frizzy and frayed out of shape.

An old and clearly fatal gunshot wound clotted up the side of his head.

His eyes burned with a cold, inhuman white light.

They'd found one of Washington's missing men. Not so missing after all.

Dodger raised his pistol and put a round through his forehead. The pistol shot was like an ice pick to the ears in the claustrophobic confines of the hallway.

The creature barely even flinched.

Dodger shot it again, this time through the mouth. Same results.

Its jaw hung low and loose. A pair of slender black tentacles slithered out of its mouth to test the air. Then it came on in a howling rush.

Scrambling, frantic, the Crows retreated back down the hallway.

And the creature gave chase.

Muzzle flashes lit up the walls as Dodger emptied his pistol into the thing. The gunfire didn't even slow it.

Izzie broke right at a t-intersection. "This way," she called. Her brothers and sisters fell in behind her.

Finch took a deep breath, set his feet long enough to center himself, and barked a spell in a commanding voice, sending a lance of will at the creature, trying to hex the abomination down.

For a second or two, the thing stopped and shuddered. Then like a broken robot, it started moving again. It bought them enough time to shove through a door and get out of the hallway and into the southern wing, but that was it. They'd gained a few steps on the creature, and no more.

They were greeted with darkness.

Dodger slammed the door shut behind them and Delilah helped Piper drag what might have been a bookshelf across it. Dodger threw his back against the shelf and held it in place.

Cussing and stumbling, they groped around until they found a light switch. They were in a big sitting room that opened onto another interior hallway.

Outside, the world rocked in a full-tilt gangland gun battle.

"What now?" Delilah barked. Immediately, the creature began to slam against the blocked door.

"Not sure," Piper replied, looking left, looking right. He trotted over to the far door and peeked out into the opposite hallway.

Then some asshole in the next room started shooting through the walls.

Drywall burst in dusty plumes. An end table lamp disintegrated.

Piper let out a yelp of pain and surprise, then clutched at his hip as he went ducking for cover.

"You motherfucker!" he snarled, jabbing his own pistol toward the wall and returning fire.

The Crows hit the floor and bullets crisscrossed back and forth through the room, punching through the walls.

Shouting and snarling, Piper ran his pistol dry. The exchange of gunfire slowed to a trickle, but every few seconds, whoever was in the next room reminded them he was still there by punching a couple more rounds through the walls at random.

"Goddammit!" Piper shouted, clenching his teeth and rocking back and forth where he lay on the floor clutching his wounded side. A bullet had hit him just above the hip and just below the vest, right at the waistline of his jeans.

The creature in the hall pounded against the blocked door. The door was coming apart. Dodger leaned into the barricading bookcase to brace it and try to keep the thing out. The door and barricade both shook and rattled with each blow, and the reality of their predicament began to settle in.

They had two scavenged pistols, one of them empty and reduced to a club, the other on its last mag. A small knife, and whatever heavy objects in the room they could swing. There was at least one armed enemy in the next room and a monster in the hallway. One that had shrugged off Finch's best effort to hex it down and Dodger's hail of gunfire. Their only other way out of this room was into a blind hallway that may or may not have been full of gangster gunmen, any of whom knew this massive estate house a hell of a lot better than they did.

And outside, where they had to go if they wanted to escape, the world was flying to pieces.

That was when they heard the windows begin to break.

Silky black wings fluttered up and down the hallways as cackling starlings begin to trickle inside. They were no longer still and silent. Outside, their shrieks and cries began to rise above the spats of barking gunfire.

Delilah was filled with the sense of something horrid turning over. Like a drowning wave breaking and coming down.

Piper growled as Finch peeled the hip of his jeans down to check the fresh hole in his side. On the other side of the room, the door splintered and the cabinet rocked. Dodger dug his heels into the carpet, but it wouldn't hold long. The thing on the other side of the barricade gave off an unearthly howl and slammed into the door again.

"God, what is that?" Delilah wondered out loud.

"I don't know," Izzie replied, her voice less than steady.

"Burn it!" Dodger shouted, desperate to keep the barricade up and the door shut.

But they'd stripped her of everything. Even her lighter. She had no fire to prime the pumps. "I can't."

"Sit still," Finch hissed, trying to ascertain how badly Piper was hit.

"Don't fucking poke at it," the gnarly old Crow snapped.

There were four more gunshots and more bullets stabbed through the walls.

Delilah felt the world collapsing into tunnel vision. Rabbit fear. Trapped. Mind racing. Run. Hide. Fight. Scream.

Then the bookcase heaved and tipped over, pile-driving Dodger into the floor with a terrific crash. The big man was stunned. Before he could right himself, the thing with the glowing white eyes lurched through the now open doorway and snagged him by the back of the jacket, wrangling him out from under the wreckage.

With a snarl, it dragged him back into the dark hallway beyond.

"No!" Delilah screamed, scrambling that direction on all fours.

More gunfire sliced through the walls, sending her sprawling to her belly and covering her head. By the time she looked up, Dodger and the creature were gone and what she could see of the hallway was empty.

Piper shoved Finch away. "We have to go! Now!" The wounded Crow dragged himself painfully to his feet. His trembling leg threatened to drop him right back to the floor.

A couple more gunshots pecked through the walls making everyone flinch.

Then *two* more raggedy, torn, disheveled figures lurched into the room through the broken door. Their eyes burned white. Inky black tentacles groped from the mouth of the one on the right and slithered down the arm and hand of the one on the left.

"Go," Piper hissed, pointing toward the opposite door, the one into the unknown hallway.

"But—" Finch protested.

"Go!" Piper shouted, giving Finch a shove in that direction. The creatures rushed into the room.

Move, move, move, Delilah thought frantically, scrambling back to her feet and darting toward the door. There was no time to think, no more time to react. No time to wonder if she was about to step out into the waiting guns of people that meant to kill her.

Good, bad, or indifferent, they couldn't stay here.

They broke out into the hallway and chose the opposite direction from the gunman who'd been pecking at them through the walls. Piper, limping along as best he could, brought up the rear. The creatures with their hateful burning white eyes gave chase.

Two more gunshots popped in the darkness behind them and Piper staggered a couple of steps, shouting out a bark of fresh pain. But they kept on moving. Then the creatures filled the hallway, and the gunfire stopped. The broken, bloodless corpses, driven by the malice possessing them, gained ground quickly.

The chase was on, blind and frantic through the house. Gunfire boomed and bellowed outside, flat and hollow sounding. In the rafters above, starlings swooped and cackled.

Three veteran spell-slingers and a wounded knight faced

off against two unknown creatures. But there was no time to mount an arcane defense. The old mantra was true. *The blade and the claw are faster.* They only needed a few seconds to work and a chance to concentrate to turn their arcane talents on the creatures pursuing them. That was a few seconds they didn't have. What they needed desperately were weapons and workings, ones that could harm or hinder the creatures—but they had none.

Shit, other than Piper's little belt-knife, they had no weapons or workings left at all. They'd been stripped of all of that and never had a chance to recover it. The mercs and Miss Althea hadn't seen fit to leave their gear behind.

They swung full circle into an empty living room and saw windows to the outside world. On the same wall was a door.

"There!" Delilah called out, pointing at what had to be an exterior door. She had no idea where it led. But out there had to be better than in here, and the outdoor gunfire seemed further away on the far side of the building.

Piper stumbled as they shoved their way into the room from the hallway, and Izzie caught hold of him, keeping him upright.

Then one of the creatures skidded into the open door behind them.

"Shit," Izzie grunted, backpedaling, pulling Piper along. She raised a hand and forked her fingers at the creature. She began to hiss a spell in a shaky voice.

There just wasn't time.

The creature sprang forward and snagged her by the wrist. An unearthly howl boiled out of its throat and the slimy black tentacles writhing from its hand wrapped greedily around Izzie's forearm. Bones snapped in her arm as it heaved her like a rag doll, bouncing her off the nearest wall. She slumped into a pile on the floor, and Delilah lost sight of her behind a sofa. She couldn't help it. She screamed.

Then the thing had a hold of Piper, and they were wrestling and shoving, but it wasn't much of a fight. Tentacles burst from the creature's mangled chest and snaked around Piper's head and neck. Screaming and cussing all the way, Piper and the creature spun out of sight to the floor.

Finch grabbed Delilah by the back of the jacket, shoved open the door, and yanked her outside into the dark night beyond. He threw the door closed behind them and it slammed shut with a loud bang.

They tumbled out into the side yard, a square patch of grass and paved patio, bordered on all sides by outbuildings and the massive stables beyond. Once outside, the sound of exchanging gunfire got louder and more urgent.

The whole world seemed to be held in terrifying chaos. A chorus of gunshots, screams, and the howling maelstrom of starlings—a black avian hurricane—was circling through Sweet Valley Ranch in mesmerizing murmurations. Spiraling clouds of black wings rose and fell, twisting and turning, magnifying the chaos and confusion. Here and there, smaller, independent tornadoes of starlings cropped up and broke off. Delilah thought she could see them harassing man shapes out there in the lamp-lit driveway, picking targets and attacking them *en masse*. The opposite direction, horses were neighing and stomping in the stables. Black birds zipped and flittered in all directions.

"Come on!" Finch shouted, dragging Delilah along behind him.

Dodger, Piper, and Izzie were all still in there. With the monsters. "We have to go back!" Delilah cried, her voice hitching in a sob.

"Dee! Come on!" Finch pleaded, pulling on her hand.

They were spell-slingers. They didn't do gunfights. And the creatures … Delilah didn't even know what they were up against. Was this what Felipe had sent against Gabriel at the Couatl's lair? No weapons. No workings. Nothing but off the cuff spells and best wishes to hold them at bay. She didn't even have her lighter. No flame, no spellfire. Everything about this was a losing proposition.

Tears welled up in her eyes, broken gears ground in her heart. Delilah gave in. She fell in with Finch, and they ran.

Thirty frantic paces ahead, ducking and pressing on through a swirling swarm of black birds, they neared the long gap between the west barn and the stables.

Thirty yards past *that* a darkened barn door lit up with the strobes of muzzle flashes.

They'd run headlong into a gun.

Bullets hissed and snapped past them, a wall of roaring gunshots washed over them. With a cry of surprise, they turned hard right and ducked behind the stables out of the hail of gunfire. Pure startled panic nipped at their heels.

Finch ran ten steps and staggered, his legs going wobbly. He clutched at his side. Then he slumped shoulder first into a great white stable door.

"Finch?" Delilah gasped, dread flooding numbness through her.

"Shit," Finch grunted in a thin, breathless voice. His face twisted in pain and shock. Then his knees buckled.

"Oh, God," Delilah said, and she caught him before he could fall.

"I got ... I got shot," Finch muttered, stunned. In the dark of the stable yard, blood poured black between his fingers. "I got shot, Dee." His voice was eerily calm. But his eyes were wild and afraid.

Delilah was slight, and Finch was a lot bigger than she was. Just as shocked and stunned as he was, she couldn't keep him on his feet. He slumped back against the bay door and slowly sank toward the ground, the exit wound through his back leaving a smear of blood down the whitewashed wood.

"I can't breathe," he wheezed.

"Goddammit, Finch, get up," Delilah said frantically, trying to get her arms locked under his. She tried but couldn't lift him. His arms and legs had gone loose and watery.

"I can't breathe," Finch wheezed again, trying to force enough strength and coordination into his legs to stand upright as Delilah pulled on him. It just wasn't happening.

Then Delilah caught motion out of the corner of her eye.

The rest happened both in a terrified blink and in bullet-time slow motion.

A gunman, hugging tight to the corner ten paces behind them, brought his rifle around into the stable yard. Delilah saw his pale face and dark hair, a surreal vision streaked black by the tornadic flight of swarming starlings. This was no neighborhood gangbanger. Not one of Dante Washington's mercs.

This was a Brother of the Helitori. Hunter. Killer.

He was low and at the ready. His muzzle tracked. Pinned on Delilah.

She ducked, dropping to a knee.

The muzzle bloomed in a flash of white as he fired.

Fire.

A bullet screamed past Delilah's ear, taking a piece out of the collar of her jacket.

On pure defensive instinct, she grabbed the faint flame of the muzzle flash and drove it back with a vulgar spike of will.

Before the gunman could squeeze the trigger again, the fire bloomed, doubled, rushed back through his weapon and into his face like a powder flash. He jerked as fire washed over his face and eyes.

The round in the chamber fired, and the bullet cracked over Delilah's head as she continued to drop to a knee. Her thrust of pyromantic will spread to the flammable propellant in the rifle's magazine.

The next round cycling into the open chamber cooked off before it seated, as did rounds in the mag. With a *pop* and *clack* and a burst of orange flame, the rifle burst at the action with a sharp *ping.*

The gunman staggered, blinded, the rifle bucking broken in his hands.

Delilah's knee hit the deck.

She wrangled in the wisp of fading fire before it could wither away. It answered her sorcerous call, and under her spike of angry will, it grew.

Before she had time to think about what she was doing, she drove the dancing mote of fire into the gunman's face like a burning fist. He screamed. When he opened his mouth, Delilah rammed it down his throat.

He dropped the blown-out rifle, clutched at his burning throat, and collapsed to his knees. His scream fell silent. His agony did not.

Rage—the kind she came by honestly from her daddy— boiled over inside of Delilah.

She bent her will, stood to her full height, raised her hands in a graceful gesture, and the fire swelled and exploded. First, it burst from the gunman's mouth like a vomiting volcano, then through his neck, and his chest, and in seconds, he was immolated.

He collapsed kicking and bucking to the ground, burning, orange flames lighting up the dark stable yard. All too reminiscent of the night she'd watched the Godfather burn one of his traitorous pack hounds alive. The flames threw long, sinister shadows, turning the whirling mass of starlings into a cloud of ink-black noise.

Finally, the gunman stopped bucking and fell still.

Delilah St. John had killed her first man.

That killing fire, that murderous black magic, it whispered at her from the inside out, a flood of feelings and dark emotions. Rage. Grief. Hate.

Wrath.

Delilah screamed and threw her will against the smoldering flames.

They burst with a roar into a bonfire. With another tearful scream, she hurled her will against that bonfire, and it became a monstrous flame-wave, rising, filling the gap between the barn and stables, scorching and biting into the buildings on either side.

The flame-wave rolled over, cresting, crashing, and spilling across the stable yard where it blew apart into half a dozen hungry, crackling torrents. Flames crawled up the walls and rushed between the outbuildings. First, the tires of nearby parked vehicles and drought-wilted shrubbery caught. Then the sagging old boughs of the sparse few trees looming overhead. Glass cracked. Walls licked in flames.

Sweet Valley Ranch was burning.

Screaming, crying, Delilah fanned the flames.

Little wicked things, hungry for the murderous black magic, groped and clawed inside her, trying to get out. The sensation was a mixture of agony and ecstasy, euphoria and horror, orgasms and broken bones.

Seen not by her eyes, but through her awareness of the hungry fire, Delilah perceived several other gunmen sheltering

on the opposite side of the barn. They retreated frantically from
her flames, and the fire gave chase, whipping and lashing.

"Dee," Finch whispered, bloody fingers groping at her pants
leg. "Stop."

She didn't hear him at first. Her arms flashed lobster red to
the elbows and blisters rose between her splayed fingers.

"Dee," Finch croaked once more. "Please. Stop."

The fire was spreading. Far beyond anything Delilah could
do to stop it.

"Dee," Finch pleaded, his voice a breathless, wounded
whisper.

This time she heard him. She stopped. Delilah had to pull
herself—mind, body, and spirit—away from the black malice of
the killing flames. Breaking that connection was a host of awful
and wonderful sensations, all at once. Rush and crash. It took
tremendous force of effort to do it willingly.

There were lines Delilah St. John had never crossed. She'd
just leaped over all them with both feet. Her arms sagged to her
sides. The expression drained from her face and tears ran down
her flushed cheeks. Her snow-white hair danced on the fire-
whipped wind. Embers, orange and hot, swirled around her in
the darkness. She turned her face away from the flaming horror
before her—the reality of the moment, now framed in rapidly
spreading fire, came home with a vengeance.

Finch sat sprawled and bloody at her feet, reaching up to her
with a shaking hand. *Finch. Oh, God, Finch.* She choked back a
sob and dropped to a knee at his side.

He touched her cheek with trembling, bloody fingers. "Stop.
Please."

All she could do was nod. Blistering pain was beginning
to surge to life in her burned hands. "We have to go," she said.

Finch was crying, but there was very little expression on
his face. Just the tears. He looked very sleepy. He was bleeding
badly from the right side of his chest, and he was struggling
to breathe. She wiped a tear away from his cheek. "Come on,
Finchy," she said urgently. "Get up."

A mixture of adrenaline, fear, and the lingering rush of
arcane energy gave her the strength to finally haul Finch

awkwardly to his feet. He was several inches taller than her, and a lot heavier. But she wedged herself under his arm and managed to get him moving forward on rubbery legs, away from the firestorm growing and swelling behind them.

She looked back once toward the lapping walls of fire. Trees swayed and burned. Buildings became black outlines, wreathed in flame. Starlings swooped and swirled, heedless of the inferno, black as slivers of night against the hellish glow. In the stables, terrified horses shrieked in panic as the fire closed in. The flames had spread to the main ranch house. Tendrils of orange flame slithered along the eaves on the near side. Dodger, Piper, and Izzie, were they still in there? *Oh, God, what have I done?*

She looked once, and then never again. She put her head down, got a hold of Finch's belt with her raw, burned hand and began to trudge forward. She turned away from the fire and limped west with Finch, away from it all.

The night was still alive with the back and forth bark of gunfire. There was a utility shed ahead, at the top of a short dirt drive on the edge of the main house grounds. An old pickup truck was parked beside it, and while its windshield had taken a stray bullet, all of its tires were still inflated. With any luck it wasn't pissing from the radiator or the gas tank. Hotwiring it would be the easy part.

Maybe that would work. She'd take anything that could get them the fuck out of here.

"Hold on Finchy," she muttered, dragging him in that direction.

A figure rose up from behind the truck.

The hellish glow behind them was just enough to show the man's face and his curly mop of straw-colored hair.

Reinhardt, Brother of the Helitori.

Delilah froze. Her mind raced and groped for a spell to defend them with.

Reinhardt's rifle wheeled up. The muzzle barked, shots rang out.

A sledgehammer blow smashed into her collarbone.

Her whole body went numb. The blow knocked the wind out of her.

The ground came up to meet her, and she wound up flat on her back.

Her memory glossed over with a confusing blank spot and she had no clear recollection of how she'd gotten laid out on the ground. Her pulse was pounding in her ears. Her left arm wouldn't obey her. Her entire chest felt heavy and numb. She looked left, slowly, drunkenly, then right.

Finch. She remembered Finch.

Finch was prone on the ground beside her, his cheek to the dirt. His hazel eyes were vacant, empty, staring off unfocused into nothing. There was a bloody crater blown out of the side of his head.

Everything in her world knotted up into a tangled ball of confusion, pain, and grief. She couldn't make sense of it. *Finch?*

He stared at nothing. There was no light. There was no Finch.

Numbness became pain. Sudden waves of it. A hot, molten black hole of pain through her left shoulder.

Then Reinhardt was there, looking down at her and Finch like a hunter looming over wounded prey, watching cautiously for it to breathe its last.

She met his gaze and saw the realization dawn on his face that she was still alive.

Reinhardt angled the muzzle of his rifle toward her head.

There was no fear or dread at all for her in that moment. Just hurt and emptiness.

Some detached part of her thought there'd be more to it.

There was a dark blur. Reinhardt's rifle jerked upward, and suddenly he wasn't alone anymore. Where there had been only one man, now she saw two. The second one was masked and hooded, with a suppressed assault rifle slung across his back.

Delilah didn't need to see his face to know him.

She could feel him.

Michael.

He caught hold of Reinhardt's rifle, twisted and jerked, a blur of fast hands and sure steps. Reinhardt lost his grip on the rifle, and as Michael twisted it away, he used the sling like a dog harness—first to pull the hunter one direction, then to whip him back the other.

As Michael jerked Reinhardt off balance, he snagged the strap under the hunter's jaw, stepped through, and heaved. Where the head goes, the body must follow. Using the strap, leverage, and technique, Michael whipped the bigger man off his feet, rolled him over his hip, and dropped him like a rock onto his back. Dropping to a knee, Michael followed him to the ground.

When Michael's other hand came around, his knife was in it, and he buried the blade to the hilt in the side of Reinhardt's exposed neck.

Reinhardt belched out a bloody, breathless cry as Michael twisted the knife. Arteries were severed and steel ground against spine. The stricken hunter kicked and thrashed, spraying blood. Then he was still.

Fast. Silent. Over.

Somewhere, far away in the cottony, shocky distance, Delilah felt relief at that.

Then Michael was there with her. He was talking, but she couldn't understand what he was saying. Then she was up and moving, bouncing along through a world washed red in fire, streaked black by swarming birds. Everything hurt, but the pain was a far away thing, like watching a thunderstorm flash soundlessly out across the nighttime horizon.

She thought of Finch. And of the man she'd killed.

Then, for a while, the darkness swallowed her.

73

Dante Washington rolled up to the Church with a crew more than a dozen men deep. He showed up to deliver the front money himself, surrounded by a posse of hard-hitting pros. Victor and Fiona stood shoulder to shoulder in the foyer with Bingo and watched them roll in.

"For some reason, I don't take this as a good sign," the Lord Crow muttered.

"Nor do I," his Lady Wife replied.

Dante Washington's caravan of big burly security SUVs pulled into the front lot, parking at strategic angles. The men dismounted and lingered by the vehicles. They stood straight, despite the attempts to look casual. Victor spotted the black assault rifles held low against their sides.

Mr. Dante Washington was one of the last to put his feet on the deck. As he swung out of his ride in his crisp gray suit one of his men handed him a zip-top duffle. The contents sagged with notable weight. Moving like a well-coordinated pack, Mr. Washington and half a dozen of his men swaggered across the parking lot toward the front doors.

Victor glanced at Bingo, "Bring him to my office."

Bingo nodded.

Victor and Fiona withdrew to the Lord's Hall.

He laid out a couple of glasses and a bottle of the good stuff and took a seat in his throne. Fiona stood at his side, her hand on his shoulder.

A few moments later, their guests entered the Lord's Hall, Bingo bringing up the rear. Victor gave him a discreet nod, and he posted up by the door.

Washington's smug vibe was unmistakable. Something had changed. And Mr. Dante Washington knew what that was before Victor. That was gangster pool, and Mr. Washington was a couple pockets ahead.

"You know," Victor said, pouring himself a glass, "it's not every day that somebody walks into my Church like they own the place."

Mr. Dante Washington held up the duffle bag, unzipping it with a brassy rasp. He tilted it forward to display the contents to the Lord Crow: strapped stacks of hundred dollar bills. He dropped it on Victor's table with a smile. It landed on the polished wood with a flat, thirty-pound thud. A million and a half in cash was heavy. Silence followed.

"Boom," Mr. Washington said softly. His smile widened. "Half of your ten percent, as requested. One point seven and some change." Washington helped himself to the chair Gabriel usually sat in. "Would you care to count it? Now's your chance."

Victor shook his head. "Nah. Not right now." He leaned back in his throne, crossed his legs, and plucked a stray piece of lint from the knee of his trousers. "So. What's with the dick measuring?"

"Well, that's the only way to know who's got the biggest one, right?" Mr. Washington said with an apologetic shrug. Then he seemed distracted by the bottle service laid out on the table. "Do you mind?"

"Knock yourself out," Victor replied.

Mr. Washington smiled and poured himself a slug. He gave it a sniff, nodded appreciatively at its fine aroma, then set it aside. "So, I want to tell you a story, Mr. St. John."

Victor grunted. "I bet you do."

Mr. Washington nodded and made himself at home. "See, it goes back about six months ago, give or take."

Victor gave a sour laugh. "Fuck the history lesson. Why don't you tell me what's going on now?"

Mr. Washington didn't look happy to be interrupted. His pleasant smile faded by a degree. But he conceded. "Okay, we can fast forward. Suffice it to say, it's a very big, very strange world. Of course, I don't have to tell you and the Addams Family here that, do I?"

Victor offered no response.

Mr. Washington continued. "Sometimes, opportunity falls right into your lap."

"And if it's too good to be true, it probably is," Victor cautioned. "My professional advice."

"Yeah, well, you weigh the risks and play the hand you're dealt, right?"

Victor nodded.

"Your friend, the late Dr. McCoy. He was a very smart man."

"Yes, he was," Victor agreed.

"But he was very hard to do business with," Mr. Washington said. "And, well, I'm accustomed to getting what I want. It's good to be king."

"I take it he had something you wanted that wasn't for sale?"

Mr. Washington nodded. "You ever look into the Outer Darkness, Mr. St. John?"

"No," Victor replied. "I've got better sense than that."

Mr. Washington chuckled. "See, that's what all you people say. You've never actually *seen* that boogeyman, but somehow, you're all experts on it."

"But you know better?"

"Yeah, I think I do, actually. It's just like any other fork in the road. Any other deal with the Devil, so to speak. You just can't flinch. You gotta own it, or it owns you."

"You think so?" Fiona asked.

"So far, I seem to be right," Mr. Washington replied.

Fiona let off a single bark of contemptuous laughter. "How do you gauge it so, Mr. Washington?"

Dante Washington shrugged. "Well, one of us is winning, and one of us is losing, so I'll let the results speak for themselves."

Victor ran his thumb against the smooth edge of his throne's armrest, the only tell that he didn't like where this was going. "Well, clearly you think you know something I don't. So, what's your angle, Mr. Washington?"

Dante Washington smiled, a grim, humorless expression.

"*You* summoned the Fifth Horror, didn't you?" Fiona said. "That's what you're talking about. This whole thing has been a smoke screen."

"We experimented with it, yes," Mr. Washington confirmed. "Results varied. Some things went better than others. Thanks to Miss Ramirez and her coven mates going against the wishes of the old man, that is. They were very helpful."

"But?" Victor asked.

Mr. Washington gave a shrug, as though the 'buts' were inconsequential. "Can't make an omelet without breaking a few eggs and all that. We gave it a test run. A little parley with the beast on the other side of the Dark. You clear that first hurdle and he gives back a little. A little taste." Dante Washington smiled. "Shit, I understand that business model. Everybody's a dealer at the end of the day."

Fiona shook her head. "Even if you succeed, and gain that kind of favor and power, what are you to possibly do with it?"

"Not to put too fine a point on it, my dear Lady Crow, but whatever the fuck I want. Yes, I would like very much to have a set of keys to the universe. Wouldn't you?"

"At that price?" Fiona replied, her brow arching. "No."

"Let me guess," Victor interjected with a grunt, "You burned up your free sample already, didn't you? Ripping off the Cartel and putting all these little pieces in motion."

"Like a nappy-ass crackhead," Mr. Washington confirmed with a smile. "And to be honest, without the cooperation of the late, great, Dr. Angus McCoy, we've gone about as far as his apprentices and my talent are able to go. That's where you and *your* talent come in."

Victor laughed. "Are you outta your fucking mind? Nobody with an ounce of sense wants to take on the kind of heat you're talking about."

Mr. Washington studied Victor for a second, then he looked to Fiona.

The Lady Crow shook her head in kind. "I don't know what you think you know, Mr. Washington. But it's just not done. There's a reason Dr. McCoy wouldn't have any of it.

There's a reason *we* won't have any of it."

Mr. Washington shrugged. "We pull this off, and money is not an obstacle."

"It's not about a price tag," Victor assured him. "It's about being alive to spend it. Surely by now, the Helitori, the Watch, Del Torro all breathing down your neck, you're figuring that out, right?"

Mr. Washington nodded. His phone vibrated in his jacket pocket. He paused, took a look at it, and fired off a three-tap-reply with his thumb. Then he returned to the conversation with his host. "I am figuring that out, yes. Known that for quite some time, actually." He nodded toward the duffle full of cash. "You sure you don't want to count that out?"

"I'm sure you're good for it," Victor replied, a dangerous glower lighting in his eye. His face turned down in a granite frown. "What have you done?"

"Well, you're right about all that heat. I certainly don't want to have to put up with it for the rest of my, hopefully, very long and productive life. And like I said before. I'm king, and the king is accustomed to getting what he wants."

Bingo had begun to inch discreetly along the wall, farther from the door and closer to Mr. Washington's back, one jump away from shouldering past his guards and being on the man himself if his Lord Crow gave the nod.

But Mr. Washington, ever the wary street soldier at heart, sensed him creeping up. He didn't even turn around. "You better tell grandpa there to be cool. Before I have the homeboys here unzip him from balls to throat right in the middle of your fancy ass table."

Victor held Bingo at bay with a flick of his eyes and a single shake of his head. He felt Fiona's hand tense on his shoulder as the whole affair began to turn south. "What do you want, Washington?"

Mr. Washington patted the duffle of cash. "To pay you for your services," he said. "As you've obviously puzzled out, I know where the money is. Always did. So, your paycheck is already written. I just need you to, uh, finish the job."

"And what job is that? We already conveniently disposed

of your patsy for you. That *was* Felipe's part in all this, yeah? Fall guy number one?"

"Well, gotta make it look convincing, right? We already made a test run at opening the Way to the Fifth Horror. I want you to finish it. Take it all the way."

Victor couldn't help but laugh. He got the picture. "This whole goddamn gig has been a frame job from the start, hasn't it?"

Mr. Washington gave a noncommittal shrug. "I'd prefer to think of it as a 'cover operation' myself."

"Bullshit," Victor replied. "You want to pin this on us—the money, the summoning—you want us to take the fall for all of it while you grab the brass ring."

"When you put it that way, it sounds kind of harsh."

"Why the fuck would we do this for you?"

"Because you like to get paid," Mr. Washington said. Then his smile turned dark and cold. "And because you love your family. I can give you both, or I can take both away ... the choice is yours."

Victor's face darkened like a storm cloud.

"Have you called and checked on your kids lately?" Mr. Washington asked, glancing back and forth between Lord and Lady Crow.

The room got very quiet.

"I will *kill* you," Fiona hissed in a low, dangerous tone.

Victor held up a hand, staying her wrath.

Guns came out in a flash around the room, muzzles locked on the Crows. Mr. Washington gave a nod to his man at the door, and he stepped out. A moment later, a couple of Washington's goons hauled Anna in at gunpoint. Bingo bristled, but she shook her head, trying to keep her daddy bear calm.

"This doesn't have to be a fight," Mr. Washington said at length. "I'm not trying to rob you. I'm just gonna fuck you a little. When it's over, you're going to take a pile of cash and go start a new life on a different continent. What's so bad about that?"

Victor glared hard at Washington in response.

"*Or*," continued Washington, "you can fuck with me, and

I can start taking your Crows apart one piece at a time until you see things my way. I can start with your kids. I can start with the old man. Shit, I can start with your cats, if you want—whatever motivates you."

The sound of Victor's teeth grinding was his only reply.

"I want you to understand this, Victor. I own you now. My people, they're all over your people. If you don't believe me, give it time. I'm sure they'll be calling to let you know they're spotting tails on them. I've got your kids. I've got your knights. I've got your talent. Swoosh. Boom. Like that." He snapped his fingers. "What took you twenty years to build, I took apart in about an hour. So, I want to you think about that before you say whatever it is you're thinking. You can't move unless I say. You can't take a shit unless I say. Now, do you wanna get paid, or do you wanna start having funerals?"

Victor was quiet for a very long time, and the room held its breath along with him. Then finally, "I want to talk to my son."

Mr. Washington nodded. "I thought you might." His thumb pecked and dialed at his cell phone then he put it on speaker with a faint, cold smile while it rang. And rang. And went to voicemail.

A tremor of worry, a hint that something wasn't going according to plan, passed over Washington's face. He picked up his phone and dialed a different number. It, also, rang ... and rang ... and finally, unanswered, went to voicemail.

"What's the matter, boss?" Victor asked. "Nobody wanna take your calls tonight? Wonder why that is."

Washington turned to one of his men. "Get Markus on the phone ... *now*."

The merc nodded and stepped out into the hall.

Victor St. John and Dante Washington spent the long silence having an old-fashioned stare down. The Lord Crow lit a smoke. Washington nipped at his scotch.

A few moments later, the merc returned. He leaned down to Mr. Washington's shoulder and whispered something into his ear. The king did not look pleased. The muscles in his jaw flexed, and irritation crept into his expression.

"Load them up and get them the fuck out of here,"

Washington ordered abruptly, his good humor gone.

Victor smiled like a wolf. "Guess it's not all quite sorted out yet, is it?"

"Not yet," Washington conceded, draining his glass. "But soon."

"I suppose we'll see about that," Fiona replied.

"I suppose we will," Washington said. "Get them out of here. Now." He rose up out of his chair and stalked toward the door. "Bring the fucking money."

Washington's men took the Crows as ordered, leaving the Church hollow and empty in their wake. They rolled out east into the desert, destination unknown.

74

Delilah faded in and out. She was distantly aware of Michael and one of his fellow Watchmen huddling over her, packing her shoulder in a pressure dressing. They were driving. Rattling around in the back of some shitty old van full of gear and shuffling boots. Somebody stepped on her fingers in the process, but it didn't really hurt. She was just aware of it, nothing more. The pain came and went with the blackness. She was so shocky that it was hard to form thoughts or control her own head, let alone move and speak.

Finch was dead. Her last sight of him, the lifeless, blood-spattered mask of his ruptured head, kept coming back to haunt her. Torn. Broken. Gone.

Time was meaningless in that condition. It was sort of like being a little kid again, high on the nitrous oxide at the dentist's office. People were doing things all around her, talking to each other, talking to her, pushing, pulling, man-handling her, but it didn't really compute though. After a while, she was carried again, and the lights got brighter.

Then there was a bed covered in plastic sheeting and a cheap print of a deer and a spotted fawn on the wall. A motel room, maybe? Overhead, her eyes fixed on the metal star shape of a fire sprinkler.

Then her lights went out again, and thankfully, there were no dreams.

When she woke up again, the world was heroin-numb. Her face itched, and her wounded body pulsed softly with her heartbeat. It didn't hurt much. She felt very floaty. Morphine, maybe. To take the edge off her bullet-broken shoulder.

There was an old, ugly Chinese woman staring down at her with a disapproving scowl, her thin lips pressed into a tight pucker.

"She need doctor," the old woman insisted in broken English. "Hospital. Hurt very bad."

"Yeah, that's not an option," Michael insisted.

The old Chinese hag shrugged. "She die."

"That's not an option either," Michael replied.

"She stink," the old woman said with a sour snort. "Full of the Black."

"I didn't call you here for a sermon," Michael said. "I need help. *She* needs help."

"Help not free."

"Listen," Michael said, taking the old hag by the elbow. "This is Fiona St. John's daughter, her blood heir. I'm sure the Lady Crow would be very grateful if you helped her daughter."

That seemed to motivate the old crone, but only grudgingly. "My price, fine. *Other* price, nobody can pay but her."

Through the fog of blood loss, shock, and morphine, Delilah had a moment of clarity. Maybe it was the mention of her parents. Maybe it was something else. All she knew was that her family needed her.

She tested her voice and found it thick, slurred, and drunk. "Just get me back on my feet."

The old crone chuckled. "You be lucky I keep you out of your coffin."

"I don't have time to die right now," Delilah managed. The moment of lucidity was already starting to fade. She held on to it desperately. "Do what you need to do. I'm good for it. Whatever it costs."

The old crone cocked a slender eyebrow. "Price very high."

"I don't care," Delilah replied. Finch's ruined head, his dead staring eyes, crawled through her doped-up mind. She imagined more and worse for the rest of her family. It hurt, and the hurt made her angry. Being high as a kite amplified all of it.

"Very much pain," the old crone warned.

Delilah summoned up all the fortitude she could muster.

"You don't scare me. Now. If you can fix it, then fix it. If you can't, then fuck off, you old witch."

The old crone looked to Michael.

"You heard the lady," he said.

She leaned in, crook-backed and rheumy-eyed. She brushed her thumb across Delilah's blood speckled cheek and slithered into her personal space. For a moment, Delilah thought the old witch might kiss her. She stank of mud, yellow sweat, and old, stale cigarette smoke.

Then she smiled a ghoulish, foul grin. Her teeth were old and rotted, black-green as swamp moss. She parted her teeth, and Delilah saw a shiny black beetle, huge and wet, scuttle up out of the crone's throat to fill her mouth.

A spike of panic hit Delilah then.

But the crone locked her lips down over Delilah's and the world exploded in pain, like molten lead pouring down her throat. What came next was little more than a blur of horror and agony playing on an endless nightmare reel.

Delilah held on. She endured it.

She screamed.

75

The captive Crows were taken east, deep into the California desert. On the shores of the Salton Sea, the crumbling ruin of an abandoned motel and marina awaited them at the end of the line. There was nothing for miles in any direction. Blue nighttime desert. Black nighttime sea. Old concrete, pale beneath the starlight. The stink of rot. The air here had a peculiar taste. Desert dust and salty brine. The only lights visible at all were more than a mile back to the west along the highway, and those were only passing headlights, which were few and far between. It was a huge, empty, lonely place full of wind and ghosts.

Last to be delivered were Victor, Fiona, Bingo, and Anna, and no word was given why they were here or what would happen next.

They encountered several Washington's men, and most of them had the numb, shocked expressions of soldiers who'd just battled through a firefight on the outskirts of Hell. Several of their vehicles bore the scars of having gone through a gauntlet of gunfire.

Victor turned to Washington with a smirk as his men removed him from the van. "Your boys having a tough night?"

Washington's mouth drew into a razor scowl, but he said nothing in return while the men escorted the last of the captives to the ruined marina.

Washington's men had searched the captured Crows from top to bottom before first loading them up at the Church. Before bringing them inside, they searched them all over again. There wasn't much chance for hiding anything.

The captives were taken into the empty, cavernous, concrete

husk, Washington trailing behind at a casual distance. Men with guns led the way by flashlight, guiding them past piles of broken concrete till and other refuse until they reached a mostly-intact room along an exterior wall.

Two guards manned the door, and soft lantern light spilled out into the hollow central hall.

They culled Fiona from the rest of the group and steered her toward a separate lantern-lit room on the far side of the complex.

When Victor realized Fiona was being separated from the others, he balked. "Not a fucking chance," he growled as Washington's men tried to lead her away. And he looked like he might be willing to fight about it. Right there. Right then.

"It's all right, love," Fiona said. "I'm sure they have nothing but the finest accommodations in mind for me, don't you boys?"

Washington's men made a point to avoid Fiona's frosty gaze. None of them would look her directly in the eye. Clearly, they'd been educated about some things, and in the last few hours, they'd seen enough to start believing some of it.

"Give me your right hand," one of the guards instructed.

"What?"

"Your right hand," the guard replied, then he grabbed Victor by the wrist and took it by force.

Victor didn't fight him, but the look in his eyes promised murder.

The guard snapped a tarnished brass cuff over Victor's right wrist and fastened it shut with a metal pin. The lantern light caught in the constellation of runes etched into its surface.

Victor chuckled. "Kinky, but I don't swing that way hotshot."

But it was Washington who sounded smug. "I told you, Mr. St. John. I got your number. Whatever little aces you think you've got up your sleeve in all that ink, they're gonna stay there. So we can be friends."

Victor chewed on that for a moment. "Well, aren't you full of surprises."

Mr. Washington gestured across the compound. "Take her where she belongs."

They threw the rest of the family in chains and delivered the Lady Crow to a room of her own.

Miss Althea was waiting for her.

The floor was drawn in a circle of runes ten feet across, deep and intricate. An Oculan Trap, a prison for mages. Straight from the pages of the Vert Grimoire of Jean-Francois Mercier. At its outer edge, a span of runes about a foot long remained unfinished, the circle not yet closed and joined.

"I see you put the grimoire to good use," Fiona quipped, flicking a glance toward Miss Althea.

The priestess nodded and gestured toward the center of the circle. "If you please."

Head held high, Fiona walked willingly into her cell.

"Perhaps you wish to sit," Miss Althea suggested. "It is my understanding that the Oculan Trap is ... excruciating."

With a fearless and stony expression, Fiona St. John sat.

Miss Althea produced a piece of chalk from a pouch at her belt and with precise strokes, she laid down the final runes to close the circle.

Fiona's cage crushed her in its eldritch embrace, and the Lady Crow endured it.

76

Bloody night faded into blue dawn. This time, the sunrise brought no respite. The terrors of the night did *not* pass. There were too many that the sun lacked the power to drive away. They lingered, staining the new day black and red for those who were still walking through the nightmare drawing breath.

The day broke golden over the City of Angels.

It brought no peace.

PART SIX

Last Pale Light

Choices have consequences. The inescapable gravity of consequence is a real son of a bitch. As anybody who'd ever jumped off a cliff can tell you, gravity kills. When the stop comes, it's sudden. Then everything breaks.

77

After the nightmare of pain and the whirlwind of power passed, unconsciousness took Delilah. When she awoke, white daylight was leaking through the motel room curtains, and she was startled and disoriented. Then the urge to vomit took over, and she sprang from the bed, tangling herself in the bloody plastic sheeting. Crumpling to the floor, she scrambled on all fours toward the toilet, clawed the lid up, and proceeded to heave her guts out.

Her stomach upended, disgorging a belly full of gore. Purple blood clots. Bits of bullet-torn meat. Chips of white bone, bile and blood. Then she choked as something big lodged in her throat. She felt her face turning purple, her blood pressure climbing like a swollen balloon inside her skull before she finally dislodged the obstruction.

The rancid, dead and rotten carcass of the black beetle plopped into the soupy mess.

Shaking and shivering, Delilah hovered over the toilet bowl until the urge to vomit had passed, then she closed the lid and sagged onto the floor, hands trembling, body quivering.

Her wounded shoulder throbbed, still pierced deep with bone-breaking pain. Her arm and hand were very weak, but they functioned. Her pinky and ring finger were almost completely numb though. So was her elbow. She dared a look at the remains of her injury and saw the grisly entrance wound scar right through her collarbone—angry, purple, and fresh. She was as black and blue as if she'd been beaten with a baseball bat. The exit wound scar was similar, but worse—about twice the size and shaped like a ragged keyhole. It all hurt so badly that she wondered if the bones were still broken inside.

Then Gabriel was there, snatching up a couple of clean towels and kneeling beside her, helping her to cover up, to get warm.

"Where'd you come from?" Delilah rasped in a raw, scratchy voice.

"Michael called me," Gabriel said. Worry lined his haggard face, lips pressed tight, brow furrowed. "Did it work?"

Delilah nodded. "I think so. As good as it's gonna get." She coughed and everything hurt. "Help me up."

He guided her out of the bathroom to the foot of the nearest bed on what felt like newborn legs. Delilah plopped down hard, immediately regretting the way the shock jarred her tender shoulder.

Across the room, Michael LeMay leaned against the wall, arms folded across his chest. By the tilt of his head and the sour expression on his face, Delilah could tell he was out of patience.

"Were you following me?" she asked.

"Something like that. Then everything went to shit."

"Thank you," she managed.

"You can thank me by telling me what's going on," Michael replied. "All of it."

Delilah grunted. "I can't."

Michael looked to Gabriel. "How about you?"

Gabriel didn't even pretend. "Sorry. Family business."

Michael rolled his eyes. "You two are something else, you know that?"

They couldn't argue.

"Maybe, just maybe, you could let me help you," Michael said.

Delilah shrugged with her good shoulder. "You did. And we said thank you."

"Let me phrase that another way. I stuck my foot in where it doesn't belong. We shouldn't have interfered. But we did. 'Thank you' isn't quite going to cover it."

Delilah's head sagged with an exhausted sigh. "There's no point in all of this."

Michael clearly agreed with her. Right up to the instant

when she raised her hand and sent him stunned to the floor with a strobing blast of eldritch energy. He never saw it coming.

"Sorry about that," Delilah muttered apologetically as Michael settled into a half-conscious sprawl on the motel carpet.

Gabriel looked a little stunned himself. But if anybody could sucker punch Michael LeMay, it was going to be Delilah. She knew him inside and out, knew every chink in his armor. Gabriel had recently learned himself just how sharp the double-edged razor of intimacy could really be.

"Trust me. That was going to end badly," Delilah said. It was all the explanation she was willing to offer.

Gabriel didn't argue. Instead, he tossed her a plastic sack of clothes he'd picked up at a Wal-Mart along the way. They weren't exactly styling threads, but they came without bullet holes and blood stains.

"Come on," Gabriel urged with a shake of his head. "Before he wakes up."

They didn't waste any time.

78

Michael LeMay awoke to the heavily accented call of "Hallo? Housekeeping?"

His head was ringing like a gong, and the last clear memory he had was of it suddenly getting very, very bright before a horse had kicked him in the skull.

The housekeeper let out a startled yelp when she found him sprawled out on the floor.

"Don't do that," Michael muttered, cupping a hand over his eyes. Shit. It was like he could *see* sound, and it fucking hurt.

The housekeeper fussed over him, kneeling beside him, trying to help, carrying on in whip-crack Spanglish and Michael did his best to reassure her in kind. Something about being fine, no worries, too much *cerveza*.

She wanted to call an ambulance or the police, but he insistently waved that notion away and struggled back to his feet on punch-drunk legs, thanking her graciously for all her help. He managed to peel a rumpled twenty-dollar bill out of the pocket of his jeans and give it to her as a tip along with his apologies for the mess and missing check-out time.

Thankfully, the missing Crows hadn't left any of Delilah's bloody wreckage behind. Small victories, he supposed, if you could count that as one.

He managed to bullshit and bribe his way out of the tangle with the frantic housekeeper long enough to round up his shit and stagger out into the desert sun anyway.

The Crows were gone. That sort of figured. "You scrawny little bitch," he grunted.

Michael didn't wait around. He pulled out his phone and

dialed, stomping straight toward his vehicle. He threw his shit inside and climbed in the driver's seat, phone to his head, ignoring the old man staring at him from the check-in counter window.

Master Dutch answered on the fourth ring.

"You remember that favor I was waiting to cash in?" Michael asked.

"I do."

"*Ka-ching*. Cash me out, boss. We got a situation here."

Dutch didn't argue. "What do you need?"

"Everything you've got."

"Let me know when you've got a place and time. We'll be there. Brief me when you can."

"Will do."

"How bad?"

Michael contemplated that. He wasn't one to cry wolf. He also wasn't one to blow sunshine up asses either. "Consider it as bad as it gets until it gets better."

"Noted."

The Watch was rolling.

79

Gabriel drove while Delilah sagged, exhausted, in the passenger seat. Sun-bleached desert rolled by outside. She rode in silence, staring off into the horizon. Her face was hollow, pale and bloodless. She was clearly still in a lot of pain. Gabriel scrounged her up a bottle of water and a palm-full of his pain pills. Being short and slight compared to her brother, but accustomed to recreational self-medication, she helped herself to two.

"You doing okay?" Gabriel asked, at a loss for what else to say.

"I got shot. Finch is gone. No. The answer is no, I'm not doing okay."

Gabriel didn't argue with her. Instead, he lit a cigarette and passed it to her. "Did, um… Did anybody else make it out?"

"I don't know. What did Michael say?"

"He didn't know either."

She took a drag, blew it out the crack in the top of the window, and said, "What have I done?" Their exploits were all over the news. They'd be dodging the fallout of this weekend in hell … forever.

He offered the best answer he could muster. "Nothing we can undo now. And nothing I haven't done too. Sometimes shit just … happens."

Her vision blurred with tears and she closed her eyes. "Where's Finchy?"

"Michael's people picked him up before it all burned out. We'll get him home."

Delilah managed a tearful chuckle. "Maybe I shouldn't have been such a bitch to him, then, huh?"

Gabriel didn't have an answer for that one.

"Can you fill me in?" Delilah asked, dreading the answer.

He did, and he didn't pull any punches.

"What happens now?" she asked, shifting gears, wiping the tears from her cheeks. Bushwhacking Michael would only buy them time—a temporary respite from having the Watch breathing down their necks, and likely a short one at that. She couldn't hide from Michael any better than he could hide from her—not with Samuel connecting them in this universe. Hopefully, it would be time enough to get their business handled before the sky came crashing down. Before they had to answer for things they didn't want to.

They were on the wrong side of Dante Washington. The wrong side of the Cartel. Probably on the wrong side of the Watch, too. And if, or *when*, the authorities connected the bloody dots back to them, they'd be on California's Most Wanted List. These were the kinds of problems that haunted you forever. They never really went away. Not until you were dead.

And everyone they loved in this world was standing on the gallows.

"We don't have the muscle to go head-to-head with Dante Washington," Gabriel said. He didn't even mention the Cartel because … what was the point? "Even if we *did*, Washington's people are all over us. If we make a move and he sees it …" Gabriel reached between the seats and produced a bundle wrapped in an undershirt and passed it to his sister. "I think *that* is what this shit is all about."

Delilah took the bundle and unwrapped it. Inside she found a fourteen-inch length of jagged, twisting iron, old and pitted, stained with blood. It resembled a long, dull dagger. Holding it was like holding a beating heart alive with the stain of Maglo. Worse. *Born* from the stain of Maglo. "God. Is *this* the relic Felipe whipped out on you the other night?"

Gabriel nodded.

"What is it?"

"I was hoping you could tell me."

But she couldn't. She could *feel* that it was a piece of the Fifth Horror—a token of power, a potent connection, a key—but none of those things shed any light on its function or its purpose. Just holding it made her feel equal parts sick and aroused. The hurt in her shoulder numbed, while the sourness in her stomach worsened. She wondered if she'd be able to skin the meat from her fingers with it.

Jesus.

Delilah wrapped it up and passed it back to Gabriel. "We need to get rid of that. *Everybody* needs to get rid of that."

"Probably not gonna happen though," Gabriel replied. "Washington sent Markus after it. He wanted it, and he was willing to kill whoever it took to get it. I don't get the impression he's gonna give up."

Delilah mulled that over. "Where do you think Felipe got it?"

"Best guess?" Gabriel asked, throwing her a sidelong glance. "Washington."

The expression on Delilah's face said that was hard to compute.

"I will bet my ass that this whole thing has been a setup. I'm not buying the story that Washington is Felipe's victim. Not anymore. Felipe and Markus had a beef to settle, and whatever it was, Felipe seemed to think Markus started it." Gabriel was quiet for a bit while he mulled it over. "I think Felipe was Washington's trigger man, and when the job was done, Washington tried to pin it all on him. But the trigger man stole the gun and ran." He shook his head. "And here we are."

"So, what do we do?" Delilah asked.

Gabriel shrugged. "I don't know."

They were quiet for a very long time. Desert highway rolled by and not a word was said.

Then, after another smoke, Delilah spoke up. "I've got an idea. At least a way to get us some muscle Washington doesn't know about."

Gabriel turned to her, weighed the sincerity in her face and nodded. "Okay, sis. Let's hear it."

Delilah laid it out and, in the end, the Captain Crow bought what she was selling, no questions asked.

"Where are we going?" Gabriel asked.

"Head to Palm Springs," Delilah replied.

80

Tracking down the Godfather was easy enough—at least for Delilah.

He had a dusty ranch house out on the edge of the Agua Caliente Indian Reservation, nestled up against the feet of the San Jacinto mountains. The house sat at the top of a long hill and in the driveway was an old four-wheel-drive pickup truck and the Godfather's Harley. He met the Crows at the door with a smile on his face, not looking the slightest bit surprised to see them.

"You causing all kinds of trouble out there in the world, little sister?" he asked.

"Maybe," Delilah replied. She didn't bullshit or bandy words. "You want a shot at squaring up that debt you owe me?"

The Godfather cocked a curious eyebrow and looked to the Captain Crow on his doorstep. "Side business getting official?"

Gabriel nodded. "Looks that way."

The Godfather motioned for them to come inside. "Let me make a phone call."

"You haven't asked me what I want," Delilah said.

"Eh," the Godfather replied with a crooked smile and a shrug. Then he stepped aside and dialed his phone, motioning for them to make themselves comfortable.

Out of the back of the house came Ruby, the hedge witch, dressed in cut-off jean shorts and wearing one of the Godfather's old t-shirts.

On the other end of the Godfather's line, somebody answered.

"Sorry to disturb you at this hour," he said, in his congenial salesman's tone, seemingly unconcerned with the fact that it was the middle of the day. "But I've got a situation here I need to run past you. Doesn't look like it can wait." He glanced to Delilah for confirmation, and she nodded.

For a moment, the Godfather listened, then he spoke once more. "I'm standing here with the prince and princess of the Crow. They need a favor. Just so happens that I owe them one."

Again, a pause while he listened.

"Yes, sir, I believe so," he said. But what he believed remained a mystery to Gabriel and Delilah. After a moment, the Godfather smiled. "I will. Yes. Thank you, sir. I'll keep you posted." That quickly he hung up.

He raised his hands and shrugged apologetically to his guests. "We all work for somebody, right?"

He offered no further elaboration on who it was *he* worked for though.

"Well?" Delilah asked.

The Godfather gave a broad, paternal smile. "How can we be of service to the Crow?"

The Crows laid it on the table, and the Godfather and his little Ruby paid heed. The first part was simple enough. They were going to need either an extraction or a rescue—muscle they could move without Dante Washington catching wind of it. It just so happened, the Godfather had that.

Then they came to Ruby's part. "What do you say, Ruby?" Delilah asked with a humorless smile. "Wanna do big girl magic?"

Of course she did.

"Then bring two shot glasses and a bottle of tequila back here," Delilah ordered.

Ruby didn't hesitate.

Delilah worked the Red blood magic with practiced grace, pricking her finger, then Ruby's and placing three drops of crimson blood into each shot glass as she whispered the incantation. The timing was poor, but Delilah was an old pro at this one. It would do.

When finished, Delilah and Ruby crossed their arms like newlyweds having their first toast and downed each other's blood-laced shots.

Where she and Gabriel were going, there weren't likely to be many opportunities to use a phone or to place a distress call. Chances are, they wouldn't even know where *there* was until they'd arrived—and by that time, it'd be too late to dial in the Godfather's Pack—so just in case other options failed, Delilah was now the Godfather's homing beacon, and Ruby, his receiver.

"Now remember. You'll be able to find me, for a little while, but I'll *always* be able to find you. This is *my* spell. You fuck with me, and I will turn you inside out. Clear?"

Ruby looked a little shocked, even opened her mouth like she might say something. But in the end, she held her tongue and gave a respectful nod. That was probably wise.

Delilah was high on the Black and numb with grief. It had turned her more surly and dangerous than usual. It grated against her guilt and pain, levered on the traumas she'd endured over the past twenty-four hours, leaving her hung on the razor edge of lashing out. Like Pacino doing Tony Montana with a head full of coke. *Say hello to my little friend!*

It would pass if she let it. Slowly burning out of her system like bad dope ... or she'd go off like a pipe bomb and the hooks would get deeper. All bets were off which would happen first. Strung out on the Black, drowning in pain and emotions that she'd never been equipped to deal with, Delilah reminded herself most of her Lord Father. In all the worst ways.

"We have a deal," she said, looking at the Godfather with stern, serious eyes. It was as much a warning as confirmation. "Let's keep it that way."

The Godfather shook on it and looked pleased. "You handle your business, little sister. We'll be there to back you up when the time comes."

With that, they got back on the road.

81

They parked it at a lonesome rest stop, like a galley lost at sea, surrounded by rolling desert scrub. Across the highway was a massive truck stop, with eighteen-wheelers turning in and out like passenger jets at a busy airport. On their side of the highway, everything had been left to die when the truck stop moved in. The sky was springtime white, and everything else was the color of Mars. Delilah went looking for a soda, but the sun-bleached vending machine was out of order and most likely had been since *Tab* was still a thing.

Gabriel sat on a rusty picnic table and stared at his phone, contemplating their final play.

He'd touched base with Twitch and Grizz, the only Crows he knew were clear of a tail, so the only Crows he dared make contact with at the moment, and he'd gotten the pulse of the street. It was pretty much what he'd been expecting.

"The word's out, boss," Twitch advised. "Washington wants to hear from *you* personally by five o'clock today. Or he's gonna start sending our people back to us in bags."

Washington wanted the dagger, and he clearly wanted something from *them*. One way or another, he was going to get it. Gabriel's preference was to give it to him with the pointy end. Time wasn't on their side, though. If they kept playing hard-to-get, Washington was going to start making people bleed.

They needed to make a move before one of their brothers or sisters wound up dumped dead in the parking lot of the Church with a sign around their neck.

"I know I can find them," Delilah said at length. "When the sun goes down, there's not going to be any hiding the shit they're doing and the shit they've done. We have the dagger, and I can find where it belongs. I can find Mom and Dad. I *know* I can. No matter what they do to stop me."

Gabriel believed her. He knew she could do it.

But, their backup, the Godfather's Pack, was just that—backup. A little operational support was a whole lot different than going in strong against an adversary like Mr. Dante Washington. And as promised, Washington's people were all over their own. That wasn't a threat. That was a fact. They couldn't even get tacos without tipping off the hounds at their heels. One thing Washington had was a tremendous advantage in manpower.

Every Crow wanted to know the same thing, should they ditch their tails and get in the fight? Gabriel's answer was a resounding *no*. Washington was on a hair trigger, and almost surely, that would provoke him. That remained Gabriel's nuclear option, though.

Right now, Washington's hostages were as good as human shields, guarding him against the wrath of the Crow. They were the only thing restraining Gabriel from giving his Crows the order to kill every last motherfucking thing with Dante Washington's name on it. If anything happened to Washington's hostages that restraint would be gone.

It wouldn't matter if it was a losing battle at that point. The Crow had scattered, flown the coop, leaving the smoldering wreckage to burn down behind them before. They could do it again if it all came crashing down. They weren't there. Yet.

But they were close. Right there on the razor's edge, as a matter of fact.

He looked at the bloated silver sun, hanging midway to the horizon in the whitewashed afternoon sky. It was already ten minutes to five.

"I think we're outta time, Sis," he said at last.

And she didn't protest, because she believed him.

Gabriel made the call.

Mr. Dante Washington answered on the third ring. "Yes?"

"Where is my family?"

"Mr. St. John, I presume?"

Gabriel repeated himself. "Where is my family?"

"Here. With me. And, no, they are *not* safe. Would you like them to be safe, Mr. St. John?"

"You let them walk, and we can talk. No dice while you're still holding them."

"Is your sister, Miss St. John, with you as well?"

"Open your ears, Washington. I already told you, I'm not talking to you until you let my family go."

Washington *tsked* at that notion. "Sorry, Mr. St. John, it's just not going to work that way. See, I am one hundred percent done fucking around with you people. So, here's what's going to happen. Starting now, I'm going to kill one of your people every thirty minutes until I get your unconditional surrender. You understand what unconditional means, don't you?"

Gabriel was silently fuming. He'd rolled the dice and thrown snake eyes. Calling Washington to measure dicks had been an automatic loss. There was a pause, and he could hear shuffling and scuffling in the background.

"Right there, gentlemen," Mr. Washington said to someone on his end of the line. "Okay, Mr. St. John. I'm going to start with your boy Piper here. I'm going to count to three, and if I don't get your surrender by then, I'm going to shoot him in the throat. Then we'll start the clock. Thirty minutes after that, I'm going to do the same thing to Bingo. Then probably your little family doctor, Miss Anna too. And so on. Until you pony up or I run out of Crows to kill."

"You piece of shit," Gabriel grunted.

"Don't you give him shit, captain!" Piper called in the background. He was wounded, hurting. Gabriel could hear the pain and bug-eyed rage in his voice. Then Piper started goading his captors. "Come on. Do it! Right here! Right now. Do it!"

"Are you ready, Mr. St. John?" Washington asked.

Gabriel remained stony, silent.

"One," Washington said calmly.

"Come on, you pussy piece of shit! Light me up!" Piper definitely had no plans to go out quietly.

"Two."

Gabriel closed his eyes and could imagine the pistol in

Piper's face, the ragged old Crow defiant and loud to the very end.

"Suck my dick! Suck my big, fat, pink dick!"

"Three—"

"Stop," Gabriel said at last. Chicken played. He lost. Check and mate. There was no direction he could move that didn't end with one his brothers or sisters getting killed *right now*.

What would his Lord Father have done? Said *fuck you* and endured the casualties.

What did Gabriel do? He closed his eyes. "Stop. I'll do it. Whatever you want."

"That sounds an awful lot like you suddenly being ready to surrender," Washington said.

"Fuck you. Just tell me what you want."

"I'm going to give you a place and a time. You and your sister both will both be there, and you will bring the dagger. Don't bother bullshitting me, because I know you've got it. My people will be there to pick you up. Once they've got you, they will let me know. If I get anything other than an 'all-clear' from them at the pickup spot and every ten minutes thereafter, I will turn your whole goddamn family into dog food.

"Not one by one. No second chances, no chance to change your mind and cooperate after all. We won't play this game again. They'll all be dead, and we'll see just how long you can run from me. Do we understand each other?"

"Yeah. We understand each other just fine," Gabriel said.

"Once you and I can sit down face to face, we'll talk about what you can do for me. Any questions?"

"Just tell us where to be."

Washington gave him the time and place. "Show up like you're planning to work."

"We'll be there." Gabriel paused before he hung up. "Washington?"

"Yes, Mr. St. John?"

"Sooner or later, this bill is gonna come due. I promise you. The Crow collects every debt. This *will* get paid."

"We'll see about that, Mr. St. John."

Then he was gone.

82

Following the directions Mr. Washington provided, they headed out and caught Highway 86. Then they followed it south off the Planet Earth and onto the Moon. They found the place easy enough. A dirt spur off the highway that dead-ended at the foot of a massive cell tower. It was easy to find because, out here, there simply wasn't anything else.

By then, the sun was low in the sky and falling fast.

A flight of pelicans winged by low overhead, flapping their slow dinosaur wings and heading east. A surreal sight in the middle of the California desert to be sure, but it told them where they were—on the outskirts of the Salton Sea.

Gabriel fished out the holding bag that Markus's dearly departed team had used to round up his possessions the night before and repeated a similar ritual with his sister.

One by one, they relieved themselves of anything they were carrying that was important and dumped it in the sack. Delilah had next to nothing. Miss Althea and her goon squad had already taken everything but her clothes, and even those old clothes were now gone. Gabriel had wadded the bloody mess up in a trash sack and set it on fire in a roadside ditch. There wasn't much else to be done with it. She had nothing left but her blood-spattered shoes and the new clothes he'd brought her.

Gabriel had already been packing light when he left on his hunt for Felipe. His inventory was easy to police up. He dropped his pistols, his last boomstick, his binding lash, and the cash in his pocket into the sack. Then he cut an empty water bottle in half to use as a spade. He walked a short distance in the shadow of the cell tower, dug a shallow hole at the foot of a prominent boulder, threw the sack in, and covered it with dirt. No sense letting Washington's cronies make off with anything worth stealing.

He saved a pack of smokes and a book of matches.

He gave Delilah his lighter, just in case, but he doubted they'd let her keep it.

Other than that, the only thing he kept was the clothes on his back, the shoes on his feet, and the jagged length of pitted iron crawling with the corruption of Maglo.

With nothing left to do but wait, Gabriel and Delilah perched on the rear bumper, side by side, and watched the sun go down. The desert turned gold, then violet.

"You don't have to do this," Gabriel said.

"Yeah, I do," she replied. And she even managed a smile.

Not long after that, two gray security SUVs turned off the highway and onto the dirt spur toward the cell tower, contrails of dust rising behind them to be slashed away by the wind.

With a deep breath, Delilah reached out and took her big brother's hand, lacing her fingers in his. He squeezed back and held on.

Washington's men took them as the last pale light bled out of the west.

83

The end of the line was the abandoned marina on the bleak shores of the Salton Sea.

In the Fifties and Sixties, this was the place where dreams of a new Las Vegas had come to die. The picturesque Salton Sea had once been home to thriving resort communities, destined to rival anything in the American West during the boom years. But the dream and the reality got divorced like angry drunks. The salinity of the lake was too high. Then came disputes over transportation, irrigation, and farming. Investors got nervous, money dried up, and with the money evaporating, the dream died the death of a thousand cuts.

Along the shores of the Salton Sea were ghost towns and half-towns, built on grids of empty streets intended to host tens of thousands but now home to only a few hundred. The fossils of failed progress littered the desert in the most improbable ways. Abandoned hotels and marinas dotted the shore. Naked foundations poked up out of the desert like dirty, rotten teeth. Buildings without names stood decaying in the never-ending wind, time having erased any sense of why they'd been there at all.

Here and there were tiny pockets of civilization, but in between, there wasn't much of anything.

A vast expanse of glassy blackness opened on the eastern horizon—a colorless void where the world seemed to come to an end—the Salton Sea at night. Then nothing for three very long miles as they drove along the shore.

The sea was a lightless inkwell as they slowed and approached an abandoned old shore-side motel. A long, empty dock jutted out into the water like the knobby old backbone of some dead dinosaur. Nothing remained of the adjoining marina except for rows of concrete pilings. The glassless windows stared out of the shell of the motel like empty jack-o-lantern eyes—black, bleak, and hollow. Some illegible metal road sign, peppered with birdshot scars and bullet holes, declared nothing discernible about the place. It had been long-since bleached white by the desert. The site was a derelict, abandoned leftover—a good place for doing bad things.

Washington's mercs pulled Gabriel and Delilah from the vehicle and ushered them inside the decrepit, sun-washed ruin through the old lobby doors. A small generator was purring along quietly by the exit, several extension cords running away from it into the gloom toward a series of harsh white shop lights on poles. Elsewhere, pale lantern glow could be seen, pinpoints of light in the dusty, hollow dark.

The interior of the old ruin had a tomb-like quality.

Inside and out, the graffiti was laid down with years and heavy hands. It wasn't like gang graffiti—this was intoxicated spray can finger painting, left over by generations of desert-wandering hippies, hipsters, and partying drunks. Most of it was talentless scrawl, the mega-sized equivalent of cocks and swastikas drawn on gas station toilet stalls. But some of the pieces visible within the halos of sparse light were noteworthy.

There was a twenty-foot-long mural: a fair representation of Dorothy and chums from the Wizard of Oz cavorting down the Yellow Brick Road. Of course, someone had come along at some point and ruined it by drawing a circle around the Scarecrow's head in red spray paint along with the words 'Tricky Dick'.

Fuck seemed to be the favorite word of spray paint artists over the years.

On the other side of the echoing central chamber, someone had taken to the walls with chalk and not too long ago at that. A leering, sneering werewolf rose, slender and horrible, up the wall, colored in over the top of a generation's worth of petty scribbles. Framed in a halo of a full yellow moon, the words "Hey There Little Red Riding Hood" were written beneath him in blocky horror house script. Some chalk artist's peyote-fueled nightmare maybe. The detail in the chalk art suggested talent, but the general irregular waviness of the outline hinted at inebriation.

There, in the harsh glow of the shop lights, Mr. Dante Washington and some of his handpicked loyalists waited to receive them.

"Cut them loose," Mr. Washington ordered, and the mercs released their bonds.

"Where are they?" Gabriel demanded at once, rubbing some feeling back into his wrists. In the empty dark, even low voices seemed large.

"They're fine," Mr. Washington assured him.

"We're not doing anything until we see them," Delilah said.

Mr. Washington looked to one of his mercs, maybe the man in charge now that Jonathan Markus was retired.

"They're clean. And we have the package," the merc said.

Mr. Washington relented. He gestured to his men and then waved off into the dark. "Take them," he ordered, sounding bored.

A mixed group of Washington's soldiers—mercs plus bangers from Silver Dollar's hood—led them by flashlight to the rest of their family.

The remainder of the Crows were being held in a chamber off the main central lobby. Much of the old marina motel was an empty concrete husk, many of the interior walls having been demoed at some point, the till piled around like burial mounds. It gave the place a cavernous honeycomb quality with strange blind corners mixed with long open stretches of dusty darkness. The room that held the captive Crows was largely intact. It didn't have a door—just four walls, a roof and armed guards posted outside. Their escorts led them into the impromptu cell.

Washington's men had shot bolts into the concrete of the far wall, run some chains through the rings, and handcuffed the prisoners in place, leaving the captives only enough room to stand or sit down against the wall.

"Jesus," Delilah sighed when she saw her family chained up like junkyard dogs.

Bingo's mouth and temper had earned him a couple of pops

to the face, so his beard was matted from a bloody nose, and his left eye was swollen, but he didn't seem too worried about it.

Anna looked angry and protective, hanging close to her brother and father, but otherwise, she looked like she was in good shape.

Dodger was seated with his back to the wall, and he looked like a rodeo rider after the bull wins. His face was swollen and cut, his bottom lip split, but he nodded upon seeing his brother and sister Crows, letting them know he was still in it to win it.

Piper didn't look so good though. He was laying on his side against the wall, curled up as best he could with his wrists in chains. Dodger's motorcycle jacket was balled up under his head. His jeans were dark with dried blood stains down the side, and a bloody pressure dressing was strapped across his hip. He licked his dry lips and gave a weak nod at their arrival, but he didn't try to get up. His wounds had caught up to him hard.

Izzie didn't look much better. Her forearm was encased in a temporary plastic splint, and her hand was swollen and purple. Her ear was puffed up with a chunk taken out of it, her nostrils caked with dried blood. One of her eyes was swollen completely shut. But she managed a strained smile. She was glad to see them.

Other than his suit being a little dusty, Victor looked no worse for wear and actually looked calm. Then again, Victor always looked calm. He was sitting against the wall when the guards led his kids into the cell, and at their arrival, he stood and dusted his hands off.

"You okay?" he asked the two of them.

Gabriel and Delilah both managed to nod.

"Where's mom?" Delilah asked.

"She's all right," Victor assured her, tilting his head towards the west. "They're keeping her down the hall. Because they're scared of a little Irish lady."

"You sure she's okay?" Gabriel asked.

Victor nodded. "Yeah."

"Where's Finchy?" Dodger asked. His deep voice carried well in the dusty dark.

Delilah swallowed a lump in her throat, but no words were willing to come out.

"He's gone," Gabriel said with a single shake of his head.

A thundercloud of hate fell over the captive Crows. Piper perked up from his wounded pile raising his head, glaring. An injured hush fell over the prisoners as they took the collective gut punch together. Dodger slowly rose to his feet, curling his arm against his bruised ribs and wincing at his stiffened injuries.

"You motherfuckers," he growled, turning toward the nearest of Washington's soldiers like he meant to strangle him with his own handcuffs.

"You better sit down and stay down," the guard warned, dropping a hand to his pistol.

But Dodger took a step forward instead.

Gabriel got between them and held Dodger back. "Not the time, brother," he said in a quiet, urgent tone. "Not the time." He looked back to the guard and held up a hand, offering peace. "Everybody just be cool, okay?"

The guard gave a skeptical grunt. "Sit your big gorilla-ass down," he ordered, looking to Dodger.

Gabriel patted Dodger in the middle of his chest. "Come on, dude. Just be cool. We'll settle it up later."

Dodger, his face twisted up like an angry demon, hocked up what spit he could muster and spat in the guard's general direction. "Fuck all of you," he snorted and then gimped back to his seat amongst a rattle of chains and grunts of angry pain.

"Are you sure about Finch?" Victor asked, his tone as stony as his expression.

Gabriel and Delilah both nodded. The haunted light in Delilah's eyes told the tale well enough. She'd been there, she'd seen it, and it had been horrible.

Victor studied his daughter's face, her posture, her expression. The subtle way she favored her left arm. She was hurt, and he could tell.

Delilah knew he saw it, so she shook her head and gave him a look, warning him away from mentioning it because now wasn't a good time to show any more weakness then they had already.

Victor bottled it. "Do you know what Washington wants?"

Before either of them could reply, Mr. Washington himself answered from the door. "Not yet they don't. But they're about to. That's enough family reunion for now. There are your people, Mr. St. John, Miss St. John. Whole as promised. You do things my way, you can take them out of here." He let the unspoken threat of what would happen if they didn't do things his way hang for a moment. "Any questions?"

They didn't have any.

"Get them out of here," Washington ordered. "We've got work to do."

84

Gabriel and Delilah were led off through the crumbling dark and taken before Miss Althea Gentles. She stood at an impromptu workbench made of portable sawhorses and a sheet of plywood. There was an assortment of workings and several battery powered lanterns laid out on the table before her.

Mahri was waiting with her.

Neither of the Crows had a word to say to Mahri, and she wasn't much on making eye contact with them either. Her left hand and forearm were bandaged all the way to the fingers. Though she'd managed to get away from the brunt of it, Gabriel's blast at the ambush had burned her, too. She looked pale in the electric lamplight, exhausted and in pain. There wasn't a Crow in the room who gave a shit.

Delilah let out a bitter bark of a laugh when she saw the massive grimoire laid out on Miss Althea's workbench. Doc McCoy's *Codex of Nine*. A study of the Outer Darkness.

Priceless, masterwork theory by a genius of the modern era. A work his apprentices were not allowed to study and one of which he only spoke to Delilah about in the theoretical, the conceptual. A book of blackest secrets, inscribed only because the Doc had been a heartfelt scholar. He hadn't believed in forbidden lore. Only that some was more appropriate for certain audiences than others. This one, he'd deemed too risky to study for any but the most right-minded. He hadn't even considered Delilah one of those. This work, he had guarded with his life. This work had *cost* him his life.

"You little cunts," Delilah said. "It was you this whole time. *You* killed the Doc."

Mahri looked toward the floor, but Miss Althea held her head high.

"Angus McCoy was a vain and prideful man, Miss St. John," the priestess replied. "It served him poorly. His vanity led him to hoard works he had no business hoarding. That vanity brought him to his fate. He made his choices and got what comes of them."

"Is that what you call peeling off his skin and pulling out his guts?" Delilah asked. Her eyes flooded with bitter anger. The lanterns dimmed and buzzed at her ire. The surrounding shadows seemed suddenly very close, and very claustrophobic.

Everyone in sight felt the hair-raising tension of it.

Delilah St. John was still poisoned on the lethal black magic that had fueled her killing fire. Still high on the grim power that had knitted her wounds. The little devils dancing in her head and in her heart were very real and very hungry. That rotten hurt was close to the surface, and she had more than enough metaphysical muscle to turn it into a tornado of horror.

Miss Althea cocked a slender eyebrow and said simply, "Choose very carefully, what you do next, Miss St. John."

By degrees, the leering darkness withdrew and returned to normal as Delilah wrangled that poisoned pain back under control. The air wasn't as close and expectant. The lanterns quit buzzing. The tension bled away. Delilah's hate-filled glare did not.

Miss Althea gave a nod, seeming to approve of her decision. "I'm assuming that Mr. Washington has explained to you what's at stake for you and your family. So, we can skip the arguments and the refusals, yes?"

"Yeah," Gabriel said. "What is this? What do you want?"

Miss Althea laid it out for them. "This is the Fang of Maglo," she said, laying her hand reverently upon the jagged sliver of pitted iron. She smiled, a look of appreciation and awe. "A gift from the darkness behind the stars for those with the will and wit to use it." Her long fingers trailed slowly across the jagged angles of the pitted blade, and Miss Althea seemed lost in her admiration of the relic.

"Is that what we're calling it?" Delilah asked. "A gift?"

Miss Althea's gaze rose from the jagged blade. "Yes." Her reverence was deep and deadly serious. The frost in her expression indicated that she took offense at Delilah's glib tone.

Delilah didn't really give a shit.

Miss Althea turned the hulking grimoire around on the table and presented it to the two captive Crows. "Doctor McCoy wrote extensively in his works about the Keys of the Nine Horrors." She tapped her finger to the open page, indicating an artistic representation of the very dagger itself. Miss Althea smiled. "The Fang of Maglo is one of the nine Keys."

"And I suppose you want to stick it in the lock?" Gabriel asked.

"Something like that," Miss Althea replied.

The light bulb went on over Delilah's head. "You tried this already. You, and Mahri, and Felipe. And you blew it."

Mahri shifted uncomfortably. Miss Althea offered no response.

Delilah shook her head. "That was why you went after the Doc. You needed the owner's manual." She looked to Mahri. "You are an incredible piece of work, you know that?"

"Where do we come in?" Gabriel asked, shaking his head.

Miss Althea smiled. A pitiless, cold expression. "I need you to turn the Key."

That was it. That was what it all came down to.

"And you just want to do this on the fly, huh?" Delilah asked with a skeptical snort.

"Everything is prepared. Meticulously. All I need you to do is push over the first domino." Miss Althea turned several heavy pages in the grimoire and stopped when the book was open to a pair of them filled with a dizzying constellation of arcane runes. The clockwork machinery of a complex spell, penned in the Doc's meticulous hand: The Key of Maglo.

Delilah looked at the spell for a full five seconds in silence. "Shit."

No one had to ask what the payoff was. They'd all seen the power of Maglo first hand. "So, you want the dirt to stick to us while you walk away with the prize," Gabriel said, cocking an eyebrow. "Sound about right?"

Miss Althea shrugged. The gesture seemed almost apologetic. "Well, in this game there are no points for second place, Mr. St. John. For someone to win, someone has to lose."

Gabriel chuckled. "Sort of like how you guys left Felipe holding the bag for the cash depot heist? You got him to do your dirty work, then you left him to twist in the wind. Guess you weren't expecting him to fuck you back though, were you?"

Miss Althea neither confirmed nor denied.

"So what happened to Silver Dollar?" Delilah asked.

Miss Althea looked to Mahri. Her expression was less than pleased.

"Dollar worked the spell with us the first time around," Mahri explained. Recalling the event made her look a little green around the gills. Or maybe that was the miserable backstabber's guilt talking. It was hard to tell.

"Dollar had talent?" Delilah asked.

Mahri shrugged. "Sort of. He was the Key Bearer."

"What does that mean?" Gabriel asked.

"Someone has to do the workings of the ritual. Someone else has to turn the key. He volunteered."

Delilah scoffed. "Guess his faith in you was a little misplaced, huh? Bet Washington's real happy that you fucked his boy up for life."

Miss Althea cut in. "He knew what he was getting into. Understood the risks."

"And you want to try this all over again?"

"We're much better equipped and much better prepared now."

"Yeah. Ever think maybe you should have learned your lesson the first time?"

"This isn't a negotiation," Miss Althea replied.

Delilah looked back down at the grimoire and the spell. "I suppose it's not."

Mahri stepped forward. "I can help you. I can—"

"You won't do *shit*," Delilah snapped. "I wouldn't trust you to take out the garbage, let alone work this ritual again. You've fucked this up enough. Time for little hedge witches to go sit on the sidelines. The grownups have work to do."

Miss Althea gave Mahri a sidelong glance. Then she looked back to Delilah.

"Get her out of here," Delilah said.

No one moved.

"Get her out of here, or I don't do this," Delilah insisted.

Miss Althea shrugged, then gestured for Mahri to leave.

Deflated and defeated, Mahri withdrew.

Delilah traced a finger around the mesmerizing web work of arcane runes on the pages before her. "I'll need a Key Bearer," she said reluctantly. She looked to Gabriel.

The Captain Crow only smiled. "I know." That was all the more that needed to be said. "When?" Gabriel asked, turning to Miss Althea.

"Now," the priestess replied.

"No pressure," Delilah muttered. Then she pulled a lantern in close, pulled one of the shop stools up to the sawhorse table, and bent low over the grimoire. Putting everything else out of her mind, she got to work.

The darkness leaned in around her. Watching. Waiting.

85

Putting the exhaustion and pain on the back burner as best she could, Delilah studied the spell. Gabriel sat with her, steady and silent. Near at hand, Miss Althea perched like a patient vulture waiting for its scavenge to finally die.

At least she wasn't alone.

The spell script was written in the Doc's favored Ptolemaic cipher, penned in meticulous strokes by his steady, educated hand.

The central glyph was a circular disk composed of a dozen different interlocking runes. *Ryhelion,* descending. It was enclosed in an outer circle of nine sequential symbols. *In the ninth order.*

A short swath of parallel bars descended at the six o'clock from the outer circle which ordered the descending *Ryhelion.* Each bar was crossed by a unique series of glyphs. The spell-scribed bars ended at a smaller circle of seven runes, connecting the two constellations of sigils. *Ryhelion, in the ninth order, descending into the House of Tor-an-mah-Calbeth.*

From there a curving tail of runes continued to sweep down the page. It ended at an hourglass shape within a triangle, within another hourglass shape, and was capped with a crown of runes. *Focused into the Eye of Am'Riga.* A two-part halo of symbols, like a set of parentheses, flanked the *Eye of Am'Riga* on either side. *The Bridge of the Binding Way.*

Delilah ran her fingertips over the descendant tail. The hair on the back of her neck stood up. Within the final primary circle, she found the representation of the Eater of Dust. "The Fifth

Horror," she whispered. *"Maglo." God. What the hell are we doing?* Delilah studied on. The night drew in, cold, quiet, and dark. She puzzled out the complex workings of the spell one piece at a time. The study of such was more than just reading the symbols and formulae. The runes themselves were magical, a conduit of power for those literate in their secret language.

Each cog in the puzzle was burned into her mind as she fitted them together. Piece by piece, she assembled the workings on the page and reconstructed them. Each gear in the engine turned the next as it was completed.

The buzzing sensation of building power grew with each piece of the spell she unraveled. The sensation itself was numbing and distracting. Each cog in the spell machinery was like a shot of whiskey. Delilah fought against getting drunk on it. The closer she came to completing her study of the spell, the harder it got to fight through the rising haze. She endured.

This was where even the most talented practitioners walked on the edge of disaster. Stretching your capabilities to their limits was like testing the maximum weight you could lift over your head. Overload yourself and drop it and get crushed beneath it.

Pushing Silver Dollar through to Veil to turn the Key had fallen on Mahri—so had bringing him back. Clearly, she'd fucked that up. It just took a little time for that chicken to come home to roost. But, oh God, when it finally did.

Delilah focused. Gabriel would be counting on her to see him there and back again. She was not going to repeat Mahri's mistakes.

She learned the gruesome truth of the Key and the Keyhole. It called for blood sacrifice with the Fang of Maglo. A mortal vessel infested with a vestige of the Fifth Horror. None of Miss Althea's grisly animated meat puppets would suffice. They were already dead. The Keyhole needed to be living. She wondered, briefly, what poor bastard they'd inflicted that fate upon the first time around. Where they'd found him and how, and if that was the event that had set this whole nightmare into motion to begin with.

None of that mattered now. They'd already used up whoever that unlucky son of a bitch was in their first attempt. There wasn't much question who they were going to be expected to use on their next attempt. Silver Dollar was the plutonium core of their nuclear bomb. And Gabriel was going to have to stick a dagger in his heart.

Silver Dollar was as close to gone as gone got by that time. He was a leaky mason jar full of nitroglycerin, waiting to cook off. Miss Althea's Merovingian Noose would hold him, *should* hold him, long enough for her and Gabriel to do what needed to be done. But it would be her brother who was at ground zero if she followed in Mahri's footsteps and fucked it up.

If Delilah couldn't protect him, he'd be destroyed, just like Silver Dollar. Probably *worse*.

Her eyes must have betrayed her doubts.

"I'm not worried," Gabriel told her with a wink.

It helped.

Delilah studied on, taking in the power of the spell through her mind's eye until her head swam and her skin crawled. It was like being high on laughing gas and coke. A little numb, a little giddy, electric vibration in her very bones. Her eyes—windows to the mind and soul, ached, now burning and quivering like a weight lifter's overtaxed muscles. The ice pick began to wiggle around inside her skull. She became increasingly aware of the grating pain in her hastily-knitted shoulder, of the dry cracking between her recently burned and healed fingers. She noticed one of the fading blisters there had actually begun to reform.

Easy, girl, she thought. *Don't let them see you sweat. And sure as shit don't kill yourself. You're no good to anybody dead.*

"You okay, kiddo?" Gabriel asked.

She dismissed his concern with a single, curt nod.

Delilah couldn't help but grudgingly give Mahri credit where credit was due. If she'd really managed to pull this ritual off, even as a ham-handed failure, she'd upped her game from *hedge witch* to *bad bitch* during recent events. Of course, Mahri was also a traitorous, lying, backstabbing twat, and Delilah wanted to do nothing more than bury the Fang of Maglo in her throat.

That thought, coupled with the dark power building in her veins, stirred the hungry little devils in Delilah's heart. She could feel the malevolent glee of the Black bubbling inside her like tar. Wanting to be out. Wanting to be fed. She kept it contained.

The clockwork runes of the Doc's ritual were as artistic and beautiful as they were brilliant. The two seemed to go hand in hand if that was how you practiced your Art. They flowed, interwoven, on the pages, giving the impression of the slow turning of the stars in the heavens above.

Of course, like the Doc, Delilah knew what was out there in the darkness behind those cold stars. Hungry things. Alien things. Cruel things.

But somehow, the Doc had managed to make even that look sublime and beautiful. Woven between the workings of the spell were artful vines of complex filigree, lending the pages a background texture of elegance that belied the ritual's grim potential.

That brought her a little peace with what she was doing. Even in this, there was something not wholly sinister. That helped her quiet the boiling Blackness eating away inside her.

Then Delilah froze.

She spotted the first sigil of the Doc's own personal cipher, hidden within the lacy web of mundane decoration. A secret runic language of his own devising—one not even known to his apprentices—but one he'd shared with her, and she knew it very well. The Doc had likely taken it to the grave.

Keeping her poker face set, giving away nothing, she followed the flow of the Doc's artful illuminations, like tracing the course of a river. That led her to another secret rune. Then another. And another. Hidden within the artwork that adorned the page was a *second* spell. A *secret* spell.

Discovering it, understanding it, made the little infernal parasites feeding on Delilah's soul rejoice in a chorus of hellish glee. She didn't deny them.

It was three in the morning when Delilah finally closed the Doc's grimoire with a dusty thud. She rubbed her burning eyes and steadied her buzzing nerves. *I got it, Doc,* she thought grimly. *I got it.* She betrayed nothing. *I see you, Doc.*

"So," Miss Althea said at length. "Can you do this?"

There was something sinister alight in Delilah's eyes when

she looked up at the priestess. She knew something they didn't. And *that*, she made no effort to hide. "Yeah," she said simply. "I can do this. Just stay out of my way." She turned to Gabriel. "Let's go."

So they did.

86

Miss Althea had not been exaggerating. In the crumbling east wing of the marina motel, Delilah found the ritual preparations laid out in meticulous order, just as the priestess had promised. The floor had been shoveled and swept clean of dirt and debris. The whole area was surrounded in a ring of low lantern light. Enough to work by, but not enough to disturb the pressing darkness. With an educated hand, the priestess had laid down a veneration to each of the Nine Horrors, and at the center of the constellation was the circle to draw the Eye of Maglo, just as the ritual prescribed.

The casket containing Silver Dollar, restrained by Miss Althea's Merovingian Noose, had been placed at the center of the ritual circle. The lid was closed, like an evil jack-in-the-box holding back a hellish surprise.

The traitorous bitch had been setting this machinery in motion the entire time, right under their noses, all the while claiming to be their ally.

One way or another, that debt would come due. The Universe abhorred a traitor in the Art. All things came full circle. But right now, it was the Crow at the gallows. That bill would have to be settled first, for good or bad.

The old roof had long since been demoed off this wing, and the concrete shell was open to the sky. Slabs of broken concrete were stacked along the walls, layered in years of graffiti. The easternmost wall was completely gone, a rubble pile leading a short distance down to the water's edge. The Salton Sea was ink black under a cloudless night sky. The air was rich with the smell of salt and wet rot. A dome of cold stars looked down on them without pity. The Eye of Maglo was upon them, dreaming. Watching. Waiting.

The small hours of the night had taken on a desert chill. It was colder still, beneath the Eye of Maglo. Cold enough to see the faint steam of breath in the air.

The ritual was attended by Mr. Washington and a dozen of his street soldiers and mercs. Miss Althea was there, as was Mahri. In the dark black corners of the ritual site, beyond the faint glow of the lantern light, four sets of cold, white eyes stared back at them, glittering faintly in the gloom—Miss Althea's monstrous zombies, animated with the frigid malice of Maglo. They stood ultimate guard over the ritual. Their presence was most definitely unsettling.

Somewhere in the ruins behind them, the rest of the captured Crows remained chained in their cell, under guard—Fiona trapped in her cage. There was nothing that could be done about it now.

The last order of business was to prepare the Key Bearer. Delilah called for the workings she would need and filled Gabriel in on his role in the ritual while they waited.

Gabriel kept it simple. "Let's get this over with."

Mahri, Miss Althea's little lap dog, brought Delilah brushes, inks, and a lantern.

"You're dead, bitch," Delilah promised as Mahri handed her the workings. "When this is all over. Whatever happens. *You're* dead."

"Dee," Gabriel said softly. "Let's just do this." Then Gabriel took off his jacket and shirt and laid them aside. He was black and blue and battered, the bandage binding the gash along his side was bloody again.

Mahri's lips moved and twitched like maybe she had something to say.

"Just go away," Gabriel said, cutting her off before she could speak.

Mahri withdrew.

In the pale glow of the lantern, Delilah took up brush and ink and layered the necessary runes across her brother's chest and shoulders. One on the back of each hand. One in the center of his forehead.

He caught the mayhem alight in her eyes then. Saw it for what it was, even if he didn't know the specifics. Little sister was up to something.

"You're just waiting for your moment," he told her in a low, confident, conspiratorial whisper. "That's all." He said nothing more about it.

Delilah nodded. She understood. "This is going to hurt," she cautioned, turning his right hand over and inking a sigil into his palm.

"I know," he replied.

When she was done, Gabriel pulled his shirt and jacket back on but didn't bother to button them. "Anybody got a cigarette?" he asked.

Mr. Washington himself came forward and brought him one, even gave him a light. "You just handle your business here. This will all be over soon."

Gabriel took a long drag and blew it through his nostrils like an angry dragon while he and the gangland king had a five-second stare-down. "Yup." One drag. Then he dropped the smoke on the floor and crushed it out under his toe. He smiled, a ghost of his father's own grim grin. "You better step back then, boss."

Mr. Washington withdrew then and nodded to his priestess to get this show on the road.

Reverently, Miss Althea brought Gabriel the jagged sliver of pitted iron, the Fang of Maglo. Drawn from cold dust and frozen metal, born in the void between the stars. A twisted, leftover sliver of an ancient celestial wanderer that long ago fell to Earth in fire.

There was a very real sense that above, from behind the light of the cold stars, the Fifth Horror focused its dreaming Eye in upon them with great interest as the dagger passed into Gabriel's spell-sealed right hand.

The watching gallery held its breath. The world was silent and empty except for the sigh of the night wind and the lapping of the black water.

They got down to it.

87

Delilah took her place at the head of the spell circle. Gabriel took his at the side of Silver Dollar's closed casket, dagger in hand. The attendees turned the lanterns out. Maglo's dead servants stared inward at them, their glittering white eyes alight in the dark.

When nothing but frigid starlight remained, Delilah St. John began the Calling of Maglo.

"Maglo et tun'y-eth," she whispered into the darkness, raising her hands before her, palms up, in supplication. *"Ah khan huath un dir, Maglo et tun'y-eth. Maglo ar khun."*

She recited again, pressing the energy of the spell bound in her mind into each word, each syllable. Each breath. With each recitation, her tone rose.

"Maglo et tun'y-eth."

The surrounding darkness drew in.

"Maglo ar khun."

The stars overhead grew brighter.

"Maglo et tun'y-eth."

The dust that had been swept to the edges of the room began to stir and rise on little eddies of air.

"Kath ruun. Huath un dir, fingrab naglo carcureth. Maglo et tun'y-eth."

An electric lantern swelled suddenly to life, bright and full, then popped and went dark.

"Eglo eathi aki. Nakul imabue. Maglo et tun'y-eth."

The casket containing Silver Dollar began to tremble, caught up in its own tiny tremor.

"Ar khun, rhaan et Maglo!"

A faint keening rose on the air, a painful barely perceptible whine at the edge of human hearing.

"Maglo et tun'y-eth!" Delilah called to the hungry stars.

"Maglo ar khun," Miss Althea whispered in reverent answer.

"Maglo et tun'y-eth!" Delilah cried again.

"Maglo ar khun," the gallery surrounding her answered, joining their voices to the alien chorus.

Delilah shouted her throat raw, allowing the power to pour out through her voice. *"Maglo! Maglo eh tuun! Maglo et tun'y-eth!"*

"MAGLO AR KHUN!" the reverent host cried.

The world exploded in a whirlwind of dust and debris.

88

Standing at the center of the ritual was like being in the eye of a tornado created from a bomb blast.

Around Gabriel, the world disappeared in a maelstrom of dust and swirling debris, a rising vortex that blocked out everything but the stars overhead.

"Shit!" he cried, dropping to his knees and taking cover against the side of the casket.

The wind rose and howled. He locked his eyes shut against the scouring blast of choking grit and held on tight, tucking his head and covering up as best he could.

The entire sensation was one of unnatural chaos. Up was down. Down was up. Inside was out. The casket quivered and squealed as it grated and slipped several inches across the floor, buffeted and displaced by the vortex.

Gabriel clutched the dagger close in his right hand and hooked his left arm into one of the caskets handles, struggling against being swept away.

The sense of time was very confusing, very surreal. Seconds. Impossibly long seconds.

A bolt broke loose from the casket handle Gabriel was clinging to, threatening to pull them apart and send them winging different directions into the howling torrent. Gabriel gritted his teeth and hung on as the handle bent, the wind pulled, the grit scoured.

Then suddenly, silence.

The howling stopped. The vortex continued to spiral and scream, but it was at best, a distant far away sound to Gabriel. The wind and dust flowed over him and the casket, but it no longer seemed to have any force behind it. It had become massless, ethereal. While it looked like utter chaos, howling in silence, it did no more than ruffle his hair and stir his shirt tails.

Shaky, disoriented, Gabriel slowly opened his eyes.

The world within the vortex was bathed in violet light from above. The stars overhead burned and swelled, pulsing like alien beacons in the purple sky. He could see nothing beyond the surrounding wall of wind and dust. Strange phantoms drifted by in the tornadic gloom, carried along at their own alien pace which defied the speed of the wind.

They waited. They watched. What they might have been, Gabriel had no idea.

The spell had pushed Gabriel and the casket a breath out of time, into the span between two beats on the clock. Through the Veil and into the grim sight of the Eye of Maglo.

It was peaceful, in a surreal, apocalyptic way.

Swallowing the dry lump in his throat, Gabriel rose and opened the casket.

Inside, he found Silver Dollar, glaring up at him with burning white eyes, hate and malice, restrained in his cage like a rabid beast raging to be free.

But the doomed man-thing couldn't so much as blink, held fast within Miss Althea's spell noose.

Gabriel gripped the dagger, the Fang of Maglo, tight in his spell-sealed right hand. His knuckles strained white.

The drifting phantoms pulled in closer. Hungry and expectant.

Gabriel raised the glittering Fang overhead, grabbing it in both hands.

The ethereal ground beneath them twisted and shifted, stretching into the shape of a great earthen maw, yawning, fangs grinding apart. But they did not fall.

"Maglo et tun'y-eth," Silver Dollar croaked in a husky, paralyzed whisper.

Bunching his shoulders and dropping with the blow, putting all of his strength and will behind it, the Captain Crow brought the blade whistling down.

It split bone and buried in Silver Dollar's heart.

The devouring maw beneath them rose up and over them like an ocean wave and slammed shut.

Everything exploded in blackness.

89

In the ritual chamber, the attendees were sent scattering and reeling by the birth of the violent tornado. Chaos. Confusion. A whirlwind of choking, blinding dust. Shouts of alarm. Lingering cries to Maglo, the Fifth Horror, who's hungry eye was upon them dreaming.

Delilah held fast, standing her ground, keeping the spell alive.

She couldn't lose her brother. *Wouldn't* lose him.

Not like Mahri had lost Silver Dollar.

A heartbeat. The time unmeasured between *then* and *now*, the *before* and *after* when the hand on the clock finally moves.

Delilah felt him, felt Gabriel.

Felt the Fang of Maglo strike home.

With a triumphant cry, equal parts victory and pain, she pulled the power driving the spell, severing the energies fueling the chaotic cold fire.

The screaming tornado collapsed. There was a terrific outward blast of wind and dirt, taking some of the attendees off their feet, sending unsecured objects scattering. Then the world suddenly stopped screaming.

Ears were left ringing.

Stunned faces coated in dust, eyes wide and staring.

Delilah quivered like a piano wire struck by the hammer.

At the eye of the storm, now silenced, Gabriel rose from beside Silver Dollar's prison and wrenched the bloody sacrificial blade from the man's heart. The hateful white light had gone out in Silver Dollar's eyes. Pitted iron grated against wet bone as the blade came free.

Haggard, covered in dust, spattered in blood, dagger clutched in his right hand, Gabriel turned and left the eye of the circle and broken casket behind. From the dagger, shadows crawled up and down his arm like tentacles. A thousand malevolent whispers echoed in his ears.

Shaken, but victorious, Miss Althea composed herself and met him in the middle. The priestess extended her hand and nodded. "Give it to me, Mr. St. John." And there she waited for him to comply.

Gabriel glanced sidelong at his sister.

She met his gaze and sketched the faintest nod.

Then a tremor rumbled underfoot. Then another.

Silver Dollar's corpse made a wet sucking noise, the mockery of a living breath. "*I see you...*" it croaked, words bubbling up and out of its bloody throat.

Miss Althea's eyes widened in shock.

With a snarl, Gabriel lunged at her, Fang of Maglo leading the way.

90

Chaos and catastrophe followed.

Miss Althea skated backward as Gabriel came on in a rush. Frantic, she hissed out a killing curse, trying to hex him down. She was fast enough on the draw, a half breath ahead of him, but the swelling power of the Fang swallowed the lethal spell whole like a shield.

A half second more was too long.

Gabriel buried the Fang of Maglo in Miss Althea's heart.

He ran her to the ground, ripping the blade out of her chest and driving it home again as he snarled. With each brutal blow, living shadows, black as pitch, slithered and swarmed into her body, flinging blood and meat.

Cries of shock and alarm, then weapons came flashing out. Fumbling confusion. The gallery clambered over each other in an effort to retreat.

Gabriel stabbed Miss Althea again. And again. His last stroke buried the jagged old iron blade through her neck. He roared in bloody, wordless rage, watching the grotesque eels of shadow burst from her throat to writhe in a bouquet from her gaping mouth.

"I see you!" The Silver Dollar thing howled.

"*Maglo et tun'y-eth!*" one of Washington's men screeched from the gallery. Then he ate his own pistol. A beat after his corpse hit the ground his eyes lit up with ghastly white fire and a groping nest of black tendrils began to wiggle from the exit wound in the back of his skull.

"*Maglo ar khun!*" another of Washington's soldier's howled. He dropped to his knees and dug his own eyes out of their sockets with his fingers. Then he slumped forward on all fours and began to bash his face into the concrete like a pile driver.

The blood pumping hot and fresh from Miss Althea's wounds coalesced into tendrils of alien shadow, rising up. They struck Gabriel away like the whipping tentacles of an enraged kraken. He was sent bouncing and sliding across the concrete. The tendrils whipped after him, groping for the Fang.

Miss Althea rose like a broken machine, a halo of writhing tentacles blooming out from her wounds. She choked and gasped on the hole torn in her throat. Then a nest of black tentacles wriggled from the gash, growing in length, whipping and snapping.

Gabriel scrambled, trying to regain his feet, to hold on to the Fang. Miss Althea surged forward, whipping and groping at him as her writhing cloud of spectral black tentacles grew.

The corruption of Maglo coursed through her, and whether she was alive or dead was impossible to tell.

A gunshot rang out. Then another.

Something hellish roared.

"I SEE YOU!" The thing inside Silver Dollar bellowed again, and with that, scarred, bloody hands grabbed either side of the casket opening, and the thing crawled out of the box and into their waking nightmares.

Miss Althea, warped and confused in a writhing mass of growing tentacles, cocked her head to the side and looked to Delilah.

Delilah.

Still fanning the flames of a very different spell.

The one she'd found hidden in the art of the Doc's grimoire.

Without hesitation, she let the Misfortune Curse fall right down on their heads. Right where it had been all along. Just as the Doc intended for anyone who meddled in his Study of the Outer Darkness.

Delilah didn't cause it, didn't cast it. She just didn't do anything to avoid it.

She'd spotted the trap, and she stomped her foot right down on top of it in defiance.

"Good luck, bitch," she said.

Miss Althea shrieked, tentacles lashing out toward both Delilah and Gabriel. Delilah managed to retreat, dodging them. Gabriel didn't. Whipping tentacles lashed and battered him, locked on the Fang, and with supernatural strength, tore it away.

Gabriel screamed in pain as the dagger was ripped from his spell-sealed right hand, enduring a sensation of meat hooks being pulled through his body, catching on bones as they went. The dagger finally broke loose from his grip and Gabriel collapsed hard with a winded grunt.

The groping tentacles delivered the Fang to Miss Althea's waiting hand, and her whole body jolted like a condemned soul in the electric chair. Her eyes blazed to life with white fire.

She howled and screamed. A nimbus of white flame erupted along the bloody blade.

Silver Dollar sprang on her like a leaping gorilla, and in a mass of writhing tentacles, streamers of white fire, and smashing fists, they went tumbling to the ground.

In the clinch, the burning dagger was thrown free, bouncing like a blazing white comet through the chaos. It came to rest on the far side of the chamber against the broken down southern wall.

The earth trembled again, shaking the old ruin, running fresh cracks up the concrete walls. Something big and heavy deeper inside the building broke free and collapsed to the floor with a terrific crash.

Delilah sprang to her brother's side and helped drag him to his feet. "Get up!" she screamed frantically. "Get up!"

Shaken, gritting his teeth, Gabriel managed to put his feet beneath him. His eyes locked on the burning form of the dagger, laying in the rubble on the far side of all the chaos.

Darting out of the shadows, Mahri scooped it up. The white fire went out.

She didn't hang around to fight. She bolted.

Gabriel dug in his heels as if he might take off after her, but Delilah pulled him back in, yanking on him until she had his attention. "No! No! No! Forget it! It's gone!" she shouted, trying to shake some sense into him.

Somewhere in Gabriel's burned mind, it seemed like that made sense. The deep hooks the gruesome relic had in him said *come get me*, but his instincts screamed *get the fuck out*.

Then the moaning, hungry Misfortunes began to boil up out of every crack and crevice in sight. Vengeful specters bled from the cracks in the floor, the walls, came spilling down from the broken rooftop overhead.

Miss Althea and Silver Dollar wrestled and roared in ruinous battle. Her corrupted guardian zombies sprang to her aid as Misfortunes zeroed in on the fray in kind. The ensuing dog pile was a vision of the Apocalypse, and anyone with any sense left at all ran away from it.

Misfortunes came on in a wave, a flood. Hellish infernal light began to bloom up out of the cracks in the floors and walls. The air filled with the reek of burning tar and fuming brimstone.

Delilah gave her brother one last, defiant shake. "Gabriel! Come on! Now!"

Willing the relic-lust and cobwebs out of his head, he did.

Everybody ran.

91

Hungry Misfortunes latched onto Washington's street soldiers at every turn, and without Miss Althea, those poor bastards had no means to fight back. Kicking and screaming, the Misfortunes pulled them apart, sucked the breath from their lungs, the beats from their hearts. Then like swarming ants, they dragged them down into the infernal cracks boiling up throughout the ruins.

Much like the Doc's house before it, the old marina motel began to crumble and burn, taking the damned and condemned with it. As the building trembled and shook, it filled with swirling dust and choking brimstone.

Staggering through the chaos, Gabriel and Delilah dashed for the edge of the growing apocalypse. The Captain Crow was still fighting to shake off the upheaval of having his metaphysical guts pulled out by losing the Fang. It took constant, conscious effort to keep putting one foot in front of the other rather than spin on his heel and go back to chase it.

They pressed on.

Along the way, he stopped long enough to pry a pistol out of a dead homeboy's hand. He patted the dead man down, looking for a spare mag, and came up with a cheap plastic lighter instead. He scratched the wheel and made sure it would produce a flame.

"Dee!" he called out and tossed her the little lighter. She caught it and held it clenched, white-knuckled, in her palm like a desperate man clutching a Rosary on a sinking ship. Bullets were becoming less and less useful by the second, but Delilah St. John with a fist full of fire was always welcome.

Gabriel gave his captured Glock a quick check. A full mag and one in the chamber. Then they were off again. Mr. Dante Washington was nowhere in sight, and there was no way they could spare the time to look for him. Payback would have to wait.

Dodging, dashing, Gabriel and Delilah took off west through the crumbling ruins, darting toward the makeshift cells where their family was being held. Dots of lantern light began to appear up ahead in the long dusty dark as they moved between piles of broken concrete and honeycomb walls.

Two dimly lit doorways became visible through the choking haze. The one on the left held the bulk of the Crows. The one on the right held Fiona. Sixty feet of broken cover, half-demolished walls, and dusty darkness separated them.

They fetched up behind a pile of debris for cover and Gabriel took a look ahead, marking the glow of the cells and the positions of the guards, then he tucked back in behind their cover.

There was no waiting, no time to hesitate. The time left before this whole compound was swarming with Misfortunes and being dragged down the cracks of hell was being counted in minutes. Or less.

There had been three nervous guards on Victor and company and two on the Lady Crow. The other guards from the west wing had either abandoned their posts or headed off toward the chaos when the shit hit the fan. The five that remained were meeting in the middle for an emergency pow-wow as the whole operation went to shit.

Gabriel looked to Delilah, his voice a whisper. "That's an awful lot of bad guys with guns, sis."

"I know," she replied softly.

In a real gunfight, being outnumbered mattered, and a pistol versus a rifle was only marginally better than using harsh language or throwing rocks. Particularly when the guys on the other end of the triggers knew what they were doing and were wearing heavy body armor.

Then there was Delilah. She had no workings, which made most of the lethal curses she knew beyond her ability, and the rest of the hexes in her arsenal were nowhere near as fast or foolproof as a trained killer on a rifle. Besides, she had just enough gas left in the tank for one last hoorah, *maybe*, before she was down to vulgar little party tricks. Opening the Way to the Fifth Horror, getting her brother there and back again, had all but used her up. She had to spend what little she had left wisely. The fire in her palm was her go-to choice. She'd just have to hope she could sling spellfire faster than five determined gunmen could kill her.

But it didn't matter. It wouldn't have mattered if the odds were good or bad, or impossible. For either one of them. Leaving here without their family wasn't an option.

"You ready, sis?" Gabriel asked.

Delilah nodded, her eyes huge and bright.

"You get mom," he instructed.

Delilah licked her lips nervously. "What are you gonna do?"

"Buy you all the time I can."

There wasn't much left to talk about.

Delilah pulled in tight behind their cover and scratched the wheel on the lighter, producing pale, impotent flame. But it was enough. Whispering to it, coaxing it, she pulled it into her palm, catching the fire for her own. She gave her brother a nod. "Go."

Gabriel posted up, drew a bead on the back of the nearest merc, and opened fire. The element of surprise was washed away in a hail of bullets. The merc flinched and staggered, and his cronies ducked, dashing for cover, reacting to Gabriel while Delilah lined up her last big shot.

Two heartbeats and one of the mercs had his rifle up, returning fire in the direction of Gabriel's muzzle flashes.

Bullets snapped and hissed around them, popping dust and debris up from their cover, screaming overhead like whip cracks. Gabriel popped a couple shots at the gunman, sliding sideways behind their cover, away from Delilah, to keep the shooter's attention on him, rather than his sister.

It worked. It bought Delilah one full second. That was all she needed.

With a cry, Delilah shoved her palm toward the sky, hurling her tiny ball of yellow flame up and over. It arced toward the mercs like a mortar shot, swooping out toward the right, growing in size, swelling to white-hot intensity. It curved and tracked like a guided missile, cutting back in and slamming into their flank.

The fireball exploded with a thunderous boom, unleashing a wave of golden flames.

Mercs scattered, some of them screaming. Two went down straight away in the blast. Then a third was overrun as Delilah's last vengeful gasp of spellfire took on a life of its own and chased him down like a hungry wolf.

The wave of living flame swept from right to left, driving them as far away from Fiona's cell as the narrow space would allow.

The dancing glow of angry orange flames filled the dusty chamber.

No one was shooting at them. For the moment.

Gabriel hazarded a quick scan of the battlefield. "Go!" he shouted.

Delilah sprang off through the dark, circling out wide to the right, tracking for Fiona's cell. Gabriel came out with her, angling to put himself between her and the remaining mercs, guarding her back. She disappeared into the darkness, while Gabriel held the last wolves at bay.

He started drawing fire almost at once as he dashed between pieces of cover, angling into the battlefield toward the nearest waylaid merc. Bobbing and weaving, he used his pistol to fight his way to a rifle and then armed himself. He had long enough to grab the fallen merc's gun and a couple of mags before incoming fire forced him to move again. He circled down the flank, and he and the last two mercs began a point-blank dance of death in the firelit dark.

One of the gunmen poked his head out from behind a line of rubble and Gabriel unzipped it for him with a double-tap, sending the merc to the ground under a gory cloud of pink mist.

But then the last merc did his level best to return the favor, driving Gabriel on the defensive. Rifles barked and flashed back and forth, deafening hammer blows that echoed sharply through the concrete halls. Maneuvering on each other through the rubble like fighter pilots dogfighting in the clouds, they jockeyed for position and traded shots. Chess with lead, trying to force the other one to make *a single* half-second mistake. The first man who broke and ran would die. The first man who zigged when he should have zagged would die. There would be no second chances.

Delilah, sprinting through the gloom, followed the edge of the outer wall and the lantern glow up ahead to her mother's cell. As her brother and the remaining mercenary gunman traded shots, stray rounds hissed and pecked through the dark, spurring her along.

As she made her way, she called a lethal curse to the tip of her tongue and hoped she had the gas left to use it if she reached her mother's cell and found that she wasn't alone.

Five steps.

A stray bullet hit the wall beside her, kicking up a shower of dust.

Three steps.

Two.

One.

She swung in through the door of the cell.

No one was home but her Lady Mother, pinned miserably in the barbed-wire rings of an Oculan Trap.

Delilah dropped the killing curse and instead, called up the last drop of juice she could muster, forming it into an angry hex with a spike of will and a snarl.

The Oculan Trap was unbreakable from the inside out.

But from the outside in, it was fragile as an eggshell.

Delilah hexed it down, and when her will hit the outer ring of the trap, the runes burned through like flashing gunpowder.

Then she staggered and had to grab the wall. The floor tried to flip over and change places with the ceiling. By the time she got her tail spinning vision under control, her mother was there, already on her feet, making sure she didn't face-plant into the concrete.

In that moment, everything that hurt, every fear, every broken bit, landed on her at once. Delilah threw her arms around her mother and crushed her in a desperate embrace. There were no tears, no cries. Just the frantic clutch of someone drowning.

Fiona returned it. "I know," she whispered into her daughter's filthy white hair. "I know, child. I know."

A flurry of rifle shots barked back and forth in the main chamber beyond, drawing their attention back to the immediate.

"Wait," Fiona cautioned, extracting herself from Delilah's frantic embrace. Before she'd even released her hold on her daughter, a spell began to form on the Lady Crow's lips. Stepping forward and placing her palm against the concrete wall, she closed her eyes, bowed her head, and whispered in the ancient tongue of her family line.

The stones beneath their feet answered with an audible hum.

Beyond the cell door, the nearest rubble pile cracked and shifted. Twisting and boiling, it rose up ten feet tall into the shape of a roaring earthen hulk. Rebar wove through it like bones, concrete and gravel becoming muscle and sinew.

Grit and dust bleeding from every grinding joint, it charged off through the fray, bellowing an earth-shaking roar.

It dashed right past Gabriel, picking up steam with each loping step like a runaway train. Without hesitation, it vectored toward the last gunman. The terrified merc pecked impotently at the monstrosity with his puny black rifle, and when his nerve broke, he turned to flee.

Fiona's elemental hulk caught him in three steps.

The merc screamed as the monster snatched him up from behind like a ragdoll. Then, with ruinous force, it dashed him against the floor and wall, pulverizing him into a sack of shattered bone and bloody hamburger.

Throwing the shattered corpse aside, the hulk turned and roared again, spoiling for challengers, standing guard over those its mistress willed it to protect.

Fiona St. John rarely took to vulgar displays of power. But when she did, they were terrifying.

Stunned and speechless, the only word Gabriel could find was, "Jesus!"

Moving with purpose, Fiona and Delilah emerged from the cell and caught up with him.

"Keys! Keys!" Victor shouted from the cell across the way, straining against his chains, stabbing his chin toward the wreckage of a burnt guard outside the door. "Blue jacket!"

Gabriel nodded, slinging the rifle over his back. When he reached the dead guard in the blue jacket, he frisked him for the keys. Once they were in hand, he rushed into the cell and began to unlock the cuffs.

Outside, but not far away, the hulk found one of the burnt mercs still alive and stomped him into paste.

"We have to go," Gabriel said urgently as he unlocked one set of shackles after another. "Now." When he got to Piper, he looked to his caregivers and asked, "How bad is he?"

"He sure as fuck don't wanna die *here*," Piper croaked in defiance, answering the question himself.

"You heard the man," Victor replied with a grim grin. Then they helped get Piper out of the cell, his legs rubber, his face knotted up in pain as his Lord and Captain hauled him out into the main hall. Once they were clear of the cell, Fiona's hulk left its gruesome business behind and scooped up the wounded Crow with surprising gentleness to bear him away.

Dodger and Izzie were both banged up pretty bad. They could walk, but Anna and Bingo stayed close to help them along. The Crows who were fit to fight armed themselves with what they could scavenge from the devastated guard post.

"I assume you've got an out?" Victor asked as Gabriel passed him one of the fallen guard's rifles.

"Yeah. We're heading north. We've got backup."

Victor cocked a curious brow. "What kind of backup?"

In the distant gloom, the first hollow-eyed Misfortunes appeared, slithering along the rubble-strewn floor like eels, hunting a reef for prey.

Then a fresh shockwave rattled the ruins, knocking dust loose from the broken ceiling above, raining pebbles down on them. The sudden calamity stopped the encroaching Misfortunes in their tracks, and as one, they all turned to look back the way they'd come.

"What the fuck is *that*?" the Lord Crow asked.

Delilah answered. "I think the Watch is here."

Yeah. It was about that time.

They didn't hang around to find out. Or take the blame.

92

Battered and bloodied, The Crow limped away from the calamity unwinding at the ritual site and headed north into the dark desert.

Over the first rise, just a few hundred yards from the chaos at the marina motel, they ran headlong into a pack of growling black hounds, bristle-backed and as big as steers. Right where they were supposed to be.

The Godfather walked among his pack on two legs tonight. He swaggered out of the desert gloom with a lopsided grin on his face, his thumbs hooked in the front pockets of his jeans. He gave the Lord and Lady Crow a respectful nod, then he turned to Delilah.

"Need a ride?" he asked, looking their motley crew up and down, giving a cautious eye to the concrete hulk cradling the wounded Crow in its tree trunk arms.

Delilah nodded and then threw a paranoid glance over her shoulder.

But the Godfather eased her mind. "Don't you worry, little sister. Ain't nobody following you. Well. Not *now* anyway." He reached out and scratched one of his half-ton hounds between the ears. It licked its bloody jaws. Then he smiled, very bright and very white in the starlit dark.

Behind them, whatever could burn was burning, and whatever could die screaming did.

"We square, little sister?" the Godfather asked.

Delilah gave a nod. "Yeah. We're square."

And that was that.

The Crows hitched a ride and got the hell out of Dodge.

PART SEVEN

Endsville

If it was easy, anybody could do it.

Victor St. John
The Lord Crow of Los Angeles

93

Mahri ran in circles for twenty-four hours, working on an out. But finding help was hard when everyone hated you. Every door she ran to was closed. Every number she called, there was no one there willing to talk to her. It was a stark reminder of all the bridge-burning she'd done, and how quickly she'd done it.

It was hour twenty-five when she came back to her ratty little motel room from her short supply run to the gas station around the corner. She knew she wasn't alone before she'd even turned on the lights. Her fingertips stopped on the switch. She froze in the door. Her makeshift wards were intact, but someone had managed to slip past them like a burglar tricking out an alarm system. That sort of thing took real talent.

Across the room, a single table lamp turned on with a click of the chain.

Sitting in the chair beside it was Gabriel St. John.

With pistol in hand resting across his right knee, a fat suppressor threaded on its muzzle, he pinned her in place with a grim, pitiless glacial blue stare. He looked rough, haggard, exhausted, cuts and bruises standing out in sharp relief on his face. He looked like a man who had forgotten what sleep was.

"Don't run," he warned.

Mahri set her crappy little plastic bag of bottled water and snacks down inside the door and kept her hands in plain sight. She shifted her canvas satchel around so it could ride on her shoulder without slipping off.

"I could scream," she said.

"But you won't," Gabriel replied. His pistol twitched ever so slightly. Mahri got the hint.

She had an out. She just needed a few more hours to lock it down. That was all. She couldn't just run. Distance was no defense against the likes of Delilah and Fiona St. John. She had to have a plan, protection. Even with the odds stacked against her, she'd managed to secure those things, but she needed to buy a few more hours to make it all come together.

Clearly, she didn't have a few more hours.

"How'd you find me?" she asked quietly.

"It's what I do for a living, remember? Come inside. Shut the door."

Mahri obeyed. Obeying the gangster with the gun in his hand and murder in his eyes was usually a good idea.

"Sit down," Gabriel instructed, nodding toward the bed.

Moving cautiously, Mahri sat on the edge of the bed across from him.

"Give it to me," Gabriel said.

She shrugged, played dumb. "What are you talking about?"

"Don't fuck with me," he warned. "Give it to me. Now."

"I don't have it," Mahri replied. "Not here. But I can get it for you."

Gabriel's pistol hand twitched again, ever so slightly. "Bullshit. *Now.* One last time. Give it to me." He nodded toward her satchel.

The light bulb went off above Mahri's head. "You didn't find *me.* You found the Fang."

Gabriel nodded, clenching his still-aching right hand into a fist. "Give the girl a prize."

There wasn't much denying it. Moving very carefully, Mahri reached toward the zipper on her bag.

Gabriel stopped her. "Why don't you just bring me the whole thing." He reached out and motioned for her to hand it over.

The thought flashed through her mind. Once. She had the power, literally, at the tips of her fingers. If she could get to the Fang, she could waylay Gabriel in a second and be out of here before he knew what hit him.

"There she is," Gabriel said.

"Who?" Mahri asked with a sour scowl.

"That nasty little witch I saw slit a kid's throat up in

Koreatown." His gun hand had gone still as death. Which was even scarier than the occasional subtle twitch. "Go ahead. Do it. You wanna find out which one of us is faster?"

No, she really didn't. She already knew the answer to that question. Reluctantly, Mahri did as he commanded. With painful effort, she stood up and handed over the bag. The look on her face was one of an addict seeing her stash confiscated and flushed down the toilet.

Gabriel took the bag in his aching right hand, his fingers wrapping tight on the strap, his knuckles going white. "Trust me. I know." His tone bordered on sympathy. Then he plopped the bag down in his lap and tugged open the zipper. He found the Fang of Maglo tucked away inside, wrapped in a white plastic grocery bag. Once he had the relic in hand, he set Mahri's bag to the floor.

"Now what?" she asked. But she had a pretty good idea. Tears welled up in her eyes, and she pushed them away. She didn't want to go out like that.

"I'm going to do what I told you I was going to do all along," Gabriel said.

Mahri blinked away the tears, looking at him in confusion.

"I'm going to put you on a plane. And we are never going to see each other again."

With a shaking hand, Mahri wiped a stray tear from her cheek. "You're going to let me go?"

Gabriel nodded.

"Why?"

"Does it matter?"

Mahri wasn't sure if she should risk an answer. "So? ... "

Gabriel stood up from the chair, bent down, and collected her bag up off the floor. Then he handed it to her. He nodded toward the door. "Let's go."

Mahri's lips trembled into a hopeful smile as she took her bag from him. Because she wanted to believe it, so she tried. She rose in kind, hooked it over her shoulder, and turned toward the door. She took a deep breath and blew it out, the tension in her bunched-up shoulders melting away. Mahri closed her eyes and wondered for a brief moment, where it was she might actually go. She knew it had nothing to do with an airplane.

Gabriel raised his pistol and put one in the back of her skull.

He didn't owe her a damn thing. But he killed her softly anyway.

Then he was gone.

94

Dante Washington was packing, the kind of packing you do when you don't plan on coming back. He rolled his suitcases into the safehouse kitchen. Threw his large locked briefcase up onto the granite counter. He *felt* as much as *saw* the two figures watching him from the deep shadows beyond the arched dining room doors.

He reached a hand toward his security radio, intent on hitting the panic buzzer.

"Don't bother," Victor St. John said with a dry chuckle. "There's nobody left to hear it anyway."

Slowly, he turned. Two figures emerged from the shadows, walking into the kitchen side by side. Victor St. John and some short, squat, swarthy little man Mr. Washington didn't recognize. He was dressed in rumpled slacks and a short sleeve button down shirt that was tight across his blubbery gut.

The foul little man was splattered with fresh blood. He grinned a lopsided, nicotine-stained grin, and even his teeth were smeared in reddish orange. He reached out a blood-soaked hand and laid a massive, pitted cleaver on the granite countertop beside the briefcase. It was dripping in gore, blood, pulverized bone and meat. It made a cold metallic *click* as the blade came to rest on the stone.

Mr. Washington nodded. "All right then."

"Planning a trip?" Victor asked as he fished his lighter and his pack of smokes from his breast pocket.

"I suppose not anymore," Mr. Washington replied.

"Pat him down," Victor ordered.

"With pleasure," Wortzworg grunted and ambled forward.

Smearing blood all over Mr. Washington's clothes as he went, he frisked him, disarmed him, and tossed everything he came up with onto the kitchen counter. A pistol and a backup. A roll of cash. A billfold. A passport. A pack of gum. A prescription for heartburn. His gold pocket watch.

Wortzworg kept the watch and the roll of cash. His massive, bloody cleaver scraped on the granite as he took it back in hand and stepped back in line beside Victor.

"I don't suppose there's any talking about this, is there?" Mr. Washington asked.

"I suppose not," Victor replied.

"So, where does that leave us, Mr. St. John?" Washington asked. His tone was calm, stoic, a king at the gallows to the very last.

The corner of Victor's mouth twitched in a smirk. "You and me? Endsville. Where the train tracks run out."

Mr. Dante Washington nodded. He understood that. He straightened his jacket and squared his shoulders, head high. "Let's get to it then."

Wortzworg smiled, an awful sight which grew less and less human by the second. A faint red light lit in the foul little man's pupils. His teeth grew sharp. His shoulders stooped. His face long. Fingers twitched as black claws stretched from skin darkening to the color of a deep, ugly bruise. As his appearance shifted and transformed, he tested the edge of the bloody cleaver against the pad of his thumb. It dripped gore in slaughterhouse awe.

Then the lights went out.

Wortzworg's eyes blazed red in the shadows. A dozen pairs of hungry red eye lights blinked into view around the darkened room to join him. Washington was surrounded.

With howls of glee, Wortzworg and his goblin pack waded in.

Then the screaming began.

Victor's lighter ratcheted and clanked. Pale orange flame bloomed up the wick into the chimney. The tip of his cigarette glowed cherry red as it took a light from the swaying flame. The orange glow spilled back across his sharp features, reflecting merrily in his dark eyes as he watched the blood flow.

95

Gabriel drove through the black desert in silence. Outside, the pre-dawn world was beginning to fade from midnight blue to rose and gray.

He did arrive at that little desert airstrip, the one Mahri hoped she might go to. The one she knew she'd never make. He watched the sun come up. Had a few smokes. Listened to the moan of the wind.

A red Jeep Wrangler came trundling out of the golden sunrise shortly after dawn.

As it approached, Gabriel got out of the car.

Michael LeMay came alone, as requested. He didn't seem pleased to find Gabriel alone as well. "Where's Mahri Ramirez?" he asked.

"She's not coming," Gabriel replied.

Michael grunted and shook his head. He looked tired and pissed. "That wasn't the deal."

"Well," Gabriel replied with a shrug. "It's the only deal you're gonna get."

"Goddammit, Gabriel."

Then Gabriel leaned down inside his car and produced the Fang of Maglo from beneath the seat. He tossed the grocery bag shroud aside into the dirt and held the jagged, twisted blade up for Michael to see. The tattered plastic sack skittered off into the wind.

Michael cocked a skeptical eyebrow. The change in his posture was subtle, but not lost on Gabriel, one gunslinger to another. Everything in Michael's body was ready to go for his weapon.

Gabriel flipped the pitted, jagged blade over and offered it hilt-first to the Knight of the Watch.

Michael was not without reservations. The Fang of Maglo was an artifact of incredible power and a value beyond priceless. It was dangerous. It was fickle. It was a treasure of the sort the Crow was not likely to ever see again. And Gabriel was offering it to him.

"Why?" Michael asked.

"Because I know a bad deal when I see one," Gabriel replied.

"Your Lord Father and Lady Mother would probably have a different opinion on that."

"Well, they don't know what I know about it. And what they don't know won't hurt them, will it? Until it *does*, if you know what I mean." Gabriel's eyes spoke volumes about the addictive, bottomless pit that was the Fang of Maglo. It *hurt* to have lost it. It *hurt* to hunt it down. And it *hurt* to give it away. There was nothing he could do to hide that.

At length, Michael nodded. With one hand ready to snap to his pistol, the other extended cautiously, he accepted the relic. For a moment, Gabriel's grip actually tightened on the blade, and he didn't let go. The grinding of his teeth was audible as he finally relinquished the Fang.

"It's all right," Michael assured him. "I get it."

"No," Gabriel said grimly. "You don't." It wasn't all right. Not even close to all right. He was a newborn junkie, and Michael was standing there with the crack pipe. "Get out of here."

Michael turned to leave, but he lingered for a moment. "Delilah …"

"Isn't your problem," Gabriel replied, cutting him off. "Her family will take care of her."

"She doesn't need anybody to *take care of her*. She needs *help*. Before it's too late." Michael paused and tilted his head to meet Gabriel's agitated gaze. "So do you."

Gabriel gave off a sour chuckle. "Yeah, well, I'll take it under advisement. Now take that thing and get the fuck out of here."

"Before you change your mind?"

"Something like that."

Michael did.

96

A few days later, late on a dusty red afternoon, the Crows buried Finch at Digger's ranch. The place was a dirt road ramshackle plot in the backcountry outside Victorville. A couple dozen goats, some dogs, a handful of cars that ran and a few that didn't clustered like a constellation of space debris around a sagging old ranch house. Flat pan desert rolled away in every direction, an empty ocean of brown and olive drab, hazy mountains dim in the distance.

Calling it a ranch was perhaps a kindness. Wind and dust and the smell of old cars rotting in the sun. Barbed wire fences snagging windblown trash. Scrub brush and rocks. Goat shit. Flapping tin. Flagpole lanyards pecking out brassy clangs in the wind. That was the ranch.

Digger was the oldest Crow anyone knew, tall and skinny and stooped, like some misplaced carnival sideshow freak. When Victor had recruited him, how and why, nobody knew for sure but the Digger and the Lord Crow himself. He'd spent the last ten years or so dying of cancer, but never quite got around to finishing up the arrangement. Dying seemed to suit the old man better than being dead. He had one job: keep the bodies in the ground, and their secrets with them. So out here, on the dusty edge of nowhere, that was what he did.

They laid Finch down beside twenty years of brothers and sisters that had met similar fates. Killed doing their duty to the house with nowhere in the outside world to honestly bury them. An unadorned chunk of sandstone was all that would mark his grave.

Bingo presided, while battered Crows, black and blue, and

Piper on crutches, gathered at the graveside—brothers and sisters who loved Finchy and wanted to send him on his way. For some, there were tears, for others not. The wind sighed and moaned, stirring the dust and whistling through the bone-bare scrub, and it didn't care either way.

Delilah didn't shed a single tear or say a single word at Finchy's funeral. Her Lord Father kissed her brow and her Lady Mother held her as tight as her wounded shoulder would allow. Bingo gave her a big, gentle hug, and he was in no hurry with it. Her brother sat with her after everyone else had gone and held her hand. "Sorry, Dee," was really all he could think to say.

It was enough. It was going to have to be.

They left Finchy in Digger's care. And the desert did what it does best, swallowed James Finch up as if he'd never been there at all.

After the funeral, Delilah went back to Los Angeles to see Xavier. He did his work with gentle hands steering clear of her tender shoulder. She sat topless in a chair at his surgically clean shop and stared a thousand-yard hole through the wall. He did his work in the fluorescent white glow—and she didn't have much of anything to say then either.

Late that night, she left with her Blood Laurel woven into the talons of the Crow across her back and a thin Ruby Cross trailing down the side of her pale neck. The Blood Laurel commemorated her first kills, and the Ruby Cross honored her wound.

They were a shitty trade for Finchy.

Then she went out into the dark and let the Los Angeles night embrace her.

She finally wept. And no one saw.

97

Michael woke up at four in the morning and knew he and Samuel were not alone. Barefoot and bare-chested, he inched out of bed, couched his Glock behind his leg, and slithered soundlessly down the dark hall. He turned on no lights. Michael was comfortable in the darkness. At Samuel's open door, he stopped.

Delilah St. John sat at Samuel's bedside, silent and grim as a grave bird, watching their snowy-haired son sleep. Her face was pale. Her mascara trailed down her cheeks, smudged dark and smoky around her eyes. She'd been weeping and scrubbing angrily at them until the tears dried up, leaving them red and raw.

She was clearly drunk and stoned, her expression numb, disconnected, and heavily medicated. Her snow-white hair was a rumpled mess, and her blouse was buttoned crooked, giving the impression that she'd recently fucked her way out of somebody's back seat.

Beneath it all, bitter darkness clung to her. Not just despair or grief. Something more present. Something sinister, malevolent. A hungry sorrow that no brooding goth girl could match. Michael had seen it before. The newly born addiction to the Black. Feasting like a bloated maggot on the open wounds of grief and the guilt. The booze and dope made it ten times worse, not better. That was Nietzsche's abyss, gazing back at her as promised. And Delilah wore that cloak like the royalty she was. A daughter of Fiona St. John's house, destiny fulfilled.

Maybe.

"Do you want to talk about it?" Michael offered gently.

"No," she whispered.

He knew she had debts to pay now, outstanding bills with forces beyond her control that were yet to be settled. Things you couldn't fix with time and money. And none of it would be easy. "It'll pass. If you let it."

"So I'm told," she said. She brushed a lock of stray hair from Samuel's forehead and the gentle little boy was unsettled in his sleep but did not awaken.

Even drunk and high, Delilah seemed to understand the subtle disquiet her presence brought to her son. Here there be monsters, after all. Not mommies.

"Don't wake him up," Michael said.

So Delilah didn't.

He leaned back out into the hallway and turned on the hall nightlight, pushing back the blue darkness with a cool white glow. But when he turned back to the room, like a shadow or a bad dream, Delilah was gone.

PART EIGHT

Scar Tissue

I know how men in exile feed on dreams of hope

Aeschylus

98

Bruises faded. Bloody bits healed. Let behind were the scars. This life left a lot of those behind. Some you could see, but most of them you couldn't.

Victor squared things up with Del Torro and the Cartel when he brought them a box full of their missing cash. Well, Dante Washington's head, anyway. Next best thing. There was always truth in the blood. The money was found, and the Crow got paid.

After the debacle at Sweet Valley Ranch, the Helitori evaporated, disappearing like ghosts back into the unknown. No one could make a full accounting of what casualties they'd suffered, or how many people, innocent and otherwise, they had killed during their witch hunt through Southland. Nothing about the debt between the Crow and the Helitori was square. That was a bill still waiting to come due. But not today.

Gabriel was there the day they buried Mahri. Her mother wept inconsolably at the funeral. A funeral which Gabriel attended and kissed her mother on the cheek as if he wasn't the man who'd murdered her baby girl. He'd hugged her brother. Shook her father's hand. There'd been a wake before, a reception after. He'd skipped them both.

Then he came back to Mahri's grave that night and did what needed to be done to make sure she kept her secrets, and his. In this world and the next. No one, not even his sister knew he did that. Mahri got what she deserved. In the end, that was all you could say about anybody. Gabriel could almost convince himself of that too.

It didn't take long before Victor asked him about the Fang.

Gabriel did what a Crow does best. He lied. "She didn't have it. She traded it for an out."

"To who?" Victor asked.

"The Watch."

"Yeah?"

"Maybe. That's the best I could get out of her, anyway. I think she thought it was the last bargaining chip keeping her alive."

Victor nodded.

Gabriel saw his Lord Father's suspicion. His doubt. "What? I thought you didn't want anything to do with it."

Victor grunted. "I don't. But that cat kinda got out of the bag, whether we wanted it to or not. Didn't it? You and your sister saw to that."

Gabriel bristled. "We were short on options."

"Yeah, you were," Victor conceded. "I know people with deep pockets who might have been interested in helping us make the best of it. When life gives you lemons and all that." There was a dangerous gleam in the Lord Crow's granite eyes. "Might have made a lot of lemonade there."

"The Watch would have burned us to the ground for it," Gabriel said.

Victor shrugged. "They'd have to catch us first."

Gabriel swallowed the lump in his throat. "Yeah. Well, like I said. By the time I got to Mahri, it was already gone."

"Hrm. Well, too bad. That was the kind of prize a whole family could retire on. Maybe someday it'll turn up."

That predatory darkness in Victor's eyes, that mild half-smile that wasn't a smile at all. It reminded Gabriel of exactly how his Lord Father dealt with people who took from him what was his. And he was not above that wrath.

But Gabriel's own poker face gave away nothing. "Maybe so, pop."

They let that sleeping dog lie and walked away from it, both of them knowing one of them was lying, and only one of them was able to prove it.

It was when things finally got quiet that the scars hurt the most.

Gabriel managed his the best way he knew how. He drank a lot, smoked a little herb, and let the medicine do its work. He got his Harley out of the garage and let the pipes rumble. Because you couldn't find time for the things you loved. You had to make it.

He called Celeste, and, just as he hoped, she answered.

Then he drowned himself in her. It was all he knew to do to survive.

For a day, they chased away memories. Hot summer nights with Mahri in a different lifetime. The maddening whispers of the Fifth Horror. The killing. The lies. Betrayal. Guilt. Fear. Doubt. Death.

Gabriel got by. He spent most of a day with Celeste. They talked, and laughed, and fucked. He took her for a ride on his bike, and they had lunch and drinks. They acted so much like normal people it was almost convincing.

At the end of their day, purple twilight settled over Los Angeles, and Gabriel got dressed. It was time to go back to the real world, and that was just as well, he supposed. He pulled on his shirt and tucked in his tails. He didn't look at the man in the mirror, and the man in the mirror didn't look at him.

Celeste lay naked on the hotel bed a few feet away, draped in the crumpled sheets, but not leaving much to the imagination. A vision from the canvas of a Renaissance master. She was as content and peaceful as a cat reclining by the evening fire.

Gabriel pushed the button of his right cuff through the hole, then he looked up, catching Celeste's gaze in the large mirror. "What are you?"

Celeste contemplated that for a moment before she answered. The question didn't seem to alarm or concern her. It made no impact on her feline contentedness at all. "Does it matter?"

Gabriel buttoned the other cuff. He put on his shoulder rig and situated his pistols. He went to the chair and retrieved his jacket. "I suppose it doesn't," he said. He took a cash-stuffed envelope out of his breast pocket, payment for her services, and laid it on the foot of the bed. "Goodnight."

She smiled, a small, sultry, sleepy expression.

Gabriel turned for the door.

"Until next time," Celeste said in parting.

He paused without looking back. Just for a moment. He nodded. Then he left.

Gabriel rode his Harley down to the Church as night fell once more over the City of Angels. And just like every other night, all the same demons and devils, shadows and sinners, came out to play.

He had been there just long enough to put the kickstand down and kill the ignition when Dodger rolled in behind him, pipes rumbling.

The big man parked it, killed it, dismounted, and ran a gloved finger along the curve of Gabriel's handlebars. "Knocking the dust off her?"

The Captain Crow nodded.

"You ride like my grandmamma. A bicycle might be safer for you." Then Dodger grinned. And it was infectious.

The corner of Gabriel's mouth twitched upward in a matching smirk. "Dick."

Dodger laughed. "Me and Pops are riding out to Vegas tonight. Spend a few days, get right. You know? We'll ride slow, stick to the kiddie lane if you wanna come with."

Gabriel contemplated that. "Vegas?"

Dodger nodded.

Yeah. Vegas would do.

MEET THE AUTHOR

Clay Sanger is a professional technogeek by day and a writer of fiction rest of the time. A life-long lover of all things wild, Clay spent much of his early adulthood wandering the four corners of the country in search of the weird and wonderful, the dark and the light. As chance would have it he found them. After meandering far and wide he returned to his native Ozarks where he lives with his dazzling wife, their sons, and a menagerie of mythical creatures both real and imagined.

Clay's short fiction can be found in *Blackguards: Tales of Assassins, Mercenaries, and Rogues* and in *Knaves: A Blackguards Anthology*.

Endsville is his debut novel.
Visit Clay's website at: www.claysanger.com